DEATH IS ALWAYS REAL . . .

"What happened to the first team? Are they dead?"

"We don't know," Jackson said.

Dalton raised his eyebrows. "What do you mean by that?"

"Their bodies are still in their isolation tanks, in a room off the main experimental chamber. The machines are keeping them in stasis at the reduced functioning status. So they're alive, I suppose. As alive as any of us when we go into those damn tanks."

"What happened to them?"

"No one knows. I don't know exactly, but I have an idea. I told Hammond but she thinks it's bull. I believe she thinks that because what I told her scared her."

"What about Raisor?"

"I think Raisor believes me. He's weird."

"What's your theory?"

"There are bodies in the isolation tanks, but there are no *people* in there, if you know what I mean. Heck, Sergeant Major, I went looking for them. I went out on the virtual plane to see if I could find them." She paused, her eyes withdrawing.

"And?" Dalton prompted.

"And I think I found them. What was left of them. Their psyches. Worn out as if they died of starvation. They were all dead there. . . ."

BOOKS BY ROBERT DOHERTY

The Rock
Area 51
Area 51: The Reply
Area 51: The Mission
Area 51: The Sphinx
Psychic Warrior

ROBERT DOHERTY

PSYCHIC WARRIOR

A DELL BOOK

Published by
Dell Publishing
a division of
Random House, Inc.
1540 Broadway
New York, New York 10036

ISBN: 0-440-23625-8

Printed in the United States of America

Published simultaneously in Canada

August 2000

10 9 8 7 6 5 4 3 2 1

OPM

To my sisters, Ellen & Jean Mayer, with love.

Acknowledgments:
With thanks to my editor Mike Shohl,
my agent Richard Curtis,
and last, but not least,
my fellow Green Berets,
the original Trojan Warriors of
2d Battalion, 10th Special Forces Group (Airborne).
De Oppresso Liber!

The Past

Prologue

April 10, 1963

The wind swept the desolate land of the Severnaya Zemlya chain of islands with no mercy for the sparse vegetation that struggled to grow among the rocks. The few plants only showed their face for a month at the height of summer. The rest of the year, the island was covered with a freezing layer of driven snow and blistered ice. The only exception was the airfield on the eastern side of the one island in the chain that held human life. The island was labeled on maps as October Revolution Island, but none of those sheets indicated that there was any habitation here, ten degrees above the Arctic Circle. The existence of the airfield and the base it served was one of the most highly kept secrets in the Soviet Union.

The men stationed on October Revolution Island, part of a unit known only by the typically bland Soviet code name Special Department Number Eight, would not have called their situation habitable; more on the order of barely survivable. The security forces were billeted in poorly constructed concrete buildings that lined the edge of the metal-grating airstrip. But it was far underground that the true essence of the work done in this forsaken spot was conducted.

Eight hundred feet down, accessible via only one large freight elevator, lay the core of Special Department Number Eight, known in inner circles simply as SD8. It was run by the GRU, the Soviet military's version of the KGB. And to keep the work done there secret from the KGB, as well as the NATO countries' spy services, was one of the reasons that this remote spot had been chosen.

The SD8 complex had been dug out by Nazi soldiers still being held prisoner by the Soviet Union in the mid-1950s. These men had been captured during the last years of the Second World War, and those in power had never seen any point in even reporting their existence, never mind repatriating them. The prisoners were useful in certain ways, such as working on this project. Upon completion of the task, the German soldiers had been summarily executed and dumped into the freezing waters of the Arctic, each of the twelve hundred bodies weighted down with a heavy iron chain.

Those Russians who worked in the complex had the highest clearances granted in the Soviet Union. Today was to be the test of whether all the time and expense they had put into the project over the last several years would bear fruit. There had already been one major disaster, and to-day's trial was to be either the beginning or the end for this particular project.

Professor Leonid Vasilev was the head of the theoretical arm of the SD8 scientific team, and as such was the second-highest-ranking scientist present on the island. But he was still number two and he often did not agree with his superior, Professor Arkady Sarovan, who had been in charge of SD8 from the day it was founded, during the dark and bitter years of the Great Patriotic War, the Soviet name for the Second World War. It was Sarovan's job to take theory and create action, and today he planned on taking that first step, over Vasilev's objections.

"It is not ready," Vasilev argued for the third time that morning. He was a tall, slender man, with thin, straight blond hair and a face badly scarred by acne. In a briefcase, he carried the master program for the project on several reels of tape.

"It is indeed ready," Sarovan said with forced patience. He was short and stocky, and the body hair poking out over the collar of his white coat made him look like a bear wrapped in human clothes. The sloping forehead belied the brilliant mind encased behind it. "It *must* be ready, because we have no more time. Those in power require a statement to be made, and this is the means they have chosen to make it. The timing is not subject to scientific realities, but political ones."

The two were riding the elevator down to the SD8 control room, and Vasilev knew this was their last chance to talk privately.

"But there is great danger. Not only if we fail, but also if we succeed."

Sarovan shrugged. "True, but if we succeed, that is for the politicians to sort out. The order for this has come from the very highest level. The very highest," he repeated with emphasis, to let the other man know that Khrushchev himself was involved.

"What will they do if it works?"

"Our leaders? Or the Americans?" Sarovan shrugged. "Either way, that is not our concern."

"No, no." The quaver in Vasilev's voice testified to the fear he felt. "Not our government or the Americans. What concerns me is what *they* might do if we succeed."

Sarovan's bushy eyebrows contracted. He knew exactly whom his colleague was referring to, and he had experienced many a sleepless night considering the problem. "It is like nuclear weapons, my friend. They are very dangerous, but as long as we keep them under positive control, they cannot harm us."

Vasilev expelled a snort of disgust. "Nuclear weapons don't *think* for themselves."

"We have positive control over the way *they* think," Sarovan said flatly.

"But we don't understand what we're dealing with! We don't really understand how they do what they do."

"We know enough to use them."

Vasilev shook his head. "No, we don't. We're meddling with unknown forces. Things beyond our knowledge."

The argument was over as the large elevator doors rumbled open. On the other side were a dozen senior GRU officers, present to oversee the test. As Sarovan walked forward, his large paw extended to greet them, Vasilev quietly walked over to the main console. He pulled the tapes out and slid them onto their spools on the large computers.

The control center was carved out of solid rock, and no matter how high the heat was turned, there was always a damp chill in the air. It was a semicircular room, over seventy feet long by twenty in depth. The front was walled in with thick blast glass overlooking the test chamber. The test chamber was also hollowed out of the rock and was two hundred feet in diameter, with a ceiling over fifty feet high. The far wall of the chamber was filled with banks of capacitors, all designed to handle the large amount of power brought in from a small nuclear reactor on the surface. On the floor in the center of the chamber lay the result of twenty years of hard work by the scientists of SD8.

There were four objects shaped like coffins, eight feet long by four in width and height, evenly spaced around a huge vertical metal tube. Their lids were open, revealing a contoured space where it was obvious a man was to lie. Numerous wires and tubes came out of the sides and top of each, running to machines that completely encircled the four. In the exact center was the shining metal tube, eight feet in diameter by thirty feet in height. The tube rested securely on a cradle, and several monitoring wires ran from the top, looping over to the control center. The bottom of the tube pointed into the floor, where a vent shaft extended over a half mile into a volcanic crack deep under the island.

The tube was hollow, with two-and-a-half-foot-thick walls. There were two openings in it. The one at the bottom led into the vent shaft; the other, near the top, was a three-foot-wide section of wall that had been unscrewed. Around the outside of the tube were numerous black wires, linked to a thin network of silver strands crisscrossing in strange patterns.

Vasilev knew all the expertise and guesswork that had gone into building the tube. Even getting it down here had been a task, requiring the removal of the freight elevator for several days as the tube was lowered down and then maneuvered into position with great difficulty. It had been built to exact specifications under a cloak of secrecy at the largest tank factory in the Soviet Union.

He checked his status board for the computers that were linked to the tube. The spools ran the tapes through, loading the program. The system was ready.

A red light began flashing in the ceiling and a buzzer sounded. The mission was a go.

Vasilev looked across the control panel. He tapped a technician on the shoulder. "The emergency neutralizer. Is it functioning?"

The technician nodded. "Yes, sir."

"Good."

A door on the far side of the experimental chamber opened.

On the other side of the globe and in a more temperate zone, the USS *Thresher*, the American Navy's most advanced nuclear attack submarine, was preparing to conduct its own set of tests: a series of deep-sea dives one hundred miles to the east of Cape Cod. On board were sixteen officers, ninety-six enlisted men, and seventeen civilian technicians to monitor her performance.

The *Thresher* was the first in a new line of submarines. It was small, less than three hundred feet long by thirty-two feet wide, and all those extra personnel made working inside quite cramped. Today the new ship was going to be tested to see how deep it could dive and operate. This new breed of attack submarine had been developed to directly counter the Soviet threat of ballistic missile submarines.

After getting approval from the commanding officer aboard the *Skylark*, the surface ship monitoring the tests, the *Thresher* began its first descent. Just over the horizon to the east, a plane circled.

Soldiers came through the door, pushing four gurneys on which were strapped the other critical component of the SD8 project. IVs ran into the arms of each of the four prone men, and sheets covered their entire body. Of all those stationed at Special SD8, these men knew they were never going to leave October Revolution Island. At least not in the way that one would normally expect.

The soldiers wheeled a gurney next to each coffin. They pulled the sheets aside and Vasilev could hear the gasps from the hardened GRU officers in the control center.

Each of the four men was horribly disfigured. All four were blind, their eye sockets empty, the gaping holes red and scarred. On each man's head four metal sockets extended out, having been surgically implanted through the skull directly into the brain. It had taken the scientists at SD8 many years to perfect the technique of implanting those sockets and to determine the correct location for each. Fortunately, they had had hundreds of prisoners to experiment on, all of whom had joined the German soldiers in their watery grave.

"Was the blinding necessary?" One of the officers had stepped back from the blast glass.

"It allows focus, Comrade Colonel," Professor Sarovan replied. "Also, you can appreciate that these men can never escape in the condition they are in."

General Vortol, the head of the GRU, gave a nasty laugh. "If only we could do such to all our prisoners. A most effective anti-escape device."

Vasilev could not control the choked noise he made, and the others heard it.

"Do you have something to say, Comrade Scientist?" General Vortol demanded.

"I don't believe it was necessary to blind these men," Vasilev said. He knew with that simple statement his career, if not his life, was over. But he could sense the mental power that was coming out of the test chamber as the soldiers lifted each of the four men into their coffins. Vasilev had no desire to be here any longer or be a part of this.

"Vasilev!" Sarovan snapped, but the general's voice overrode his.

"These men are criminals, are they not?" Vortol stared at Vasilev. He waited. "Are they not, Comrade Scientist?"

"Yes, General," Vasilev finally answered.

Vortol had a file folder in his hand, and he glanced at it. "And we could not be assured of their cooperation, correct?"

Vasilev could see that each of the four men was inside his case. Scientists were hooking wires to each body, picking up different colored leads that looked very similar to those going to a car's spark plugs. The colors corresponded to those on the four metal sockets. They attached the leads to the sockets and screwed them down tight. None of the four men moved; they were guinea pigs used to being treated as such.

"Comrade General," Vasilev said, "perhaps then we

should have waited until we found four men whose patriotism we could be assured of?"

"And who would volunteer to allow this to be done to them?" Vortol laughed. "You scientists are quite naive. This is still in the experimental stage. If you succeed today, then perhaps we could allow you to use different subjects."

"Sir, we–" Vasilev began.

"Enough!" Sarovan snapped. "You are to stand down, Comrade Vasilev. We will deal with you later."

Vasilev looked into the chamber once more. Earphones were securely fastened onto each man's ears. Rhythmic music was being pumped in through the wires at a very high volume. Vasilev knew the purpose of the music was to keep each man's attention and also to prepare the harmonics of the brain. He had spent three years simply determining what type of music worked best, amid all the other aspects of this project he had worked on.

The red flashing light ceased its activity, and the experimental chamber was plunged into darkness except for a single searchlight, centered on the metal tube. At a signal from Sarovan, the lids on each of the coffins slowly swung shut. Fluid pumped in, floating the men inside, while air from the chamber was delivered to them through a tube clamped onto their mouths. The liquid was heated to exactly body temperature and furthered the subject's sensory deprivation.

Vasilev was ignored as the party gathered around a machine in the control room. Sarovan placed a photograph of a submarine, the *Thresher*, on a piece of plate glass that was on the top of one of the machines. A light glowed upward, taking in the picture.

"This image is being fed through the machines directly into the occipital lobes of each of the four men," Sarovan explained to the military officers. "They see it as if it were before their eyes. It is the only 'light' they have seen in weeks. They *have* to see this image. They have no choice. We are also intermittently sending them the location of the submarine in a series of image stages from large scale to small—Atlantic Ocean first, then narrowing down to the exact location."

"So they see it and they have the location," Vortol growled. "I still do not understand how this works."

Sarovan did his best to swallow his sigh. "Comrade General, what we are dealing with here is a new physics. We call it the Many-Worlds Interpretation of quantum mechanics. We have been studying it for a while." He spoke from rote memory, while the active part of his mind focused on the equipment in front of him.

"In normal quantum mechanics, you have electricity, which is the emission and absorption of virtual photons. You have AM radio, which is electromagnetic modulation of photons, and you have FM radio, which changes the frequency of the photons into what you call radio waves." He glanced up. He knew he'd already begun to lose the general, but he always believed in starting from a known before moving into the unknown.

"But can you see a radio wave?" Sarovan continued. "Feel it? It is the virtual photon that propagates these waves. This virtual world is all around you, the waves passing through you all the time, yet you are not aware of it.

"What we are doing here is modulating the individual photons, one by one, that make up a virtual wave. However, we are not doing an electromagnetic modulation exactly or a frequency modulation, but rather we are affecting the virtual state of the photon, the virtual world that the photon, which has action but not substance, exists in."

Sarovan spared a glance at his audience. They were trying to look like they understood, but he knew they didn't. He himself had a Ph.D. in physics and had been working in this field for decades, and he still wasn't exactly sure how the virtual world worked. He just knew they had stuck their toe in the door and, through sheer luck, had been able to accomplish some things.

"What we have to do," Sarovan continued, "is generate a coherent virtual wave of photons inside the tube, what we call phased displacement, which absorbs any physical material, taking it from the real plane to the virtual. That is what the computers and phased-displacement generator–the metal tube–are for.

"Then, like a radio station, we can send a signal of the photons which carry the object. The phased-displacement generator is not enough, however, for us to have an effective weapons system. The problem is then twofold. Think how a radio wave goes in all directions as far as the strength of the signal will propagate. There is no focus, no direction.

"To have a weapon, we must direct the object once it is on the wave, and then re-form the object in the real world once at the target. That is what we use the men below–what we call remote viewers–for. We went through over twenty thousand prisoners to find these four, men who have the ability to 'see' on the virtual or psychic plane. Who can find our target and direct the object on the wave the proper direction and distance. Both parts–the generator and the remote viewers–are needed to make the weapon system complete."

Something else was being brought into the chamber below. Four soldiers wheeled a platform up to the tube. Two of the men climbed onto the platform, next to a wooden crate. The bottom of the platform scissored, raising it up to a level with the open hatch near the top of the tube. They picked up a round, green-painted shell and carefully slid it into the opening. Reaching in, they attached four leads on the inside of the tube to the shell, then, with great difficulty, they swung shut the thick door and began screwing it into place using long levers on the outside handles.

"As you may well recognize, that is a nuclear warhead designed for the S-23, 180-millimeter Lowitzer," Professor Sarovan informed the GRU officers. "Its yield is the smallest possible, just under one kiloton."

There was a nervous rustling among the officers.

"Are we safe?" General Vortol demanded.

"The tube can contain the explosion if need be, venting it down into the earth," Sarovan lied to them. "But it will not be a problem. The warhead will not be in there when it explodes."

The GRU officers looked at one another, their skepticism quite apparent—both about the explosion being contained and the bomb no longer being in the chamber.

"Your explanation is not sufficient," Vortol said. "It seems to be a pile of scientific excrement designed to befuddle the listener."

Sarovan shrugged his massive shoulders. "I explained as best we understand, Comrade General. There is much we don't understand. Could you explain the physics of how one of your tank guns works? Or a jet fighter flying? You cannot, but you do know those weapons work. We know this works."

"It did not work the last time you attempted this," Vortol noted.

"That was *not* the last time we tested this. We have run four tests in the past two years, and all have been successful."

Vortol's voice was cold. "Let me correct myself, Comrade Scientist. The last time you used a nuclear warhead, it failed. With terrible consequences."

Silence filled the control room. They all had sufficient clearances to know what had happened in late 1958. In fact, both Sarovan and Vasilev had been extremely fortunate to have survived the disaster, mainly because they had manned the remote-viewing site, overseeing where the warhead was supposed to have gone. Those stationed where the warhead was initiated had all perished in a terrific explosion that had devastated a large portion of Russian countryside to the east of the Ural Mountains, just north of the city of Chelyabinsk. The dead had numbered in the thousands. That disaster had led to Department Eight's exile to this remote site.

One of the scientists below indicated all was ready. The experimental chamber was evacuated and the doors shut, leaving only the four men in the coffins.

"We are now seeking to gain a coherent balance in the hyperspatial flux inside and placing the bomb in the virtual field," Sarovan informed the military men. "Building our virtual wave and containing it before release, so to speak. We must achieve this before proceeding further. That is what those computers"–he pointed to a bank of machines along the back wall of the control center, manned by a dozen white-coated technicians–"are for."

Vasilev could sense the growing unease among the soldiers as the minutes passed and nothing apparent happened. A green light flickered on the console in front of Sarovan.

"We have coherence." There was a quiver to the scientist's normally calm voice. "Initiating phase two."

Sarovan leaned slightly forward toward a microphone. His voice was low, almost soothing as it spoke to the four subjects. "The target. You must find the target." He repeated the two sentences for almost a minute, but nothing happened. Still speaking, he gestured with his right hand.

One of the other scientists turned a knob.

Sarovan momentarily shut off the microphone to address the GRU officers. "Current is being sent directly into the brain center of each man. To the place that regulates pain. You could not even begin to imagine what they are experiencing right now."

"Ahh," General Vortol said. "Motivation. We have used that direct stimulation technique on prisoners. Most effective torture, with no actual physical harm other than the probe into the brain."

"These men are special," Sarovan said. "They were tested at our Institute along with thousands of others, and these four had the highest rating on our psychic ability scale. We have long known that certain people have an ability to do what we call remote viewing–to 'see' places that are physically distant from them, using their minds. That is how these men will find the target for us and 'aim'– so to speak–the weapon."

Sarovan turned the mike back on. "The target. You must find the target." He repeated that several times.

"We have a lock," one of the scientists announced from his desk, watching a panel.

"Show me the target," Sarovan said into the microphone. "Show me the target."

Above the tube, something flickered. A long black object appeared, the image hazy and unclear, floating in the middle of the experimental chamber, slowly gaining more form and substance.

One of the GRU officers swore under his breath as the forty-foot-long image became clear: a submarine. They could even see the propellers moving in the air. It was an exact copy of the picture on the machine: the USS *Thresher*. The image was not totally solid, as they could faintly make out the other side of the cavern through it. It was nose down, diving.

"That is the *Thresher* as it is operating right now in the Atlantic Ocean," Sarovan told the officers. His knuckles were white as they gripped the edge of his desk. "Center the target," he whispered into the mike, then cut it off.

"Arm the warhead," he ordered the man next to him, who threw a switch and flipped open a cover, revealing a red button underneath. The GRU officers all unconsciously took a step back from the window. Vasilev's hand hovered over a button on his console, the neutralizer switch, his eyes focused on the chamber below.

"Center the target," Sarovan repeated to the four men below.

Slowly the image descended, until the tube was centered in the middle of the image.

"Initiate ten-second countdown on warhead detonation," Sarovan ordered. The man next to him slammed his fist down on the red button.

When the countdown hit five, Sarovan leaned forward to the mike. "Project!" he yelled. "Project!"

There was a bright flash of light.

The image faded.

One of the scientists monitoring a panel spun about. "The warhead is gone!"

That was confirmed as the countdown passed through zero and nothing happened in the chamber.

Sarovan's broad smile showed his exultation. "The wave carried the warhead to the target. We have succeeded!"

Vasilev realized he had stopped breathing and had gone completely rigid, waiting for the explosion in the chamber. He untensed his muscles, taking a deep breath.

"That is it?" General Vortol asked suspiciously.

Sarovan pointed at a radio. "Call your plane monitoring the area."

Alarms rang on the *Skylark*. The *Thresher* had been at depth for fifteen minutes without a problem, but now garbled reports were coming of electrical trouble. Then suddenly the communication was gone. The sonar men on the *Skylark* threw down their headsets as a tremendous explosion roared into their ears.

The captain of the *Skylark* ran to the side of his bridge.

He staggered back as the surface of the ocean erupted in a massive mound of white water two kilometers off his starboard bow. The fountain went up two hundred feet, then slowly subsided. The large wave hit the *Skylark*, rolling it thirty degrees over, and then passed.

"Get me contact with *Thresher*!" the captain yelled as he ran back into the bridge. The sonar men put their headsets back on, but all they heard were noises that everyone associated with submarines prayed they'd never hear: the sound, like popcorn popping in the depths, of bulkheads giving way, and the high-pressure noise of air escaping into the ocean.

That noise meant that what remained of the *Thresher* was headed for the bottom and 129 men had just died.

Far overhead, circling to the east, a Soviet TU-20 Bear-D reconnaissance plane noted what had happened.

General Vortol put the radiophone down. A broad smile crossed his face. "They saw the explosion reach the surface!" He grabbed Professor Sarovan by the shoulders and gave him a vigorous hug. "You did it!"

The doors in the chamber below opened, and soldiers and scientists walked in. At the other end of the control center, Vasilev slowly relaxed. He walked over to the computers and pulled the tapes off, putting them back in their case. He turned and walked to the elevator, knowing he was done here. He stepped in as the sounds of the celebration behind him rose. The doors swung shut and blocked out the noise. With a jolt, the elevator began going up.

In the control room, Sarovan pulled a bottle of vodka out of a drawer, and drinks were poured all around. What no one remembered in the excitement was that power was still being fed to the four men through the leads to their heads.

General Vortol was beside himself. "We cannot be

defeated now! We have the ultimate weapon! We do not need Cuba to base our missiles. We can strike anywhere in the world from right here."

On the surface, Vasilev stepped out of the elevator, the heavy doors sliding shut behind him. The bitter arctic wind cut into the exposed skin on his face.

Inside the experimental chamber, the scientist closest to one of the coffins reached forward to open the lid, when his right hand suddenly jerked upward. The scientist didn't have time to ponder this strange development for long, because the arm snapped like a twig, bone protruding from the forearm. He screamed, staggering back.

At another coffin, one of the other scientists jerked backward, his hands going to his eyes, tearing at them. Fingers came forth dripping blood, holding two eyeballs, the occipital nerves still dangling.

There was a moment of shock in the control room, then Sarovan dropped the bottle and sprinted to the panel Vasilev had been at. He slammed his fist down on the button Vasilev had watched over. Canisters exploded, pouring gas into the chamber. The surviving scientists and soldiers in the experimental chamber turned and ran for the door, but it slid shut in their face, locking them in.

Sarovan watched as the scientists at the last two coffins grabbed each other around the throat. The gas was now rising inside the chamber. It was fast acting and Sarovan almost regretted having to use it, but there would always be other bodies to use now that they had had this success. The men trying to get out slumped to the floor, bodies twitching as the gas tore into their nervous system.

"What is happening?" Vortol demanded.

"Everything is under control," Sarovan said. He pointed at the coffinlike objects in the chamber. "They will be dead in twenty seconds. The—" Sarovan's jaw dropped open in shock as the heavy lids to all four coffins flew off, spinning through the air and crashing down. The four men inside all sat bolt upright, their heads turned in his direction, eyeless sockets fixing him with their dead gaze through the gas swirling about them. The wires still dangled from the sockets in their heads. Something formed in the air above the men—a black vortex, five feet in diameter. Sarovan had never seen anything as dark, as if the universe had opened up and was showing him its deepest depth.

Sarovan stepped back from the blast glass, hands raised in futile defense. Lightning crackled around the vortex, arcing outward. Then the vortex exploded and all was consumed.

On the surface, Vasilev spun about as the massive elevator doors buckled as if a huge hand had punched them from the inside. The earth beneath his feet trembled violently, and he fell to his knees on the icy runway.

The Present

Chapter One

Wires and tubes crisscrossed on the bed, and Sergeant Major Jimmy Dalton carefully scooted them aside as he gingerly sat on the edge. With a callused hand he tenderly brushed a stray lock of gray hair off the face of the woman lying there.

He could feel the press of her thin thigh against his hip, and he stared at her face, letting his hand lightly trace over every wrinkle and line etched there by the years, lingering on the closed eyelids. He let out a deep breath and took her hand in his, careful not to disturb the IV line in the back of it. He leaned over, his lips close to her ear. His voice was a low, gravelly one, one that gave an immediate sense of confidence to the listener.

"Well, my Treasure, another great day in airborne country. The colonel gives his regards. He was by last night. Lots of people are worried, but I know you're going to be all right.

"The Christmas formal is only six weeks away and, well, I was wondering if you might want to escort this old soldier there." Dalton waited, head cocked as if listening to an answer, before speaking again.

"You've been away from home for four months now. I think it's time to be coming back. I miss you."

Dalton felt her skin under his fingers. He remembered the long years when he had so yearned for just this sensation, to be able to feel her once more. He leaned close and put his lips to her ear. "You waited for me for five years when I was a POW, I'll wait forever for you. So we can be together once more."

"Sergeant Major Dalton?"

Dalton slowly straightened and looked over his shoulder at the door. A young woman, at least by his standards young, somewhere in her thirties, stood there. She held a metal clipboard in her hand. "I'm sorry to disturb you. I'm Dr. Kairns. I was assigned yesterday to take care of your wife. I assume you know that Dr. Inhout, who was caring for your wife, was transferred."

Dalton slid off the bed, his highly polished boots making contact with the tile floor. Dalton was a little less than average height, five foot nine inches tall, and had a stocky, well-muscled build. His face was dark and well tanned, cut with deep lines, his hair heavily peppered with gray and cut very short. He walked across and held out his hand. Kairns, after a moment of surprise, took it.

"Thank you for taking care of Marie, ma'am," Dalton said.

"Well, you're welcome, but I haven't really done anything yet." She held up the chart. "I have—"

Dalton took her elbow. "Perhaps we should talk outside."

Kairns looked over at the bed. She knew the woman could not hear them, but she allowed herself to be escorted out of the room. They walked down the hallway to an empty waiting room. Large windows revealed Cheyenne Mountain to the west, the sides covered in snow. Between the window and the mountain lay rows and rows of barracks, motor pools, and housing areas, all comprising Fort Carson, home to the 4th Infantry Division and the 10th Special Forces Group. Behind and to the right of Cheyenne Mountain, and barely visible, was the bright white top of

Pikes Peak, catching the first rays of the rising sun coming over the Great Plains of Colorado from the east.

Kairns flipped open the chart once more. "We took another MRI and there's no doubt your wife suffered an aneurysm in the anterior portion of the frontal lobe." Kairns looked up at the sergeant major. He nodded, indicating he knew what an aneurysm was.

Kairns showed him the MRI. "It happened here. Fortunately, there wasn't too much bleeding or swelling of the brain, but I have to warn you it could happen at any moment even though she's been in here a while. The brain is very strange. Very delicate at times, very tough at others, and there's much we don't know about it."

"Why is she unconscious?" Dalton asked. Ever since being admitted four months ago, his wife had been in a coma.

"In effect, she also suffered a stroke. I thought Dr. Inhout would have explained all that."

"He did, but I'd like to know what you think the situation is, given that you are the one who is going to be caring for her."

Kairns said, "Even if your wife regains consciousness, there is a high likelihood of some brain damage. The blood that came from the burst blood vessel, well, that flow was interrupted, obviously, and the part of the brain that blood vessel feeds did not get enough oxygen for an extended period of time."

Dalton nodded to indicate he understood. He walked over to a hard plastic seat and sank down in it. He wore heavily starched camouflage fatigues that were covered with insignia: The Combat Infantry badge with two stars and the Master Parachutist badge were sewn above his name tag. Below it was sewn the small dive-mask badge indicating Dalton was scuba qualified. On his left shoulder was a Special Forces patch, of subdued green and black to match the fatigues. Above it was a Ranger tab and a Special Forces tab. He wore an identical Special Forces patch on his right shoulder, indicating combat service in the unit.

The patch was in the shape of an arrowhead, homage to the stealthiness and craftiness of Indian warriors. An upright dagger was in the center, to indicate the covert way Special Forces operated. Three lightning bolts ripped across the dagger, representing the three means by which Special Forces soldiers infiltrated their objective: by air, sea, and land. The patch, and the green beret that went along with it, were the insignia of the elite of the United States Army. Sergeant Major Dalton had served thirty years in the unit, one of the very few left on active service who had served in Vietnam. Mornings like this he felt the cumulative effect of those thirty years.

Kairns grabbed another seat and pulled it nearby.

"What's the prognosis, ma'am?" Kairns had an oak leaf on her white collar, and despite the twenty-year age difference between them, she held the higher rank. Other than her rank, the only other insignia she wore was the abacus of the Medical Corps. On his collar, Dalton had pinned the three chevrons and three rockers, with a star circled by a wreath in the center, indicating he was a sergeant major, the highest enlisted rank in the Army.

Kairns looked down at the chart once more, but Dalton was aware she didn't need it for the information. She knew, she just didn't want eye-to-eye contact when she told him. He knew, even before she spoke, that the answer would not be good. The previous doctor had been full of crap, in Dalton's opinion. Even when Dalton had asked the man to level with him, the doctor had hidden behind a flurry of medical terms, most of which, despite his own medical training, Dalton had had to go to the library and look up. He knew more about aneurysms now than he particularly cared to. As he did about the other afflictions ravaging his wife's body.

"There is most likely some permanent damage to the brain. We won't know exactly how much or what kind until your wife regains consciousness."

Dalton could hear the "if" in her voice. He had always been able to read people, and the skill was one he had honed over the years.

"When do you think that's likely to occur?" he asked.

"That's hard to say."

"There's a possibility she might not regain consciousness at all, isn't there?" Dalton asked in a quiet voice.

Kairns leaned back in her seat and looked directly at him. Dalton noted she had soft green eyes, just like Marie's. He knew his wife would have liked this woman. Marie had always made friends so easily.

"Yes, that is a possibility." Kairns cleared her throat.

"Go ahead," Dalton said.

"This setback on top of your wife's advanced amyotrophic lateral sclerosis . . ." The doctor paused.

"Her body has been gone for two years due to ALS," Dalton said. "All she's had is her mind and now you're telling me that's probably not going to come back?"

"No, it's not."

Dalton tried to keep his voice steady. "She's not going to regain consciousness, is she?"

Kairns slowly shook her head. "No, I don't think she will."

Even though he had long expected those words, their impact surprised Dalton.

"There's the issue . . ." Kairns paused again.

"Go on," Dalton dully said.

"There's the issue of whether you want to continue the life support," Kairns said.

Dalton rubbed his chin, feeling the slight stubble there, aware that he would have to shave when he got to work. He felt a rapid beating in his chest. He dipped his head and put his hand on his forehead, hiding his eyes from the doctor. He slowed his heartbeat as he'd been trained, forcing his mind to accept the reality. His hands felt cold and clammy and in a remote part of his mind he knew that the blood vessels were closing, choking the flow of blood, and he knew he could reverse that process, he'd been taught that, but he didn't care right now. A tear rolled out of his right eye, down his weathered cheek.

He heard movement, and when he looked up a minute later, he was alone. He looked down the hallway. Kairns was standing twenty feet away, writing something into the chart. Dalton stood and walked over to her.

"My wife appreciates all you've done for her." Dalton caught the quick quiver of her eyes and said, "I'm not nuts, Major. When you spend thirty years with someone, you know what they *would* be thinking, so I just thought I'd let you know that. And *I* certainly appreciate all your efforts."

Kairns nodded.

"There's nothing you can do?" he asked.

Kairns let the chart hang at her side and met his gaze. "No. We have to hope the brain can stabilize itself, and that can take quite a long time. If there's a turn for the worse, we might have to go in to reduce pressure, but let's hope that doesn't occur. It's been four months now and things haven't gotten worse, so in a way, that's a good sign. I am sorry, Sergeant Major."

"Keep her as comfortable as possible," Dalton said. "I have to think about what to do."

"I didn't mean to pressure you," Kairns hurriedly said. "There's certainly no—"

Dalton held up his hand. "I know. I'm glad you were frank with me. I appreciate the honesty."

Dalton bid the doctor good-bye and walked down the corridor. He paused outside his wife's room and watched her from the doorway for ten minutes, then reluctantly continued on, his morning visit done.

Chapter Two

She was beautiful. Tall, six feet from her bare feet to her shining blond hair. Smooth skin, very pale, except for a red blush on her cheeks. Icy blue eyes that softened as they looked at him. Her body was exquisite, the breasts those of a nubile young girl, the belly flat, the legs those of a trained dancer, the figure barely sheathed in a white flowing gown that was transparent.

Another figure appeared behind the woman. A dark-haired twin to the first. This one wore only garters and stockings, carrying her body without the slightest hint of modesty.

The first woman circled to his left, the second to his right. He felt himself pressed between them, the hard and soft of their bodies molding into his, but there was a barrier between, more than the flimsy clothes, like a thin layer of warm air. It felt smooth and caressing, but it wasn't the same as bare flesh.

The woman behind him ran her hands over his chest while the one in front reached over his shoulder and kissed the other, before coming back to kiss him.

Feteror checked the time with irritation as the women continued their caresses. He controlled himself, not allowing his true feelings to surface. He had no choice and it was best to let this event go to its programmed conclusion.

Finally, the two women faded away, disappearing into a fog, the controllers satisfied that they had satisfied Feteror.

He felt full power come back on, the charge flowing into him like a cleansing waterfall, filling the pool of his soul.

"We can change the women."

Feteror recognized the invisible voice, even though it came through electronic channels. General Rurik, his captor and commander.

"We have a new programmer," Rurik continued. "He is most skilled. He assures me he can design whatever you desire." Rurik laughed. "Or perhaps you would like a man? That just occurred to me. You Spetsnatz warriors are a strange breed. Fancy yourself Spartans. But Spartans had no time for women, only each other. This is something perhaps we should consider?"

Feteror's "eyes" clicked on. He could see Rurik now, standing at the main control console. The general was tall and distinguished looking, with white hair combed straight back. His chest was covered in medals and he walked with a slight limp.

"I am satisfied," Feteror said. He could hear the echo of his own voice, tinny and raspy, coming out of the speaker. He knew that Rurik could change the voice, make it more realistic, more human, but he also knew the general didn't to taunt him, to keep an edge.

"Satisfied?" Rurik laughed once more. "You had better be. The good doctor says it is important that you have everything as a normal person should. To keep your sanity, but I doubt if you have ever been sane." Rurik paused. "Tell me, Feteror. Do you dream? The doctor tells me he puts you to sleep, that you must sleep for your sanity. That you must dream. But if you dream, what do you dream? Of the body that was once yours?"

Feteror heard Rurik but his concentration was on his status. Power was at 94 percent. Good enough. All systems were functioning. He checked the backup programs.

General Rurik's voice intruded once more. "We need

more information. The Ministry is concerned about your previous intelligence report regarding the treaty exchange with Kazakhstan."

"Concerned?" Feteror would have laughed but there was no laughter configured for his voice program.

"You will do your duty for the State," Rurik said. "You can access the tasking now."

The State. What was the State? Feteror wondered. The one that had sent him to Afghanistan years ago and cost him everything? But that State no longer existed. The farce that had replaced it? A husk of the empire he had served so proudly? Where criminals were now more powerful than the government? That was an impotent bear on the international scene?

He accessed the tasking that had been put into his database. As expected, he was to surveil the Mafia and find whether they planned to intercept a shipment of nuclear weapons that Kazakhstan was required to send back to Russia as part of the internal strategic arms agreement between the various states that had once comprised the Soviet Union. In return, Kazakhstan would get several ships of the Baltic fleet.

"There is something else." General Rurik walked in front of the camera that was hooked to what remained of Feteror. The general's left hand was on his right wrist, lightly touching a metal band. There was a small green light steadily blinking on the band. That band was Feteror's leash. On the ring finger of that hand was a thick gold band set with several diamonds.

"One of our undercover men has picked up a report that a Mafia gang is making some inquiries about old research programs."

Feteror waited.

"We don't have much information other than that there has been a contact made with a ranking officer in GRU research files. We are a bit concerned and I want you to check this out also."

"I need more information than that," Feteror said. "Do you know which Mafia gang it is? My database indicates several operate in Moscow."

"Yes, the group run by someone with the rather interesting title of 'Oma,' " Rurik said.

"Do you have the name of the GRU officer who has been contacted?"

"No. We are, of course, investigating."

"Do you know the nature of the research they are inquiring into?"

"No."

"How do you know about the Mafia group, then, or that there was a contact, if you didn't get it from your end?" Feteror asked.

"We have an agent inside this Oma group. A man posing as a bodyguard. He knows only that there is a meeting set with the GRU traitor. He doesn't know where the meeting will occur, but it is to happen shortly. I want the name of the traitor."

"I will investigate," Feteror said.

"You may go now," Rurik said. He signaled to one of the technicians.

A circle of light appeared, a long white tunnel beckoning. Feteror gathered himself, then leapt for the circle.

The old man had fouled himself hours ago. There was a steel collar around his neck, attached to an iron chain, welded to a pin set in the center of the concrete floor. He had determined all that by feel, as he was in complete darkness and had been so ever since being thrown into this pit.

He had no idea how long he had been here. He estimated about two days, but he was aware that he was very disoriented. His last memory before this hole was of walking down the stairs to the subway in Moscow, going to work at the Institute. Hands grabbed him from behind, something was pressed over his mouth, and then he awoke here in the darkness.

There was a bucket of stale water that he had drunk from carefully, not sure when it would be refilled. No food and no sign of his captors either.

He was naked and cold. The concrete was damp, and there was a dripping noise in one direction, but the chain wouldn't allow him to reach any wall. Just twenty feet of rough concrete floor in every direction.

He sensed something change. A presence. He looked about but he could see nothing.

He started when the voice came out of the darkness. "Professor Vasilev."

The old man spun about but could see nothing.

"Professor Vasilev." The voice was deep, deeper than any voice Vasilev had ever heard, with a rough edge to it that made the hair on the back of his neck stand on end.

The old man wet his lips with a swollen tongue. "Yes?" His voice was weak, quavering, bouncing into the walls and being absorbed. His heart rate increased dramatically as two red objects appeared, about seven feet above the floor, glowing like coals in the darkness. Eyes.

"Who are you?" Vasilev whispered.

"I am Chyort," the voice rasped. "The devil."

Vasilev's gaze was focused on those red dots staring at him. "What do you want?"

"Where are the computer tapes from October Revolution Island?"

Vasilev swallowed. "What are you talking about?"

"The tapes for the phased-displacement generator you took with you when you left."

"There is—"

"Do not lie to me," the voice warned. "There are many

things worse than dying, and I am intimate with all of them. Where are the tapes?"

Vasilev closed his eyes. "They were updated and transferred onto floppy first, then CD-ROM three years ago."

"Where is the CD stored?"

"With everything else. GRU records."

"Is the program current?"

Vasilev frowned. "Current?"

"Has it been updated to run with current operating systems in modern computers?"

Vasilev sighed. "As of a few years ago, yes, but I don't know if it is current with today's operating systems." He looked up at the two inhuman eyes. "Where am I? Why am I here?"

"This is hell," the voice said. "And you are here to pay retribution for your sins."

As the rough, evil voice faded, so did the two coals, and Vasilev was left in darkness once more.

Chapter Three

The walls of the conference room were covered with plaques and photos from Special Operations units all over the world. From the Royal Danish Navy's Fromandskorpset, to the now defunct Canadian Parachute Regiment, to the Norwegian Jaegers, the plaques were tokens of goodwill to the men of the 2nd Battalion, 10th Special Forces Group (Airborne) for various training and operational missions conducted with those elite units.

Dalton knew that each of those plaques represented a lot of sweat and time, and in some cases blood. He knew that because he'd been to every country represented on the wall and had taken part in practically every type of exercise with the A-Teams of 10th Group. What he also knew was that there were plenty of exercises and deployments that would never have a plaque to commemorate because they were too classified to be acknowledged.

Dalton had been in 10th Group, off and on, for twenty years, with some other assignments sprinkled in over the years. He considered the unit to be his home in the Army, although he had served in it at four different places. Fort Carson, Colorado, was a new posting for 10th Group, the unit being transferred there in the mid-nineties during a round of base closures that had shut down its longtime home at Fort Devens, Massachusetts. The 1st Battalion of the 10th Group had been staged forward in Germany since the unit had come into existence in the late fifties. First at

Bad Tolz, a former SS training barracks, where Dalton had done two tours, then, more recently, when Bad Tolz was given back to the Germans, at Stuttgart.

If there was one constant in Dalton's military life, it was change, and this morning he was ready for whatever was going to be laid on the table. As soon as he'd come to work, he'd been grabbed by the battalion adjutant and told that there was an important meeting in five minutes in the conference room and the colonel wanted him to sit in on it.

Since the briefing hadn't yet started, he had no idea what this was about, but he had a bad feeling, mainly due to the glimpse he'd had of the two people in the colonel's office, which adjoined his. The man wore civilian clothes—a black turtleneck under an expensive blazer—but it was more than just the usual military distrust of those not in uniform that generated Dalton's negative feelings. Dalton had been in Special Operations for over thirty years now, and he could read Agency in a man as easily as if he had the letters of his organization imprinted on his forehead with a bright red tattoo. The man was either CIA, DIA, or NSA. The other person in the colonel's office was a woman, dressed in a tailored suit, her blond hair drawn tight. Dalton hadn't been able to get a read on her.

When Dalton had walked into the conference room, he'd noted there were two other people already there: Captain Anderson and Master Sergeant Trilly, a combination that Dalton found strange. Anderson was the battalion assistant operations officer. Trilly was the team sergeant for ODA 054. Dalton had greeted them both, then taken his usual seat next to the head of the table.

ODA stood for Operational Detachment Alpha and was the official designation for the basic organizational element of Special Forces, more commonly called an A-Team. The company headquarters, one hierarchical level below Dalton but one above the ODA, was the ODB, or B-Team, each of which commanded five ODAs. Dalton was the sergeant major of the battalion, or ODC, which had three ODBs in it, and fifteen ODAs. Anderson was the man who helped plan the missions all those teams went on.

What set the Special Forces units apart from the rest of the Army was that SF troopers rarely operated tactically at any higher level than the A-Team. The B and C teams existed mainly for command and support purposes. This placed a great deal of responsibility on those at the lowest levels and was the major reason Special Forces looked for very mature soldiers to fill its ranks.

Dalton had a lot of respect for Captain Anderson, who had commanded a team for two years before being brought up to battalion for the past year, but not as much for Trilly. Anderson was a West Pointer who had commanded a company in the Infantry before going through Special Forces training. He was six feet tall and in great shape, able to keep up with the physical demands of the training a team went through. He had dark hair cut tight against his skull, flecks of gray already appearing along the sides. The most important traits Anderson had, in Dalton's opinion, were the ability to know what he could do and what he couldn't and his willingness to trust his men to do their jobs. Too many officers that Dalton had served with over the years had held back their implicit trust from those they commanded, and in a self-fulfilling prophecy, that lack had eaten away at the integrity of the unit.

The problem with Trilly, in Dalton's opinion, was that he simply didn't have enough Special Forces experience. Trilly had gone through the Special Forces qualification course as a senior E-7, after fifteen years of duty in the air defense artillery. He'd come to 10th Group three years ago, been promoted to E-8 six months ago, and, despite Dalton's misgivings, been given the team sergeant slot based on his rank. Dalton had convinced Colonel Metter to assign Trilly to 054, which he felt had the strongest team leader in the battalion, commanding what was probably the best team. But where was the team leader? Dalton wondered. If 054 was going to be used in some sort of operation, the team leader should have been present.

Dalton knew both of the men from a training experience they had gone through as part of a two-team contingent three years ago—a classified experience that was not represented by a plaque on the wall.

Dalton turned his attention from the other men as the colonel and two civilians came in.

"All right," Colonel Metter said as he walked to the end of the conference table. "Let's get this going." He pointed to his right. "This is Mr. Raisor, from the Central Intelligence Agency. He's brought us a high-level tasking direct from Washington for one A-Team to participate in some rather unique training. Accompanying Mr. Raisor is Dr. Hammond." Metter pointed to the woman. "Mr. Raisor, Dr. Hammond, this is Captain Anderson and Master Sergeant Trilly. As you've requested."

That answered one of Dalton's first questions.

Raisor and Hammond leaned across the conference table and shook each man's hand. Raisor's grip was strong, his body lean. He had thinning black hair and a thin face that was bland in a way that Dalton associated with bureaucratic spies. But the man's eyes caught Dalton's attention. They were flat and emotionless, almost bored. Dalton had seen that look before. Dead eyes, the sign of someone who had done dirty work in the covert world, and the only time eyes like that came alive was when someone's life was on the line. Dalton had worked with men like that, who relished combat, not concerned about the cost in terms of human suffering and death. That put Dalton on alert, because it meant the CIA had assigned one of its few killers to this project. Raisor had something in his hand that he was fingering, but Dalton couldn't make out exactly what it was, only catching a glint of gold.

"And this is Sergeant Major Dalton, my senior enlisted man."

Raisor met his gaze briefly and Dalton swore there was the hint of a cold smile on the agent's lips, as if recognizing a kindred spirit.

Raisor pulled a manila folder out of his briefcase. There was a red Top Secret cover stapled to it. "Gentlemen, what I'm going to brief you on is classified top secret, special compartmentalization. You may not discuss this with anyone, even if they have a top secret clearance." Raisor's voice was low and smooth, one used to speaking in dark rooms about secret material.

"The subject matter may seem a bit, shall we say, strange, outrageous even, but let me assure you that this is a very serious issue. First, though, let me make sure we can get the right people." He slid a piece of paper to the colonel. "Besides the two men we requested be here, we need a complete team, drawn from those who participated in Trojan Warrior."

"Trojan Warrior?" Metter asked. He had taken command a year and a half ago.

"It was a classified training program two of our teams—054 and 055—participated in three years ago," Dalton quickly told the colonel.

Metter didn't even look at the list, passing it to Dalton. Raisor's statement answered the question as to why 054's team leader wasn't here; he hadn't been on the team when it had gone through the Trojan Warrior training program. Anderson had gone through the training as the team leader of 055. Dalton didn't need to look at the list—he knew every man who had gone through that training and how many were left in the battalion from the twenty-five original members.

"It would be advantageous if you picked men from that list who did not have families," Raisor added.

Dalton put the paper down in front of him. "Because you think men without families are expendable?"

"Because we think men without families are better security risks for the duration of the operation," Raisor answered.

"Do you need a full team?" Dalton asked.

"Yes," Raisor said.

"We can't do that. Of the twenty-five names on this list," Dalton said, still not looking at the paper, "there are only seven left in the battalion. The others have either left the service or moved to other assignments."

"Then give me all seven." Raisor sounded irritated.

Dalton held up the list. "What does Trojan Warrior have to do with this briefing? That program was dropped two years ago."

"We'll get to that later in the briefing," Raisor said.

"Then why don't we get started so we know what we're getting these men into?" Colonel Metter suggested.

Raisor looked at the other three Special Forces men. "I assume those of you who were in Trojan Warrior heard of Operation Grill Flame?"

Dalton glanced at Captain Anderson, who returned the look with a roll of his eyes. Trilly looked like he was about to answer, but Dalton beat him to it. "That was the code name for a Defense Intelligence Agency operation using remote viewers."

Raisor nodded. "That is correct."

"Remote viewers?" Metter asked.

"Psychics," Dalton said. "People who supposedly could see things at a distance just by using their minds."

"Not supposedly," Raisor said. "Grill Flame was real. And, contrary to what people believe, it still exists. We just

renamed it. It's called Bright Gate now and we've taken
over operational control of it from the military."

Dalton didn't blink at the implied slam from the
younger man. "Besides Trojan Warrior, I know about Grill
Flame from an operational standpoint."

That gave Raisor pause. "What was that?"

"When I was in Lebanon in the early eighties, your
people brought in some Grill Flame operators to help
search for the hostages in Beirut. We busted a few doors
where they told us they 'saw' the hostages being held. We
came up with nothing and almost got our asses shot off a
few times."

"The success rate has increased dramatically since
then," Raisor said. "So much so, that we're ready to take the
next step. Combine Trojan Warrior with Grill Flame for
something completely new."

The others in the room waited as Raisor stood. He
walked to the podium in the front of the room. Using a
remote, he turned down the lights. Dalton could see that
the object Raisor had been playing with was a ring, which
he had slipped over his left pinky. It looked like a college
ring but it was much too small for Raisor. The slide projector came on.

TOP SECRET

**PSYCHIC
WARRIOR**

TOP SECRET

Raisor's voice came out of the darkness next to the
screen. "Gentlemen, we are passing into a new age of war-

fare. We are literally entering a new dimension. One where the commonly accepted limitations of physics and the way combat has been conducted no longer apply."

Dalton sighed and leaned back in his seat. He could just see Raisor briefing the Select Intelligence Committee in Congress with the same words and the same slides. It was the same way the initial briefings for Trojan Warrior had been conducted. He knew the slides hadn't been made up to impress a bunch of green beanies who were going to have to do what they were ordered.

"There has never been a jump in warfare such as the one we are making with Psychic Warrior. The commonly accepted nexus points of war technology—the use of iron, the invention of the firearm, the plane, the tank, even the atomic bomb—all pale against the radical nature of Psychic Warrior."

A new slide came up with the words *Grill Flame* written in bold black, with red flames encircling the letters.

"A little background is necessary in order to understand where we are now," Raisor said. "Operation Grill Flame was started in 1981 as a joint Army-CIA program to examine the potential of remote viewing, or RVing—the ability to psychically see objects or locations at a distance. The primary responsibility for the project lay with the Army and the unit was based at Fort Meade.

"As your sergeant major has noted, the project had some growing pains. In fact, to read open source material on the project, you would think that the Army disbanded it four years ago and that no government organization is currently conducting research into any form of psychic operation.

"However, I can assure you, gentlemen, that while our government has publicly disavowed any current psychic operation, four years ago Grill Flame, under the auspices of a group called Bright Gate, went deep underground at a very classified level.

"At the same time as it appeared Grill Flame was gone, we used Bright Gate to instigate the Trojan Warrior program here in the 10th Special Forces Group. Three years ago Trojan Warrior was conducted here. It was a six-month training program designed to significantly enhance the capabilities of the participants through the application of emergent human technologies and concepts."

Raisor flashed a humorless smile. "At least that is what we told you it was. In reality, the training you men received in Trojan Warrior on such subjects as biofeedback, visualization, conscious psychological control, meditative states, cognitive task enhancement, visual control, and other subject matter"—Raisor waved his hands—"all that was part of the master plan to prepare you for Psychic Warrior."

Dalton felt a flush of anger. He'd wondered himself at the time what the purpose of some of the Trojan Warrior training had been for—six months of intense work on all the areas Raisor had mentioned, along with martial arts training. Dalton had no doubt it had made him not only a better soldier but a better person. However, there had been aspects, like the biofeedback and visualization training, that he had never quite understood the purpose of—until now. He'd seen the obvious reason for the martial arts training, but many of the subjects had seemed esoteric. He'd been lied to before in his military career, but he'd never grown used to it.

Raisor continued. "Psychic Warrior takes Trojan Warrior another step. It merges two programs, one psychic, the other medical, to come up with something completely different from the original Grill Flame operation in remote viewing and Trojan Warrior's training. Something that we feel it best to keep classified to prevent both disclosure of our capabilities and to protect those involved.

"While the Trojan Warrior training was being conducted, the remote-viewing program itself became much more efficient after years of modifying its personnel and operating procedures. Remote viewing has become an accepted intelligence-gathering apparatus of our government, and as such we must keep the extent of that capability secure from potential enemies."

"It's been over two years since we went through that training," Dalton said. "When were you going to let us in on all this?"

"When Psychic Warrior was ready for you and when we needed you," Raisor said. "Recently, an external factor has entered the scene which brings a new sense of urgency to this entire operation."

Dalton just wanted to smack the CIA man upside the head and tell him to get on with it, to tell the facts and details and stop being so melodramatic. If one of the battalion's A-Teams had conducted a briefing like that, Dalton had no doubt that Colonel Metter would have a boot up the team leader's ass in a heartbeat. The fact that Metter sat silently next to him told Dalton that his commander's secure phone to the Pentagon must have rung in conjunction with this visit and Metter was under strict orders to support the CIA.

"If you had let us know Trojan Warrior was preparation for further training," Dalton said, "we could have kept most of those men in the battalion and we wouldn't have only seven left."

"The ball was dropped on that," Raisor conceded. "My predecessor did not have much faith that Psychic Warrior would ever become operational. He was wrong. When Grill Flame was first brought into being, it was very much an experimental operation and more concerned with testing concepts than actually conducting operations. In places such as Lebanon, it was used, but only as a last resort, and the results were mixed."

Dalton could sense Raisor looking at him from the shadows. "At times," the CIA man went on, "Grill Flame personnel were used before they were trained sufficiently or prepared to conduct live operations.

"During the Gulf War, Grill Flame was employed to find Iraqi Scud missiles. The success rate was about forty percent, which actually is not that bad."

The slide changed and a picture of a destroyed Scud missile launcher was displayed.

"More recently, we have been using Grill Flame to surveil Iraqi weapons sites. Some of the recent tensions in that area have been the result of things the RVs–remote viewers–have picked up in places that satellites or even the UN human inspectors on the ground cannot gain access to."

Another slide, this one of a fenced compound in a desert region. Dalton heard Colonel Metter shift in his seat impatiently.

"You must have been planning on using my people for a while," Metter said.

Raisor nodded. "Bringing some Special Operations soldiers from Trojan Warrior on board has always been part of the master plan."

"But you didn't plan on it happening this soon," Dalton interjected.

"The timetable has been moved up somewhat," Raisor acknowledged.

Dalton held up the list. "You still haven't said exactly what you want these men for."

"To be Psychic Warriors, of course." Raisor clicked the remote. The next slide showed a large, clear, vertical tube, with Dr. Hammond standing next to it, giving some idea of its dimensions, about ten feet high by four in diameter.

There was a thick-looking, greenish liquid inside. And floating inside the greenish liquid was a man wearing just a black bodysuit with no sleeves or legs. Various lines and leads went to his body. His head was totally enclosed in an oversized black helmet out of which ran several tubes and wires. He floated freely, arms akimbo, his back slightly hunched over.

Everyone in the room sat up a little straighter and leaned forward.

"Gentlemen, this is a picture taken of an RVer working under the auspices of Bright Gate just last week. As you can see, we have come a long way from the days of sitting in a dark room with subdued music playing. This is the direction Bright Gate has gone, combining natural psychic power with technological breakthroughs in physiological psychology.

"With proper input, Bright Gate RVers can now view with a seventy-two percent success rate of finding the correct target, with sixty-eight percent accuracy in the intelligence picked up."

Dalton combined those numbers in his head and he wasn't that impressed. He'd conducted special operations, including reconnaissance missions at the strategic level, and he knew nothing could beat a set of eyeballs on target. Real eyeballs. With a thinking brain behind them. He wasn't too keen on technology either—if Grill Flame or the high-speed satellites that the National Reconnaissance Office boasted of were so great, why had Special Forces soldiers had to go deep into Iraq during the Gulf War to do live reconnaissance missions?

"Gentlemen," Raisor said, his voice rising slightly, "we are now ready to move to the next stage of military action: Operation Psychic Warrior. We will no longer just remote view, we plan to conduct actual combat operations on the psychic level."

There was a long silence before Colonel Metter spoke. "How?"

Raisor stepped in front of the screen. "That is Dr. Hammond's area of expertise." He sat down.

Hammond took his place. She was tall, maybe an inch shy of six foot, and in her mid-thirties, with very pale skin and an angular face. Her voice held the slightest tint of a New York accent. "First, let me tell you, Colonel, that three years ago when I initially learned we were to take soldiers, men with no background in the field, and make Psychic Warriors out of them, I thought the plan would not work. But when my people checked out how the soldiers in your battalion did during their Trojan Warrior training, we were extremely impressed with the quality. The names on that list, each of those men, could possibly be one of my Bright Gate personnel."

Colonel Metter stared at the woman. "Ma'am, with all due respect to you, and I don't know you or what your role in this whole thing is, the men in my battalion are the best soldiers in the world. They are some of the best *people* in the world. Don't stand up there and try to put me waist deep in bullshit. Just tell me what I need to know."

A red flush had climbed Hammond's cheeks, her face tightening. "All right, Colonel. Much of the science we are dealing with on the psychometric or virtual plane is unproven, or even if proven, not completely understood. Our philosophy at Bright Gate is to concern ourselves with what works, sometimes well before we even have a clue as to why or exactly how it works. Unlike our counterparts at the universities, we are pragmatic first and foremost. While they dabble in theory, we have gone places they only chat about over a glass of wine at academic receptions.

"As Agent Raisor has indicated, Operation Psychic Warrior has been under development for many years. The basic concept is to project not just a remote-viewing capability into the psychometric plane, which we have already accomplished, but an actual capability to project an avatar into the virtual plane, travel along jump points to the target, or far point, and then out of the virtual or psychometric plane into the real plane at the far point."

"Whoa!" Colonel Metter interrupted. "Some background and definitions would be helpful. What the hell is an avatar?"

"An avatar is a form that represents the original in the virtual plane," Hammond answered. "If you play a computer game, whatever form you take in the game is your avatar. In Psychic Warrior we go one step further. We can take that avatar from the virtual plane into the real plane at the far point. We make the avatar real."

"What the hell is the virtual plane?" Metter asked. "And the real plane?"

Hammond considered her audience for a few seconds, then spoke. "Scientists in the last couple of hundred years have been digging deeper into the physics of what makes up reality. If you'd asked a scientist two hundred years ago what they thought reality was, you would have gotten a very different answer than a hundred years ago, and fifty years ago, and so on.

"For centuries the most learned men of their age believed that matter and reality consisted of four basic substances: fire, earth, water, and air. We have made great strides since then, but it is foolish to believe we have reached the end of that path of knowledge. In some ways, people two hundred years from now may look at us as we look at those who believed in the four base elements composing all matter.

"Early in this century it was believed that the atomic level was the basic building block of matter, and thus of reality. But with the discovery of such things as quarks and further research into quantum physics, the realm of reality has been extended further into levels that couldn't even be conceptualized by the early atomic scientists.

"We at Bright Gate believe the psychometric plane is beyond the plane of quantum physics, which scientists are still groping to understand. We call it the astral or virtual plane, and there are *some* proven laws of physics we can connect to it." She smiled. "I don't think we need to get into the nuts and bolts of the theory, do you?"

Colonel Metter glanced at Dalton, who returned the look, his face telling the colonel what he thought. "As a matter of fact," Metter said, "I think we do."

Hammond frowned. "Well, let me see if I can lay it out moving from the known to the unknown. You are all aware that there is such a thing as a magnetic field, which your compasses work off of?" With four heads nodding, she continued. "You are also aware that electricity can produce an electromagnetic field. But have you ever wondered what produces the electromagnetic field? What *it* is made of?"

She didn't wait for an answer. "We call fields which produce the electromagnetic field, hyperfields. Quantum physics, with its quarks and wave theory, is a hyperfield. But there are others. They are around you all the time. In fact, there is a concurrent hyperfield to the quantum physical one. A virtual field. It is this virtual field that is the psychometric plane; the two terms are synonymous. Existing side by side at times with the real plane, at other times existing very separately from each other. It is the boundary between these two planes that is the entire focus of our efforts at Bright Gate.

"And without getting into the philosophy of it, a mental field—what you perceive in your brain—is a virtual field. If you perceive something to be with your mind, then it exists in the virtual field."

"But not in reality," Dalton interjected.

"Most physicists would say no, not in reality as it is

currently defined," Hammond said. "But if our thoughts are not reality, what are they? Everything man has ever invented or done has come out of his thoughts. So they are real in some way. So I say yes. I say that there is a link between the virtual world and the real world. That the line between the two is an artificial one that is constantly being breached. And that, with the proper equipment and training, we are able to breach at Bright Gate and will continue to go through with Psychic Warrior."

"You say?" Colonel Metter said. "Is there any proof?"

"I've been there," Hammond said. "I've been on the psychometric plane."

"And what happened?" Captain Anderson asked.

"I RVed—remote viewed—at several points on the globe."

"An out-of-body experience?" Dalton asked.

"You could call it that," Hammond said, "but that is a crude simplification of a complex process."

"How do you know it wasn't just a hallucination?" Dalton asked.

Hammond smiled, revealing even white teeth. "It might have been what you call a hallucination, but does that make it any less real? When we checked, we found out that what I saw was real, so *how* I saw is not as important as the fact that I saw it. I existed in the virtual world and saw the real."

She tapped the side of her head. "We must stop limiting our minds with the boundaries of our physical brains. We accept that we can impart what exists in our minds to others through speech, or through the visual spectrum, or any of the senses in various modes. To understand Psychic Warrior, you have to consider that there is another way to bring our minds out of the physical limitations of our bodies beyond the methods that we use every day. Those of you who were in Trojan Warrior were introduced to these concepts."

Hammond clicked through the slides quickly until she came to the one she wanted.

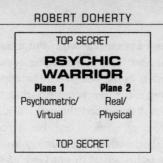

"These are the two planes I am talking about. Think about it. They quite clearly exist inside each of us. We have our minds, which operate on the psychometric plane, and then we have our bodies, which operate in the real plane. And somehow they are connected, are they not? We can take ideas from the psychometric/virtual plane of our imagination and make them real in the physical world, say in a painting. And we can process things from the physical world into our brains, remember them, even change them with our thoughts!

"What my remote viewers are able to do is travel outside of the confines of their physical brains on the psychometric plane and observe what is happening at a distance on the real plane. It is the greatest journey man has ever made! Far more significant than the first travelers across the oceans or even our journey to the moon."

"But you're talking about something very different with Psychic Warrior," Captain Anderson noted.

Hammond nodded. "Yes. What we plan to do with the Psychic Warrior is travel along the psychometric plane, then not only 'see' into the real world at a remote location, but act in it through the projected avatar."

"Is there any precedence for this?" Colonel Metter asked.

"You've all probably seen or heard of psychics who can bend a spoon with only the power of their mind? Well, some of those are frauds who employ trickery, but some of them are quite real. This is a very base-level effort, given that the psychic is in the same room as the spoon and can physically see it. We're going much further than that."

"But this is theoretical, correct?" Colonel Metter pressed.

Dalton caught the glance Hammond exchanged with Raisor. "We've conducted some limited trials," she said.

"And?" Metter prompted.

"And the trials were indeed successful."

From long experience in the covert world, Dalton knew she was both lying and telling the truth.

"Amplify your answer," Colonel Metter prompted.

"We sent an individual into the psychometric plane. That individual was able to, at a remote point, come out of the psychometric virtual plane as an avatar and influence the real, physical plane."

"Doing what?" Metter asked.

"A simple task. Rearranging some blocks in a room on the other side of the country from where he—his physical body—was located."

"Like a child in kindergarten," Metter noted.

A flush swept Hammond's face. "Yes, like in kindergarten, Colonel. We had to start somewhere and we started with the very basics."

"What went wrong?" Dalton asked.

"Excuse me?" Hammond again looked at Raisor. The CIA agent gave a very slight shake of his head.

"I asked, what went wrong?"

"You have to understand"—Hammond was picking her words carefully—"that the psychometric plane is very much unlike our reality. In some ways it is much more complex; in some ways it is much simpler. The biggest thing to know, though, is that we hardly understand it at all.

"One thing we do know is that distance can be very

confusing on the psychometric plane. Just because you are here, that doesn't preclude you from being right next to something occurring on the other side of the world in the virtual plane. Something which we are only beginning to understand is that this space, the line"—she pointed at the empty spot in the center of the slide—"between the psychometric and the real plane, is very unique. We don't know exactly what separates the two, even though we can travel through it. But in going through, there is some cause and effect, it appears." Hammond paused, as if considering how to continue.

"Sometimes our RVers can travel great distances in an instant by 'jumping' from one known point to another. At other times, though, especially if the end point desired is not clearly defined to the RVer, the trip may take time. Sometimes, the trip cannot even be completed." Hammond shrugged. "It is quite complex and requires an understanding of very complex math to even begin to understand."

"Who else is over there?" Dalton suddenly asked.

Hammond was startled, as was everyone else in the room. "No one is over there."

"But your man ran into someone or something, didn't he?" Dalton pressed.

Raisor shook his head as he spoke up. "No, he didn't run into anyone. Something happened and his mission ended before we would have liked it to. But by moving those blocks you make so little of, he did prove that it is possible to come out of the virtual world and into the real at a remote distance."

"Where is this guy?" Dalton asked.

"That's classified information," Raisor said.

"This is a classified briefing," Colonel Metter noted.

"That first trial with Psychic Warrior," Raisor said, "occurred a month ago. Since that time we have been refining the procedure." He gestured toward his partner. "Dr. Hammond has–"

"What happened to your man a month ago?" Colonel Metter's voice was flat, but it caused Raisor to pause.

"We had a problem with our equipment," Dr. Hammond said. "The problem occurred in the real world on our end. A mistake was made, a mistake which I take responsibility for and which will not occur again because I have corrected the problem."

There was silence as everyone in the room stared at her, waiting.

"Our man died. He drowned in the embryonic solution you saw on the slide."

Chapter Four

"No one knows, but more importantly, no one really cares," the man in the long black leather coat said irritably. "You soldiers are fools caught in the past. Don't you realize the State has changed?"

The other man wore an olive drab greatcoat, the three stars on the shoulder boards indicating he was a colonel in the army, the small insignia on his collar the symbol of the once dreaded GRU, the military's KGB. The two men were meeting in a remote park on the edge of Kiev. The snow had been dusted off the concrete table they were seated at. A black Mercedes, smoke coiling out of the exhaust pipe, was idling on the nearby road, a hundred meters away. The car rode low, due to the armor plating built into it. The windows were tinted, hiding the interior.

Three men, also in long black leather coats with fur-lined collars, waited outside the car, their right hands suspiciously inside the front of their coats. The park had been chosen because it was very broad and open. Anyone approaching could be seen a mile away. It had originally been built for the power elite under Communism, those who summered in the villas along the river nearby. Given the fall of Communism and the bitter winter temperatures on this day, they had the park to themselves.

Colonel Seogky didn't trust the man across from him, but he didn't really trust anyone anymore, so that mattered little. His focus was on the metal briefcase the man had next to him on the bench.

The other man, Leonid Barsk, followed that gaze and knew the colonel would not be any trouble. "All is ready? You have the papers?"

Seogky rubbed his rough leather gloves together. "Yes. I've told you that."

"The CD-ROM?"

"You did not give me much time," the colonel said.

"Do you have it?"

"I have it," Seogky said. "But it will cost you more."

Barsk tapped a finger against his upper lip, showing off the expensive Italian-made gloves he wore, a further contrast between the wealth of the Russian Mafia and the poverty of the Russian Army. "We will not have any unforeseen problems, will we?"

"I have done what you wanted me to," Seogky protested. "What happens beyond that is not my responsibility."

Barsk waved a finger. "Ah, that is where you are wrong, my colonel." He ran his hand over the metal case. "When I give you this and you give me what you say you have, you become responsible. Even for those things that happen that you know nothing about."

Seogky twisted on the cold bench, anxious to be going. His vehicle was parked over two miles away. It would be a miserable walk through the snow and ice. Barsk had told him to park that far away, citing security reasons, but then why was Barsk's car here? Seogky knew the reality of the situation was that Barsk had made him walk in and would make him walk back out as a sign of power. Seogky's feeling of cold was replaced with a warm glow of anger in his gut, not so much at Barsk but at the breakdown of the system and the fools who had allowed it to collapse to the point where he was sitting in this park today negotiating with this reptile of a man.

Seogky stood. "I have done what you have asked. If you wish to ask more, it will cost you more."

Barsk also stood. "No, that is where you are also wrong, Colonel. If I ask, you will do as I say. You are ours now." He held out the briefcase.

Seogky hesitated, realizing the truth and import of what Barsk had just said, but he also knew that he had crossed too many lines already. He might as well be comfortably situated in his new position. Still he didn't take the case.

"Why do you want this?" he reached in his coat, pulling out a sheaf of papers wrapped in plastic and bound by a rubber band. With his other hand, he pulled a plastic CD case out and put it next to the papers.

"That is my business," Barsk said.

"This information is old. Surely—"

"You are thinking too much, Colonel. Just give me the papers and the CD-ROM."

Seogky hesitated. "Is the money in American dollars?"

"It is, as we agreed."

Seogky threw the papers and the CD on the tabletop and picked up the briefcase. Barsk stuffed the items into an inside pocket of his coat.

Seogky paused. "You're not going to check them?"

"Even you wouldn't be that stupid," Barsk said. "I assume you want to be able to spend your hard-earned money."

Seogky turned and began walking across the park. He had gone less than ten feet when he felt pain explode in his right side, doubling him over. His first thought was that he'd been shot. His second that the firer had used a silencer, as he had heard no sound of a weapon. His hands were over the spot of the pain and he brought them up before his eyes—no blood. The pain came again and Seogky sank to his knees.

"What is it?" Barsk yelled.

Seogky turned his head. The Mafia man was backing toward the Mercedes. The three guards had submachine guns out, and they were turning to and fro, searching for the attacker.

Seogky went bolt upright as pain ripped up his spine, as if a fire were burning inside. His hands extended out in front of him on their own, the fingers rigid in a claw, as if there were someone stronger behind him, moving his body. As they came up toward his face of their own volition, he finally knew what was happening. It had only been a story, whispered about in the dark corners of barracks and officers' quarters, only after much cheap vodka had been drunk, but he knew now the rumor was true.

His fingers closed on his face, despite his most strenuous efforts to stop them. He could see through them that Barsk had paused before getting in his car and was watching from a hundred meters away. It was the last thing Seogky ever saw as his fingers ripped into his own eyes, gouging the orbs out of the sockets.

Seogky's scream jolted Barsk. "What is it?" he hissed at his guards.

"I don't know," Dmitri, his chief bodyguard, replied, a finger pressed against the plug in his ear, listening to the reports from the outer rim of security they had deployed around the park. "Our perimeter guards report we are secure. No one has passed. And I know no one was here."

"What the hell is he doing?" Barsk stared at the colonel's hands as they ripped at his own face. "Come on," he said, tapping Dmitri on the shoulder. "He has our money."

The two carefully walked across the snow to the colonel, who was still on his knees, bent at the waist, rocking back and forth and moaning in pain. Barsk paused as he saw the blood-covered hands.

"What is that?" he asked, nudging his hand-tooled boot toward something dark and red in the snow.

Dmitri took a closer look. "His eyes."

"His *eyes*?" Barsk scanned the surrounding area. "What is going on?"

Dmitri knelt in the snow and grabbed Colonel Seogky's shoulders. "What happened?"

Seogky moaned. Dmitri pressed down on the colonel's shoulder, but that produced no response.

"What happened? Why did you do this to yourself?"

"Chyort," Seogky whispered.

"What did you say?" Barsk stepped closer, avoiding stepping on the eyeballs out of concern for his boots.

"Chyort," Seogky repeated, then he screamed, his head snapping back, his bloody sockets pointing skyward. His hands slapped against his ears. "Make it stop!" he shouted, then blood bubbled out over his hands from his ears while a gush of red also came out of his nose. The colonel collapsed forward into the snow, the area around the body slowly turning red.

Dmitri felt the colonel's neck. "He's dead."

"Take the money. Let us go."

Dmitri looked around suspiciously. "What did he mean, Chyort? What devil is he speaking of?"

"Let's move," Barsk snapped.

Dmitri scooped up the case, and they were walking quickly toward the Mercedes when Barsk suddenly paused. "Did you hear that?"

"Hear what?" Dmitri held the briefcase, his submachine gun slung over his shoulder.

"The voice." Barsk turned to and fro. "There's a voice."

Dmitri gave his boss a worried look. First the colonel

tearing his eyes out and dying in front of them, now this. "I hear no voice."

Barsk held his hand up, silencing his bodyguard, straining to hear. Dmitri grabbed his arm and pointed at the snow to their left. A line was being drawn in it, but there was nothing visible that could be doing it.

The drawing turned into Cyrillic letters, rapidly appearing in the fresh white surface.

BETRAYAL

"What the hell does that mean?" Barsk asked as the first word was completed.

The invisible marker kept writing.

DMITRI

Barsk turned to his bodyguard. The man's face had gone white. His mouth flopped open as he searched for words.

"You can't–" Dmitri began. He shook his head. "This is not possible. Words cannot appear in snow."

"And men don't rip their own eyeballs out," Barsk noted.

GRU

Barsk reached for his pistol, but Dmitri was faster, dropping the suitcase in the snow and swinging the submachine gun up. The two other guards aimed their weapons at Dmitri.

"Don't!" Dmitri yelled. "Tell them to back off," he ordered Barsk.

"Wait," Barsk ordered the guards. He stared at the bodyguard. "It is true. The words are true."

"You will find out how true when I take you in," Dmitri said. "I've listened to–" He paused as he and Barsk heard the sound of something moving in the snow to the right. They both turned. Footprints, large ones leaving the impression of clawed feet, appeared in the virgin snow. They were moving, circling in. But there was nothing there.

Dmitri fired a quick burst in the direction of the footprints. Now they both could sense more than see something moving, almost faster than their eyeballs could track, a hazy silhouette of something big, over seven feet tall, with two arms and two legs and what appeared to their disbelieving eyes to be wings on the back. It was on Dmitri before he could fire again. One of the arms flashed forward, into Dmitri's gut.

Barsk could hear the skin rip. Dmitri screamed as his body was lifted into the air. The other arm of the shadow creature whirled down, and the two halves of Dmitri's body flew in opposite directions. They fell into the snow, twenty feet apart, blood slowly staining the white.

Barsk had forgotten how to breathe. He stared up, the vague outline of the creature rippling, but still he could see through to what was behind it. Except for the eyes. Two bright red eyes, seven feet above the ground, glared at him.

Then it was gone, just as quickly. Barsk took a step back. He paused, still holding his breath, but nothing happened. He darted forward and scooped up the case Dmitri had dropped, then ran for the Mercedes, not caring how wet or torn up his boots got. He jumped into the backseat as the guards got into the front, one of them taking the wheel. The car skidded as the driver hit the accelerator too quickly, then the studded tires caught and the car raced for the park's gate.

Behind, near the two bloody bodies, a whirlwind began to circle faster and faster, the unnatural wind blowing out the writing in the snow and the strange footprints, until all that was left were the two dead men. And then all was still.

Chapter Five

"What exactly do you want from my men?" Colonel Metter asked.

"We want your people to continue the Psychic Warrior project," Raisor replied. "We need trained personnel from Trojan Warrior. People who once they go into the virtual world and then come out are capable of conducting military operations. As you know from your superiors, Colonel Metter, the Pentagon is very interested in this program and desires you give me your complete support."

"I understand that, but you've just informed me that the last person to do this died," Colonel Metter said.

"That problem has been corrected," Dr. Hammond interjected. "It was a freak accident."

"Doesn't this RV stuff you're talking about take a special person and specific training?"

"Yes," Hammond said. "But as we discussed, the men on this list are ready due to their Trojan Warrior training. Also, we've simplified the procedure to a large extent and we have a very sophisticated computer that provides the vast majority of the support needed."

"You also said at the beginning that there was an urgency to all this," Metter said. "The Chief of Staff also told me the same thing when he called this morning. Perhaps you could tell us what is causing this urgency to implement Psychic Warrior?"

Raisor answered that. "We have a live mission that

needs to be conducted in eight days. That is why we need your people right away."

"What is the live mission?" Metter asked.

"I can't tell you that," Raisor said. "Only those actually participating have a need to know."

"Eight days is not much time," Metter said. "Can you train men to do this Psychic Warrior stuff in eight days?"

Raisor said, "We're here because your men have years of training as Special Operations soldiers and they've been prepped to do this through their Trojan Warrior training. Dr. Hammond's people will get them 'over the fence' into the virtual world. That is the big breakthrough and the part of the program that came from the medical side. We can tap directly into the brain and give it the extra help it needs to go over."

"I don't like the sound of that," Metter said.

Raisor pulled a sheet of paper out of his briefcase. He slid it across the table to Colonel Metter. "That is my authorization to task you to support this mission. I'd love to stay here and answer questions, but time is of the essence. We have to get back, with the team, to our headquarters and begin training." Raisor looked at his watch. "We have two helicopters due in at the airfield in an hour. We don't have much time if your team"—he pointed at Captain Anderson—"is going to get their gear together."

Metter didn't touch the copy of the orders. "These are my men. My responsibility. I will do as I am ordered, but let me tell you both something." A muscle in Metter's jaw quivered. "You screw with my men and I will not simply stand by."

"That's very noble, Colonel," Raisor said, his tone overly polite. "I assure you, we all want Psychic Warrior to succeed."

For the first time, Dalton picked up a sense of sincerity in the agent's tone, which he found as disturbing as the previous lack of emotion. Raisor cared about this mission, Dalton realized.

"Can you tell me what the real-world urgency is?" Metter asked.

"I am afraid not."

Colonel Metter stood. "All right. Captain Anderson, Master Sergeant Trilly, get the men Sergeant Major Dalton selects and all their equipment together and move to the airfield."

Anderson and Trilly saluted and walked out of the conference room to wait for Dalton in his office. Raisor began breaking down his slide projector with Hammond's help.

Dalton walked out of the room with Metter. "Sir, I request permission to participate in this training and the mission to follow."

Metter paused in the door separating his office from the sergeant major's. "What about your wife?"

"Sir, it doesn't look like her situation is going to change any time soon. She's in the hospital and doesn't need me at home like she used to, to take care of her," Dalton said. "I've been here two years without going on a deployment, and I appreciate you allowing me that and your concern. But I think it's time I earned my pay."

"I don't know," Metter said. "I'd hate—"

"Sir," Dalton cut in, "I would rather be doing something than sitting here with too much time on my hands. Plus, if I don't go, that knocks them down to only six men. I think they're going to need every body they can get."

Metter folded his arms. "You know something's jumping for them to be tasking a team like this."

Dalton nodded. "I don't think they planned on bringing us in on Psychic Warrior for a while. Or even at all, given they dropped the ball on it the last couple of years. Something real serious has caused their timetable to get moved up."

Metter still had his arms folded, his eyes staring hard at the sergeant major. "I want you to come back from this."

"I plan on it, sir."

"Do you?" Metter didn't wait for an answer. "All right. But you might be stepping on Trilly's toes. That should be his team."

"Trilly's weak, sir, and this is a composite team. I think rank will have to prevail. I'll work it out with Captain Anderson."

Metter smiled. "Good. I don't have a warm fuzzy feeling about Raisor or Hammond, and I certainly don't think either of them are going to be updating me on what's happening with the team."

Dalton knew there were many commanders who would just wave good-bye to the team and then drop the whole thing from their plate, focusing on things that were of more immediate concern.

Metter nodded. "All right. Go with them. Make sure they don't get screwed. I'll check on your wife."

"Yes, sir."

"A weapon!" Barsk threw the papers and CD-ROM disk down on the desk. "That is what you wanted. Not this. Seogky double-crossed us! This is nothing but old papers from the archives."

The person across the desk reached out and picked up the papers and CD-ROM. The hand was old and wrinkled, the skin mottled with liver spots. A lace cuff covered the wrist, part of a rather old-fashioned dress the owner of the hand wore. She was a woman in her mid-seventies, almost the archetype of the stolid woman of the Soviet days, with a blocky body and gray hair pinned in a bun. She did not seem to fit the room she was in, a modern office with teak furniture and walls lined with bookcases. The large, bullet-proof window behind her showed a view from the top floor of the tallest office building in Moscow. Steel shutters were adjusted inside the window, deflecting the evening light.

There had always been crime in Russia. Under the Communists, the top criminals had been in bed with the government, their actions controlled. A good case might be made that during the rule of Stalin, the worst criminal in the country's history had been in charge of the government. But with the fall of the Berlin Wall and the collapse of the Soviet Union, it had been the government that had fallen out of the bed, leaving the Mafia holding the reins in a country whose populace was totally unprepared for a free market economy. The unbridled Russian Mafia stepped forward with a vengeance.

In the decade following the fall, the Mafia grew to the point where it rivaled the government for control of the country. The woman behind the desk had been at the very forefront of the growth. In fact, she knew that the Mafia was stronger than the government in many ways, especially with regard to the economy. The previous year, the country had imported a total of sixty billion dollars in Western goods; over half of that had been imported illegally by the Mafia. In Moscow, the murder rate was standing at approximately one hundred Mafia-related killings a *day*. No one was being arrested for these crimes.

The old woman knew the numbers. She read the Western papers that wrote stories about her country, because Russian papers were under the control of the Mafia and printed lies. She was one of the seven major chiefs in the Moscow Mafia. She had gotten where she was by being smart and by being farsighted. And that vision told her they were milking the cow to death. Even the Russian people, dulled as they were by centuries of oppression and hardship, could not bear up under the weight of such crime much longer. The last time it had gotten this bad, there had been a revolution in the midst of a world war and three quarters of a century of Communism. But there were other cows to be milked, beyond Russia's borders, and that was where her sight was aimed.

The woman adjusted her bifocals as she scanned the documents that Barsk had gotten from Colonel Seogky.

"This is exactly what we wanted," she said.

"But—" Barsk was surprised. "But that talks of something old, decades old. I don't—"

"Do you think I would have sent you on a wild-goose chase?"

Barsk straightened. "No, Oma." The word was the Russian familiar for grandmother, and the woman behind the highly polished desk was indeed related in that way to Barsk. But she was called that by all in her inner circle, a sign of respect in the Russian matriarchal society; and in the dark and brutal world of the Russian Mafia, it was a word spoken with deep respect and fear.

Oma held the papers up. "Do you think that whatever killed Colonel Seogky would have done so if these were worthless? Or given up Dmitri to you?"

Barsk shook his head. "No, Oma."

Oma sighed. "Grandson, I have tried to teach you, but you are thickheaded. You must understand that where there is smoke, there *is* fire. None of those things would have happened if these papers were not very important. The GRU turned Dmitri and there was a reason for that."

"You knew about Dmitri?" Barsk asked.

Oma looked over the rim of her glasses. "Of course. But he was your responsibility."

"He could have killed me!" Barsk objected.

"He could have. It was a risk but I felt it was a good learning point for you. One cannot learn from words. Experience is the best teacher. If one does not survive the experience, then that is also best."

Barsk bowed his head to hide his anger. "Yes, Oma."

She turned to a specific page. "This is what we want. The phased-displacement generator."

"What is it, Oma?"

"Part of a very powerful weapon in the right hands."

"Part of?" Dmitri asked.

Oma put the papers down on the desk. "What do you think it was that attacked Seogky and killed Dmitri?"

Barsk swallowed. "I don't know, Oma."

The old woman smiled, revealing steel-capped teeth, ruining the matronly image. "You've thought about it on the drive back here. Tell me your best guess."

"A devil—a Chyort as Seogky said—such as my mother used to tell me about," Barsk said.

"A Chyort?" Oma did not laugh. "Your mother was a good woman but prone to flights of fancy. I kept her well insulated from the real world. However, you are not far off." She tapped the papers with a finger. "These give information about the location of a piece of a weapon that will give us power beyond anything you can imagine. I want you to prepare a mission to the site listed in these papers and recover the phased-displacement generator."

Barsk had already been reprimanded once. He knew better than to risk twice, even though he knew the difficulty in executing what she had just ordered. "Yes, Oma."

"This is very important, Barsk," Oma said. "I will give you more than enough support to accomplish this."

"Yes, Oma."

"I will send Leksi with you. Listen to him."

Barsk's jaw tightened. Leksi was his grandmother's chief assassin. A man with no soul. Barsk had seen and dealt much death, but every time he was in Leksi's presence he felt a chill in his heart. "Yes, Oma."

She interlaced her fingers on her lap as she sat back in the deeply padded leather chair. "Barsk, you must understand some things. You thought you were going after information that would lead you to nuclear weapons, did you not?"

Barsk hesitated, then nodded.

"Nuclear weapons are another piece of the puzzle we need, but Leksi is in charge of doing that and he is close to achieving it," Oma said. "I anticipate, if all goes well, having nuclear warheads under my control shortly."

Barsk kept his face expressionless, although his stomach was churning at the implications. "Yes, Oma."

"The problem here in Russia has never been getting the nuclear bombs. There are many left over from the Cold War. The problem has been, what is the point in having them if you cannot do anything with them? There have been thousands of nuclear weapons here in Russia. Have the Americans ever been truly afraid of them? During the Cold War, yes, but not recently. Because the biggest bomb in the world here in Russia is not a threat. But the smallest bomb, in the United States, that is a threat, yes?"

"Yes, Oma."

"That is what you are looking for. A means for us to be able to use the bombs once we have them. Do you understand?"

Barsk shook his head. "No."

Oma smiled. "Good. You are learning. Just do as I ask."

"This phased-displacement generator," Barsk said. "It can fire a nuclear bomb to America?"

Oma shook her head. "Not by itself. But it is a necessary piece."

"But how?"

"That is beyond you." She slid the papers and CD across to him. "Have you wondered how I knew to contact Seogky and how I knew he had access to these highly classified papers?"

Barsk shook his head. "No, Oma."

"You lie." The words were said lightly, with an edge of

humor. Oma smiled. "You've thought about it and you assumed my information came in the usual way. From a spy,
from a paid informant." She leaned forward. "But this information did not come to me in the usual way."

"How did you find out, Oma?"

"Why, from the Chyort you met in the park, of course."

Chapter Six

In all directions, white-coated mountains covered the countryside below the helicopter. Seated in the cargo bay of the Blackhawk, Dalton leaned back and took in the sights, every now and then spotting a ski slope he'd visited over the course of the last few years.

He had not only skied the mountains they were flying over, he had spent many days and nights traversing them. Part of the Trojan Warrior program had consisted of long, overland movements to put some of the theories they had learned to the test. Dalton had participated in the training for two reasons—one was the same reason he was on board this chopper: to make sure the men were taken care of. The other was because the limited information they had received beforehand about the content of the training had interested him.

The six months of intensive work had been interesting and frustrating. Some of what they were taught by the various instructors clearly had a connection to their warfighting mission. But other subjects, such as the biocybernetics, had seemed more radical. That training had concentrated on mental alertness, strength of concentration and focus, and control of the body's voluntary and involuntary systems, all while getting feedback from various machines they were hooked to. They had learned to do such things as mentally increasing the blood flow to their extremities, which was of some use during winter warfare training, but at the time had not seemed worth the amount of time they had invested. They'd also learned to reduce levels of muscle tension.

One aspect that had seemed very strange at the time was the training spent hooked to a machine that gave them feedback on their alpha brain waves. They'd learned to increase those waves, which the trainers said resulted in decreases in anxiety and apprehension and allowed them to master stressful and life-threatening situations, something Dalton thought he had gone a long way toward achieving in Vietnam.

All the men who had gone through Trojan Warrior—named after the figure on the crest of the 10th Special Forces Group when it was first formed in 1958—had changed, mostly for the better.

But then the training had ended, the instructors were gone, and everyone seemed to lose interest in the entire program. Life went back to the normal cycle of training and deployment Special Forces was used to.

Dalton looked around the interior of the Blackhawk, mentally cataloguing the other seven members of the team. It was a thing he found strange about the military, the sort of lottery that resulted in one man's getting chosen to go on a mission while another didn't get picked. One man died on the luck of the draw while another lived. It was something he had struggled with over the years, having too much imagination to simply accept as others did that it was just fate.

Captain Anderson was, of course, the highest-ranking man and the team leader. But Dalton had worked with Anderson and he knew that the younger man would defer a lot of responsibility and decision making to him due to his experience. It was the traditional Special Forces way of doing business.

Master Sergeant Trilly had not questioned Dalton's

position or attempted to take charge of the team during the load-out. Dalton's major concern was whether the man would pull his own weight, never mind take responsibility. Trilly had been the weakest link during the Trojan Warrior training.

Seated next to Trilly was Sergeant Barnes, the medic. Barnes was a tall, well-built man with dark hair, in his mid-thirties. His slate gray eyes were his most distinguishing feature. Of all those that had gone through the Trojan Warrior training, Barnes had been the one most deeply affected.

Staff Sergeant Stith, an engineer/demo man, was a quiet black man who, Dalton knew, had plans to get out and go back to college to get a degree in architecture with his GI Bill money. Sergeant Monroe, a hulking presence in the helicopter, over six and a half feet tall with a completely shaved skull, was known for his imaginative work with weapons.

The last two members were an intelligence sergeant and an executive officer. Sergeant First Class Egan was a quiet man who wore wire-rimmed glasses. Dalton knew Egan's passion was reading military history, and he felt the man was a strong asset to any team. Warrant Officer Novelli, a large, slow-moving man, was the second-weakest man on the team, in Dalton's opinion. Dalton felt Novelli had somehow slipped through the cracks over the years. As with Trilly, Dalton simply hoped Novelli would hold his own.

The chopper turned and Dalton looked out. He spotted the distinctive white cross of snow on the Mount of the Holy Cross to the north. From that, he knew they were somewhere in the White River National Forest, south of Vail, north of Aspen, and west of Leadville, in the heart of the Rocky Mountains.

"Check it out." Barnes nudged him, pointing forward.

Straight ahead, a large door, camouflaged to look like part of the mountainside, was sliding up, a level metal grating coming out at the bottom. A dark hole appeared on the side of the mountain.

"Some high-speed stuff, Sergeant Major," Barnes said. "Who the hell are these people?"

Dalton knew that Anderson and Trilly had not had a chance to fully brief the team, but Special Forces men were used to missions with vague parameters.

The blades flared and the chopper settled onto the metal grating. Dalton grabbed the door handle and slid it to the rear. He felt the chill blast of air as he stepped out.

"Gentlemen, welcome to Bright Gate." Raisor waved the team off the helicopter. Dr. Hammond was next to him, holding her coat against the chopper blast.

It had taken them two hours to reach this location deep in the spine of the Rocky Mountains. The helipad was extended out of the side of a massive, thirteen-thousand-foot peak. The entire platform shuddered, then began retracting into the hangar cut into the side of the mountain, taking the helicopter and its passengers with it. As they cleared the side of the mountain, the door slid down, cutting them off from the outside world.

"This way." Raisor gestured toward a large door on the side of the hangar furthest into the mountain. He and Hammond led the way, the team following, carrying their gear in large green rucksacks. Raisor paused before the door, a large circular steel structure, over eighteen feet in diameter. It was strangely formed, with rings of concentric strips of black metal spaced evenly out from the center on the polished steel. Dalton noticed that strips of the same black metal were attached to the rock wall that extended left and right the length of the hangar, disappearing into holes drilled into the rock where the hangar ended.

Dalton looked closely. There was something strange about the door, in fact the whole wall the door was set in; a shimmering effect that was barely noticeable.

Raisor punched a code into the panel on the right side. Dalton blinked. The shimmering seemed to have stopped. The door rolled sideways into a recessed port. A corridor lit with dim red lights beckoned. Raisor made a sweeping gesture with his hand and the team trooped through. The door rolled shut behind them and Raisor again punched a code into the inside panel. Dalton swore that the shimmering came back, this time on the inside of the door. And the inside was also covered with the black metal circles, branching off into holes drilled on this side into the rock.

Dalton followed the rest of the team down the corridor. They walked through a door, then down a hallway cut out of the stone. Hammond opened a door and showed them a large room with gray painted walls and several bunk beds.

"I'm sorry the arrangements aren't the greatest," Hammond said, sounding not sorry at all as the team members threw their rucks down. "I'd like to get started right away," she added.

They followed Raisor and the doctor down another corridor deeper into the mountain. The corridor opened into a large chamber. They all stopped, taking in the view. There were two rows of ten of the large cylinders that had been on the slide. Two had people in them, floating in the green liquid, a man and a woman, like full-grown fetuses in suspended animation. Each wore a slick black one-piece suit over their torso.

The team silently walked up and stared at the two bodies.

"Don't touch the glass," Hammond warned. "The fluid inside is supercooled and your hand would freeze to the glass."

Dalton looked closely and now he saw a thin haze in the air surrounding the glass as the ambient room temperature met the much lower temperature.

"Supercooled?" Anderson asked.

"It's necessary to slow the body's processes down to allow the brain to function at a higher level."

"How do they breathe?" Master Sergeant Trilly asked.

"Actually, they're not breathing as you know it," Hammond said, a statement which caused a ripple of concern among the team.

Hammond pointed. "You see the center tube going into the helmet?" Next she pointed to a bulky machine on the outside. Clear lines coiled around the outside of a pump moving so slowly, the action was almost imperceptible. The liquid in the lines was a dark blue.

"A mouthpiece is attached to that lung machine. It doesn't send oxygen in the gaseous form as you are used to, but rather a cooled, special liquid-oxygen mixture directly to their lungs. The machine actually does the work for the lungs, because we can't count on the autonomic nervous system to function properly."

"They're breathing that blue stuff?" Trilly asked in astonishment.

Hammond nodded. "It's similar to what some extreme-deep-sea divers use to get the exact right mixture of gases to handle the depth. It's difficult to take at first, but you get used to it."

"Breathing a liquid?" Trilly asked.

"You don't even notice after you go over," Hammond said.

"Yeah, right," someone muttered from the back of the team.

"The autonomic nervous system?" Captain Anderson asked.

"All right," Hammond said. "Listen up. Now is when we move you from what you learned in Trojan Warrior to Psychic Warrior. Where you learn what you need in order to be able to go in there." She jerked a thumb over her shoulder at the tanks. "We call these isolation tanks. The embryonic fluid not only cools your body, but suspends you so that you have no sense of physical contact with the outside world, not even gravity."

Dalton could read the mood of the team. Hammond had not led into this well at all. He stepped up next to her.

"Remember how you all felt in airborne school at Fort Benning," Dalton said, "the night before your first jump?"

Hammond turned in surprise at his interruption.

"I don't know about you guys, but I was scared," Dalton continued. "Not so much of jumping, but because I had never done it before. It was a new experience and everyone gets a little nervous before trying something new." Dalton turned sideways so that he was half facing the team and half facing the tanks. "But as you can see, it works. Just like you knew at Benning that all those people before had jumped and been all right. That doesn't mean it's perfectly safe," Dalton added. "But the more you learn about it, the safer it will be for you." Dalton turned back to Hammond. "Sorry, Doctor. Go ahead."

"Let me explain why these isolation tanks are important," Hammond said, walking between the team and the tubes. "Your brain works on several levels. What we want to do with the machines is allow you to remove all other inputs and distractions to your brain and allow you to concentrate on the virtual plane."

"I don't call breathing a distraction," Staff Sergeant Stith remarked.

Hammond ignored the comment. "There will be two major aspects to your training here. In the mornings, we will work on adapting you to the equipment. In the afternoons, we will work on adapting you to your own bodies and minds.

"Come with me." Hammond guided the team out of the main chamber into a classroom. She waited until they had all found seats. There was a large table in the front of the room, crowded with various machines.

She picked up a helmet, the twin of the one on the bodies in the isolation tanks. It was solid black and large, about twice the size of a football helmet on the outside.

"This is the key." Hammond turned it so that they could see inside. She shone a light into it. There was a thick lining that she ran her finger across. "This is the thermocouple and cryoprobe projection assistance device, or TACPAD for short. This is the breakthrough that has changed everything and makes the Psychic Warrior concept possible.

"We will be fitting each of you shortly for your own TACPAD. What the TACPAD and the isolation tank allow us to do is—" Hammond paused, looking at the eight men in camouflage fatigues. She sat on the edge of the desk. "All right, let me try to explain this as best I can.

"What we tried to do in Trojan Warrior was focus your brain. To bring out capabilities that each of you has but that have remained dormant. But it goes beyond the training you received there. I know you may not believe it, but trust me when I tell you there is a residual telepathic capability in every person.

"Many, many thousands of years ago the first human beings did not have a verbal language. We were just a step, a slight step, up from being monkeys. But there was a big difference: our brain. It was larger and more complex than that of any other species on the face of the planet. At some point, the human brain made a fantastic leap. We became telepathic."

Dalton raised his eyebrows. "I've never heard of this."

"Most people haven't," Hammond said. "But if you went to a university and talked to a physiology professor, he or she would tell you that this was indeed likely but it was still only an unproven theory. But we aren't in a university here, and I'm telling you the breakthroughs we have made prove to me that this theory is valid.

"This telepathy was not as big of a deal as you might think. It wasn't like these early people could 'talk' to each other with their minds. The reason they couldn't was they couldn't talk verbally–they had no language–so the telepathic communication was emotional. If someone saw a large tiger approaching the group, that person could use their mind to warn the others by sending their fear into the others' minds. There are even some examples of this 'pack mentality' in the animal world today."

"What happened to this ability?" Captain Anderson asked.

"It's still there in some people but regressed," Hammond said. "Once we developed a verbal language, it wasn't as important. The person who saw the tiger could yell 'Tiger!' which was just as quick and more effective in that it specifically identified the threat. Since this was a better mode of communication, evolution took over and the verbal mode of communication became dominant.

"So as humans used the verbal language more and more, the telepathic capability waned and became residual. It's not entirely gone. All of you have had moments when you sensed things despite the fact that there were no specific normal sensory inputs that gave you that information. A sixth sense."

Hammond stood up. "Especially you men. Each of you has an even stronger residual mental capability than the norm. Significantly stronger. That's why you were chosen for Trojan Warrior three years ago.

"First, each of you is left-handed or ambidextrous. The brain consists of two hemispheres." Hammond pointed at her neck. "At the base of our brain, our nervous system does a switch. So the right side of your brain is responsible for the left side of your body and vice versa. Thus a left-handed person is right hemisphere dominant.

"Both sides of your brain are pretty much the same. That makes for redundancy. There have been clinical examples of people who have suffered tremendous damage to one hemisphere, or had extensive surgery, who were still able to rehabilitate to almost a normal level of functioning."

Dalton thought about Marie, lying in her hospital bed. Whatever damage the aneurysm had done, perhaps there was hope that she would recover. Hope. Dalton knew what a two-edged sword that was from bitter personal experience. He forced himself to accept reality: Even if by some miracle she did regain consciousness, the ALS would be that much worse, the disease still progressing even as she lay in the coma. And he knew Dr. Kairns had leveled with him—Marie was never going to wake up.

Hammond walked to the front of the room and pulled a chart down. It was a top view of a brain. She pointed to the right side. "But there is something very interesting that doctors have always wondered about right here. The speech center on the right side appears to not work. All our speech comes from the left side. But the same parts are present on the right. Why?" She didn't wait for an answer and tapped the chart. "This is where the residual telepathic ability resides. This is where we focus our efforts to get you into the virtual plane."

Hammond went back to the desk and picked up the TACPAD. "This machine amplifies the parts of your brain that can allow you to get to and operate on the virtual plane. We've used the TACPAD successfully for two years.

"What the TACPAD does in conjunction with the isolation chamber is the following—" She grabbed a marker and begin writing on the board.

1 — Isolation Chamber
Emphasize parasympathetic

Hammond pointed with the marker. "When the para-sympathetic nervous system is operating, your body relaxes. Your pupils constrict, your heart rate slows, your digestive system practically shuts down, your muscles relax. You did some of this consciously in Trojan Warrior, as you remember. The isolation chamber does this by lowering your body temperature to the point where your body is almost totally inactive."

She pointed at the wall plug. "Your brain operates on such a low voltage that its power is almost negligible. We can't exactly increase the voltage into your brain, as that would fry the cells, so we focus the power that is already there by reducing the need for it to be expended on unnecessary outputs. As I told you earlier, the isolation tube even does your breathing for you. It will also control your heartbeat."

"How?" Barnes asked.

"We do direct electrical stimulation to control and maintain your heartbeat and also control the nervous system in the brain."

Dalton glanced at the other men in the room. No one looked particularly happy.

The pen squeaked against the board again.

2 — TACPAD
Cryoprobe

She turned the helmet once more so that they could see the thick lining inside. "The cryoprobe is a device that surgeons have used for a decade or so to target certain areas of the brain. It's a very fine probe that reduces the temperature in the target area to ninety-three degrees. This causes the neurons there to cease firing, effectively shutting that area down."

"What parts of the brain do you shut down?" Dalton asked.

"Those connected with the parasympathetic nervous system, since those bodily functions are taken care of by the isolation tank," Hammond said. "Every milliamp of power we can save is critical."

"What exactly is the microprobe?" Captain Anderson asked.

"A microscopic wire that is inserted directly into the targeted areas of the brain." As there was an uneasy rustle in the room, Hammond quickly elaborated. "The wire is so small that you won't even feel it go in, and when it's removed there is no bleeding. Less than .008 millimeters in diameter. The fact that there have been so many breakthroughs in microtechnology in the last several years has been one of the reasons we've been able to develop the TACPAD." She held up the helmet. "It's so thin, you can't even see the probe with the naked eye."

She wrote again.

3 — TACPAD
Thermocouple

"The thermocouple does the opposite of the cryoprobe. It targets those areas we want to activate and emphasize. It raises the temperature of the designated area, which facilitates its functioning."

"Isn't that dangerous?" Barnes asked. "Wouldn't that be like someone suffering heat exhaustion, where the body temperature goes too high? I've seen guys get their brains fried like that."

Hammond shook her head. "No. It's very controlled and specific. There is a low-grade electrical current running through the thermocouple that does slightly over half the emphasizing."

"Hold on," Dalton interrupted. "You just said that it's not a good idea to up the voltage or amperage in the brain."

"In an uncontrolled or nonspecific manner, yes. But here, we're talking about less power than you would get from a double-A battery. It's safe, I assure you," Hammond said. "Doctors have been using this technique in brain research for years."

"Do you use wires into the brain for that too?" Anderson asked.

"Yes. Again, so fine that you can't see it or feel it." She went back to the board.

4 — TACPAD
Cyberlink

"Not only has this technology been used by experimental psychologists, everything I've talked about up to now has also been used for the past couple of years in the Bright Gate program by our remote viewers. It is only in the past six months that we have developed the critical piece of technology that takes us one step beyond.

"The last component that makes the Psychic Warrior program possible is the cyberlink." Hammond paused for a second in thought. "You've all seen or used simulators that act like the outside environment, such as pilots practice on?"

Everyone nodded.

"In a way, the cyberlink reverses the simulator process." Hammond reached into the TACPAD and held up a black pad about two feet long by eight inches in width with numerous wires coming out of the back. "We can use our mainframe computer, code-named Sybyl, to help you locate where you are going on the virtual plane and also to orient you. More importantly, the computer gives you form—what we call an avatar—in hyperspace that you can project into real space."

"Form?" Anderson asked.

"That is the key to being a Psychic Warrior," Hammond said. "You have to be able to come out of hyperspace, or virtual reality, and into the real world. By using the precoded avatar formats that our programmers have developed with Sybyl, you will be able to stay oriented while in the virtual world and come out into the real.

"Sybyl is one of the most powerful computers in the world, perhaps the most powerful. She is able to calculate at a rate that was unheard of even six months ago. Because of that, she is capable of the vast number of concurrent calculations needed to give your virtual reality avatar enough substance so that you can project it into the real world. She also projects the power into the virtual plane that you reconfigure into mass when you want your avatar to materialize. The power she sends out is critical—that's what allows us to make the transition from simply remote viewing into being able to project the avatar form in both the virtual and real planes."

Hammond was now walking back and forth across the front of the classroom, her eyes gleaming. "But Sybyl does more than that. She is also your communications link back to our operations base here. You can also access the computer's database for information as needed." Hammond's words were tumbling over each other as she raced to get them out. "It's truly remarkable. You've never experienced anything like it. Through the link, you can get whatever knowledge you could ever possibly need. It's like you are part of the computer."

"As long as the computer has it in its database," Dalton cautioned. "Correct?"

Hammond stared at him. "Sybyl has over—" She paused.

"Suffice it to say I can't think of any information you would need that Sybyl doesn't have somewhere in its memory and couldn't access through the Internet."

Raisor had been standing in the back of the class. "Time, Doctor," he said.

Hammond nodded. "All right. You've seen the equipment that you will use in the isolation tank, and I've told you how it will help you. The other part of your classes here will consist of some refresher training on mind control techniques." She pulled down another chart. "These are some of the techniques our experts will be reintroducing you to:"

BIOFEEDBACK
ATTITUDE
VISUALIZATION
RELAXATION
COGNITIVE TASK ENHANCEMENT
CONSCIOUS PHYSIOLOGICAL CONTROL
MEDITATIVE STATES
DEATH AND DYING
MISSION COMMITMENT

"Whoa," Dalton said, reading down the list. "What the heck is death and dying? And mission commitment?"

Hammond held up her hands, palms out. " 'Going over' is transcending to another level. A level most people never experience. In fact, the closest experience to 'going over' that I've heard of is those people who have near-death experiences. Who travel out-of-body while their physical self passes into what is often physical death. Some of our RVers experience an initial panic when they go on missions. The feeling that they may never return to their bodies, that they have indeed died.

"We have found the best way to deal with that is to

train you on the emotional problem you will experience, to make you feel more comfortable with the theoretical concept of death and dying."

"I don't find death to be theoretical," Dalton said. "I've seen it many times and it's damn real."

Hammond shook her head. "But it's not real when you go to the virtual plane. There's another aspect to it. We're talking about the concept of virtual death also. That you might encounter some conflict on one of your missions and your virtual self is wounded or killed but your real self is still alive. We want you to be prepared for that so you can come back to your real self."

"So," Dalton said, "what you are in essence saying is that you want to teach us to accept the virtual death?"

"Correct."

Dalton shook his head. "I don't like that. To me that means you want us to give up. To surrender our will. There's a big difference between accepting a situation and surrendering one's will."

Hammond sighed. "It is what we think will be best."

"Has anyone ever been 'killed' in cyberspace?" Dalton asked.

"We haven't had that occurrence." Hammond's eyes shifted once more to Raisor.

Dalton caught that look. He also noted that the CIA agent was no longer leaning against the wall. "So this, like the other stuff you're talking about," Dalton said, "is still theoretical. For all you know, if someone's cyberself, their psyche, gets killed, they are dead."

"Well, that's theoretically possible," Hammond said, "but the body will still be alive. The structure of the brain will still be intact. So there's no reason to believe the self can't be restored."

Dalton shook his head. "But if you turned that thinking around, wouldn't that be like saying if you programmed everything a person knew into a computer, that computer would be alive? Would be that person?"

"I think if you were truly able to do such a program," Hammond said, "that the computer would indeed be alive. But no one's been able to accomplish that yet, so your argument holds no weight. As you noted, the situation is exactly the opposite here—your real self remains here at Bright Gate, while the projected self, with the aid of the computer, will be out there on the mission."

"Enough theorizing," Raisor snapped. "We have a very tight schedule, Dr. Hammond. We should get started."

She nodded. "The first thing we need to do is fit all of you for your TACPADs."

Oma had dismissed Barsk, letting him rest after his journey from Kiev. She turned to the window and looked out on Moscow, a city she could rightly call hers. She knew if she so desired, she could wipe out the other six clans that also worked the city. But there was no point to that. Because the effort required would not be worth the reward gained. It would be like a jackal fighting the others over an already eaten carcass. Oma had no trouble seeing herself as a jackal. She believed that self-awareness was the trait that had led her to her current level of success. One always had to be aware of one's capabilities and limitations, or else any other kind of awareness was worthless. She knew she could not judge others unless she was very certain where her own perspective was coming from.

In the midst of her musings, she felt the hairs on the back of her neck tingle and she turned, recognizing the feeling. A shadow flickered in the corner of her office. She waited as the shadow took on the form of a large creature—Chyort.

"Yes?" she said.

"Very careless to have a GRU turncoat be your grandson's bodyguard."

The voice echoed in her head, the rough edge giving it an inhuman quality.

"Really?" Oma said. There was a rumbling sound that she supposed was the creature's laughter. It caused even her hardened stomach to feel queasy.

"Ah, so maybe it was not such a mistake? Wheels within wheels perhaps?"

"What I do with my personnel is none of your business," Oma said.

"It is if it threatens this operation."

"I felt confident you could deal with it if there was a problem," Oma said. "And you did. So shall we move on?" There was a pause. She felt the red eyes burning into her.

"So perhaps you are bluffing. Maybe you didn't know about Dmitri. Maybe I am working with the wrong people."

"You're working with me," Oma said, "because I am the most powerful and because you know that we can achieve our goals together."

"Remember, old hag, that *my* goals are the only ones I care about."

"I assumed that long ago," Oma replied. "My main concern is who else you are working for. Who made you what you are? The KGB? The GRU?"

"Perhaps I am from the devil."

Oma shook her head. "I know there is no God and I need no Satan to accept the evil that men do. I saw enough horror in the Great Patriotic War to convince me of both of those things. When I saw what the Nazis did to my sons, my village, I knew that man could make greater evil than anything written in the Bible. Men made you, of that I am sure."

The shadow seemed to grow behind the monster. "Keep in mind that I know what you fear. Everyone has something that controls them. A chain in their own mind that if someone takes, they can make you do what they will. I know what controls you inside your own head."

Oma stared at him. "If you knew such a thing, I think we would be talking differently."

The creature moved, shadows shifting in the corner. Oma had never really been sure of the form other than it had two arms and two legs. Occasionally she thought she could make out claws at the end of the huge hands, and a ridged spine on the back flaring into two large, leathery wings, but it was like trying to watch the water come in with a wave, always changing a little bit, nothing of permanence.

"The Americans are aware that there is a plot."

She clenched her steel teeth together. "Was there a leak from my organization?"

"If there was, I would not be here right now," Chyort said. "They found out from the same source that led to them stopping the beryllium shipment in Vilnius last year. The Americans put a very high priority on maintaining an eye on nuclear material. They do not trust our government—should we be surprised by that? They know how incompetent those fools truly are."

"Do the Americans know of Phase Two?" she asked.

"Not yet."

Oma considered the way that answer had been phrased. "I will move up the timetable."

"That would be prudent."

She stared at the demon. "Was Dmitri really working for the GRU? I suspected, but I had no proof."

"Is proof necessary? But, yes, he was turned by the GRU. Your grandson needed a lesson, one that the death of Seogky was not enough for. Also, it reduces his power, does it not? Which keeps your hand strong, does it not?"

"This is my organization," Oma said, surprised at the

demon's insight. "I have run it for over forty years. I do not need your help."

"I care nothing for your organization. Only that you keep it together long enough for me to accomplish my goal. The target will be at the location I gave you at 0800 local time two days from now."

"Two days? You told me it would be seven!"

Chyort moved again. Oma swore she could hear the click of claws on the hardwood floor. A scaly hand with three-inch claws came into the light and picked up a Fabergé egg that rested on the desk. She could see the egg through the claw. It took all her willpower to not move her chair back.

"The GRU is not as stupid as you would like to think," Chyort said. "They have moved up the timetable while keeping a train on the original schedule as a decoy. They hope to move the bombs before anyone can plan anything. I suggest you call that big Navy ape of yours."

"I can handle it."

"You have the papers on the weapon's location?"

"Yes."

"And the computer program to run the weapon?"

"Yes."

The egg dropped back into its holder. The room seemed to expand again to normal size as the shadow disappeared. Oma's anger at being told what to do had never even had a chance to get started. She was simply grateful the demon was gone.

Oma sat still for several moments, reflecting on the conversation. It was something her husband had taught her how to do many years ago. To always go over every encounter or conversation immediately, to sift through and find the hidden meanings, the things said that had not been meant to be said. And what had not been said.

She didn't know who the creature was. For all she

knew, he was Chyort, the devil, but as she'd told him, she didn't believe in such things. The first time he had appeared in her office, three months ago, it had taken all her considerable willpower to control her fear. Chyort was the name he had given himself or someone had given him. She had had some of her people make inquiries, and they had learned of a myth in the army, a myth about a creature with such a name that dated back to the war in Afghanistan. But there was nothing more than those vague rumors. She had them checking further, trying to uncover the truth behind the myth.

The only thing she held on to was that Chyort wanted something. And he needed her help to achieve his goal. That told her his power was limited. She had long ago learned that every relationship, whether it be personal or business, was a rope that pulled both ways. So far, Chyort had done all the pulling, but in doing so he had firmly handed her the other end of the rope. Oma smiled. She would wait and pull when it was most opportune for her own goals.

She didn't know exactly what Chyort's objective was, but each encounter they had she learned something more. Another thing he had said today that she found curious was the comment about the "Navy ape." That meant he knew about Leksi, which was not surprising—everyone knew Leksi worked for her; what was more interesting was the way he had said it. She had picked up a note of derision. She considered that. Afghanistan and dislike of the Navy. That pointed to an army man, someone who was in an elite unit and thus able to sneer at Leksi's naval commando background. That meant Spetsnatz, the Russian version of the American Special Forces. Oma marked that mentally for further investigation.

She hit a number on her phone and it automatically summoned who she needed. Then she leaned back in the comfort of her chair, feeling the ache in her spine as she continued to consider what she had learned in this latest encounter. She was still pondering that when a green light flashed on the edge of her desk. She pushed a button and the wood-paneled steel door slid open.

The man who walked in drew attention wherever he went. He was just shy of seven feet tall, and his head was completely shaved, revealing a jagged scar running from the crown down the left side, disappearing inside the black turtleneck he wore. He was not only tall, he was wide, his broad chest and thick arms indicating extreme strength. He walked to the front of her desk and halted, waiting, his manner indicating his military training.

"We must move up our timetable," Oma said.

Leksi waited.

Oma's left hand moved, writing the information Chyort had given her onto a piece of paper. She slid it across the desk. One of Leksi's massive hands reached down and carefully picked it up. He peered at the Cyrillic writing, read it a second time, then handed it back to her. She tossed it in an opening on the left side of her desk and there was a flash, destroying the paper.

"I know it is not much time, but the window of opportunity grows tighter. You must accompany Barsk on Phase Two first. Then you must immediately return and complete Phase One."

Leksi still had not said a word, a trait that Oma valued. He was a former naval commando, an expert in weapons and martial arts. But more importantly, he would do whatever she asked, without the slightest hesitation. He was not particularly imaginative but he was thorough. She had already gone over the plan for this operation with him several times and felt secure that he would follow it through to the letter. Today's news only changed the timetable and the order of events, not the mode of execution.

She held out the papers. "This is the location you must go to for Phase Two."

He took the papers.

She slid the CD-ROM across the desk. "Take that. I will supply you with the man who knows how to use it."

Leksi put the CD-ROM in his pocket.

"Go," she said.

Leksi went out the way he had come, still not having spoken a single word. The door slid shut behind him, leaving her alone in her high aerie.

A door slid open twenty feet up and food was thrown down, the first indication to Vasilev that he wasn't really in a metaphysical hell. There were only torn pieces of bread and some meat that was suspicious at best, but Vasilev wolfed it down.

When he was done, he was disappointed with himself. He should have eaten more slowly. What else did he have to do?

The air crackled. Vasilev rose to his feet, swaying from weakness. The two red-coal eyes appeared. Vasilev squinted but all he could sense in the darkness was a deeper shadow in the black of the pit.

Vasilev waited, not saying anything, but the eyes only watched him for a while. Finally the voice came.

"You should have died."

Vasilev blinked. "What?"

"You should have died with the others. You were as guilty as those who did die."

Vasilev swallowed, trying to get moisture to his dry throat. "I don't know—"

"Special Department Number Eight."

Vasilev's throat seized and he could only make a strangling noise.

"You must pay for what you did."

Vasilev fell to his knees, curling into a ball, whimpering his apologies, his sorrow for what had happened over thirty years ago.

"You will do what I tell you to do and forgiveness will be yours. Only then will you know peace. Do you understand?"

Vasilev could only nod, while his mouth moved in half-articulated apologies.

Then, just as suddenly as they had appeared, the red eyes were gone and he was alone once more.

Chapter Seven

Dalton was surprised the embryonic solution was warm. It felt like molasses as his feet sank into it. He resisted the urge to shake his head; the TACPAD helmet weighed heavily on his neck, and his vision was blocked by the pad of the cyberlink completely covering his eyes and wrapping around his head. The helmet was fastened on very securely, the location determined after four hours of fitting by two members of Hammond's staff in a white room that was completely sterile. They had told him the location had to be exact, within one hundredth of a millimeter. And they had only been able to do that after doing complete MRI, CAT, and PET scans of his brain.

As they worked, the two technicians had talked in a lingo that Dalton had not understood. They had sent cryoprobes and thermocouples into his brain to test locations, reading results off a bank of machines and then making adjustments to the inside of the TACPAD. Hammond had been right–the insertion of the little wires had caused no pain, or any other sensation for that matter. Still, it had been disconcerting to simply lie there, knowing that they were penetrating directly into his brain, over and over again.

Just putting the fitted TACPAD on had taken forty-five minutes, with another thirty of testing, before they had strapped him into the lift harness in the main experimental chamber and lifted him into the air and swung him over the isolation tank.

He wore a slick black suit that covered his torso, leaving his arms and legs free. An electrical lead was attached directly to his chest, and a microprobe had been slipped through the material and into his chest just before they'd lifted him. Even though Hammond assured him as she slipped the probe in that the wire was so thin he couldn't possibly feel it, Dalton was very aware that something had gone into his heart, a distinctly uncomfortable feeling. The last thing he considered himself capable of doing, encumbered as he was, was conducting a mission. Of course, he still didn't know the mission they were being prepared for, but it wasn't the first time in his career he'd received training without knowing exactly what it was to be used for.

Dalton took steady, deep breaths through the mouthpiece as he was lowered further into the isolation tank. He knew that a few members of the team were gathered around, watching, as he was first to experience being inside. The others were still being fitted.

The solution came around his waist, up his chest, then he was all the way in. The worst feeling so far, other than the microprobe into the heart, was the feeling of the embryonic fluid seeping into the TACPAD, pressing up against his face. Dalton also didn't like the fact that he could see nothing. He felt neutral buoyancy, something he was used to from his scuba training.

"All right?" Dr. Hammond's voice was loud and clear in his ears.

Dalton gave a thumbs-up. It was extremely hard to move in the solution. Dalton was surprised at the viscosity of the liquid. He wasn't able to speak with the lung tube stuck down his throat. It was irritating, but the hardest part had been when Hammond had put it in, getting past his gag reflex with one practiced push. Dalton had been on the other end of that technique several times in his army career during his medical training.

"Okay, we're going to do several things, all at the same time. Just relax. Let us do it all right now."

Dalton concentrated on his breathing. He felt a buzzing inside his head. A light flickered in his eyes. He didn't know if it was the cyberlink pad over his eyes or the thermocouple projecting directly into his brain. The light became a white dot.

"Follow the dot," Hammond said.

The dot moved slowly to the left.

"Don't move your head," Hammond warned.

Dalton moved his eyes and they followed the dot. Or was his brain following it? he wondered. His eyes were covered, so they couldn't be. . . . The dot was moving the other way and Dalton had to stop his wondering and follow it.

This went on for a while, how long Dalton couldn't know, but he gradually became aware that he was cold. The buzzing in his head was still there, but he was hardly noticing it; it had become the norm.

"You're doing good." Hammond's voice was more distant. "Give me a thumbs-up if you hear me clearly."

Dalton was shocked to find that he couldn't feel his hand. He couldn't feel any part of his body. He made the mental effort anyway. He tried to feel his eyelids, to determine whether they were open or not, but there was no way he could tell.

"At this point," Hammond said, "your peripheral nervous system is just about shut down, so you shouldn't be able to feel your extremities. You're doing fine. We're doing the last part of the physical aspect now, taking over for your central nervous system. Relax. Relax."

Dalton felt a twinge in the tube in his throat. His chest spasmed as liquid slithered into his lungs.

"Relax."

Dalton was drowning, his lungs filling.

"The dot, follow the dot."

There was a flash of brightness. Then the dot re... peared, now moving in a circle.

Dalton felt as if his chest were being crushed. He tried to expel the liquid coming in, the dot forgotten.

"Relax."

Dalton wanted to tell her to shut the hell up as he concentrated on accepting the foreign substance pouring into his lungs. He focused on the knowledge that he wasn't drowning, that this liquid was sustaining his life. The body didn't buy it. He was drowning.

"You're all right. That's done," Hammond said. "The machine is breathing for you."

Dalton halted the panic with a firm mental slam on the runaway emotion. He was breathing. He couldn't feel his lungs but he accepted that he was getting the oxygen he needed. He'd actually passed out several times in scuba school, drowned, so he knew what it was like to go under without oxygen.

"The dot. Look at the dot."

Dalton went back to following the dot. He felt very small, as if his entire being had closed in around the core of him, the "I" that rattled around inside his skull.

"The dot, find and stay with the dot. It will be your connection with Sybyl, along with my voice."

Dalton was startled out of his lethargy. During winter warfare training, he'd seen men, tough soldiers, curl up into small balls inside their snow caves and totally withdraw from the outside world. Just wanting to fall asleep and then slip into frozen death.

Dalton focused on the dot.

"All right," Hammond said. "You're in good shape. We're doing your breathing for you. We've got your heart regulated and beating in the correct rhythm. Everything is fine."

Yeah, right, Dalton thought. He noted that her voice was growing fainter, as if she were very far away.

"Your senses are shutting down. Soon you will no longer be consciously processing information from your normal senses."

Dalton had to strain to hear her.

"You'll be hearing me on Sybyl's link next. Just give me . . ." The voice faded out. A deep, profound silence ensued.

Dalton felt himself start to drift away, and he snapped to.

There was a buzz, then silence. Then a clicking sound that really caught Dalton's attention.

He felt a stab of pain above his left eye. The pain grew stronger, almost to the point where he couldn't take it anymore, then it disappeared, to come back just as strong.

The dot was still there, but Dalton didn't care. He went back further inside his memories, to a dark hole. Dank, dripping, concrete walls. The surface pitted. Dalton knew every little divot, every scratch in those walls. The four low corners, each one of significance to him. The ceiling too low for him to stand up, only four feet high.

He could reach his arms out and touch wall to wall. Exactly square. He'd measure it by using his thumbs. Sixty-three thumb widths wide each way. He had spent a long time considering how whoever had built this thing could have been so exact in their measurements, because when he was taken out, he could see the entire building that was his prison and how poorly constructed it was. The Hanoi Hilton the media had called it, but those who spent years of their lives inside had had other names for the hellhole.

"Sergeant Major Dalton."

The voice was raspy, echoing, intruding. The pain that had been so distant was back, although not quite as sharp.

"Sergeant Major Dalton."

Dalton tried to answer.

"Sergeant Major Dalton." There was a change to the tone and timbre of the voice.

Dalton didn't know how to speak. He had no throat. No mouth.

"Sergeant Major Dalton." The voice was smoother now, almost human.

Dalton tried to figure it out, how to answer with no voice of his own.

"Sergeant Major Dalton." It was recognizable as a human voice now. A woman's, but there was a timbre to it that was unnatural.

"Sergeant Major Dalton. This is Dr. Hammond. I'm talking to you through Sybyl now. Through the computer directly into your brain. You have to focus your mind to answer. This may take a while, as we have to adjust your program link to your brain."

Dalton tried to reply.

"To answer, you must focus on the dot."

The damn dot, Dalton thought. He did as instructed. The dot was still now, centered.

"Now, say hello."

Dalton tried, but he knew it wasn't working.

"It takes time to learn. Relax."

Dalton thought that humorous. How could he relax when he had no control?

A sharp stab of pain right between his eyes caused Dalton to start.

"Good. The computer heard that," Hammond said.

The pain came again, but Dalton was ready.

"I didn't hear that," Hammond said. *"You must relax and allow your emotions to pass through."*

The pain once more.

"Screw you," Dalton projected.

There was a long pause. *"We must do a series of tests now*

to format your program. I'm going to have Sybyl run you through a program we've prepared for this. Do what she tells you to.

Sybyl's voice was a flat mechanical one, barking out directions. Dalton did as instructed, feeling like a child as he responded, sometimes feeling a little silly.

A series of grid lines appeared. Sybyl had him focus on various coordinates. After a while, the computer guided him in moving along the grid line, a task that Dalton was able to accomplish only after many tries. He had no idea how long this went on until finally Sybyl told him he was done. For now.

Dalton felt a snap, followed by an echoing pain that slid back and forth across his head like a slow-moving tide. The pain wound down, but then he began feeling a tingling sensation in his forehead.

The dot disappeared.

The tingling turned to itching. The extent of the feeling came down his forehead, across his face. To his neck. He could feel the obstruction in his throat.

Soon his entire body itched as if armies of ants were marching across every square inch. And Dalton squirmed, since he couldn't scratch.

But then the cold came. Worse than the most bitter cold he had ever experienced in all his winter warfare training. He'd been in Norway above the Arctic Circle on exercises with the wind chill hitting under seventy below zero, and it hadn't been this bad.

Hammond's voice exploded in his head. "I know you're cold. We're warming you up." The volume went down during the second sentence. "We're going to get you back on oxygen shortly."

Dalton sensed some uncertainty in Hammond's voice. Was this where they had had their accident and lost their man?

"It take a little bit of time to get the fluid out of your

lungs, and when we start, you won't breathe again until your lungs are clear and we can get oxygen in. It takes about two minutes. Trust us. We'll get it done.

"We'll keep your heartbeat slow. You can go ten minutes without oxygen at your present physiological rate."

A fist hit Dalton in the chest. Then a drill began ripping a hole right through him. He screamed, the sound resounding in his skull but not making it out his mouth.

A claw was ripping his lungs up through his throat. Dalton felt darkness closing down as he struggled for air. The only thing keeping him conscious was the pain.

Then the oxygen came and the pain got worse, shocking Dalton with its intensity. But he could breathe. He took in a deep breath, then began choking, hacking, trying to spit.

"The machine will get the rest of the liquid out," Hammond's voice informed him. "Relax."

Screw your relax, Dalton thought. He took another deep breath, relishing the feel of the oxygen as the tube fought his breathing, trying to suck out the last of the liquid on each exhale.

He was still cold, but he could tell that the fluid around him was warming rapidly.

"We're pulling you out."

He felt straps tighten around his shoulders as he was lifted. The fluid let go of him reluctantly, and with a sucking noise he was dangling in the air. He was swung over and lowered.

His knees buckled as his feet hit the ground. He felt hands supporting him. Arms went around him, keeping him still.

"We're extracting the cryoprobes and thermocouples," Hammond informed him. "You have to remain still. It will take a few minutes."

To Dalton nothing appeared to happen, but then fingers

reached under the neck seal of the TACPAD helmet. It
ripped open. The helmet was lifted off slowly. Someone
delicately peeled the cyberlink pad off his skin.

Dalton blinked, trying to get oriented. All he saw was
white. He closed his eyes for a few seconds, then opened
them again. This time he could make out hazy forms
around him. He shook his head, clearing his vision a little.
Staff Sergeant Barnes was still holding him up. Dalton
slowly regained control of his legs. He looked about. Dr.
Hammond and Raisor were standing at the main control
console.

There were three bodies in other tubes.

"Damn it, I told Anderson to wait until I was done,"
Dalton said, his voice hoarse and cracking.

Barnes frowned. "I know, Sergeant Major, but you were
in there five hours and they said they had to get this thing
going."

Five hours. To Dalton it had seemed no more than an
hour. His throat hurt where the tube had been. He shivered
and Barnes draped a blanket over his shoulders.

"You okay, Sergeant Major?"

"Yeah, I'm all right. Whole bunch of fun," Dalton said.
He stared at the other men in their isolation tanks. He
could see one of them quivering inside the green liquid.
Under the blanket he peeled the suit off, down to his shorts.

"Geez, Sergeant Major, what happened to your back?"
Barnes was looking at the bare skin the blanket didn't cover.
A jagged scar six inches long reached up from the waist-
band of his shorts. The skin was rough and purple.

"Bayonet," Dalton said.

"Bayonet?" Barnes repeated.

"It's a long story from a long time ago." Dalton shivered
once more, violently, as if the cold would never leave his
bones.

"Here," Barnes held out a cup of coffee.

Dalton took it, wrapping his hands around the mug, grateful for the warmth. He walked over and stared into the closest isolation tube. He recognized the body in the tank: Staff Sergeant Stith, the demo man.

"How long have they been in?" he asked Barnes.

"They put the first one in two hours after you. Stith just went in twenty minutes ago. Captain Anderson was the first one after you."

Dalton stared through the glass at the body floating in the green liquid. He shivered once more, but not from the cold.

The town of Markovo lay one hundred kilometers south of the Arctic Circle, centered in the land mass just north of the Kamchatka Peninsula, in the far eastern wasteland of Russia. This practically unknown and almost uninhabited land beyond Siberia was one step removed in the wrong direction from the worst stretches of hinterland on the planet.

The population of the town was less than five hundred hardy souls, half of them natives, the other half the progeny of political prisoners who had survived the local gulag long enough to bring forth life. The inhabitants of the gulag had dug out, under the year-round ice, the holes that now held the prefab components of Special Department Number Eight's Far-Field Experimental Unit—SD8-FFEU.

It was set underneath the tip of a rounded mountain that overlooked the town. One narrow road switchbacked up the side of the mountain, ending at two massive steel doors that led down into the station. Signs at the start of the road and circling the mountain at the base warned that intruders would be shot without warning.

There were six prefab components that made up SD8-FFEU, each buried fifty feet under the rock and ice. The communications center, enlisted men's quarters, mess hall/gym, officers' quarters, and science quarters were all spaced around the central compartment, known as the Brain Center. A five-hundred-meter tunnel led to the small nuclear reactor that supplied the power needs for the station. The supplies were stacked in a large tunnel that was over two hundred meters long. It also was the corridor to the ramp that led to the surface.

Here, hidden from the spying eyes of satellites, SD8 conducted its most secret operation, under the command of its most ruthless officer.

General Rurik paced back and forth, the track worn in the carpet showing that this wasn't the first time his feet had traveled that path. He paused, looking to the center of the room. His right hand was on his left, twisting the wedding band on his ring finger around and around.

A four-foot-high steel cylinder was set in the center of the room on a base of eight shock absorbers. Inside, carefully preserved, was what remained of Major Feteror, formerly of the Soviet Spetsnatz. Who—or what—he was now, was open to debate.

Rurik had been involved with SD8 for fourteen years. He'd been present as a senior captain at the newly constructed FFEU facility when Feteror had been flown in directly from Afghanistan in 1986. The report from the GRU colonel who had accompanied the body had been brief. Feteror had been recovered in a rescue mission responding to a radio call the major had made just prior to being captured. It had taken the GRU some time to locate the village, and during that gap, the major had been horribly tortured.

Rurik, an experienced interrogator, had been both impressed and disgusted when he saw Feteror's body being wheeled into the operating room. Impressed that the man was still alive, disgusted at the vulgar means the Afghanis had employed. Of course, he knew their goal had not been to extract information but rather to inflict punishment, and on those terms they had succeeded.

Department Eight had been looking for someone in Feteror's situation for half a year. Like ghoulish vultures, they'd put the word out to the commands in the field.

Feteror's condition had been critical when he arrived, but in a way, some of what the *mujahideen* had done to him had also kept him alive. Leather tourniquets had been wrapped tight around Feteror's limbs, so tight they had sliced through the skin. The extent of bone and nerve damage had been so great that the leather had never been cut on the eight-hour flight to Department Eight's facility. Since no blood had flowed to the limbs, they were effectively dead when Feteror arrived, and the surgeons lopped them off immediately, adding to the carnage the Afghanis had begun.

But that was only the beginning. Like sculptures working on a grotesque masterpiece, the surgeons continued to slice away, removing everything that wasn't absolutely essential to keeping Feteror's brain functioning. His digestive tract was completely removed. His heart and lungs, which had been badly torn by broken ribs, were also removed, once they were able to get him completely dependent on a heart-lung machine. What was left of his eyeballs was removed, the nerves capped, then eventually shunted to a computer for direct input. All this was done, in the words of the senior physiologist, to remove any "extraneous nervous input."

What remained of Feteror, all twenty-six pounds, was encased in the steel cylinder. Over three dozen lines and tubes ran into the cylinder. About half of those were biological, half mechanical.

Several of the tubes, carefully suspended, ran to a row of machines, the best the Western world had to offer to the highest bidder on the worldwide, very extensive, medical black market. The heart-lung machine handled the blood, keeping it at the right temperature and making sure the proper oxygen level was maintained. Another machine performed the functions of the intestinal tract by the expedient manner of injecting minute quantities of nutrients directly into the bloodstream on the way in from the H-L machine.

Inside the steel cylinder lay the bare minimum of a human being. A spinal cord suspended in solution. A head held firmly in place by screws drilled directly into the bone. Leads passed through the skull directly into the brain, the frightful legacy of the research done by SD8 over the years. All the medical equipment served only one function—to keep Feteror's brain alive—and little else. There were no eyes to see, no ears to listen, no skin to feel, no tongue to taste, no nose to smell. All inputs into the brain were controlled by the leads attached to the master computer.

It was a "living" arrangement General Rurik had no doubt Western medicine was capable of making, yet had not done so for the simple reason that no one could see a need for such a horrible existence. And Rurik also knew that the West—because of ethical considerations and the lack of bodies to experiment on—had not done the direct brain interface work that Department Eight had spent decades experimenting with.

Working their way from rats to monkeys to humans, Department Eight scientists had fine-tuned their ability to send electrical impulses directly to the brain, mimicking those of the central nervous system. They had also done the reverse, learning how to pick out the nerve impulses sent out of the brain stem, which gave Feteror the ability to "speak" with the aid of an external voice box and conduct other limited actions through the computer.

That limited ability, of course, was not the key to what made Feteror the Chyort, the demon of legend and mystery who had carried out Department Eight operations for the past decade. The key was the results of the work on October Revolution Island that the lone survivor, Dr. Vasilev, had brought out with him. Feteror's isolated brain, enhanced by the computer, could go onto the psychic plane with power far exceeding anything that had been done before. The computer could produce the harmonics to open a window to the virtual plane and then Feteror, his psyche, could travel there, drawing power from the computer.

Because he lacked a physical body, Feteror could concentrate every milliamp of mental energy on the virtual plane. And he had achieved something the scientists in Department Eight had only speculated about—he could come out of the virtual plane at a distant point and assemble an avatar, the Chyort, and influence physical objects on the real plane.

How he did this, the scientists were not able to exactly tell General Rurik, much as they had not been able to fully explain the operation of the phased-displacement generator three decades previously. Even more mystifying was the fact that they were not able to duplicate Feteror's unique ability. Three other "volunteers" had gone under the knife and been placed in their own cylinders hooked to a similar computer. None had managed to do what Feteror could.

The others had managed some limited remote viewing, but nothing beyond what regular remote viewers could do. Feteror was different, there was no doubt about that. In the end, Rurik and the scientists had only been able to conclude that either Feteror had had some innate ability that they had happened to tap into, or that Feteror's horrific experience just before being brought to Department Eight had changed him in some fundamental way.

The bottom line was, they knew that Feteror worked, and the major concern had been to develop a way both to control Feteror and to protect themselves, the legacy of the disasters at Chelyabinsk and October Revolution Island very much in the forefront of General Rurik's concerns.

A small box, with a blinking green light that matched

the one on Rurik's wrist, was on the machine on the other side of the cylinder from the medical machines. This was an advanced computer, again the best the West sold. The box was wired into the master program that controlled all the computer's interfaces with regard to Feteror.

The monitor Rurik wore had a very sensitive pressure pad on the inside, against his skin. It monitored his pulse. If Rurik's heart stopped for more than ten seconds, the light would turn red, meaning that the master computer had "frozen" the cyberlink with Feteror. That would effectively isolate Feteror's brain from both inputs and outputs.

Rurik knew that Feteror did not fear death; indeed he knew that Feteror yearned to be released from his almost nonhuman prison and the only way out was to die, but there was something he knew the Spetsnatz major did fear: the darkness of isolation inside his own brain, with no sensory input coming from the computer, no ability to "leave" on the psychic plane without the support of the computer. Such a netherworld existence horrified even the hardened Feteror, who had experienced two years of such a life while they completed all the surgical procedures, and while Department Eight technicians worked on the programming necessary for the project. Of course, at the time, they had not known that Feteror had been conscious those long two years, screaming into the darkness where he had no voice. Not knowing if he was dead or alive, if he was now in some sort of hell or purgatory, his last memories those of the brutal torture he'd undergone in the Afghani village.

Only when they completed the first rudimentary cyberlink had they found out that the major's brain had been conscious the entire time. The psychologists were amazed that Feteror had retained his sanity, but General Rurik was not so sure that Feteror had been sane to start with. As soon as they had gotten Feteror on-line, to demonstrate his power, Rurik had locked Feteror down for another month into the netherworld abyss.

Rurik would take no chances even with a decorated war hero. He knew that his predecessor, on the cusp of his own great success after sinking the *Thresher*, had died in a mysterious blast at Department Eight's earlier site. It didn't take a genius to look over what they did know and the results of the interrogation of Dr. Vasilev and conclude that the subjects had rebelled and killed their captors to free themselves through death. History would not repeat itself as far as General Rurik was concerned.

There was not only the issue of the human beings they were dealing with, there was also the danger of the equipment. Before the disaster on October Revolution Island, there had been the even greater disaster at Chelyabinsk in 1958 during a weapons test on the virtual plane. There had been no survivors at the test site from that one.

But Rurik believed in what he was doing. To get powerful weapons, one had to take great risks.

Besides the cyber-lockdown, Rurik had another ace in the hole, so to speak. The entire complex, buried deep under the ice above the Arctic Circle, was surrounded by a static, psychic "wall" that had only one "window" in it. The window went directly to the cylinder and allowed Feteror his virtual exit to the world, and Rurik controlled whether that window was open or closed. Closing it prevented Feteror from turning and attacking his home base. He could only return to his own physical mind through the window. When the psychic window was closed, Department Eight, where Feteror's physical self lay, was the one place where he couldn't go psychically, as far as Rurik knew.

Other than the fact that it required tremendous amounts of power from the nuclear reactor, Rurik didn't know how the psychic wall worked, but he didn't care. That was the job of the scientists. However, the wall had several interesting side effects that they'd discovered quite by accident. The wall was generated outward by lines surrounding the mountain halfway up; the lines were connected underneath SD8-FFEU through small tunnels that had been drilled. The field, as far as their recording instruments could tell, extended about two hundred meters into the air above the station, projected by steel towers built around the perimeter. Nothing living could go through that wall. They had first noticed the bodies of birds and small animals in the first days after the wall went up. Rurik had been interested and gotten a prisoner from the gulag. He'd turned off the automatic, conventional defenses that surrounded the base, and had the prisoner walk up the side of the mountain, into the psychic wall.

The effect had been startling. The second he hit the slightly shimmering wall, the man had grabbed his head, collapsed to his knees, and begun screaming in a high-pitched voice. Blood had streamed through his fingers, then his body had jerked upright, held in that position for a few seconds, then simply collapsed.

Rurik had had the wall turned off and the body recovered for autopsy. The doctors discovered that the structure of the man's brain had literally dissolved.

Another side effect, not so beneficial to security in Rurik's opinion, was the fact that once the psychic wall was turned on, they could no longer communicate with the outside world. Radio waves would not pass through. Even their best shielded cable and telephone lines would not function.

They kept the psychic wall on all the time for protection. It was breached only for two reasons: one was to make the twice-a-day radio contact with GRU headquarters outside Moscow; the second was to open the window to allow Feteror out or to bring him back in.

Rurik's job was to be Feteror's handler. So far, the Spetsnatz man had come up with quite a bit of good intelligence for the GRU.

Besides the psychic wall, there was another special aspect to FFEU that made it unique and more secure. Because they weren't totally sure of the exact nature of what they were doing, and its great value to the national intelligence structure, the entire complex was physically guarded in a most unique manner.

A complex set of weapons, ranging from machine guns to air defense heat-seeking missiles, was layered around the complex and controlled not by human hands, but by a computer. The targeting computer was hooked to a series of sensors that watched across the spectrum from infrared to ultraviolet. Anything that approached the base–or tried to get out of it–would be spotted and targeted automatically. And, once the guardian system was activated, there was nothing anyone inside the base or outside could do to stop it. The base would effectively be isolated. The system automatically came on whenever Feteror was "out." This prevented Feteror from using any outside comrades to try to break in, or from subverting anyone inside to help him.

Despite the strong security measures, one thing did worry Rurik, though, and that was why he had worn the path in the rug every time Feteror was "out." And that was that the scientists couldn't exactly tell him how Feteror operated. They knew he could remote view and come out of the psychic plane in his demon form, but they also suspected he was capable of much more. But Feteror had not exactly been forthcoming over the years as to his capabilities, and an uneasy truce existed between Rurik and Feteror. The latter got the information requested, but there were limits even Rurik could not push him beyond. In return, there was much Feteror could not get from his captor.

What also bothered Rurik was that he didn't know where Feteror went when he left SD8-FFEU. There was no way of tracking him on the psychic plane. That task was something that Rurik had the scientists working hard on.

Right now a red light was flashing from the top support beam that ran from the floor on one side, to the roof, around to the floor on the other side of the semicircular room. It was a visual signal to everyone that Feteror was out. Besides not knowing exactly what Feteror was capable of and where he was, another thing that disturbed Rurik was he didn't know what Feteror's time sense was. Just as the time spent being cut off in the virtual world inside the cylinder seemed like forever to Feteror, Rurik had to wonder how time in the virtual world outside of the cylinder seemed.

Rurik was startled out of his ruminations by a junior officer approaching.

"Sir, we received some intelligence from Moscow in the last communiqué." A young lieutenant held out a piece of paper.

Rurik took it and read. The GRU counteragent who had infiltrated the Oma group had been found dead in a park near Kiev, along with a GRU colonel named Seogky.

The condition of the bodies was most strange. Seogky had had his eyes torn out and died from a brain hemorrhage. And the counteragent had been cut into two pieces. Rurik crumpled the paper. The filthy Mafia.

Rurik knew Seogky. The man worked in Central Files in GRU headquarters in Moscow. What did the Mafia want from Central Files? Correction, Rurik thought as he reread the message, what did the Mafia now have from Central Files?

He looked up at the red flashing light and frowned.

Chapter Eight

"What's wrong?"

Dr. Hammond was focused on her computer screen, not the isolation tank that Dalton was pointing to. "We're having some trouble." She leaned forward and spoke into the microphone. "Sergeant Stith, this is Dr. Hammond. Focus on the white dot."

"What kind of trouble?" Dalton demanded. He was dressed in his fatigues, only an hour out of the isolation tank and still feeling the shakes.

Stith's body spasmed, bending at the waist until his head, encased in the TACPAD, was almost touching his knees.

"Get him out of there!" Dalton ordered.

"We can't right away," Hammond said. "Sergeant Stith, this is Dr. Hammond. You have to focus on the white dot." Her hand pushed a button on her console.

Raisor was behind her, watching. Dalton walked to the front of her console. "Get him out."

Stith suddenly jerked upright, his legs and arms spreading as wide as they could go, slamming against the side of the isolation tube.

"There's an interface problem," Hammond said. Her fingers were flying over the keyboard.

"Who has control?" Raisor asked.

"I don't," she said shortly. "Yet," she added.

"Is he locked into Sybyl?" Raisor asked.

"We haven't completed pass off."

"If you don't have contact and Sybyl doesn't," Dalton demanded, "then who does?"

"Sergeant Stith"–Hammond pushed the red button,– "you have got to focus on the white dot."

Stith's body was twisting. His left arm jerked hard, slamming into the glass with a sound that reverberated through the chamber. The arm jerked back in an unnatural manner.

"Oh, shit," Barnes exclaimed as a sliver of white poked out of Stith's forearm. "His muscle spasms are breaking his bones! He's got a compound fracture." A slow swirl of red spread into the embryonic solution.

"Get him out of there now!" Dalton slammed his fist on top of the console.

"We just can't pull him out," Hammond said. "He's breathing the liquid mixture and his body has been cooled. He'll die if we just pull him out," she said, her focus still on her console.

"He'll die if he stays in there," Dalton said as Stith spasmed again, this time the uncontrolled force of the muscles breaking his left leg, the misshapen shape of the thigh indicating the damage.

"Damn it," Hammond said, reading something on her screen. "He's vomiting the breathing mixture. Some of it must have gotten into his stomach."

"Sergeant Major!" Sergeant Monroe had grabbed a fire ax. He stood ready next to the isolation tube with his teammate, the ax looking like a toy in his massive hands.

Dalton turned to Barnes. "What do you think?"

"Breathing, bleeding, and broken," Barnes said succinctly.

Dalton knew exactly what he meant. The three priorities when treating a wounded man. And Stith was in bad shape on all three.

"Get him out now or we will," he told Hammond.

"All right, all right." Hammond shoved her keyboard back. She threw several switches. "I'm warming the embryonic solution as fast as possible and extracting the liquid mixture from his lungs."

Dalton stood in front of the isolation tube, next to Monroe. "Take it easy, Pete," Dalton said to Monroe in a low voice.

Dalton reached up with his hands and placed them on the glass, feeling the cold stab into his palms. "Hang in there, Louis. Hang in there."

"His lungs are clear, but he's not breathing oxygen," Hammond said. "His nervous system isn't responding. I'm forcing oxygen in and keeping his heart pumping with the microprobe."

"Too slow," Monroe muttered, lifting the ax.

Dalton reached under his fatigue shirt and pulled out his nine-millimeter pistol. He stepped back from the isolation tube, aiming.

"What the hell do you people think you're doing?" Raisor was running down from behind the console.

"I'm going to break this goddamn thing!" Dalton yelled. "Pull him out or we get him out our way. Now!"

"He's still too cold!" Hammond protested.

"He's not *breathing*!" Dalton yelled. He shifted his aim from the glass to Raisor.

The CIA agent stared at Dalton's eyes for a second. Raisor wheeled toward Hammond. "Do it."

Hammond slammed her fist down on a lever. With a hum of motors, the winch began reeling in the nylon strap that was attached to Stith's harness. The body came up out of the tube, dripping embryonic solution. Hammond pushed on the lever and Stith swung over the ground, his body twitching.

Dalton holstered his pistol and had his arms up. With Monroe, he caught Stith's body as it came down. Dalton

could feel the chill. "Get this thing off him," he said, pointing at the TACPAD.

Hammond was kneeling over the body. She spoke to
herself as she worked. "Extracting cryoprobes." She pressed
a small button set on the outside of the TACPAD.

"Hurry!" Dalton yelled.

"You can't take it off until they've fully retracted. You'll
break them off." Her hands kept moving, hitting another
button. "Extracting thermocouples."

Hammond reached down and slid the microprobe out
of Stith's chest. With Barnes's help, she pulled the TACPAD
off his head.

Dalton leaned over and ran his fingers through the sergeant's mouth. They came out dripping blue fluid.

"Shit," Dalton muttered. He leaned over, locked his
mouth onto Stith's, and blew. Nothing. He threw Stith over
his knee, face-down. He slammed into the man's back with
both fists. A large pile of embryonic fluid gushed out of
Stith's mouth onto the floor. Dalton hit him again, then put
him on the floor on his back. He breathed into his mouth;
this time the sergeant's lungs came up.

Barnes was across from Dalton, feeling for a pulse.
"Nothing," he said, then slammed his fist down onto Stith's
chest. He began compressions in ratio to Dalton's
breathing.

Dalton fell into the rhythm. In between Barnes's compressions, someone draped a blanket over the body. Dalton
pulled up for a second and looked into Stith's face. It
was blue. He slid the eyebrows up. The eyes were open
and vacant, the pupils dilated. He bent back down and continued.

"He's gone, Sergeant Major. He's gone." Barnes had his
hand on Stith's neck. "He's gone."

The words were a litany, slowly sinking into Dalton's

consciousness. Finally he paused in his breathing and looked up. Barnes shook his head.

"He's gone. Fifteen minutes and no oxygen. Even if we brought him back, he'd be a vegetable."

Dalton's head snapped back and he glared at the younger medic, causing him to step back in surprise.

"What about his mind being frozen?" Sergeant Monroe asked. He was now on his knees, cradling the body in his large arms. "Like someone who falls into freezing water."

"His mind wasn't frozen," Hammond said. She was standing over them, her face tight. "Just his body. The TACPAD and helmet kept the brain at normal temperature."

Barnes slid a poncho liner over the body.

Dalton stood. There were the three other men still in the isolation tubes. "I want to know what happened. What killed him?"

Hammond was back behind her console. "I'm not sure."

"Take a goddamn guess!" Dalton snapped.

Hammond stepped back. "As nearly as I can tell, his psyche got lost going from our world to the virtual world. I lost contact and Sybyl never established contact. That affected his entire brain and his autonomic nervous system went nuts. That's what caused his death."

"Are you certain of that?" Dalton asked.

Raisor stepped between the two of them. "We don't have the time to stand around and argue. We—"

"We'd damn well better know what killed Sergeant Stith before we go any further," Dalton said. "Or we're not going any further."

"Don't you threaten me or this project," Raisor said.

"Is this what happened to the man you lost?" Dalton ignored the CIA man and focused on the doctor.

"No," Hammond said. She seemed more sure of herself. "*His* death was caused by mechanical failure. This was different. This happened on the line between the physical and psychic planes." She shook her head. "We're moving too fast. We should have had—"

"We have to move fast," Raisor said. He moved to a position between her and the Special Forces men.

Dalton pointed at the other isolation tanks. "We need to get those other men out."

Raisor shook his head. "I'm afraid we don't have time for that."

Dalton glared at Raisor. "You'd better make time."

"It's not up to me," Raisor said. "We're on a tight time schedule dictated by others. It was a training accident. You have them all the time. A parachute fails to open. A man is knocked unconscious during scuba training and loses his mouthpiece and drowns."

"We have training accidents," Dalton acknowledged, "but we work hard to make sure they don't happen after we figure out what went wrong. We don't know what went wrong here."

"You are under orders, Sergeant Major," Raisor said. "This mission has top priority."

"I think it's time to let us in on the secret," Dalton said. He walked over and stood by Stith's body. "Seeing as we're putting our lives on the line for this. I want to know why this man had to die. Why we're in such a damn rush."

Raisor met Dalton's glare, then nodded. "All right. I'll tell you. Because one of our RVers has discovered that someone is going to try to steal twenty nuclear warheads in eight"—Raisor looked up at the large clock—"make that seven days."

Feteror was tired, but he had one more place to check before going back. He felt the link to SD8-FFEU, a line growing more tenuous the longer he was out. It was a flow of power and information into his psyche, without which he was impotent.

Feteror accessed the satellite imagery of the area he wanted. He centered it in his "vision" and then, with a burst of energy, he was there, looking down on a railyard.

He paused, feeling the vision fade with a loss of power. He had prioritized his missions, knowing this would happen. Damn Rurik and his leashes and limitations.

The vision came back and Feteror scanned the railyard. There were troops all over the place, armed with automatic weapons. He could see the national insignia of the Kazakhstan army on their lapels, but the uniforms were still the dull color of the former Soviet Union.

Feteror swooped down to the railmaster's shack on the edge of one of the sidings. The wall was just a brief blip and then he was inside. There were two soldiers in the room, but he ignored them. A routing schedule lay open on the desk. Feteror checked it and got the information he needed. The two soldiers looked about, disturbed by something they could sense but not see, since Feteror was staying invisible in the virtual plane. He had no need to do anything on the real plane here.

He paused. There was another presence in the room. Another being on the virtual plane. Feteror reached out and probed the presence. He hit a protective psychic wall, but he knew he could break through. He gathered his strength to— Feteror froze as darkness closed on his consciousness. A dark tide swept in, then back out. Damn General Rurik, Feteror thought. The old fox was cutting his power to bring him back.

The other presence was gone.

Feteror let the dwindling power link to SD8-FFEU draw him home.

Chapter Nine

"Why don't you just tell the Russians about the threat?" Dalton asked.

He was in a conference room, just off the main experimental chamber, with Raisor and Hammond. The other members of the team who had not yet gone into the isolation tubes had carried Stith's body to the dispensary. So far none of the other three still under had experienced any problems, and Hammond had told him that all had successfully integrated with Sybyl and that they were developing their virtual programs.

Raisor shook his head. "We can't. It's the classic problem of sharing intelligence—by doing so you disclose your capabilities. You know about Coventry, don't you?"

Dalton had read extensively in the area of military history, and he knew exactly what Raisor was referring to. During World War II, the Allies had broken the German Enigma code with their Ultra machine. Doing so had given them access to all German transmissions and a wealth of information. However, to make sure that the Germans didn't realize that they had broken the code, the Allies had to be very careful what they did with the intelligence. When the Ultra scientists had decrypted a communiqué indicating that the city of Coventry was going to be heavily bombed, they had passed that warning on to Churchill. Who had done nothing with it. The city wasn't evacuated and hundreds lost their lives and the six-hundred-year-old cathedral in the center of town burned to the ground. But the secret of Ultra was maintained.

"We're not at war with the Russians," Dalton said.

"We're always at war," Raisor said. "That's the only way to look at the world in the spectrum of intelligence operations."

"Bullshit," was Dalton's take on that.

"We're in a double bind," Raisor continued as if nothing had been said. "We can't pass the intelligence to the Russians. And we can't act overtly. Both would disclose too much of our capabilities."

"So let's keep a secret and get nuked?" Dalton said.

"It won't come to that," Raisor said. "Even if the warheads are stolen, they'll still be in Russia. We would prefer not to have the first event happen, but push comes to shove, it's not worth disclosing our capabilities for unless it appears the warheads will be crossing borders."

"Do you know who is going to try to steal the warheads?" Dalton asked.

"We're not certain," Raisor said. "We suspect it might be the Russian Mafia, but if that is the case, that most likely means that they are just middlemen and will be passing the warheads on." Raisor leaned across the conference table. "Just imagine twenty nukes being on the open market, going to the highest bidder."

"I am imagining it," Dalton said, "and it seems that this would be worth disclosing your Bright Gate capability in order to stop."

Raisor shook his head once more. "Which brings us to the other problem with passing the information to Russian intelligence. The Russian military is heavily compromised by the Mafia. For all we know, we might tip our hand to those who are going to do the attack."

Dalton rubbed his forehead. "So we're going to descend on this attack out of the virtual plane and stop it?"

"That's the idea. It's more secure than trying a conventional assault which could cause a war to break out. If there's one thing the Russians will not tolerate, it's American soldiers on their soil. We have to avoid that at all costs. That's why the President—and the Pentagon—has chosen to use this option."

Dalton rolled his eyes. "We've lost one man and we haven't done jack yet. You think we're going to be able to do something no one's ever done before in seven days? You're gambling everything on that?"

"It wasn't my decision," Raisor said. "I can assure you that this was discussed at the highest levels, and the decision was made to move up the timetable on Psychic Warrior to deal with this threat. I am just implementing that decision."

"Why can't the RVers here do it?"

"Several reasons," Raisor said. "First, they're not trained soldiers. They're intelligence gatherers. Second, and more importantly, this Psychic Warrior technology, the cyberlink in conjunction with Sybyl, is new."

"Have you ever sent somebody into the virtual plane and then have them come out in the real at a remote location and conduct a mission?" Dalton asked.

"Not conduct a mission," Raisor said, "but as Dr. Hammond told you, we have successfully tested it."

"Yeah, by playing with blocks. I'm sure that will scare the crap out of the Mafia guys trying to take down these nukes."

"You'll be able to do more than that," Dr. Hammond said.

"I'm a little fuzzy on that," Dalton said. "So far I don't feel like I've accomplished much of anything other than having one of my men die."

"You'll be working on your virtual forms next," Raisor

said. "From what Dr. Hammond has told me, that will give you something to conduct your mission with."

"How does that work exactly?" Dalton asked.

"I don't know *exactly*," Raisor's voice was taking on an edge. "All I know is that it *does* work."

"We're gambling lives on untested tactics."

"Isn't every war a trial of untested tactics?" Raisor said.

"Yes," Dalton agreed, "and they're usually big screwups. Millions of men dead and the generals in the First World War never really adjusted to the fact that machine guns made frontal assaults obsolete. They were still ordering cavalry charges in the early days of World War II."

Raisor slapped the tabletop. "That's why we want to use the technology we have here correctly! To move us into the modern age."

"When they introduced the tank in the First World War, the generals still never really adjusted. It takes more than new technology," Dalton added.

"We have adjusted with Psychic Warrior," Raisor said. "For the first time, we are ahead of the technological-tactical interface."

"It sounds like we're too far ahead and it killed Stith." Dalton stared at the CIA representative. "Do you believe the bull you speak?"

"It's the way the world is," Raisor said.

Hammond had been watching the heated exchange. She leaned forward between the two men. "It works, Sergeant Major Dalton. We know it works."

"It didn't work with Sergeant Stith!" Dalton yelled.

"Every new technology has its dangers," Raisor said. "Do you know how many test pilots have died testing new aircraft? This is new and—"

"Don't give me bullshit," Dalton snapped.

"Sergeant Major, this is going forward whether you are on board or not," Raisor said.

"Do the Russians have remote viewers?" Dalton asked.

"We don't know," Hammond said.

"You don't know?" Dalton didn't buy that. "Come on. Seems like that's the first thing your RVers would check on."

Raisor answered. "We have checked. And we don't know. We suspect they do." Seeing Dalton's look, he amplified his answer. "Dr. Hammond believes it's possible to block psychic viewing with either technology or with other psychic viewers putting up a wall. So if the Russians do have psychic viewers, they're blocking us from being able to see that capability. As we are blocking our own capability from them, if they have it." Raisor waved his hand about. "This entire facility is shielded on the virtual plane from intrusion."

Dalton remembered the black metal on the vault door and along the walls. "How do you do that?"

Raisor looked at Hammond, who answered.

"We have Sybyl generate a virtual field and run it through specially adapted lines. The parameters of the field are disharmonic to the human mind's psychometric rhythms, so any RVers trying to get through would–" She shrugged. "Well, we've never tested it on an actual person, but I would assume it would cause severe if not fatal damage to a person's psyche. Even a person trying to walk through the field would be affected in the same manner. We have had our RVers approach the field and they report extreme discomfort when they come within a few meters of it."

"That's why we only have the one entrance to this base," Raisor said.

"One physical entrance," Hammond corrected him. "That's the door you came in through, off the hangar. We also have the entrance our RVers use. That's a narrow opening–which we call the Bright Gate–in the psychic wall that

Sybyl controls. She can let you out Bright Gate to the initial jump point on top of the mountain and she can also let RVers in when they return to the initial jump point."

"What does this field do to other things?" Dalton asked. "Once it's running, do we have communications?"

"We're not the only place that uses this field," Raisor said. "Every top secret secure site our country has is surrounded by a psychic field just in case the Russians do have an RV capability. Once we developed the wall, our scientists were able to develop a special cable that can shield a link from inside to outside and allow uninterrupted communications. That's something we don't think the Russians have managed to do yet, so we have an advantage there."

"Let's get back to the other side's capabilities then," Dalton said. "If the Russians do have RVers," he asked, "wouldn't they know about this plot in their neck of the woods?"

"If they have remote viewers and if the remote viewers happened to catch this plot, yes, then they would know. But we were lucky; our RVer who picked this up literally stumbled across it checking on some other information on a different tasking. The odds that a Russian RVer found the same thing are unknown."

"What about—" Dalton began, but the door swung open and a technician stuck her head in.

"Lieutenant Jackson is back."

Raisor and Hammond headed for the door.

"Who is Lieutenant Jackson?" Dalton asked, following them.

"One of the RVers you saw in a tank when you got here. She's been out on a mission."

They entered the main room. The last two Special Forces men, Barnes and Monroe, had gone into the tanks, leaving Dalton the only one out. At the far end, a woman was shivering, a blanket over her shoulder, wiping embryonic fluid off her face with a towel.

"Lieutenant Jackson," Raisor said as he came up to her. "Your report?"

Jackson didn't respond right away. She spit, none too elegantly, and coughed, a dribble of dark liquid rolling down her chin before she wiped it off. She was a tall, slight woman, in her middle twenties, short blond hair plastered to her skull, her skin pale and covered with goosebumps.

"Is everything static?" Raisor asked.

Jackson coughed. "No, sir, it's not. They've changed the schedule." She looked at Dalton, then back to Raisor.

Dalton had seen that look before—she had information she wasn't sure she should share in front of people she had never seen before.

"You take care of your men," Raisor said to Dalton. He grabbed Jackson's arm and helped her to her feet. "Come with me."

"Hold on!" Dalton put his hand up. "I want to talk to my commander. I have to inform him about what happened to Sergeant Stith."

Raisor stared at him for a few seconds, then nodded. "You can use the secure line down the hall there. But make sure you don't say a word about the mission. Is that clear, Sergeant Major?"

"I hear you," Dalton said.

"You can inform Colonel Metter about Sergeant Stith, but he has to hold official notification until we can implement a cover story."

"I know the way the game is played."

The red light went out. General Rurik relaxed slightly, knowing that Feteror was back inside his metal home and the window was shut.

"Report!" Rurik snapped into the microphone that

linked him directly to Feteror's auditory center. There was no way Feteror could escape the noise, and Rurik relished that power.

"I've done as you requested. There has been no change." The tinny voice that came out of a speaker on the master console actually sounded tired.

"The Mafia?"

"They still plan to attack in seven days."

Rurik smiled. "What do you know of a Colonel Seogky of the GRU?"

"I've never heard of him."

"We believe he had a meeting with the same Mafia group. His body was found in a park near Kiev along with that of a member of the Mafia."

"I know nothing of this."

"Anything else?"

"No."

"Good night." Rurik threw a switch and the power to the cylinder went down to bare life-support levels. "Pleasant nightmares," Rurik whispered into the mike as he shut it off.

Barsk stared out the window of the plane at the ocean twenty thousand feet below, where white dots indicating icebergs drifted in the Arctic Ocean.

"We drop at fifteen thousand." Leksi's voice was hoarse from too many cigarettes and too much vodka. The men gathered around him all had the same hard look; they were former Soviet Special Operations soldiers, searching for a better life outside of the military.

Leksi unfolded a map. "This island holds the target."

One of the men laughed. "October Revolution Island. Perfect."

Leksi pointed at the map. "The GRU has an observation post here, on this mountain, overlooking our target."

"I thought you said this place has been abandoned for thirty-five years," a mercenary noted.

"It has been."

"And the GRU is *still* watching it?"

"Our target holds something very important," Leksi said.

"What can be that important?"

Leksi looked up from the map and stared at the man. Then he continued the briefing. Barsk listened, but he wasn't jumping with the team. He was to stay on board the aircraft with the pilot and wait until Leksi gave the all-clear signal. Then they would land on the old runway that had serviced the abandoned base.

"Let's rig," Leksi ordered at the conclusion. He looked at his watch. "We're fifteen minutes out."

The plane was a military AN-12 Cub, surplus that Oma had bought off some Air Force personnel eager to make money. Barsk considered it interesting that in the blink of an eye the former Soviet Union had embraced capitalism fiercely; the problem was that there were none of the established checks and balances that Western societies had developed.

In the front half of the cargo bay, a large backhoe was chained down along with other excavating equipment. A pallet full of explosives was tied down just in front of the backhoe. Knowing that he was riding in a plane with a load of C-4 and detonating devices didn't do much for Barsk's emotional health.

The plane banked and Barsk eyed the pallet warily.

Leksi thrust a mask at Barsk. "Put it on."

Barsk slipped it over his head. He felt the cool oxygen flow.

The mercenaries were hooked into small tanks on their chests, bulky parachutes on their backs. Weapons were tied off on their left shoulder. Leksi had a headset on, listening to the pilot. He pushed his mask aside to yell.

"Depressurizing!"

With a shudder, the back of the plane began opening. The bottom half lowered, making a platform, while the top slid up into the large space under the tail.

The twenty men followed Leksi as he walked onto the platform. Barsk shivered from the freezing air swirling in. He edged closer to the heat duct over his head. Leksi moved a large bundle to the edge of the ramp.

A green light flashed. Leksi pushed the bundle, and the men tumbled off the ramp, following it.

Fifteen thousand feet below, First Lieutenant Gregor Potsk was concerned about wood. With winter coming, heat was the first priority, and resupply had gotten so strained that they were lucky to get enough food, never mind kerosene for the heater built into the concrete-and-log bunker set high on the side of the mountain. Two years ago they'd converted to wood, but the problem was, they had already cut down all trees within two miles. More wood meant going further.

Potsk shrugged his greatcoat on and picked up an AK-74 and a large band saw. He waited. Two of his detail of eight men stood.

"Let us go," Potsk said, opening the heavy door. He knew he could order his men to do this, but the situation here was strained at best. He believed in leading by example.

They'd been here for eight months already, having been flown in as soon as the weather had cleared the previous spring. They had four months left on their tour of duty, and morale was plummeting with the pending onset of winter. Especially since there seemed to be no purpose to this tasking—watching an abandoned airstrip and the blocked entrance to a long out-of-use underground bunker. Ice crackled underfoot as Potsk traversed the hillside, heading for a valley where the closest trees were.

"Sir!" one of the men said, tapping him on the arm and then pointing upwards.

Out of the low-hanging gray clouds a parachutist appeared, then another. Soon there were twenty chutes in sight as the first one touched down about two hundred meters away, tumbling down the hillside until the man got his feet under him and cut away the chute.

"Sir?" The soldiers with Potsk were waiting on his orders.

Potsk looked from the closest jumper to the bunker, now over a quarter mile away. He knew they would never beat the paratroopers there. And he had no idea who these men were. Perhaps Spetsnatz running some sort of training exercise. But then he should have been notified. Of course, he immediately thought, things were so disorganized in the military that whoever was jumping might not have known the island was occupied. In fact, Potsk thought as he started walking toward the jumpers, these men shouldn't know about this place at all, because it was highly classified.

"Hello!" Potsk called out.

The man stared at him. He was wearing a black jump-suit with no markings or insignia.

"This is a classified area. There is to be no trespassing. Who is your commander?" Potsk demanded.

"I am." The voice came from the right, and Potsk spun around.

Potsk stepped back. The man towered above him, and Potsk noted that there was a scar running down the side of his face. "I said—"

The man brought up a submachine gun and fired a burst, blowing back one of the soldiers with Potsk. He swung the smoking muzzle toward Potsk. "Drop your weapons."

Potsk swallowed, dropping his AK-74, the other soldier doing the same. Behind the large man, some of the paratroopers were setting up a tripod and opening a case.

"Who are you?"

"Are all the rest of your men in the bunker?" Leksi demanded.

Potsk glanced toward the bunker, then back at Leksi.

"Tell me the truth." Leksi shifted the aim of his gun and fired. The round caught the other soldier in the leg, spinning him down to the ground. The man moaned in pain, looking up at Potsk.

"They are all in the bunker," Potsk said. He knew the shots would have alerted his men.

"Don't lie to me." Leksi fired again, this time right between the soldier's eyes. Potsk was stunned at the sight of the brains splattered onto the icy ground. The muzzle of Leksi's submachine gun turned in his direction. "Are they all in the bunker?"

"Yes."

Leksi signaled. The paratroopers had placed a missile on top of the tripod. With a flash the missile was off. One man watched through a sight, leading the wire-guided missile. It smashed into the front of the bunker, the armor-piercing nose punching through, the charge going off inside, making puree of the inhabitants.

"You pig!" Potsk yelled.

Leksi fired, almost negligently with one hand, the bullet taking off the top of Potsk's head.

Leksi grabbed his commo man. "Bring the plane in. We don't have much time."

Chapter Ten

"I don't give a damn what this guy says." Colonel Metter's voice was harsh, even with the dampener of the secure phone line. "I'm running this up the flagpole before we lose anyone else."

"Raisor said that we have to keep quiet about Sergeant Stith's death until he gives us the release," Dalton said. He was standing in a room off the experimental chamber, talking to his commander on a direct satellite link phone. "I don't think running it up the flagpole is going to do any good," he added.

"How are the rest of the men?" Metter asked.

Looking around the door, Dalton could see into the chamber. "They just pulled the first two after me out. Both are okay. The rest seem to be doing all right."

"You know they're going to tell me to forget about it." Metter was calming down, thinking about the reality of the situation.

Dalton knew what his commander meant. No matter what the colonel said, the Pentagon was going forward with this. "It's the nature of the job, sir."

"But I'm still going on record against this. From what you're telling me, they haven't got a good handle on what they're trying to do."

"No, sir, I don't think they have." Dalton hadn't told Metter about the nukes, and he knew he couldn't. "But they do have a high-priority mission that all this is aimed for. And it's got a short fuse."

"Is the mission worth losing men over?"

Dalton thought briefly of all the various missions he had been on where men had died. Few had been worth it. "Yes, sir, it is."

There was a long silence. Dalton could hear the slight crackling in the earpiece, indicating the MILSTARS satellite the call was going through was frequency hopping, making sure the transmission couldn't be intercepted. Dalton could see Raisor walking toward him across the experimental chamber. "Got to go, sir."

"Good luck."

The phone went dead.

"I assume you didn't reveal any information you weren't supposed to," Raisor said.

Dalton glanced around. No one was close. He stepped close to the CIA man, invading his personal space. "Listen to me very carefully, because we are not having this conversation again. I know you're holding information back from us. I highly recommend you stop doing that. Because what we don't know could get us killed."

Raisor started to say something, but Dalton got even closer. "I was doing special operations while you were still in diapers. Don't treat me or these men like we're just pieces of the machine to be used. We're not. And we won't accept being treated that way."

Raisor met his eyes. "What are you going to do? Complain to your colonel?"

Dalton didn't say anything. He remained perfectly still, looking deep into the other man's eyes, until finally Raisor nodded. "I understand where you're coming from." He changed the subject abruptly. "We've got new information that changes things. You want to be informed, follow me."

Dalton trailed the man across the experimental

chamber. Captain Anderson was pulling on his fatigue shirt, his face drawn. Dalton gestured for the captain while Raisor called out for Dr. Hammond to join them.

The four entered the classroom. Raisor and Hammond sat behind the front desk while Dalton and Anderson took other seats.

"The nuclear weapons convoy has been moved up five days," Raisor said.

Silence greeted that statement.

"We're going to have to be operational in forty-seven hours," Raisor continued.

Dalton waited on Hammond, as it was clear this was the first she had heard of this also.

She finally spoke. "That will be hard."

"We have no option," Raisor said.

"There are plenty of options," Dalton countered.

"No, there aren't." Raisor leaned back in his seat, putting more distance between the two. "This is not open for discussion. We are going in forty-seven hours. The only issue is how do we prepare."

"*We?*" Dalton repeated.

"I'm going with you, of course," Raisor said. He turned to Captain Anderson. "*You* are the ranking man here, not the sergeant major. You are under orders to comply with any and all instructions I give you."

"What the sergeant major is saying makes sense," Anderson said. "I don't think we can do this in two days. We've already lost a man."

"It's not up to you," Raisor said. "Plus the person who knows if you can or can't do it in two days is Dr. Hammond, not you or the sergeant major. And if you can't follow orders, I'll relieve you and find someone who can."

Dalton remained silent, as did Captain Anderson. They knew that by doing so, they were assenting to the mission, but there really wasn't much choice now. They'd pushed it as far as they could short of disobeying orders and getting court-martialed.

"We can do it," Hammond interjected. "But we have to really accelerate the schedule. I'd like to get moving on developing avatars immediately."

"Good," Raisor said. "I'll get as much intelligence as possible regarding our target." He threw a satellite photo down on the desk. "Right now all we have is that the state of Kazakhstan is transferring twenty nuclear warheads via rail to Russia in accordance with the latest arms agreement signed between the two countries.

"The warheads will be on a train traveling from Semipalatinsk to Novosibirsk." His finger traced a black line. "Along this rail line. Our analysts believe that the attack will occur just after the handover occurs on the Russian side of the border."

"Why then?" Captain Anderson asked. "Why not on the Kazakhstan side?"

"Because we believe it is the Russian Mafia who will be conducting the raid. They have more power on the Russian side. They might even have infiltrated some of the soldiers who will be guarding the warheads."

"What kind of security will the Russians have?" Anderson asked.

"One understrength company of infantry," Raisor said. "About fifty men. The train itself will be armored."

"That's a pretty tough nut to crack," Anderson noted. "How do you figure the Mafia will be able to take it down?"

"We don't know," Raisor said. "But you do need to understand that the Mafia in Russia is very much unlike anything you've heard about here in the States. They are very powerful and well armed. There is a tremendous amount of firepower available on the black market in that part of the world. We've had reports of the Mafia having tanks and attack helicopters. Along with the trained personnel to use them. I have no doubt that if the Mafia wants to take down that train, they will do it."

"What about the codes that arm the warheads–the PAL codes?" Dalton asked. He had some knowledge of nuclear weapons, having served on a "backpack nuke" team for a while. That was before Special Forces gave up the mission of infiltrating tactical nuclear weapons in backpacks with the advent of cruise missiles, which could do the job more efficiently. "Even if the Mafia gets the warheads, I'm sure even the Russian army isn't stupid enough to ship the PAL codes on the same train."

"And the Russian Mafia isn't stupid enough to attack this target if it didn't feel confident it could get the arming codes somehow," Raisor said.

That was the first thing Raisor had said that made sense to Dalton. "How do we stop them?"

Raisor turned to Hammond. "That's your area of expertise."

Hammond nodded. "What we're going to do is design combat forms for each of your men using Sybyl. These forms, which we call avatars, will be what you use when you come out of the virtual plane into the real."

"What exactly is an avatar?" Captain Anderson asked.

"An avatar," Hammond said, "is a representation of a person in virtual reality. Gamers use it when they participate in a virtual reality session. For our purposes, we use the term for the cyber-self that goes into the virtual world. We also use the term for the form that comes out of the virtual world at the far point. Let me show you what I mean."

She stood up and walked to a TV on a cart in the corner of the room and wheeled it to the front. She took a videocassette from the rack on the bottom and slid it in the VCR.

"This is a tape of the avatar used during our test run." The screen showed an empty room, the floor covered with various objects. For a minute nothing happened, then there was a shimmer in the air, about four feet above the center of the room.

Raisor spoke up. "The RVer who conducted this operation was in an isolation tank here at Bright Gate. This room—the far point—was in the basement of CIA headquarters at Langley."

Hammond tapped the screen. "Our man has now found the room and is beginning to gain coherence. The avatar used here was very basic. A program that copies a mechanical arm. Two joints, you could say an elbow and wrist, and five digits. The arm is about ten feet long, which makes each finger eight inches long."

Dalton could now make out the vague outline of the arm Hammond had described, but he could still see straight through it. Then, from the high end, the arm began to solidify in small squares, each one about four inches on each side, the colors ranging from red to orange, each one slightly different.

"We added the color in order to be able to see the avatar," Hammond said.

"Can it remain invisible?" Dalton asked.

"Not quite invisible, as you saw when it first started to appear," Hammond said. "You can remain invisible if you stay in the virtual world, but once you enter the real world, there will be some disturbance of the light spectrum. The light goes through, but it is affected. There is also a disturbance of the electromagnetic field, but that can only be noticed with special imagers."

"So if you wanted, you could keep our forms—avatars—relatively invisible?" Dalton pressed.

"I have a tape of the avatar operating when we don't add color," Hammond said. "You'll be able to see what it looks like."

The arm was now solid, floating in air. The long fingers,

actually looking more like a series of rectangles, began moving.

"Our man is testing the avatar now," Hammond said.

The arm bent at the elbow, then at the wrist. The fingers continued to move.

Then the hand reached down and picked up a block of wood about four inches square. It moved through the air and deposited the block on the other side of the room. Hammond hit the fast-forward and the arm raced through a series of maneuvers.

"What was the heaviest weight the arm moved?" Dalton asked.

"Four hundred pounds," Hammond answered. "That was the heaviest we tested it for. Really there is no limit to what it can do as long as the power coming from Sybyl is sufficient to support the proposed action."

"What's the limit of the power, then, that you can send from Sybyl?" Dalton asked.

"We're not exactly sure," Hammond said, "but based on our data, we have set up some basic parameters. The limit on avatar size will be about eight hundred parts per projected unit."

"Parts?" Anderson asked.

"It's a power unit that flows into size for Sybyl. To put it in terms you can understand, eight hundred parts would equal a 170-pound human being."

"Not exactly Godzilla," Dalton noted.

"It's the best we can do right now," Hammond said. "Eventually we might be able to produce Godzilla-like avatars, but there seem to be some limits on what can be sent through the virtual plane and then reassembled in a coherent form at the target."

"And power?" Dalton asked.

Hammond frowned. "That is a problem. Using Sybyl, we can only send a set limit. That one arm could lift four hundred pounds, but if we'd put another similar arm into the room, also powered by Sybyl, each one could only lift two hundred pounds."

"So the more men we send over," Dalton summarized, "the less power they will have?"

"Yes," Hammond said. "I've got our computer people working round the clock to increase the flow, but there seem to be some mathematical limits to the virtual physics that we don't quite understand."

"There seems to be a hell of a lot that you don't understand about all of this," Dalton said.

Hammond pointed at the screen. "It works."

"It picks up blocks," Dalton countered. He tapped the satellite imagery on the desk. "This will be real, Doctor. With real people. And real nuclear warheads. Your stuff had better work then."

"It will."

"I'm a little confused," Captain Anderson said. "You told us it could do only eight hundred parts. How many different avatars can you send over?"

"We're not sure," Hammond said. "We do know, though, that the total power is limited and the amount allocated to each avatar is inversely proportional to the number of avatars generated."

"Can you get the entire team operational?" Dalton asked.

"I think we can," Hammond answered.

"What about weapons?" Dalton asked. "We reappear as 170-pound 'forms' in our birthday suits, we're asking for trouble."

Hammond smiled. "That's something I think you will be very happy with." She grabbed another tape off the rack.

Dalton and Anderson leaned forward as a small, hovering sphere appeared in a different room. They recognized it as an indoor pistol range.

"That's the range at Langley," Raisor said. "The RVer was here at Bright Gate."

The avatar elongated until it was a tube about six feet long by six inches in diameter, bright red in color, the surface pulsing.

"We only gave it this form in order to get some idea of aim."

There was a glow on one end of the tube. Then, faster than they could see, the glow shot along the tube and down range. The wooden target exploded in a shower of splinters.

"How much power is that?" Anderson asked.

"Enough to punch through an inch of plate steel," Raisor said. "More than sufficient to go through any type of body armor a target might be wearing."

"How often can it fire?" Dalton asked.

"We're working on that," Hammond said. "There is a direct correlation between power and frequency of firing."

"If I wanted enough power to kill someone," Dalton said, "how often can I fire?"

"Once every two seconds," Hammond said.

"Jesus." Dalton shook his head. Two seconds was forever in combat. "We're back to the days of lever action rifles."

"Is that the best weapon you have for us?" Anderson asked.

"We have some other options in terms of power and rate," Hammond said defensively.

"What about if we have to take out armor?" Dalton asked.

"Then you materialize *inside* the tank," Raisor said, "and you kill the crew."

"Could I then use the tank?" Dalton asked.

"You can use anything you can retrieve," Raisor said. "That's one of the beauties of this type of operation. You will have the element of surprise and then of shock. You'll materialize out of nowhere, in a form that can hardly be seen, and what they do see will scare the piss out of them. Your weapons will be something they've also never experienced before. You'll have more than enough advantage."

"Against a force that's going to attack a company of infantry?" Dalton asked. "With only seven of us?"

"Eight. And all we have to do is stop them from taking the warheads," Raisor said. "That means just disrupt the attack."

"I think you are severely underestimating your advantages," Dr. Hammond said. "You will be able to move anywhere you want in an instant. And your physical selves will be here, at Bright Gate, safe. That's a tremendous advantage. You can't get killed, like a kid playing a video game on 'God' mode."

"What about the avatars?" Dalton asked, not thrilled with comparison to a video game. He'd been hearing about "push-button" warfare for over two decades now and he didn't buy into it. Sooner or later it always came down to some guy with a gun in his hand standing on a piece of terrain over the body of another guy with a gun. "What if one of the avatars is shot? How does that affect our physical selves and the form?"

"Your physical self will be fine," Hammond said. "The virtual form you project will be disrupted. What you are basically doing is transforming energy into matter. If the matter gets disrupted, it will backflow to the energy field. But you'll be able to 'dissolve' your avatar and re-form it again, so in effect, you will be indestructible."

"So why can't we just go as those tubes and fire everyone up?" Captain Anderson wanted to know.

"Because it's difficult to maneuver such a form," Hammond said. "We much prefer to give you an avatar that can actually make contact with the ground and any other surface. That can move physically if you need to. To disappear and re-form takes time and practice, neither of which we have much of right now.

"Also, you are used to having two arms and two legs and having your head on top of your shoulders. That might sound funny to you, but we try to approximate the human form as much as possible because it is the way you are used to getting sensory input and also the way you are used to moving. We could give you four arms, but how would you use the extra two? Where in your mind would you direct the commands for those arms to function? Perhaps with a lot of practice you might, but for a long time any additions or differences would only be a distraction. Trust me on this. A human-type form is the best for you to have as your avatar."

Raisor stood. "The best thing to do is for you to experience it firsthand. Perhaps that will answer many of the questions you might have. Let's get going. The clock is ticking."

Feteror remembered the plane ride out of Afghanistan. It was the last memory he had of the time before the long darkness. The last memory of being a man, even a wounded, dying shell of a man.

He had learned over the years to be able to put his memories into the mainframe computer he was hooked to. It was the only way he could "experience" a real life—replaying his memories, reliving them inside the computer. They were as "real" as the women the programmers sent to him for his "relief."

He often regretted that he didn't know more about computers, but at the time he had been shipped to Afghanistan, computers had barely appeared in the Russian world, other than those the government used.

The scientists called the master computer at SD8-FFEU Zivon, which was a Russian name that meant alive.

The scientists had great respect for the computer that assisted Feteror in accomplishing his missions, but Feteror knew the computer to be stupid and unimaginative. He supposed that as machines went, it was quite an impressive piece of equipment, but it was poor companionship for all the years he had spent hooked to it.

Of course, Feteror knew, the scientists also had named Zivon thusly because they considered Feteror to be part of the computer. They saw no clear separation between the human brain and remaining body floating in a solution inside the metal cylinder and the circuitry and memory boards that surrounded it. Feteror himself often wondered where the line was as he wandered the electronic corridors of Zivon.

The Russians had long worked at direct interfaces between the human mind and the machine mind. Ethical considerations had limited what could be done in the West, even though their machines were so much superior. SD8 had no such considerations to worry about and they had had access to all the other work being done in secret Soviet labs on cyborgs.

Feteror had looked up the word *cyborg* early in his new life after overhearing the technicians using it. The most interesting thing he had discovered about the definition was the part where it said that the human, once it became a cyborg, was then reliant on the machinery that was part of it for its survival.

During one of his maintenance periods, the technicians had turned his video eye–since his virtual demon's eye could never enter SD8-FFEU–on the metal cylinder that held him and the surrounding machinery. It had been hard for Feteror to accept that what he saw was his "self."

He remembered seeing himself in a training film when he had still been fully human and being surprised at what he saw, as many people were, not used to seeing themselves and having developed an unconscious representation in their own mind of what they looked like, sometimes at odds with the reality. Much as people were always surprised to hear their voice on tape, as it sounded different somehow. But seeing the machines that made him up had been far beyond anything any human had ever experienced.

Feteror had long ago ceased thinking of himself as he had been in human form, but he had not been willing or able to translate that concept to the machines that surrounded the husk of his body. He preferred instead to view himself as Chyort, the demon avatar he went on missions as. But that didn't mean he had been able to completely close the door on his past.

Feteror was very careful with his memories. They were all he had and he had made sure to encode them and hide them deep inside Zivon. Everyone he had known, and how he had known them, was in there. Everything he had ever done. Everywhere he had ever been. Even when Rurik cut his power down to minimum, Feteror was free to roam those parts of Zivon that were accessible to him, the space he was allowed for his own use.

And those parts of Zivon that the scientists had blocked off from him—Rurik was no fool—Feteror was still trying to get to. Like a prisoner slowly chipping away at a prison wall with a spoon, Feteror had been working on breaking through the circuit walls that surrounded him, trying to get to the outer world of Zivon, which he knew would give him access to the entire world of the Internet and beyond. His goal was simply to be able to shut Zivon down, and in the process kill himself, but he had become aware of the incredible electronic virtual world that had sprung up in the past decade and it had piqued his interest.

Rurik never gave Feteror access to any information other than what was needed to accomplish his missions, but each time he was out on one of those missions, Feteror always made sure to try to gain more data. Several times he had materialized and accessed into computers, "surfing" the Internet, a phrase he found most amusing, and an experience he had found quite stimulating. He had learned much, more than General Rurik could even begin to suspect. He had learned much about Rurik also, because he believed one of the keys to his plan was to understand his captor completely in order to be able to manipulate him.

In the past year he had even begun to contemplate trying to get to Zivon from the outside, hack his way into his own outer self, but the safeguards put in place seemed overwhelming, as did those on the inside, keeping him from hacking out. Even when he penetrated the GRU system, he had not even been able to get close to SD8, and he had been afraid of tripping alarms. If there was one tenet he had accepted early in his army career, it was that surprise and stealth were the most important tactical considerations when preparing an attack.

So he had accepted that another way had to be found.

But for now he was tired. He had accomplished much in the past few days, and his plan was gathering momentum.

He wandered aimlessly through the electronic archives that held his memory. When he paused to see where he was, he was surprised to discover that he was next to the place where he had encoded memories of his grandfather and his childhood.

He'd never known his father, not really. A vague figure who'd come home every once in a while wearing a smelly greatcoat. A large man who preferred the rough life of the army to the bitter life of the farm. Home on leave for a few days every few years, until finally he stopped coming and Feteror's mother stopped talking about him coming home.

Feteror saw little of his mother, as she worked in a factory in the city, six days a week for sixteen hours a day,

and it was too far to come back to the small farm each
night. So he saw her maybe once a week, usually less. It was
just he and his grandfather on the farm.

His grandfather—Opa in the Russian familiar—had told
him of the Great Patriotic War and how the Germans had
come and killed everyone in their village that they had
caught, including Feteror's grandmother and his own
mother's two brothers and three sisters. Only his grandfather, out in the woods hunting for game, and his mother, a
young girl then, accompanying him to help carry it back,
had survived. They had then joined one of the many guer-
rilla groups and spent the rest of the war hiding and killing
when they could.

Unlike many of the other old men whose stories Feteror
had heard, his grandfather had not spoken of the war
fondly, or boasted of great feats of arms. He had spoken of
the loss, the boredom of waiting, and the terror of the quick
clash of combat.

But mostly they had simply worked the farm, raising
enough food to eat and make the quotas from the State that
grew larger every year. When Feteror had turned sixteen,
his grandfather had died and Feteror had seen the writing
on the wall. He had known he could never make the increasing quotas, even if his grandfather were still alive to
help. Feteror had gone for the only thing he knew, immediately signing up to serve his required time in the military.

He'd found that the disciplined life was for him. In
many ways, it was easier than the farm had been, and
Feteror gained a better understanding of why his father had
been gone so much.

Feteror had done well, finally being sent to the elite
Airborne. Even there, among the best, he had excelled, and
he had been sent, after a few years of service, to officer
training. He'd returned to the Airborne and served as an

officer, before putting in enough time and gaining enough experience to join the Spetsnatz.

Feteror remembered the last time he had gone to the farm. He accessed that memory and the virtual area around him began to take on a form.

The collective had gobbled the farm up, but the small shady spot next to the stream where he and his grandfather had spent Sunday afternoons was still there, surrounded by acres and acres of open fields. Feteror closed his eyes and lay down in the shady spot, feeling the cool breeze, the itch of the grass underneath, hearing the murmur of the water going by. He had spent many, many hours perfecting this location in the computer's memory.

Feteror heard footsteps and when he opened his eyes, he was not surprised to see his grandfather standing there, a flask in his hand and a bright smile of crooked teeth amidst the wrinkles in his face.

Feteror sat up and greeted Opa and began to talk to him of what he had planned. He knew the old man would understand.

When the mercenaries complained about having to dig, Leksi threw money at them. Literally. He had a briefcase full of American dollars, and he tossed a thick band to each man.

"A bonus for the labor," he said.

But Barsk knew it was not so much the money, but Leksi himself, overseeing the digging, that made the ex-soldiers work like madmen. They wanted to be done with this and away from Leksi as quickly as possible.

There was also the problem that the GRU unit they had wiped out most likely made some sort of regularly scheduled radio contact with its higher headquarters. When they failed to call in, it was inevitable some sort of alarm would be raised. Barsk knew the remoteness of this site would preclude any investigation soon, but eventually someone would check.

The backhoe had worked through the rubble in the entrance to the elevator shaft relatively quickly. The shaft had suffered some damage but was unblocked except for debris at the bottom, which the mercenaries were digging out and placing on a small cage pulled out by the backhoe. An arc welder was cutting through the steel doors, which had been buckled by some sort of explosion.

When the welder finally cut through, Barsk could see that the doors were two inches thick. What Barsk really didn't understand was why this generator was so far underground.

With a solid thud, one of the doors fell inward. Leksi was through, followed immediately by Barsk. The welder went to work on the other door while they walked into the blasted shambles of what the papers called the control room.

"What did this?" Barsk whispered. There were skeletons strewn across the floor, the flesh seared from the bones. The blast glass overlooking the experimental pit had been completely blown away. The walls were scorched as if from an intense heat. Barsk ran his hand along the top of what had once been a computer but was now melted metal and plastic.

Leksi snapped a finger, and one of his men opened a case and took a reading with the machine inside.

"It is clean," the man said. "No radiation."

Leksi knelt and picked up a skull, peered at it for a few moments, then tossed it aside. "High heat," he said. "A very powerful explosion. Not nuclear though. Most interesting."

It was a shock for Barsk to see the ex–naval commando almost reflective as they both looked about.

Leksi crooked a long finger from his position near the blast wall. Barsk joined him. On the floor below was the

gleaming steel tube of the generator, still standing straight
and tall, the silver still shining amidst the black coils that fed
power to it. More skeletons littered that floor.

"What are those things?" Barsk asked. There were four
coffins next to the tube, a skeleton lying in each open container.

Leksi was turning the pages on the papers. "They're
called sensory deprivation tanks in here."

"Why did they need those?"

Leksi waved some of his men forward, ignoring the
question. "We need to unbolt that tube and then we're going to have to winch it to the surface. I want you five to
work on freeing the tube. You others, prepare a brace on the
surface so we can use both the plane and the backhoe to
haul that thing out of here."

Barsk was looking more closely at the coffins. He could
see the metal sockets implanted in each skull.

"What were they doing here?" he whispered.

Leksi frowned. "I hope we can take off with that weight
inside," he said in a lower voice to Barsk. "Move!" he yelled
at the men. "Move faster!"

Chapter Eleven

Knowing what to expect didn't make it any easier. In fact, the dread of what was to come always made things worse, in Dalton's opinion. The hardest part this time was the breathing crossover, but eventually he was past that and Hammond had him linked to Sybyl, who was going to introduce him to the avatar form that Hammond's team had crash-designed with the help of the computer.

Dalton had slept for two hours, if one could call it that. Hammond had given him a shot that had knocked him out for that time period. Dalton didn't feel rested, but as they used to say in Ranger School so many years ago when he'd gone through that training, he could rest when he was dead.

Remembering Ranger School, Dalton's lips curled in a slight smile inside the TACPAD and around the tube shoved into his mouth as he followed the instructions of Dr. Hammond. It was the same routine he had done the first time: focusing on the white dot, followed by moving along the grid line. What would his grizzled Ranger instructors have thought of this new form of soldiering? Floating in a freezing tank, connected to a computer? They would have liked the freezing-tank part—it seemed like every military school Dalton had gone through had always had immersion into cold water as part of the curriculum.

"Now we fit you to your basic avatar," Hammond said, her "voice" filtered through Sybyl. *"Are you ready?"*

"Yes." Dalton found this talking inside of his own head to Hammond very strange.

The grid lines disappeared. A stick figure replaced them after a brief blackout.

"This is you."

"Lost some weight," Dalton said.

"This form has no mass at present, although once projected out of the virtual and into the real world, it will have mass out of the energy we will send using Sybyl."

"It was a joke," Dalton said.

There was a long pause.

"We will proceed. Sybyl will run you through a series of maneuvers to familiarize you with your avatar."

Dalton waited patiently. He had no idea how much time had already elapsed. That was something he was going to have to ask Hammond—how could one keep track of time in the virtual world?

"Move your left arm," Sybyl commanded.

Dalton tried to do as he was told, but he could feel nothing from his left arm.

"Again."

They went through this how many times Dalton didn't know, until suddenly he felt a painful twinge in his arm. *"Hey!"* Dalton yelled.

"You are getting feedback?" Hammond asked.

"I can feel my arm."

"You feel your virtual arm," Hammond said. *"Now you can move it. We have to make sure you have feedback before we allow movement. Now we will allow your nervous system to interact more fully with the form."*

Dalton focused on moving his arm forward. The stick figure in front of him slowly moved its right arm forward. Dalton felt his arm move at the same time. It was very confusing, since he knew that his arm had not moved in reality.

"Experiment," Sybyl told him. *"Practice."*

Dalton did just that for a while before he noticed something. *"What about my hands?"*

"We must start with the basics," Hammond said. *"This form is the barest outline of the avatar you will eventually employ. Try the other arm."*

Soon Dalton could move all of his limbs individually. Sybyl then tested him in much the same manner that she had with the grid lines. A light would flash next to one of the limbs and he had to move in the direction of the light. The computer would also rotate the figure left and right, so that he had to move forward and back.

As the practice went on, Sybyl started flashing lights in combination and at a fast pace. Dalton found himself totally immersed in trying to keep up. It was like when he had first learned martial arts, the practice at making all movements a routine, an instinct.

Hammond's voice came back. *"The goal is so that you can move the avatar as naturally as you move your own body. For example, if you were to do a forward roll, you would not be thinking how each of your arms and legs moved. You would do the roll. The avatar needs to be as much a part of you, so that you can move in combination in an unconscious mode. The major thing keeping you from that right now is the belief in your mind that you are not really the form you see. You must suspend your disbelief and believe you are looking into a mirror. But focus on what you feel, not what you see."*

Dalton did as she instructed and found that his action became more natural. It felt as if he were floating in the tank at scuba school, weightless and free. He rolled forward.

"Whoa!" Dalton yelled. The figure in front of him was tumbling and he felt like he was spinning out of control. With great effort he brought himself to a halt.

"How do I know which way is up?" Dalton said. *"I've got*

no feeling of weight. Even in water, I can tell direction by check-ing out my air bubbles. Here there is nothing."

A red line appeared next to the figure, arrows on it slowly going by pointing up. *"Orient on the arrows,"* Hammond suggested.

Dalton did the roll again, but this time he focused on the red arrows. He did two complete revolutions, then halted himself.

"Very good."

Dalton felt like he was gasping for breath, but he knew now that it was only a part of the virtual feedback.

"Now feet and hands," Sybyl said.

Dalton found that more difficult. He had never truly realized how complex the human hand was and how many moving parts it had. The foot was also hard to master.

Soon Sybyl had him mimicking the act of walking, the stick figure moving jerkily along. One thing Dalton found disconcerting was the lack of resistance, particularly to his feet.

"Right now you might consider what you are doing walking in space, much like an astronaut," Hammond said. *"As you may have noted you have no weight. You are acting against no object. You are totally free. It is important to learn this type of movement, first because it is the most strange for you and also because it is the way you will feel while you travel on the virtual plane."*

"Can I go somewhere?" Dalton asked.

There was a pause. *"I must check with Raisor."*

"Why?"

There was another pause. *"Because he's in charge."*

"Forget it," Dalton said.

"You have completed this phase of training," Hammond said. *"We are pulling you out."*

"The fools will never succeed," Feteror's grandfather said as he stood at the edge of their glade, peering in the direction of the open fields. There was the distant heavy coughing sound of the Combine's tractors working the land. Even in the virtual world, the State intruded, Feteror thought wryly. He knew he could delete the sound, but it was the way he had last been in the glade.

Feteror frowned. He had told his grandfather his entire plan and this was his response?

"Did you hear me, Opa?"

"I heard you. I know little of such matters, so you must do what you deem is best." His grandfather shook his head, his heavy gray beard slowly swinging back and forth. "They think the group is stronger than the individual, but it is not so. Because the group is only as strong as the weakest individual. A good person can beat any group."

"Then you believe I will succeed?" Feteror asked.

"Even in the war," the old man went on as if he had not heard a word. "The generals used us as if none of us mattered. They threw us against the Germans like so many pieces of garbage to be tossed onto the scrap heap. They'd keep our artillery fire so close that we lost as many of our own as the Germans did to our shells. But what did the generals care about us? We weren't them. More importantly, from their perspective, they weren't us. They had a goal and we were the means to achieve that goal."

Feteror stared at the construct of his grandfather. Zivon had developed this persona out of the memories that Feteror had poured into the computer, but in the past year or so, Feteror had slowly become aware that the persona had grown beyond the memories. It used words his grandfather had never known, but underneath, Feteror still felt that the essence of the construct was his grandfather.

"And we did win," Opa continued. "But what did we win?"

"You defeated the Nazis," Feteror said.

"Yes, we won *that*," the old man acknowledged. "But

what was the total result? The entirety? We thought we
were fighting for good." His withered hand swept around,
taking in what Feteror knew was supposed to be the farm.
"We produce less now than we did when we worked the
land, *our land*, with just a sickle and horses to pull the carts.
Sometimes you can think you win but actually lose if the
price you pay for winning is too high. You can lose your
soul."

"What–" Feteror began, but the old man cut him off.

"I want to know what happened to you, grandson. Tell
me of your last battle." He waved the hand about. "I do not
understand all this. I must know where you have come
from."

That memory was in Zivon also, a recollection that
Feteror was loath to go into. Feteror felt a spasm pass
through a nonexistent stomach, his mind reacting.

The glade faded and he and Opa were over a village set
in the mountains. Feteror knew the when and where: Afghanistan, August 29, 1986. Feteror realized he didn't have
control over this playback, that his grandfather would see
the true extent of what had happened:

*A dry wind blew down off the mountain peaks that surrounded
the valley, kicking up small dust storms. Feteror pulled the cloth
tighter over his face and narrowed his eyes as his men drew
closer, stepping onto the dirt road that served as the village's main
thoroughfare.*

*Feteror knew that because of the war, the people of the village
had seen much pain and suffering but to them that was simply
the way life was. The Soviets had invaded Afghanistan seven
years ago and still the war dragged on, but he had learned that it
was not of much concern, since if it was not the Russians, then the
people would be fighting another village or some other foreign
power. War was an integral part of life for the* mujahideen *who*

controlled the countryside, and it mattered little to them who claimed rulership of the country in Kabul.

The mujahideen *did, however, enjoy the new weapons that the Americans were sending in through Pakistan, especially the Stinger missiles. Just a week ago, a passing band of* mujahideen *had downed a Russian helicopter flying by low in the valley. When the villagers had come upon the crash site, they'd found eight dead Russians. Feteror had a good idea of what had happened next from other villages he'd raided. The Afghanis had cut the heads off and brought them back to the village to be used later when playing the Afghani version of polo, the heads replacing the ball in the Western game. The game, of course, would have to wait until the men of the village returned. Most of the men were gone, either dead or off fighting. Feteror knew there was little concern in the village about the Russians or their Afghani Army lackeys because the village didn't sit astride any route of communication nor did it have any resource of great value. The war had been going on for long enough now that the Soviets no longer sought out conflict, but stayed inside their fortified positions, fighting only when forced to. Feteror was counting on the villagers' complacent attitude to get his disguised band of men into their midst.*

Thus, when the small group of eight men was spotted walking up the valley floor toward the village in the early morning light by a young boy tending his flock, there was not much concern. The elder, summoned out of his house, could see that the men coming up the valley were dressed in the traditional robes and turban of the mujahideen *fighter and that they were moving openly. As they approached, he ordered the eleven remaining families to contribute some food so that the fighters might be nourished as they passed through.*

It was too late when the elder turned to yell for his youngest son to get his weapon, as Feteror's men whipped aside their robes. AK-74 assault rifles began firing, killing the few villagers who had weapons. Resistance was destroyed in less than thirty seconds.

The elder had not moved throughout the entire time. Feteror knew he knew that to do so would invite death and his duty was to the village and the people as a whole. Feteror's men spread out, mopping up.

Feteror walked directly toward the elder, his rifle held loosely in strong hands, while yelling commands to his men in Russian. With one hand, he ripped off the turban he had been wearing. He pulled a pale blue beret out of his robe and set it on his head. The other men did the same.

The elder raised his hands wide apart. Feteror brought the weapon up and fired, the round ripping through the elder's right leg, knocking him to the ground.

"Any other men?" Feteror asked in Pashto, the language of the mujahideen, which surprised the elder.

"No."

"Order everyone into the street. You have ten seconds. I will kill anyone who hides or runs."

Ignoring his pain, the elder yelled at the top of his lungs, ordering all into the street.

There was a burst of automatic fire as the middle son of the elder's brother ran out, firing an old rifle, and was cut down in a hail of bullets from the Russians, his body tumbling down the street like a rag doll. The old man's black eyes watched this, but he said nothing, nor did he show any sign of the pain radiating up from his leg.

Slowly the rest of the villagers came out until there were seventeen women, twenty-two children, and four other old men standing under the watchful guns of the invaders.

"Is that everyone?" Feteror asked.

"Yes."

"The men are all away fighting." Feteror made it a statement, not a question. "You thought yourself safe here, high in the mountains, didn't you?"

The elder remained quiet, feeling the deep throb of pain from the wound on his leg.

"My name is Major Feteror." He was a slight man, his body lean like a blade under the robes he wore. But it was his face that the elder focused on. There were scars running down the left side, and he had ice-blue eyes under straight blond hair. Those eyes worried the elder. Feteror reached up and touched the beret. "We are Spetsnatz. Special Forces. Your fighters call us the 'black soldiers.' You would do well to–"

Feteror paused as there was a sudden consternation among the Russian soldiers. One of them came forward carrying a dirty burlap sack. He laid it at the feet of Feteror and opened it. Inside lay the battered heads of the eight Russian soldiers from the helicopter.

The elder closed his eyes, waiting for the bullet, but seconds passed and he slowly opened them, to look into Feteror's. The major's face was expressionless, only the glint of the eyes showing his anger. He reached down and picked up one of the heads. The face was contorted, but it was easy to see that it had been a young man who had not yet reached his twentieth birthday. The elder had heard that the Soviets were sending younger and younger men to fight the war. He felt nothing about that. His brother's middle son had been only eleven. A man was a warrior when he was big enough to pick up a rifle.

"It will not be that easy, old man." Feteror barked some commands in Russian as he placed the head back onto the bag. His men lined the villagers against the mud wall of the elder's house, then stepped back on the other side of the street. They put their weapons to their shoulder and aimed, waiting.

The elder was proud that his people stood still, glaring back. There was no crying, no pleading. One woman spit, then the rest did the same, while also putting their children behind them. The four old men walked to the very front.

Feteror yelled some more orders. The muzzles of the seven

AK-74s moved back and forth, sighting in on one person, then moving to another. And another. But still no bullets came.

"Tell me when, old man," Feteror said.

The elder couldn't keep track of all seven weapons. He looked at his wife, whom he had been married to for thirty-two years. His four grandchildren. His two daughters.

"Tell me when, old man, or they fire on full automatic. As it is now, they will each shoot only once at your command."

The elder ran his tongue along his lips, feeling the dryness. He knew that in the long run it would not matter. "Now."

Feteror yelled a single word and seven rifles fired in one sharp volley. Seven bodies slammed back under the impact of the bullets. The elder saw that one of the seven was his wife, and in a way he was grateful that she would be spared whatever else was to come.

"You play well," Feteror noted.

The Russian fired as the old man swung the knife he had slid out from under his robe. The round caught the elder in his upper right shoulder, knocking him back onto the ground, the knife falling harmlessly to the dirt.

"But you don't fight so well." Feteror kicked the knife away. "So we will have to keep playing and not fight." Feteror leaned and smiled, revealing even teeth. "You are a disgrace and a coward." As the elder struggled to rise up, he kicked him down with a heavy boot. "Watch my men play, old man. It was what you were going to do with them," he said, pointing toward the heads. "You have your games, we have ours."

While four of the Russians stood guard, the others dragged the women into one of the huts. The elder listened to the screams and curses of the women for several hours as the soldiers raped and sodomized them. When they were done with a woman, they slit her throat, throwing the body out the back onto the refuse pile. Halfway through, they simply killed the women, no longer able to force themselves on them. The old man noted Feteror took no part in that sport.

While that was going on, Feteror had each of the children tied with a blue cord cinched tightly around their necks and made to stand in the center of the street under the bright sun, ignoring their cries for water.

It was early afternoon by the time all the women were dead. Feteror had the old men executed, a bullet to the back of each head, and then only the children were left. The elder had watched the sun slowly climb across the horizon with a growing feeling of contentment.

Feteror attached a small green plastic tube to the end of one of the blue cords and walked over to the elder, who was now weak and dizzy from the loss of blood.

"I am being merciful, old man," Feteror said as he handed the green tube to him. The elder slowly followed the cord; it was tied around the neck of his six-year-old grandson. He looked to the Russian in confusion.

"Pull the ring," Feteror ordered.

Still not comprehending, the elder did as he was told. The detonating cord ignited instantly, and with a flash and small pop, the elder's grandson's head lay in the street, the body still standing for a few seconds before slowly toppling over.

"I think sometimes that the heads can see their own bodies if they fall in the right direction," Feteror commented as he inserted the next length of blue cord into the green tube.

"No!" the elder protested as Feteror held the tube out to him. "I will not!"

"Ah, then I will not be so merciful." Feteror gestured to the guards. While two kept their rifles ready, the others drew knives out of scabbards and approached the closest child.

"I will peel them alive if you do not play," Feteror warned.

The elder took the green tube and pulled the ring. A second head lay in the street. The Soviet slid another end of blue cord in. The elder closed his ears to the cries of the children who were left. His hands worked automatically, taking the ignitor each time the

Soviet gave it to him and quickly pulling the ring. He lost count, but mercifully there were no more lengths of blue cord.

The elder turned to the Russian leader. "Kill me."

"I would," Feteror said, "but then who would tell the others what I have done here?" Feteror grabbed the old man's chin. "This was a warning. You take heads, we take heads. I think I have made that perfectly clear."

"Kill me," the elder insisted.

"No. I will have my medic bandage you and tie you so that you cannot hurt yourself. When the men come back, you will tell them how you failed the village and what I have done. Then they will kill you. And the war will go on, but there will be that many less"—Feteror gestured at the heads lying in the street—"to grow up and fight us and that many less women to bear more spawn to grow up and fight us."

"You are the devil!" The elder tried to work up spit in his mouth, but it was dry. He had expected to die now. The thought of facing the men in the midst of this was unbearable.

Feteror smiled. "The devil—Chyort. I like that." He suddenly straightened and looked to the north, toward the mountains. Then he glared down at the elder. "You kept me here. You knew they were coming. That is why you didn't fight me when I first came."

The elder smiled as Feteror slammed the stock of his weapon into the old man's head, knocking him out. Yelling orders, Feteror turned and ran for the southern end of the village, his men falling in line behind him. The radio man ran next to Feteror, proffering the handset. From the north there came a sound like thunder, hundreds of horses' hooves striking the hard-packed ground and closing on the village.

Feteror took the handset and began calling for extraction when the earth exploded in front of him.

When Feteror regained consciousness, he was greeted by the stare of a line of lifeless eyes. The heads of all the children he had had killed were arranged around him in a circle. He slowly took an inventory of his body. He could feel pain in his chest, from both the ropes wrapped around it and several broken ribs. He could sense something hard and straight against his back and realized he was tied upright to a thick pole. He was naked, the cool night air brushing against his skin.

Carefully he tested, but the stake was set deep into the earth and solid. The ropes were thick and well tied.

It was dark outside the circle of heads, the only light coming from a lantern set on the ground three feet in front of him. But Feteror could sense the people lurking there, watching, the hate washing over him in waves. Feteror smiled.

A whip snapped out of the dark, the leather knots on the edge slashing into his skin, peeling back a long slice on his chest.

Feteror's only response was a sharp intake of breath, the smile still on his face. The whip came again. And again. The smile disappeared only when he slid into unconsciousness, the skin flayed from waist to neck.

When he came to, it felt as if his upper body were on fire. Just taking a breath caused his wounds to reopen and agony to surge into his brain. He looked about. Night still blanketed the countryside and the heads were still watching him. He leaned his head back and looked up to the stars. He remembered seeing those same stars as a child while riding on the open steppes. His grandfather telling him the stories of the animals the various stars represented. He also remembered seeing that same sky often while in the field during training. He had traveled by those stars many times on operations all over the world, but he knew tonight he would be taking his last journey.

Movement drew his attention back to earth. A woman came out of the shadows. She was small, wrapped in robes, only her dark eyes showing through a slit in her turban. In her hand she held a short curved knife, the firelight glinting off the highly polished surface. She was one of the women who accompanied the men when they went to war.

Feteror knew what to expect. The woman reached and grabbed him between the legs, pulling none too gently. The knife flashed. Surprisingly, Feteror felt little. Despite the pain he was able to think quite clearly with a part of his mind. He figured that any pain from below his waist would have trouble overriding the tide of agony from his flayed skin. The woman held up his severed penis in her hand and, with a shrill scream, carried it back into the darkness to throw it to the dogs. Another woman came out with a dirty rag and a piece of rope. She pressed the rag up against the new wound, tying it in place with the rope. Feteror knew they weren't concerned with infection but they didn't want him to bleed to death. Not yet.

A man appeared, large, as tall as Feteror's six and a half feet. He carried something long in his hand. Feteror forced himself to focus. It was a sledgehammer. He could even see the Cyrillic writing on the side as the man came closer. It must have been taken off of a Russian tank that the mujahideen had destroyed. Forged in a factory back in the motherland. Feteror found that strangely amusing. That he and this sledgehammer, both forged far to the north and west, would end up here at the same place at the same time in this godforsaken land.

The man gestured and the same woman who had tied the crude bandage in place came up, carrying another piece of cloth. She folded it over several times, then knelt, pressing it up against the front of Feteror's right knee.

Feteror's thoughts on fate and his newly developed theory on pain below the waist were both gone in an instant as the man swung the sledgehammer into Feteror's right kneecap, smashing it against the thick stake he was tied to, the sound of the bone underneath the cloth being crushed as devastating as the pain.

Feteror screamed for the first time.

The sledgehammer went back once more. And again. And again.

Feteror, the essence of him, retreated from the pain, climbing into the recesses of his mind, praying for death or at least unconsciousness, but each time the latter came, the mujahideen would bring him alert with pain to a previously undamaged part of his body. And they kept death at bay by searing shut any bleeding wound with a hot knife, although the use of the cloth kept the hammer from opening too many wounds. Feteror's only hope lay in the possibility that they would run out of things to do to him or that they would grow bored and kill him.

But as dawn touched the eastern sky, neither appeared to be close.

He could now see past the circle of severed heads. He was at the edge of the village. A crowd of mujahideen watched him silently, the hate in their eyes not abated in the least. Feteror was now in some other place, someplace removed even from his own mind, floating above, able to look down on his own body tied to the stake. He wondered if he was dead, but the body–his body– still twitched with life.

The old man, the village elder, was tied to a stake on the other side of the circle of heads. A leather band was stretched around his forehead, forcing him to look directly ahead. His eye-lids had been sliced off. A man stood next to the elder, speaking in a low voice that Feteror could not make out. The elder was also naked. Several leather bands were wrapped around his body and limbs.

A woman came up, several similar strips of wet leather in her hand. From above, Feteror dully felt her tying bands around his arms and legs, a most strange experience.

The man who had been speaking to the elder came over. "The leather shrinks as it dries. It will take a few hours." He pointed at the elder. "We put the bands on him two hours ago. It is beginning to dry. The sun will quicken this. You think you know pain now. Watch."

As the sun came up, the elder began screaming, begging. The leather tightened down on his flesh, compressing all beneath. Something gave way in the old man's legs and he gave forth an undulating cry that didn't stop. For fifteen minutes it went on. A young man talked to the man who had spoken to Feteror. The man reluctantly nodded. The young man went over to the elder and slit his throat, stopping the cry.

"You will not be so lucky," the man informed Feteror.

Feteror could tell that the straps were tightening. The pain was drawing him back to his body, something he fought with all his will.

Feteror began praying for death, calling on a God he knew only from the stories Opa had told him many years ago. He was back in his body as the agony reached levels he had never thought possible.

Through the pain, he heard something. Very distant. His eyes flickered up, his mouth wide open as he took careful breaths. Yes. He could hear it. He wondered why the mujahideen didn't. The sound of helicopter blades cutting through the thin air.

One of the mujahideen was coming close, holding the red-hot knife just pulled out of the fire. But this time it was not to close a wound. Feteror pushed his head back against the stake as the man brought the knifepoint toward his face. Feteror ripped muscles in his neck, trying to avoid the knife. The man called for help in dealing with the Chyort, the devil man.

Two others ran up, grabbing his head and holding it still with all their strength as Feteror fought them with every once of energy he had left. The night had been too long, the damage too great. It was a lost battle.

The knife came forward. Feteror felt it touch his eyeball, and pain, far beyond anything he had felt so far, hit his brain like a spear splitting it straight through. He screamed, his battered and sliced body straining against the ropes, which brought even more pain and deepened the primeval essence to the shivering cry he let loose.

But still he could hear the sound of the helicopters so close, and machine-gun fire. And screams coming from others. And then there was only blessed darkness.

———

The village was gone. They were back in the glade. Opa was crying, tears flowing down his weathered cheeks.

"Do you see now?" Feteror asked. "Why I must do this thing?"

Opa opened his mouth to say something, when the sky and glade disappeared along with the old man.

"Time to work." General Rurik's voice was harsh. There was a bright glaring light in Feteror's face. He knew that was a construct the programmers used to get his attention, feeding the input directly into his occipital lobe.

"What is it?" Feteror was disconcerted.

"We have lost contact with one of our surveillance units," Rurik said. "We want you to see what has happened."

"Why don't you send a plane?"

"Because it is very far from the closest plane," Rurik said. "And more importantly, the surveillance team was watching where we used to be headquartered."

Feteror waited.

"We are inputting the coordinates."

Feteror read them as they came in. Information about the history of Department Eight had always been strictly withheld from him by Zivon on General Rurik's order, under the theory that knowledge was power and the less Feteror knew, the weaker he would be.

Feteror could have gotten this information from Oma, after she had received the papers and CD from Colonel Seogky, but he had not wanted her to know that he wasn't aware of the information contained in them. It had taken him four years to simply find out that the phased-displacement generator had been built, and that had only been because of a most fortunate meeting. The location of the generator had been something for which he had needed Oma and her organization. He had pointed her to the man in GRU records who would know that information. He could have taken it out of Vasilev, but the added fact that they would need the CD-ROM to program the computers to work the phased-displacement generator—and Vasilev himself, the only survivor among those who had invented the machine, to properly operate the computers—had precluded Feteror from pushing the old man too far, too soon. Vasilev would pay, but only after he made penance.

Feteror translated the grid coordinates as they came in. The far north!

"Find out why the surveillance unit has not reported in and come back immediately. You are to observe only."

"Why is there still a surveillance unit there?" Feteror asked.

"That is not your concern."

"Why was Department Eight moved from there to here?"

"That is also not your concern. Just do as you are tasked."

The tunnel beckoned and Feteror jumped. He felt the weightless feeling of flying as he roared into the virtual plane, assuming his winged-demon shape. It was what he felt comfortable in. The first time he had been like this was in the village in Afghanistan. Rurik and his minions thought they were so brilliant! The computer link only gave him more power, more information.

The body was basically humanoid, except larger, more powerful, and armed with sharp claws at the end of each hand. The wings were something he had worked out with Zivon. He had not liked the feeling of floating free or moving from place to place without a sense of spatial orientation. The wings gave him that, although it had taken him much time to get used to them. They gave him a solid way to control his orientation, direction, and speed. And they helped scare the piss out of anyone he appeared to on the real plane.

Feteror stretched his wings wider, moving faster, the virtual plane going by in a rush, his mind focused on the location he had been given.

The virtual plane was a strange place. There were times when even Feteror felt concern as he traversed it. It was a gray world, and traversing it was like moving in a vast mist, but references from the real world could be spotted poking through here and there if he made an effort to see. If there were no references, then Feteror would have to stop and come out of the virtual, into the real, and align himself. Sometimes he sensed other shadows, forms, moving in the fog.

Some he recognized–psychics, real ones–plying their trade. Sometimes he knew they were Americans, from their Bright Gate operation. He knew the presence in the rail station had been a Bright Gater. How much the Americans knew he could not tell. He was also unsure exactly what their capabilities were. He knew they could remote view but he had picked up some different disturbances at times that indicated the Americans were doing something more advanced than just RVing. He had tried once to breach their facility in the state they called Colorado, but it was well protected from psychic probing.

He had given General Rurik the information about the Mafia in order to move the timetable of everything up, so that whatever the Americans might plan would occur too late. But now he knew they also knew the timetable was sooner rather than later.

Feteror sensed he was over Siberia. He could feel the vast emptiness of that land reflected around him. He could not explain how he knew where he was, he just knew it. It was one of the strange aspects of the virtual plane. Often the emotion of an area was what passed through to him, not the physical realities. Feteror oriented himself and continued his flight.

He had no idea how quickly he moved. Sometimes he arrived at a place "instantaneously" in real time, yet it seemed like it took an hour on the virtual plane. Other times, going to the same place, real time had elapsed. There was no way to tell. He had asked the scientists, and their mumbo-jumbo answers had told him they didn't have a clue why that was. He knew they didn't even really know why he was able to do what he did.

Feeling he was in the right place and sensing death–something he was very familiar with–below, Feteror halted and focused so that he could see the real world. The island appeared below. Feteror could see the Cub transport plane parked on the edge of the runway. He swooped around in a large circle, going lower. He could see the backhoe and lines going from it into a hole in the side of a mountain.

Claws on the end of his feet splayed, Feteror landed right next to the hole. He bared his fangs in a grin as a couple of the mercenaries looked around, sensing something, not sure what it was, only that they felt danger in the air around them like a faint scent at the edge of their consciousness. Feteror could clearly sense their fear, like a wild dog near its prey.

Feteror was still in the virtual plane, the demon shape only something he felt, not something that was really there with the soldiers, but he knew the line between the two worlds was not solid and fixed.

He folded his wings and walked forward, into the hole. The ropes disappeared into a large elevator shaft. He looked down. There was a glint of light on steel far below. The phased-displacement generator.

"Careful, you pigs!"

Feteror looked at the man who stood on the other side of the shaft opening. Leksi. Feteror had seen the man before. And next to him the boy-man who had taken the papers from Colonel Seogky. Who was so stupid he had not listened when Feteror had whispered in his mind that his bodyguard was a double agent. Feteror remembered the name: Barsk, Oma's flesh and blood.

Feteror blinked as an image of his grandfather passed across his mind.

"Even pressure on both cables!" Leksi was yelling.

Feteror threw himself back, spreading his wings wide and hovering. He felt a strong desire to gain solid form, to match his power against Leksi. To rip the man to pieces, to make him bleed and suffer.

But there was not enough power coming from Zivon. Only the beckoning signal to return from Rurik. And he needed Leksi for now.

Feteror tightened his wings and dove into the shaft. He landed on top of the generator. Looking beyond, he could see the skeletons and devastation in the control center. He could feel spirits floating about. Feteror stepped back in surprise. He had felt spirits before, but always very distantly, but these came at him. He "saw" nothing, but he knew they were all around him. Four men, long dead, who whispered to him of revenge, of pain and suffering. He felt an immediate affinity for their suffering. He promised them he would avenge their pain.

Feteror pivoted over on one wing and flew out of the cave, up into the virtual sky.

Vasilev screamed as he scrambled away from the demon that pursued him. Its red eyes speared him with their malice, and he could hear the creature's claws against the floor. He scuttled sideways, trying to put as much distance as he could between himself and the monster.

It had halted and Vasilev did too. He breathed deeply, then almost smiled. This was just a bad dream. All he had to do was waken and the nightmare would be over. He would be home in bed, ready to wake up and go to the university for another day of teaching.

He opened his eyes and blinked. It was dark.

Then he saw the eyes and knew the nightmare was real. The demon came forward once more. Vasilev ran away, so hard that when the chain reached its end, the collar around his neck snapped him back so badly, he tore muscles in his neck and he flopped back onto the concrete like a rag doll.

"Please, please," Vasilev pleaded as the creature leaned over him. He swore he could smell its fetid breath. "Mercy!" Vasilev begged.

"You gave no mercy on October Revolution Island," the creature hissed.

Vasilev's eyes widened in shock. How did this thing know of that? Those thoughts were brutally interrupted as a claw ripped up his right side, parting flesh with one smooth stroke.

The pain was like acid. He screamed once more.

"You will not have death until you atone," the creature said.

"I am sorry!" Vasilev whimpered.

"Atonement requires action." The creature drew back, leaving Vasilev holding his bleeding side.

"I am sorry," Vasilev whispered as the demon once more disappeared.

Chapter Twelve

Dalton had refused the shot from Dr. Hammond this time. He had always been able to sleep when he needed to. He had slept on many an aircraft, fully rigged with 48 pounds of parachute, 140 pounds of rucksack attached to the rig dangling between his knees on the cargo bay floor, helmet pulled down over his eyes, weapon tied off to his right shoulder, while men threw up around him from the turbulence of a low-level-flight infiltration.

Sleep when you could was a lesson that had been beaten into him from too many missions when he hadn't been able to. But sleep was coming slowly right now for different reasons. He lay back on the bunk and stared at the concrete ceiling.

Dalton closed his eyes. The image of the concrete ceiling remained. But this one was smooth, not like the other one. The one where Dalton had counted every single mark on it. Memorized them, then begun using his imagination, the only thing he had left, on it. He'd made a world out of that ceiling only four feet above his mat on the floor. He couldn't stand in the cell, so he'd lie there, legs always bent, and stare at the ceiling.

There were the faintest outlines on the ceiling, brown marks from some time when water had been in the cell, perhaps when the nearby river had flooded, that made up the continents and oceans of Dalton's imaginary world.

He put countries inside those continents. His favorite

land had been Far Country, a land settled by the persecuted of Old Country. Dalton had invented the entire history of those people leaving the homeland, the travel across the huge Middle Ocean, to arrive in Far Country. A land where there was no war. No need for armies, because no one would follow them across the Middle Ocean.

It was not a land of plenty, but rather a hard land. Another reason no one would dare the terrible ocean to come there. There was nothing to conquer but empty space. Endless plains, running into the High Mountains. And beyond the High Mountains were even more wonderful and strange lands.

But in Dalton's history the people of Far Country loved their land. And the peace made any hardship brought on by the land or weather more than bearable. Because there was nothing that nature could do that could be worse than what men did to other men.

Dalton could see the High Mountains, particularly Dunnigan's Peak, the white summit shimmering to the west. He'd climbed the mountain numerous times, using a different approach each time. The view from the top reached back over the Plains to the Middle Ocean, the water—

"Sergeant Major!"

Dalton was alert in an instant, rolling to the side away from the voice, hand reaching behind his back, pulling out his nine-millimeter pistol, before his eyes focused on Lieutenant Jackson's face. The RVer looked exhausted.

Dalton took a deep breath. "What?"

Jackson looked to her left and right. "I have to talk to you."

"Talk," Dalton said, lowering the hammer on the gun and putting it back in its holster.

"I'm Army," Jackson said. "Most of these people are CIA or NSA. But there's a couple of us from the service here. We were part of the original Grill Flame operation.

And we were good, so they kept us when they switched over to Bright Gate."

"What's your point, ma'am?"

"You can't trust Raisor."

Dalton leaned back on his bunk. "You woke me to tell me that?"

"Did he tell you what happened to the first team?"

"The first team?" Dalton swung his feet over to the floor on the same side that Jackson was crouched. "Dr. Hammond said someone died when there was an equipment malfunction. She didn't say anything about a team."

"Dr. Hammond doesn't know diddly," Jackson said vehemently. "She'll lie when Raisor tells her to, but a lot of the time she talks out her ass because she doesn't understand a lot of what she's working with. Hell, no one does. At least *we* admit it. She has to act like she knows more than she does because her ego won't allow her to admit her ignorance. They've sold a whole pile of crap to the Oversight Committee and the Pentagon. You don't think they'd be bringing you and your men in unless they were desperate, do you?"

"I figured that," Dalton said.

Jackson nodded. "Raisor put together the first Psychic Warrior team using NSA and CIA operatives. They tried to keep us RVers in the dark, but since we were both using the same facilities here, it was kind of hard to do. Plus we'd run a lot of the early tests for Psychic Warrior, gathering the data Hammond needed to make the next step. But obviously Raisor wanted to keep it in house, so he brought his own people in to make up the first team."

Dalton waited. He knew he'd been lied to; now he was beginning to get an idea of the extent. "What happened to the first team? Are they dead?"

"We don't know," Jackson said.

Dalton raised his eyebrows. "What do you mean by that?"

"Their bodies are still in their isolation tanks, in a room off the main experimental chamber. The machines are keeping them in stasis at the reduced-functioning status. So they're alive, I suppose. As alive as any of us when we go into those damn tanks."

"What happened to them?"

"No one knows. I don't know exactly, but I have an idea. I told Hammond but she thinks it's bull. I believe she thinks that because what I told her scared her."

"What about Raisor?"

"I think Raisor believes me. He's weird."

"What's your theory?"

"There are bodies in the isolation tanks, but there are no *people* in there, if you know what I mean. Heck, Sergeant Major, I went looking for them. I went out on the virtual plane to see if I could find them." She paused, her eyes withdrawing.

"And?" Dalton prompted.

"And I think I found the team. What was left of them. Their psyches. Worn out as if they'd died of starvation. They were all dead there."

"Wait a second." Dalton held up his hand. "You're talking about a thing that's not real in a place that doesn't exist."

"Oh, you know it exists," Jackson said. "Or you will once Sybyl passes you over. It's as real as this room."

"If this avatar is a construct, how can remains of the psyche exist? Wouldn't it just disappear?"

"I don't know," Jackson said. "I'm just telling you what I found. I don't pretend to understand this stuff like Hammond does."

"But . . . how could their avatars have 'starved,' as you put it?"

"Loss of power from Sybyl. They got cut off."

"How?"

"I don't know. Like I said, whenever Psychic Warrior was operating, we were locked down."

Dalton considered what she had just told him. What mission had the first team been on? Or had they been lost in training and that explained Raisor's reaction to what had happened to Stith?

"There's something else I think you should know," Jackson said.

"What?"

"There's something, or someone, else over there," Jackson said.

"Who?"

"Chyort," the lieutenant whispered.

"What?"

"The devil. I translated it using Sybyl. *Chyort* is the Russian word for 'devil.' The CIA picked up reports about such a thing several times but they dismissed it. I don't."

Dalton bit back his reaction. He could tell the lieutenant wasn't making this up. That she believed what she was saying.

"Not the devil like most people think of him," Jackson said, then she paused, as if hearing her own words. "Well, maybe I'm wrong there. Maybe it *is* the devil like most people think of him. But whatever you might think, I'm telling you there is someone else in the virtual world."

"Any idea who?" Dalton asked.

"Most likely the Russians," Jackson said. "We know they've been working with remote viewing longer than we have. And I heard rumors when I first got to Grill Flame from some of the old hands that the Russians had gone way beyond what we had been doing. That they had taken psychic warfare very seriously a long time ago and have been putting a lot of resources into it.

"Also, we get blocked when we try to see into certain places in Russia. It seems pretty logical to me that if the Russians know enough to block us psychically, then they know enough to RV. You can't have an antidote without a poison."

"So this devil is a Russian avatar?"

"I think so. I met him earlier today. When I went on the recon to check out the nuke warheads shipment. He was there. In the same room at the railhead. I couldn't see him and I don't think he saw me, but he was there. I felt him. And I know he felt me."

"Does Raisor know this?"

"I told him. He didn't seem that interested. The CIA reports are unsubstantiated according to him. And he chooses to disbelieve reports we give him that he doesn't want to hear."

"But this means the Russians probably know about the planned attack," Dalton said.

"There's a high probability of that," Jackson said. "I've read numerous unclassified reports of the strong Russian interest in remote viewing and psychic phenomena. In fact–" She paused, but Dalton indicated for her to continue. "In fact, there's some evidence that the Russians were trying to tap into psychic weapons a long time ago. In 1958 there was a tremendous explosion of undetermined origins just north of Chelyabinsk in the central Soviet Union that devastated a large amount of countryside. The CIA formally reported it as a nuclear mishap, but there was quite a bit of speculation that it was caused when some sort of psychic weapon misfired.

"There's a scientist, a Dr. Vasilev, at the Moscow Institute of Physiological Psychology, who has written several papers that, if you read between the lines, indicate strong Russian experimentation in psychic weapons. I think this

Chyort, this devil, may be the latest generation of such a weapon."

The lieutenant shivered and Dalton put an arm on her shoulder. He could feel the shaking, something he had felt before from soldiers who had been pushed too far and couldn't handle it anymore. Combat stress.

Jackson leaned her head into his arm, her voice no longer that of the woman, but the girl who had been scared. "I don't know what this thing is. I met the devil today and now he knows me. And he'll get me next time I go over there."

"Listen to me," Dalton said in a low voice. "Listen to me. I know you're afraid and it's okay to be afraid. Because you got something to be afraid of and you just had something real bad happen.

"When I was a POW in Vietnam, they brought in a pilot late one afternoon. They carried him down the corridor past my cell, and I could see that he was in bad shape. He still had his flight suit on but it was all torn up and he was bleeding. He must have come down near a village. In a way, he was lucky to be alive, because once the villagers got hold of one of those who brought death out of the sky—as they called pilots—they usually hacked him to pieces before he could even get out of his parachute harness. But the NVA must have gotten to him in time. They liked pilots because they could get some good intelligence off them and they had publicity value."

Dalton heard Jackson sniffle. He kept speaking.

"They put him in the cell next to me. I heard him crying that night. Hell, I remember crying my first night after I came to."

Jackson looked up at the sergeant major in surprise.

Dalton smiled. "Anyone who wasn't scared or didn't feel afraid in such a situation would have to be nuts. I've met a few guys who weren't afraid in combat, who actually enjoyed it—they were sociopaths. And those guys scared the piss out of me.

"Anyway, I reached through the bars and called to him. I got him to put his hand out and I held it. All night long. Because the thing we're afraid of more than anything else is being alone."

Jackson pulled back slightly and Dalton took his arm off her shoulders. "This devil doesn't scare you as much as the thought of facing him alone. But that isn't going to happen. Next time you meet this Chyort, this devil, you won't be alone. We'll be there with you."

Jackson stood up.

"Okay?" Dalton asked.

Jackson nodded, her eyes red.

"Get some rest," Dalton said. "I'd take one of Hammond's shots if I was you."

Dalton watched her walk away. Jackson reminded him in a way of Marie. He tried to pinpoint what the semblance was, then realized there was nothing in particular except that Jackson had needed him.

He sat in the dark of the bunk room, his mind not on the upcoming mission, but on the past. The first time he had been under fire. The day that had torn him away from Marie for five long years.

"He must keep this bandage on for three days."

Specialist Fourth Class Jimmy Dalton listened as the interpreter relayed his instructions to the mother. Dalton spoke Vietnamese, not fluently, but well enough so that he could have given the information himself, but he had learned that it went over better coming from the interpreter. It was scary enough for these people to come with their medical problems to the large foreigners and allow themselves to be exposed to treatments they could not understand. The concept of one of the foreigners speaking their language was something that took a while for most to assimilate and accept, and Dalton's priority was his patient's health, not immediate cultural acceptance. He knew the latter would require time and patience, and he was going to be here for a year, so he was prepared to take it slow.

Dalton was dressed in plain green jungle fatigues, a Special Forces patch sewn onto the left shoulder, the gold dagger and three lightning bolts standing out against the teal blue background on the arrowhead-shaped patch. On his head, his green beret felt stiff and new, unlike the battered and faded ones the other members of the team wore.

Dalton looked up from the young boy as the northeastern sky flickered. Seconds later the manmade thunder that went with the light rolled over the camp. The sound of mortars and artillery pounding Khe Sanh had been a nightly serenade for the past seventeen days. Located less than four miles to the southwest of the bombarded Marine Corps base, the Special Forces camp at Lang Vei was an inviting target to the NVA forces as the Tet Offensive exploded in earnest throughout South Vietnam. Every man assigned to Lang Vei knew it, but so far, they had been left alone other than an occasional mortar attack.

"You should all leave," the woman told the interpreter in Vietnamese.

Ba To, the interpreter, glanced at Dalton, knowing he had heard. "Why is that?"

The woman swept her hand at the dark jungle that surrounded the camp. "Many, many soldiers from the north. And their large metal beasts. They will kill all of you."

"Tell her she's welcome," Dalton told Ba To. He rubbed a rag across his forehead, then proceeded to repack his M-3 medical bag. Metal beasts. They'd captured an NVA officer a week ago who'd told intelligence that tanks were being brought up to the Laotian border, only a kilometer and a half down Route 9, which ran along the southern perimeter of the camp. The report had been greeted with skepticism by the brass and concern by the rank and file. Dalton's team sergeant, Mike Terrence, had sent an urgent

request for LAWs, light antitank weapons, to their B-Team head-quarters. They'd received a hundred of the plastic tubes just two days ago. The LAWs, in addition to the 106-millimeter recoilless rifle in the camp's center weapon pit, was the extent of their antiarmor capability.

Dalton looked across the berm and the rows of barbed wire at the jungle, less than two hundred meters away. The NVA using tanks was unheard of. At worst, the intelligence rep had insisted, if there were tanks, the NVA would use them for covering fire from the treeline. That made no sense to Dalton, but then again he was only a nineteen-year-old medic, straight out of the Special Forces Qualification Course at Fort Bragg. He'd been in-country only three weeks and the most dangerous thing he'd done was make the resupply run to Khe Sanh the first week he was at Lang Vei and hunker down in a Marine bunker while mortar and artillery rounds came in.

From the sound of the firefight to the northeast, there was no doubt that the Marines were catching hell. Since the offensive had begun, the only way in and out of Khe Sanh was by air. The same was true of the Special Forces camp. Highway 9 was cut to the east of Lang Vei, essentially isolating the A-Camp other than for helicopter resupply for the past two weeks.

The mother and son walked off toward the huts holding the Laotian refugees who had flooded into the camp in the past week, running before the NVA forces who were using their country as a free zone to organize their assault. Dalton wished Ba To a good evening, and they headed in opposite directions to turn in for the night.

Besides the American A-team, Detachment A-101, there was a mobile strike force company of the local Civilian Irregular Defense Group, CIDG, inside the walls of the dog-bone-shaped camp along with the battered remains of the Laotian battalion that had briefly fought the NVA before running to Lang Vei. Twelve Americans and three hundred indigenous troops, at the remotest edge of South Vietnam, close to the borders of both Laos to the west and North Vietnam just to the north.

This was what Dalton had been trained for: to work with the indigenous people of a country to teach them how to take care of and protect themselves. As a medic, Dalton had spent most of the past several weeks not walking combat patrols, but plying his medical skills among the never-ending line of patients. He'd already performed more minor surgery than most interns back in the United States. There was nowhere else for these people to go for treatment.

Dalton walked along the inside of camp, passing the dark forms of soldiers manning their posts. His goal was the command bunker that also held the small dispensary where he and the senior medical sergeant kept their supplies and bunked down.

Halfway there, right in the center of the camp, Dalton halted. His back felt like there was an army of small ants climbing up it, and he reached back to brush them off, when he realized that the feeling was inside his head, not actually on his skin.

The flat thump of a mortar round leaving a tube interrupted this strange feeling. Dalton had been in-country long enough to know that by the time one heard the sound of the mortar firing from outside the camp, the projectile was already over its apogee and on the way down. He ran for the nearest sandbagged position, the 106-millimeter recoilless rifle pit. Dalton jumped over the top of the four-foot-high sandbag wall as the first mortar round hit just outside the perimeter.

"Mind your p's and q's and watch where you put your feet, laddie," a voice with a thick Boston accent greeted Dalton as he sat up, dusting dirt off his shirt.

Staff Sergeant Herman Dunnigan was the team's junior weapons man, and the 106 was his pride and joy. He'd stolen it from the Marines two months ago, and Captain Farrel, the detachment commander, had already been called on the carpet twice for the return of the weapon. With the reports of NVA armor, the entire team knew that Farrel is is no rush to return the rifle to the Leathernecks, who were much better prepared at their firebase for any sort of armor attack.

Dalton slid across the base of the pit until he was next to Dunnigan, who handed him an already lit cigarette, pulling its replacement out of his fatigue shirt pocket. Two more rounds went off in rapid succession, somewhere in the south side of the camp. Dalton flinched at each explosion.

"They got the range," Dunnigan commented. "They most certainly do, the little bastards. Of course, they're probably getting adjusted by someone in the CIDG, so why the hell shouldn't they have the range?"

It was accepted that the NVA had spies in both the CIDG and in the Laotian battalion. It was a bitch having to guard against attack from the outside and betrayal on the inside of the wire, but it was the nature of the Special Forces' job. Dalton knew that some of the soldiers he was patching up could be shooting him in the back that very evening.

Dalton didn't answer as he took a deep drag on the smoke. His hand was trembling. He was scratching his neck before he realized that, again, the itchy feeling was coming from inside.

"Something's coming," Dalton said as he carefully snuffed the cigarette out and put the remains in his pocket. He swiveled around on his knees and peered over the barrier toward the jungle.

"You don't need to see 'em," Dunnigan said. "We'll be hearing them first." He gripped Dalton's shoulder. "Listen."

Dalton held his breath, just as he'd been taught when getting ready to fire his rifle. There was a very low roar, an engine running. Dalton's first thought was that it was the camp's generator, but then he realized it was of a deeper pitch and coming from outside the perimeter.

Dunnigan was on the hand-cranked phone, calling the mortar pit. "I need illumination. West side. Over the treeline."

"Tanks?" Dalton asked as he hung up the phone.

"Damn straight, laddie. Didn't you feel 'em moving up earlier?"

Dalton looked at the other man. It hadn't occurred to him to wonder why Dunnigan was in the pit this late in the evening. *"Feel them?"*

"You live long enough, you'll know." Dunnigan's head was cocked listening for the sound of the 4.2-inch mortar on the north side of the camp to fire. *"Sometimes I wonder, though, if it isn't you know, and you'll live long enough."*

Dalton was still puzzling over that when they heard the heavy thump of the camp's four-deuce mortar. Seconds later a flare burst high overhead, illuminating the western side of the camp.

"High explosive, load!" Dunnigan was looking down the barrel of the 106-millimeter, aiming it.

Dalton grabbed a round out of its cardboard container and slid it in the back of the rifle, shutting the trap on it. Only then did he look where the other man was aiming.

Four PT-76 tanks were rumbling out of the treeline and heading straight for the wire. They weren't top-of-the-line battle tanks, but rather armored reconnaissance vehicles built by the Soviet Union, with a 76-millimeter gun mounted on top in a small turret. Still, coming straight at him, the tanks more than impressed Dalton.

The recoilless rifle spit flame. A burst of fire on the front slope of one of the tanks was followed immediately by a secondary explosion, popping the turret off.

"H.E., load!"

Dalton fell into the rhythm, loading as fast as Dunnigan fired. They flamed a second tank as four more came out of the trees. By the time Dunnigan had fired for the fifth time, the lead tank was in the wire, less than fifty feet away. It paused, the 76-millimeter gun in the turret turning in their direction.

Dalton felt like time was suspended as he slid a fresh round into the rear of the rifle and locked it down. Dunnigan had his *eye pressed up against the aiming scope. Both guns fired at the same time.*

A shock wave hit Dalton in the chest, knocking him back. The sandbags in the front of the pit had taken the impact of the NVA round, and all that remained was a large divot in their protective barrier. The PT-76 that had fired was in flames.

A hand slapped Dalton on the back, bringing his attention back into the pit.

"H.E. Load!" Dunnigan was mouthing the words but Dalton couldn't hear anything other than a loud ringing in his ears.

He slid a round in but everything suddenly went dark other than the burning tanks as the flare expired. Dalton could see tracer rounds flying by overhead and he knew that one of the tanks was firing its coaxial machine gun at them.

Dalton shook his head trying to clear the ringing. Dunnigan was on the phone, screaming for more illumination.

Dalton saw figures running, silhouetted by the last tank they'd hit. He suddenly realized they were sappers in the wire. He threw his M-16 to his shoulder and fired, finger pulling back on the trigger smoothly, aiming quickly, not able to tell if he was hitting anyone, there were so many. His finger pulled and there was no recoil. Dalton's training took over as he pushed the button on the side of the magazine well, letting the empty one fall out. He pulled a fresh one out of his pouch and slammed it home.

Another flare burst overhead. Dunnigan had his shoulder into the recoilless rifle. Dalton stopped firing long enough to scan the area. There were three tanks bearing down on their pit. He could see the blinking flashes on the side of the turrets–their co-ax machine guns. And all three were pointed straight at him and Dunnigan. In front of them, Dalton saw sandbags being torn apart by the machine-gun bullets.

Dunnigan fired. The shell skidded off the deck of the lead tank. Then there was a bright flash of light and Dalton felt his breath get sucked out of his lungs as he was lifted into the air and then slammed into the ground on his back. He struggled for air,

*his brain momentarily not functioning, and then his lungs worked
again.*

*Dalton opened his eyes and saw a bright shining candle. A
flare, high overhead, slowly drifting down under its parachute.
Dalton sat up, surprisingly unhurt, it appeared. He looked about
the pit. The recoilless rifle was smashed, the barrel bent. Dunnigan was sitting against the rear of the pit, his chest covered in red
from a jet of blood pulsing out of his neck. Dalton scooted over to
him, ripping the bandage out of the case on his web gear.*

*He pressed down on the severed artery, and the white gauze
was immediately soaked through with the deep red of blood coming straight from the heart and lungs. "Hang in there!" Dalton
yelled, unable to hear his own voice over the ringing in his ears.
"You're gonna be all right!"*

*Dunnigan's eyes went wide and Dalton knew there was
someone behind him, but he also knew that if he stopped the
pressure Dunnigan was dead.*

*Dalton felt the bayonet puncture his lower back, like a sliver
of freezing cold entering his body. He arched forward, reacting
even as his mind forced his hands to keep the pressure on Dunnigan's wound. Dalton turned his head to the left, just in time to see
the stock of an AK-47 heading straight for his face.*

*There was a flash of bright light, then there was only
darkness.*

Dalton looked down. His hands were clenching the
edge of the bed, his knuckles white. He forced his fingers to
let go. Slowly he let go of the memories of Vietnam. He
cleared his mind and passed into an uneasy slumber.

Feteror's demon avatar slowly materialized as he stalked
down the empty corridor. The dull glow of the dim night
lighting in the building rippled through his form, the sound
of his claws on the tile floor a low clicking noise echoing

into silence. He paused at a door. He reached down. It was locked.

His form disappeared as he reentered the virtual plane and flowed through the thick steel, coming out the other side and reforming on the real plane. The room was lit with the glow of a dozen screensaver programs. Feteror walked to the center console. He reached out a long claw and carefully tapped on the keyboard, accessing the program he wanted.

It had taken him two months to get the code word he needed to enter the GRU classified database. Two months of hovering unseen on the virtual plane in the background at various GRU sites, waiting for someone to log on in front of him.

The screen cleared and the main menu came up. Feteror's right arm dematerialized as he reached forward, sliding it through the screen and directly into the computer. He could sense the inner workings and tapped directly into the mainframe. Suddenly his entire form disappeared and he flowed into the computer. He raced through the inner workings, a shadow passing on the border between the real world and virtual until he found what he was looking for. He absorbed the information, imprinting a copy into his own psyche. The data was encrypted, but that wasn't a problem—he could always get Zivon to help break the code.

There was one more thing. When the maintenance workers had accidentally allowed him access to the security cameras inside SD8-FFEU, Feteror had taken full advantage of the opportunity. He had accessed the small camera inside of General Rurik's quarters—no one was exempt from security's eye in the GRU—and scanned it. He had zoomed in on the photo next to the army bed: a woman with two children. The woman whose ring Rurik wore.

Feteror scanned through GRU personnel files until he found the information he needed.

Satisfied, Feteror headed back out of the computer and headed for SD8-FFEU.

"Sergeant Major, I can't do it."

Dalton rubbed his eyes. First Jackson waking him, now this. Sergeant Trilly was standing in front of him, head down. Dalton finished zipping up his black isolation tank suit. He had five minutes before his next session. He could see a couple of the other bunks were now occupied by men who had finished their second training session.

"Can't do what, Trilly?" Dalton knew the answer, but he was also aware he had to play this out.

"I can't go in there again," Trilly said, his voice quavering. "I can't breathe that shit they put in your lungs. I can't get shut off like a light switch and frozen. I just can't do it."

Dalton looked the sergeant over. He was shivering, a blanket about his shoulders. His hair still wet, his skin covered in goosebumps. He remembered how Trilly had missed most of the Trojan Warrior training after getting his collarbone broken during the aikido training.

"You don't have any choice," Dalton said. "You're the team sergeant. Your team goes on a mission in thirty-six hours. Can't is not an option."

Trilly made a choked sound. "I can't go in there again, Sergeant Major. I can't. I know I can't. You can order me and make me put that stuff on, but I can't do it."

Dalton felt the soreness in his throat where the tube had twice gone down. His body was covered with small welts, from what he had no idea. He had just noticed them when getting dressed.

Dalton stepped close to the other man and kept his voice very low and level. "Get some sleep, Master Sergeant Trilly. You'll feel better."

Trilly looked up. Dalton could see the shadows in the

others man's eyes. "I'm not going to feel better. It's not going to make any difference."

"Trilly, you're Special Forces. We may not like where we get sent or what we get ordered to do, but by God, we go there and we get the job done."

"Like Stith?"

Dalton resisted the urge to grab Trilly's shoulders and shake him. "Yes, like Stith. Who the hell do you think all those names on the Special Operations monument outside of SOCOM headquarters are? Nobodies? They were men just like you and me. They got killed doing the job they volunteered for. That you volunteered for. You want the easy life, you should have stayed in Air Defense. You put that green beret on, you choose a different path from most. Now it's our turn in the breach."

"I can't do it."

"Don't say that." Dalton kept his voice firm. "You think negative, you won't be able to. You've got to think of the team, not yourself. The team needs you."

"I can't—"

"Shut up," Dalton hissed. "Get your head out of your ass, Trilly. Think about somebody else for once. You got the stripes on your collar, you do the job. You flake out on this, we're another man short, and sometimes one man can make all the difference."

Dalton could see the clock over Trilly's shoulder. He had no more time. "Get some sleep."

Trilly turned without a word and went to his bunk. Dalton watched him, then walked into the corridor and to the experimental center. He noted the doors on the wall that he had not been through. He wondered which one hid the bodies of the first team.

Two of Hammond's technicians had his TACPAD waiting. They rigged him, the process going somewhat faster now that he was used to it. He still wasn't thrilled when they shoved the tube down his throat or his head was encased in the TACPAD, but he hardly noticed the microprobes going in anymore.

"We're going to send you over to the virtual plane this time," Hammond told him through the computer.

He was lifted up, then lowered into the isolation tank six minutes ahead of the new schedule. The handoff to Sybyl went smoothly.

The computer quickly ran through a check of his stick man form, insuring that he had control.

"It is time now," Hammond finally announced, satisfied. *"You will feel power. It'll feel good. A feeling of strength. Do not do anything until I tell you. Do not do anything unless I tell you specifically to do it. Is that clear?"*

"Clear," Dalton replied.

"I am giving you ten percent."

Like a jolt of adrenaline, power coursed through him. Dalton felt giddy. He began to lift this arm.

"Do not do anything until I tell you."

Dalton forced himself to remain still. The feeling grew stronger.

"Turn to your left."

Dalton did as instructed.

"Do you see the light?"

There was a bright glowing tunnel straight ahead. All else was dull gray fog. Dalton paused as he realized what he had just done, or what had been done for him by Sybyl–he was inside the avatar, looking about–not in his own head looking at the form.

"I see it."

"Walk toward it. I am giving you a surface to walk on and a feeling of weight."

Dalton did feel ground beneath his feet. Slightly spongy, like walking on a gym mat, but it gave him something to push off of. The tunnel got closer. Then it was right in front of him.

"*Wait,*" Hammond said.

Dalton paused.

Hammond's voice, filtered by the computer link, came through. "*When you step into the virtual plane, there will be nothing beneath your feet. It will be like floating in a mist. You will have no sense of orientation. It will take us a little while to get you both oriented and able to move. Some have difficulty with this.*"

Dalton remembered the first time he had free-fall-jumped out of a plane. It was much different from static line parachuting. He had tumbled in the air as he fell; the only orientation he had had was the ground far below that he was rapidly plummeting toward and the air whistling by. He had an idea what Hammond was talking about. He had seen men panic in such a situation, unable to deploy their chutes as they tumbled, saved only when their automatic opener activated at a predetermined altitude.

"*All right. I'm ready.*"

"*Step into the tunnel,*" Hammond ordered.

Dalton moved his leg forward. There was nothing to put it on. But he didn't fall as he lifted his other leg. He felt himself drawn forward and then he was in.

His stomach spasmed his last meal ready to come back up as he floated in a fog. He had no idea how far he was able to see, because there was nothing to see.

"*I feel like I'm going to throw up,*" Dalton said.

"*That's a psychological reaction,*" Hammond said. "*And a very good one.*"

"*Good?*" Dalton swallowed.

"*Yes. Because you can't really feel your real stomach. So this is a subconscious psychological reaction, which means your mind is very attuned to the virtual world. That your mind believes the world you are in now, the form that you are taking, is real.*"

"That's nice."

"Take some time and get adjusted to being there."

Dalton did as Hammond instructed. More than free-fall parachuting, it reminded him of scuba diving at night, when there was no way to determine which way was up. Neutral buoyancy in the netherworld; Dalton found that concept interesting. He looked about, but everything was the same grayish mist. He had no idea if he was seeing fifty meters into it or ten. He put a hand in front of his face, but all that was there was the stick arm of the avatar. He had no idea where he was either.

"Now we will teach you how to fly," Hammond said.

"Fly?"

"How else do you think you will be able to get around?" Hammond asked. *"Although possible, it is very hard to jump with just your mind, especially on your first time. It is much easier using the avatar form."*

"All right," Dalton said. *"How do I fly?"*

"With your wings, of course."

Dalton's stick arms transformed into two wide wings, white feathers glistening. *"Sweet Lord,"* Dalton whispered. He swept them down and felt himself lift. He swooped, tried to turn and felt himself lose control, before regaining his balance. He looked down. He still had the stick figure he'd originally had, but the wings had replaced his arms.

A black level space appeared ahead.

"I've had Sybyl make a place for you to stand," Hammond said. *"We must work on the rest of your avatar. I'm passing you to Sybyl for training."*

Dalton landed on the black plane. His felt his "feet" sink into the surface slightly.

"I will show you the various forms we have computer gener-ated," Hammond said. *"You must pick the one you prefer in accordance with your own physical shape and size."*

Dalton watched as a series of forms appeared in front of

him. All were man-shaped, but there were a number of subtle differences among them, ranging from the basic size to the lengths of the arms and legs. One of the forms was moved out in front of the others.

"The data indicates this would be the best fit, as it most closely approximates your own body shape," Hammond said.

The form was featureless, the skin a pure white. The eyes were two black spots on the face. There was no mouth or nose. Dalton assumed that Sybyl had the form that way because there would be no need for mouth or nose in the virtual plane, but he wondered what they would look like when they came out into the real plane. He saw a certain advantage to not having an entirely human appearance in such a situation.

"Will I be visible in the real plane?" Dalton wanted to check what Raisor had told him.

"You will cause a disturbance in the electromagnetic spectrum," Hammond said. *"Despite the fact that the human eye does not see into that spectrum, we have noted that people in the real plane do sense something when an avatar materializes.*

"You also will have the option to add color and pattern to your form if you have a need for your form to be seen."

The form in front of him disappeared. Dalton felt a wave of something pass through him, and he staggered back. When he looked down, he now had the form that Sybyl had built.

He looked down at his hands, spreading the fingers, flexing them. His movements felt smoother than they had in stick form. He walked around. He felt like he had shed thirty years. His body—avatar—felt alive and vibrant. And powerful. He reached his smooth hands up, stretching. He slid one leg out in front of the other and did the basic first kata of aikido that he had learned in the Trojan Warrior training. At first he had some difficulty, but he tried again and again, until the arms and legs began functioning smoothly, without conscious thought. He worked his way through the eight katas up to black belt level before he felt satisfied.

"Weapons?" he asked.

There was a tingle in Dalton's right arm. He looked down, watching the forearm and hand dissolve into a tube about three feet long from the elbow joint.

"Aim and fire," Hammond said.

A target silhouette appeared about thirty feet away.

Dalton extended his arm, then paused. *"How do I fire?"*

"Think it and it will happen," Hammond said. *"Think about making a fist with the arm that is now the weapon. Aiming is easy as you will see a thin red dot on the aim point of your weapon much like a laser sight."*

Dalton focused. He saw the red dot, moved it on target. He sent the impulse to clench his nonexistent fist, and he felt a slight recoil in the arm/weapon. A glowing ball raced toward the silhouette and hit. The target shattered.

Several more silhouettes popped up. Dalton fired.

He found the tube to be extremely easy to aim–it was like pointing his arm, and the red aiming dot was dead on with where the round hit. But he was disturbed by the lag between aiming and firing. He found himself pointing at a target and waiting as the power built up to firing level. It took about two seconds between each firing, an eternity in combat in Dalton's experience.

"The rate of firing is dependent on power?" Dalton checked.

"Yes."

"Give me minimum power to kill a man with a shot to the head."

There was a short pause, then Hammond responded. *"Done."*

Dalton fired at the array of silhouettes, moving at the same time, diving to his right, rolling. Coming to his knees and continuing to fire. This lower power setting was better, firing with what Dalton estimated was slightly more than a second between each shot. The accuracy was superb, as Dalton placed each power ball into the head of each silhouette.

"Can you equip my team with an array of power settings?" Dalton asked. *"I want most of them able to fire this rapidly, but I want others firing on the stronger setting."*

"I can have Sybyl do that."

"If you decrease rate and increase power," Dalton wanted to know, *"can you also fire a spread of balls?"*

"At the same time?" Hammond asked.

"Like a shotgun shell," Dalton said.

"Yes."

"I also want some of my men to be armed with a focused, powerful shot that can punch through armor."

"I can program that also."

Dalton concentrated and the tube shrunk, dissolving into his avatar arm once more.

"What about the wings?" he asked.

"If you are ready, you can change your arms to the wings. Just concentrate like you did with the power tube."

Dalton paused, closing his eyes. He concentrated; his arms felt like he was flexing the shoulder muscles. When he opened his eyes, he had the wings back.

"Where would you like to go?" Hammond asked. *"I must keep you within a certain area in the virtual world until you are more proficient. Consider the borders of the state of Colorado as your current limits. Where would you like to go in Colorado?"*

Dalton knew the answer to that, but he didn't bother to tell Hammond as he moved into the virtual plane.

Chapter Thirteen

"What is this place?" Barsk asked as the wheels of the plane touched the runway. They had flown for several hours after getting the generator on board. The plane had taken the weight, but the pilots had been forced to use every foot of runway to get them into the air.

"An old airbase," Leksi said.

"I can see that." Barsk was tired and his fear of the large man had diminished in proportion to his weariness. He could clearly see that the buildings and hangars had long been out of use. The plane was slowing.

"This is one of the bases where the planes the Americans sent over during the Great Patriotic War were flown to," Leksi said. He pointed out the small window. "In that building the American insignia was painted over and the Soviet star was painted on. A crew of our people then manned the plane and flew it to the front."

"And why are we here?" Barsk asked as the plane came to a halt, then slowly turned and began taxiing toward a hangar, with an open door.

"This is where I was told to take the generator for the first stop," Leksi said simply.

Barsk could now see there were several helicopters inside the hangar next to the one they were headed for. Men dressed in black fatigues stood in the shadows, weapons slung over their shoulders, watching.

"Who are they?"

"The men and equipment we will need for the next phase." Leksi stood as the back ramp began coming down. "But do not concern yourself, you go elsewhere from here. I'll take care of the next phase without your help. There's something you need to see."

Barsk followed as Leksi disembarked, walked out of the hangar, and headed for a hangar that stood some distance from the other buildings. Its large door was opened by two men dressed in black fatigues. Leksi led the way to a trap door in the floor. He threw it open, pointing his flashlight into the hole.

Barsk peered down. A naked old man chained to a metal post was lying on the floor. The old man stirred, holding a hand up to protect his eyes from the light.

"Who is that?" Barsk asked.

"Professor Vasilev," Leksi said. He threw the door shut. "You are to take him with you to the next site. He will be responsible for setting up the phased-displacement generator."

"What is the cylinder?" Feteror asked. He had finished his report, telling the general that a group of mercenaries had killed the GRU surveillance team and had loaded a strange steel cylinder and other equipment onto a plane and flown off to the south.

"That is not your concern," Rurik said. "You do not know who these people were?"

"Ex-military," Feteror said. "They wore unmarked uniforms and acted like soldiers. They didn't exactly line up and tell me their names."

"Your report is insufficient," Rurik snapped.

"It is insufficient because you didn't give me enough power to cross over and find things out. I could have ripped open a throat or two and gotten someone to talk. I could have stopped them if you'd given me the power, and we wouldn't be having this conversation. It is insufficient because you pulled me back too soon. Before I could see where the plane went."

"Do not lecture me!" General Rurik screamed. Everyone stopped working and stared at their commanding officer. Rurik lowered his voice. "You do what I tell you to."

"Then you should be satisfied with my report." Inside his steel housing, Feteror felt better than he had in years. All was progressing quite well. Tapping his data banks, he brought up a picture and could see the general's pretty young wife. And the young children. Two boys. Perfect.

"Get back in your pit!" Rurik slammed his fist down on the power level.

Feteror's electric eyes and ears shut off.

Dalton sideslipped and began falling, tumbling out of control.

"Relax," Hammond said. *"Spread your wings."*

Dalton arched his back and spread his arms—wings—wide. They caught and the descent slowed. *"Am I outside?"*

"You will have to look to see."

"How do I do that?"

"This is where you must look into the real world from the virtual," Hammond said.

"How do I do that?" Dalton asked once more, slowly circling where he was, in the middle of the same fog he'd been in since entering the virtual world.

"Concentrate. It is just like focusing on the white dot."

"Great." Dalton did as Hammond said. Gradually the fog began clearing. He saw white peaks, mountains.

"When you do this, your psyche is on the line between the virtual and the real world," Hammond said. *"But your avatar is still in the virtual. If you know where you are and you know where you are going, you can 'fold' the virtual world and 'jump' there."*

"I don't understand," Dalton said. He was beginning to see the peaks more clearly.

"You know where you are, and you know where you want to be. Traveling in the virtual world is different than the real. Sometimes you can cover great distances in an instant."

"Sometimes?" Dalton asked. He saw the white cross of the Mount of the Holy Cross.

"We're not exactly sure how it works," Hammond admitted.

"Great."

Dalton turned his face to the east. He pictured where he wanted to be and dove in that direction. There was a bright flash of light and then he was over the Plains to the east of the Rockies. Banking, he turned and could see Pikes Peak to the west, Cheyenne Mountain to the left.

Dalton headed down toward a large building. *"What about walls?"*

"From what RVers have reported, it will be disconcerting but you can pass right through walls on the virtual plane."

Despite that assurance, Dalton flinched as the outside wall of the building rushed up. There was a moment of blackness, a feeling of hitting something not quite solid, passing through, and then he was inside. He hit the floor of a hallway and was halfway into it before he stopped and drew himself up.

He floated down until he found the right room. He slid in, then paused. There was someone else inside. Dr. Kairns was standing there, staring at Marie. She straightened for a second, as if sensing his presence. Kairns reached down and gently moved a stray lock of gray hair off Marie's face, then turned to walk out of the room. She hesitated at the door, looking back into the room, then left.

Dalton looked down at Marie. What he saw wasn't the person in the bed, but the young woman he had met thirty-four years ago. The woman who had been waiting for him after five years of separation, standing on the tarmac as he got off the plane bringing him back with the other POWs. Who had withstood his long absences and always been there when he came back. And now he was gone when she needed him the most. He couldn't hide from his responsibility any longer.

Dalton looked at his wife and concentrated. Then he really did see her, standing over the body in the bed. As she had been, her long blond hair flowing over her shoulders, her face smooth and unwrinkled, her green eyes bright and happy. She was as Dalton had always seen her in his cell, in his memory.

"Treasure?" Dalton projected the word toward the vision.

She turned. *"Jimmy?"* A broad smile lit up her face. *"Oh, Jimmy, it's been so long this time."*

"I know."

Marie frowned. *"But I'm the one who's been away, haven't I?"*

Dalton nodded. He was afraid to get closer to her, afraid her form, which he could see through, would break apart and float away like a mist before a strong wind.

Before his eyes the young woman aged, lines that Dalton knew his army career had contributed to greatly began to materialize, flowing across her, giving her an imprint of the years she had lived, producing in Dalton a deep sense of sadness.

Marie smiled again, this time with sadness resonating through. *"I'm hurt too bad to come back Jimmy."*

Dalton nodded once more, not trusting even his mental voice.

"Is it all right if I go? It feels so much better like this, being free, rather than trapped like I've been."

She had always been there for him, but she had always

done what she wanted also. The question was the courtesy the two had always given each other over the years.

"I think it's fine if you go, Treasure."

"You look like an angel," Marie said. *"Are you all right?"*

"I'm fine," Dalton said. He reached his hand up. The image of Marie did the same. The two hands flowed into each other. Dalton felt an electric shock run up his arm/wing.

"You've always been my Treasure," Dalton said.

"I know," Marie said, *"and you've been mine."*

Chapter Fourteen

Feteror dumped the data he'd stolen out of the GRU mainframe into one of his memory cells inside Zivon. He found it ironic that the code for the encrypted information he had was also most likely inside of Zivon, but inaccessible to him, even though the scientists considered him part of the computer. He activated a decoding program and the mechanical part of Zivon went to work on the data while Feteror waited.

It didn't take long.

Feteror was impressed. The GRU was taking no chances with the arming codes for the nuclear weapons. They were shipping them via military helicopter direct from Kazakhstan to Moscow. There would be a four-fighter escort. Feteror noted the time of departure and the proposed flight route. And the name of the officer who would have the codes: Colonel Verochka.

Now he only had one problem—being on the outside during the flight—but the other data he had stolen would help with that.

A bright light flashed. Feteror would have smiled if he could—Rurik wanted him.

Feteror accessed his outside links.

"Yes?"

Rurik wasted no time. "We need you to find something."

"What?"

"I'm having the data loaded."

Feteror was not surprised to note the physical description for the phased-displacement generator entered into his data banks.

"What is this thing?" he asked.

"A weapon."

"What kind of weapon?"

"That is not your concern," Rurik snapped. "Just find it. As you reported, it was stolen from the site you just checked. So find the men you saw there and you will find the weapon."

"That will be very difficult," Feteror lied. "Practically impossible."

"Do it!" General Rurik yelled.

"I will try." The tunnel opened and he was gone.

In the chamber the red light began flashing. General Rurik stared at it for a few moments, then turned to his senior technician.

"What was Feteror doing before I summoned him?"

The technician typed into his keyboard. "He was working within the hardware, running a program."

"What kind of program?"

The technician didn't answer right away, checking the machine. "A decryption program."

Rurik leaned forward. "What is he trying to decrypt?"

The expert shook his head. "We don't know. It's inside his memory database section."

"Can we access his memory section?"

The technician shook his head. "He has cyber-locked and encrypted all that data."

"We can't access our own damn computer?"

The technician backtracked. "We can access it, but I don't think we can get the data stored there out in legible form. Also, the way I am reading what Feteror has done, it would cause some permanent damage to Zivon for us to do that."

The technician saw the look on the general's face and hurriedly continued, "For security reasons, Feteror only has access to certain parts of Zivon. We have, in effect, put a wall up to keep him from having free access. But you must remember, General, that when you build a wall, it blocks traffic both ways. That wall also keeps us from freely going into his part of Zivon."

Rurik looked at the steel cylinder. "He's up to something," he whispered.

"Excuse me, sir?"

Rurik spoke in a louder voice. "I want you to find out what Feteror has stored. In a way that can't be detected and will cause no damage to Zivon. I want to know what is happening on Feteror's side of the wall."

The technician opened his mouth to say something, but his teeth snapped shut as he saw the expression on his superior's face. He nodded and turned to his computer console.

"You're down to six," Raisor said accusingly.

Dalton wiped the embryonic fluid off his face and threw the towel to the floor. He felt a chill spasm through his body and he shivered uncontrollably for a few seconds. He felt an empty space in his chest, a sick feeling.

"Six what?" His mind was elsewhere, Raisor's words registering distantly on his conscious mind.

"Six men," Raisor said. "One of your so-called special men has flaked out on us."

"You talked to Trilly?" Dalton asked dully. He could still see Marie fading away, her spirit disappearing, growing ever fainter until there was nothing there. He'd stayed in the room as the medical alarms had gone off and Dr. Kairns had rushed in. He was grateful the doctor had obeyed his written wishes that Marie not be resuscitated. He had finally left when Kairns had tenderly pulled the sheet over Marie's body.

"He came to me," Raisor replied. "Said he had talked to you and told you he wasn't going in the tank again."

"That's not his decision," Dalton said.

"If he's not willing, there's not—"

"It's also not your place to talk to my men," Dalton said, cutting the CIA man off.

Raisor shook his head. "I'm in charge here, Sergeant Major, not you. You may be in command of your men, but I'm in charge of you. So in effect, I'm in charge of your men too."

Dalton jerked a thumb over his shoulder at the isolation tank he had just come out of. "Fine. Then you go in there and lead the team."

"I just might do that," Raisor said.

Dalton realized Raisor *would* take over. "Let me lead my team," Dalton said.

"You go over one more time for practice," Raisor said, "then it's for real."

"Fine," Dalton said. He didn't particularly care one way or the other at the moment.

"Can you do it with six?" Raisor asked.

"I didn't think we could do it with eight," Dalton said. "But we'll have seven. Orders are not optional. Trilly's going with us."

"I'll supplement your team with some of the RVers," Raisor said.

"I thought the reason we're here is because they couldn't do the mission," Dalton said.

"They can't—by themselves. But three of them are military and have had basic military training. I'm sure with your leadership, they'll be of help." Raisor's cold smile matched his tone. "And they have experience in the virtual plane."

"They're more likely to get in the way," Dalton said.

"You can't have it both ways," Raisor said. "Do you want the help or not?"

"We'll take them."

"Be ready to go in two hours," Raisor said. "We've set up the practice range as you requested."

"Fine." Dalton was tired. He wanted the blessed relief of sleep.

He turned to Dr. Hammond, who was at her master control station. She looked exhausted, her face drawn, dark rings under her eyes. She'd been on duty practically non-stop since the team had arrived.

"I'd like for all of us to go over at the same time in the next practice," Dalton told her.

Hammond nodded. "I'm bringing the rest back. We'll shut down for a couple of hours, then send you all over together with your advanced avatars to practice your weaponry skills and your team coordination."

"Fine," Dalton said. Despite his exhaustion, he went to the communications room. He dialed on the secure line.

"Colonel Metter."

"Sir, it's Dalton."

There was a short pause. "Jimmy, I've got some bad news. I was trying to get through to you but–"

"Sir, I know about Marie."

There was an even longer pause before Metter spoke again. "But it just happened thirty minutes ago. How–"

"Sir, how is not important. I need you to take care of the arrangements. I had everything ready, you just need to check on it all."

"I can get you back from there," Metter said.

"No, sir, I don't think you can," Dalton said. "And I

can't come back anyway. I'm needed here. Marie understood." Dalton leaned against the wall. "I have to go, sir."

"Jimmy, I'm sorry about Marie."

"Thank you, sir."

"Take care of the team, Jimmy."

"I will, sir."

Chapter Fifteen

Deputy Commander Oskar Bredond slapped the young Chechen with the steel wire butt of his AK-74, ripping four teeth out of the young man's mouth in the process. The Chechen spit blood at the officer, his arms bound by two sets of handcuffs, ratcheted down so tight on his wrists that his hands were turning blue.

"Fuck you, pig."

Bredond smiled. "No, I think it is you who will get fucked. A nice young piece of meat like you will be received quite nicely in our prison."

Bredond wore mottled camouflage fatigues with a thick bulletproof vest buckled over his chest. His men wore the same, along with black Kevlar helmets. They were the elite strike force arm of the Moscow police, known as the Omon, more heavily armed than their western SWAT counterparts and with broader powers of arrest.

There was another way that the Omon differed greatly from police in the West, and that was that they focused only on certain criminals while ignoring others. Moscow, if one took out Mafia-related crime, was one of the safest cities in the world. But whenever the Mafia was involved, the Omon and the rest of the Moscow police turned a blind eye.

Bredond, despite being a deputy commander, took home the equivalent of $250 a month. They all supplemented their income with second jobs. Bredond, seeing the writing on the wall, had chosen the most lucrative and easiest way to supplement his income.

He kicked the Chechen once more. The man was a freelancer. He had come to Moscow from his home state, stolen a vehicle, and driven it home, where he had sold it. Unfortunately for him, the Moscow Mafia was growing weary of freelancers working on their turf. Bredond had been tipped off about this man and his stolen vehicle an hour ago. Bredond, not a stupid man, wondered if the Chechen had been set up.

The cellular phone in Bredond's pocket buzzed, halting him in the middle of another kick. He walked away, pulling the phone out.

"Bredond."

"We have a job for you." The voice on the other end was filled with static. Bredond knew that was because it was sent through several relays and scrambled. Not that the person calling him was concerned about the police, but rather the other Mafia clans listening in.

"Yes?" Bredond waited.

"We want you to pick someone up."

When Bredond heard the name and address, he gritted his teeth. He knew what that address meant.

"That will be difficult," he said. There was no answer. He licked his lips and continued. "There will be strong repercussions if we take action in that neighborhood."

"I didn't *ask* you to do this," the voice said. The phone went dead.

Bredond cursed. He yelled for his men to gear up. They left the Chechen lying in a pool of his own blood, still whispering curses at the Omon as they drove off.

At the abandoned airbase, Barsk watched as Leksi's mercenaries pulled four Hind-D helicopters out of hangars, along with two MI-8 Hips. He was surprised at the number of aircraft, wondering how much his grandmother had paid to obtain them. Even with the glut of military material on the black market, these would still cost quite a few dollars.

The Hinds were combination attack/transport helicopters. They could carry eight combat-equipped troops in the back, while the pods on either side carried numerous rockets, and a 12.7-millimeter machine gun was mounted in the nose. The Hip helicopters could carry twenty-eight men each, and it looked like Leksi had enough men to fill all six helicopters, judging by the number of black-clad men in the hangar. The pilots began walking around, doing their preflight checks, as the men loaded magazines with bullets and sharpened their knives.

Leksi interrupted Barsk's musings on the cost of this operation by slapping a map down in front of him. "You will take the cargo plane, the generator, and the old man, and transport all to here."

Barsk looked at the map. The location was two hundred miles away from where they were. An airfield next to a large dam.

"What is this?" Barsk demanded.

"It is where Oma said for you to take the weapon. We will meet you there."

Barsk stabbed a finger down at the map. "But there is a town nearby. The authorities will be notified."

Leksi shrugged. "It is what Oma has ordered."

Dalton looked over the other six Special Forces men. They were all wearing the black one-piece suit that fit them like a second skin. Trilly looked like a dog that had been kicked once too often, but Dalton didn't have time to soothe the sergeant's feelings. He'd told him to suit and brooked no resistance.

A door on the side of the room opened and three more people walked in, two men and Lieutenant Jackson, the fillers promised by Raisor. The CIA man followed them, also in the black suit.

Eleven altogether. Captain Anderson had ceded command of the team to him without outright saying so. Not out of lack of leadership, but more out of recognition of Dalton's combat experience and natural authority. It was the strongest and smartest leadership decision the captain could make under these circumstances.

"All right," Dalton said, now that his entire team was gathered together. "We need to accomplish two things and we don't have much time to do it. We need to work on developing our avatars and projecting them into the real world, using their weapons. And we need to work on our teamwork."

He looked at Lieutenant Jackson and the other two RVers. "You have experience in the former and we have the experience in the latter. So let's all contribute and work together. We only have one shot at getting our act together before we go for real, so let's not waste any time." He turned to Raisor. "Where do you want to be?"

"I'll be overseeing the operation; don't concern yourself with me."

"Let's load," Dr. Hammond called out from her console.

The Psychic Warriors headed for their isolation tanks.

Feteror watched the Omon smash the front door in. The house was well built, but the Omon used a shotgun to blast out the locks, then two men swung a small battering ram, splintering the wood. Feteror was in the virtual plane, hovering overhead.

The team, led by Deputy Commander Bredond, sprinted through the doorway. Feteror swooped down, passing through the roof, flitting from room to room, watching as the Omon did his dirty work.

There were three people in the house—a woman and two children. The Omon had them gagged, hooded, and cuffed, ignoring the woman's screams about who her husband was and how important he was.

The Omon hustled the three out of the house and into one of their cars. Feteror followed overhead as they drove through the streets of Moscow until they arrived at an old warehouse near the railyard.

Bredond exited the car, dragging the woman with her as two of his men brought the kids. Two armored BMWs waited in the shadows. Four men emerged from the lead one and took custody of the woman and two children. They pulled the hood off the woman and checked her photograph against one they had with them. Satisfied, they threw the woman into the trunk of the car, then crammed the two children in on top of her and closed the trunk, ignoring the muted cries and jerkings of the bound bodies.

As the men started to get back in the still-open doors, Bredond stepped forward. All four men paused, hands hovering near the front of their long black leather coats.

"This is going too far!" Bredond yelled toward the rear BMW.

Overhead, Feteror began forming in the real plane, his clawed hands hooked onto one of the large support beams holding the roof up, his wings folded in tight, unseen and unnoticed by those below.

There was no reply, either from the guards or whoever was seated behind the tinted glass in the second BMW.

Bredond shifted uncomfortably, his three men holding their AK-74s uncertainly.

"Her husband is a GRU general. We were seen picking her and the children up. There will be inquiries. I will have to answer for this."

One of the bodyguards from the lead BMW put a finger to his ear. Feteror could see the thin wire, indicating he had a small receiver there. The man snapped a command and all four slipped inside the car.

Bredond raised his hand. His men pointed their weapons at the two BMWs, blocking the exit.

Feteror spread his wings and leaped. He swooped down, both arms out to his side, and went right between two of the Omon, claws ripping throats open in a gush of blood.

Feteror landed as Bredond and the last surviving Omon policeman spun about, searching for the cause of the other half of their party's death.

Feteror stepped forward and swung low. The last Omon man caught a glimpse of Feteror's form even as the claws punched through skin, into warm viscera. Feteror felt the man's spine and he gripped it, practically ripping the man in two in the process. He lifted the man up, then threw him onto the car the Omon had driven.

Bredond stepped back, weapon raised. He could see the intermittent form of some large creature, the two glowing red eyes unmistakable, the red blood dripping off an almost invisible clawed hand very clear.

Feteror drew in more power and he slowly materialized, adding color to his form. His scaled skin was black, his wings streaked with red, his demon features hard and angular.

Bredond's eyes opened wide, the weapon falling from his fingers as he dropped to his knees, hands raised in supplication. "Chyort! Please! Spare me!"

Feteror spun so quickly that those watching from the other cars only saw a blur. He lashed a backhand strike with his right wing, the six-inch claw on his middle finger extended. It sliced through Bredond's neck like a paring knife through bread. Bredond's head tilted back, held in place only by the spinal cord. The body flopped back, blood still pumping from the heart.

Feteror turned to the second BMW. A window slid down and the cracked face of Oma peered out.

"He was useful," she said.

"His usefulness was over." Feteror liked the sound of the avatar voice he had worked hard on. It was deeper than a human voice, with a rough edge. A true demon's voice. "The Omon's being involved will cause confusion. Their bodies found dead will make even more confusion. It will take the GRU a while to sort through. By then it will be too late."

"Why do we need them?" Oma asked, indicating the trunk.

Feteror extended the same claw that had almost decapitated Bredond toward the first BMW. "They are important to our plan."

"How?" Oma asked. "I did as you asked but I don't see how a GRU general's wife and children help us."

Feteror glared at the old woman. He could see the fear in her guards' eyes, the four men having jumped out of the front BMW, weapons at the ready at his appearance. He could not tell her why, because doing so would expose a weakness.

"Do as you are told, old woman."

"You need me," Oma hissed.

Feteror extended his wings, putting the car in the dark shadow they created. "Oh, yes, old woman, I need you."

Feteror leapt up, translating from the real to the virtual plane in an instant and, in doing so, disappearing before the eyes of those watching, leaving behind the bodies he had torn apart as the only evidence that what they had seen had been real.

Chapter Sixteen

Dalton looked around. He was in a large open space, the horizon limitless. The ground beneath his feet was flat and a featureless gray. The air was filled with a white fog, making him wonder how far he was really seeing.

"I am bringing all of you here in your forms in the virtual plane first," Hammond said.

Dalton noticed something above him. He looked up and saw a falcon and two eagles soaring. He immediately knew from Sybyl's input that they were Jackson and the other two RVers, Sergeant Williams and Chief Warrant Officer Auer.

More forms began appearing on the ground around him. Dalton was slightly surprised that he could recognize each of his men, their forms very similar to what they were in reality, even though their facial features were white masks without features. There was enough variance in size and shape to allow him to separate them.

"Your weapons," Hammond announced.

Right arms formed into tubes from the elbow forward. Dalton's tube was about four inches in diameter, tapering to a smooth muzzle about a half inch wide. Two others were similar to what Dalton carried, two were the "shotguns" he had asked Hammond for, and two were the more powerful, slower-firing tubes.

"What about you?" Dalton projected the question to the RVers circling overhead.

Lieutenant Jackson's voice answered inside of his head. *"We need the power to fly. We can be your eyes for this mission. If we had weapons, we would take away power from yours."*

"All right."

He saw another figure, Raisor, standing not far away, blank face watching.

The avatars gathered round. It was eerie to watch the bird forms of the RVers simply come to a halt overhead, wings folded. But Dalton knew that if he tried, he could hover off the floor and hang next to them.

"Mr. Raisor has set up a practice scenario for us at Fort Hood, Texas. They've closed off a tank range there and put in a bunch of targets, both stationary and moving, for us to attack. We have no idea right now what form the Mafia assault on the nuclear weapons train will take, but this is the best we can come up with on short notice."

"Do we fire on full power?" Captain Anderson asked.

"Yes," Dalton said. *"We act as if this is the real thing. Dr. Hammond?"*

"Yes?"

"Show us the computer mock-up of what's been set up for us at Fort Hood."

A line of old railcars appeared, towed into place on a dusty, scrub-covered range. Several armored vehicles, relics towed off other ranges, were lined around it. Scores of silhouettes, some red, some blue, were spaced all around. The terrain around was the hill country of mid-Texas that Dalton remembered from a tour of duty at Fort Hood.

"The blue are friendly. The red are the enemy," Hammond said.

"All right. Here's what we're going to do." Dalton led his men through his plan for the assault on the attackers.

Feteror was out of time. The link back to SD8-FFEU was weakening, General Rurik's way of drawing him back. The longest Rurik had ever allowed him to be out on a mission had been six hours in real time. It was another way the general tried to keep a leash on his demon and one that had worked very effectively over the years.

Feteror headed back to SD8-FFEU, sliding down the tunnel, feeling the virtual window shut behind him. He settled in and immediately accessed his inner eyes and ears, somewhat surprised to find them on. There was no sign of General Rurik in the center, which didn't surprise Feteror. He assumed Rurik had had him called back as soon as he got called about his wife and children, and that the general was still trying to find out what had happened.

Feteror paused as he moved through his electronic home. Something was wrong. Like a tracker noting a blade of grass disturbed here, a broken stick there, Feteror did a detailed search of his domain.

His scream of anger echoed along the wires of Zivon as he found that the intruder had tried to get into his memory files.

"Tell me about the phased-displacement generator," Barsk ordered.

The old man was blinking, not used to the light even though the interior of the hangar was dim. Barsk looked past the man toward the runway, where the blades on all six helicopters were turning. The first one, with Leksi on board, lifted and headed south. The others followed.

The old man gulped down the water one of Barsk's bodyguards handed him, finishing the canteen in one long swallow. Barsk waited.

The old man put the empty canteen down and squinted in Barsk's direction. Getting out of the hole seemed to have bolstered the man's confidence somewhat. Or, Barsk thought, he had simply given up. He had seen both reactions over the years among those who knew the end was near.

"Who are you?"

"I ask the questions, old man," Barsk reminded him. "What is this phased-displacement generator? How does it work?"

Vasilev worked his tongue around his mouth, feeling how swollen it was. "It is a weapon."

"What kind of weapon?"

"It can take a physical object and move it into the virtual plane and then bring it out of the virtual plane."

"What the hell are you talking about?"

Vasilev, despite his condition, drew himself up. "I would have to teach you four years of graduate physics for you to grasp the basics, and then I would have to be honest and tell you I do not know exactly how it works."

"How do you know it works at all, then?"

"We tested it a long time ago."

"At October Revolution Island?"

Vasilev nodded, his eyes distant.

Barsk remembered the bodies in the cavern. "What happened?"

"We succeeded and we failed," Vasilev said.

"I don't have time for word games," Barsk warned.

"We sank an American submarine in the Atlantic Ocean with a nuclear warhead."

Barsk looked at his bodyguards and signaled for them to back up, out of earshot. "If this generator is so effective, why was it abandoned?"

"Because–" Vasilev paused, then continued, "Because, as I said, we also failed. Part of the system, shall we say, malfunctioned, and all those involved were killed."

"The bodies in the coffins. They were mutilated. Were they the cause of the malfunction?"

Vasilev raised an eyebrow. "Yes."

Barsk sat back, considering the old man. "Can you make it work now?"

"Not without—" He paused. A sense of dread overcame him. Had they done it again?

"Without what?"

"The remote viewers to fix the target."

Barsk assumed Oma had thought of that. "If you have that part, can you do it?"

"With the proper computers, enough power, the generator, the proper program, I suppose—"

"You had better do better than suppose," Barsk warned.

"You are working with the demon?" Vasilev asked.

Barsk leaned forward. "What do you know of this demon?"

"He visited me there." Vasilev pointed at the pit.

"Who exactly is the demon?"

"It is more a question of *what* is this demon," Vasilev said. "I suspect he is a creature that exists on the psychic plane."

"Explain as much as you know to me," Barsk ordered.

Vasilev gave a weak laugh. "That won't take long."

"Go!" Dalton ordered.

The three RVers unfurled their wings and took off. Dalton watched them until they suddenly disappeared from view.

"Hammond?" Dalton checked.

"Here."

"You can have Sybyl relay information from Lieutenant Jackson and the others?"

"Yes."

Dalton shook his head. This was all happening too fast. He had little idea what their capabilities and limitations were. But he knew that Raisor and Hammond had little idea also. He had to consider so many factors that he knew he was missing some important aspects. He also knew from his combat experience that it was the details that were over-looked that got people killed. And whatever could screw up was going to. Murphy's law had been a maxim of military operations since the first man had clubbed a guy over the head in the next cave.

Dalton broke his seven-man team into two three-man fireteams. He put Captain Anderson in charge of one. Each fireteam had one fast firer, one "shotgunner," and one heavy firer.

The plan was as simple as Dalton could make it. He had to guess what the Mafia's plan would be, but he figured they had to have military men working for them and thus he felt reasonably sure about what would happen. The Mafia force would set up what was called an ORP, objective rally point, near the attack site, but out of direct line of sight. They would launch their attack from there. Dalton's plan was to use Captain Anderson's fireteam to attack the ORP while his team assaulted the attacking force. That would force the Mafia to fight on three fronts: the Russian troops guarding the train in front of them, Anderson's team from behind, and Dalton's team right among them.

"We're closing on Fort Hood." Jackson's voice was inside his head, as loud and clear as Hammond's, startling him out of his military speculating.

"Entering the real plane," Jackson said.

Dalton waited.

"Okay, we're here." There was a difference to Jackson's voice. As if she were in a large, empty space, her voice echoing strangely. *"It's like the mock-up but there's also some more armor in the ORP area. About fifty 'men' in the ORP. Another force of about a hundred stretched out between the ORP and the train. Hold on, I'll show it to you."*

Dalton blinked as an image flickered across his vision, momentarily blocking out the featureless area of virtual space around him. He focused and he could see the range target area as Jackson saw it, circling overhead.

"All right," Dalton said. *"Captain Anderson, designate targets for your men."*

"Roger that," Anderson answered.

Dalton did the same, able to use the views forwarded from Lieutenant Jackson and the two other RVers to give each of his men specific targets. As he did this, a part of Dalton started feeling more confident. He'd been on many military operations in his time in the Army, but this one, while undoubtedly the strangest, also was presenting him with advantages he hadn't even dreamed of. Being able to see the target like this and then being able to mentally communicate with each of his men, letting them know his plan by *seeing* it, instead of just telling them what he wanted, was something every military commander would give anything for.

"Are we ready?"

He received an affirmative from each man.

"Sybyl, give us the visual checkpoints," Dalton ordered.

It was a technique the RVers had perfected. Sybyl could access the NSA's satellite imagery database and pick easily identifiable spots on the earth's surface between their present location and the target. They could then project themselves through virtual space from checkpoint to checkpoint by imaging the picture.

"Let's do it."

The Special Forces men's avatars lost their weapons as their arms shifted into wings. They entered the virtual plane and headed south.

Dalton found himself alone once more, moving through the virtual sky with his virtual wings. He hit the first checkpoint and spotted two other of his men passing through. He kept going, until he was at the last checkpoint, less than a kilometer from the target. At that point, he pulled in power from Sybyl and materialized on a hillside, the bulk of the mountain between him and the target. He watched as the other men showed up within a couple of minutes of each other.

"Hell of a way to infiltrate a target area," Captain Anderson noted as he gained his feet and took a few tentative steps, refamiliarizing himself with operating in the real world with his avatar.

"Any change in the target?" Dalton asked Jackson.

"Negative," Jackson responded. *"Here's the current image."*

Dalton checked it. *"All right,"* he said to the men of his fireteam, Trilly, Egan, and Barnes. *"We will go back into the virtual plane from here and I want us to come out into the real world right here–"* He picked a spot on the image. It was about a hundred meters from the railcar, in the midst of numerous red silhouettes indicating the attacking force.

"When you come out, come out blasting," Dalton said. *"Ready, Captain Anderson?"*

"Ready."

"Let's go."

Dalton released his hold on the real world and dematerialized. He focused on the image of the spot he had picked. And then he was there. He materialized, the power tube flowing out of his right arm as he flickered into existence in the real world.

He fired at the closest red silhouette.

On a hill to the south a wide-angle video camera had been set up on orders from the CIA to send an image back to Bright Gate. The range area was supposed to be completely evacuated, but two officers from Fort Hood had stayed in the observation post, curious to see what the results of all the strange, high-level orders they had received would be. They had expected to see parachutes come out of the sky, perhaps carrying members of a Ranger battalion practicing a train takedown.

They were stunned when strange men appeared out of nothingness, firing with what looked like tubes in place of forearms and hands. Silhouettes splintered as small fireballs hit them.

Through his binoculars, one of the officers watched as a derelict tank was hit by a larger fireball that smashed through the front armor and exploded inside.

"Who the hell are these guys?" the officer asked his partner.

"*What* the hell are they?" the other officer asked in return as he focused in on one of the forms, seeing that the face was a featureless white mask.

It was going very well. Of course, Dalton reflected as he moved and fired, the silhouettes weren't shooting back. That was perhaps the biggest concern he had. Despite Dr. Hammond's assurances, he wasn't absolutely confident that the avatars could sustain much damage or that they could be reconstituted as easily as she imagined. There was the issue of what had happened to Stith lurking in the back of his mind.

He did a forward roll behind a berm and fired, slicing a red silhouette in half. *"Anderson?"* he asked through Sybyl.

"We've wiped the ORP out. No problem!" Anderson's voice was excited, like a kid who had just won a big ball game.

Dalton didn't blame him. It was intoxicating, being able to move and fire, to communicate instantly, to come in and out of reality. As he thought that, Dalton looked at a tank hulk fifty meters away. He faded out of the real, sped through the virtual, and popped into existence inside the tank. He "killed" all the crew, then "jumped" again to another position.

Without being asked, Sybyl was updating him on the position of the other members of the team, pushing the data through his consciousness without interfering with what he was doing. He could see that Anderson's team was moving slowly in his direction, clearing out the terrain between them.

That was when the drones came in overhead. Three of them, flying in triangular formation, they were firing off flares to simulate weapons. Each was programmed with their flight route and had a wingspan of twenty feet. They were flying at two hundred miles an hour, low out of the setting sun.

Even as Dalton noted this unexpected development, he was getting the exact positions, directions, and speeds of the drones from Lieutenant Jackson. He swung up his tube and fired, as did Barnes. The drones were blasted out of the sky less than two seconds after they had been spotted.

"Behind you!" One of the RVers warned him.

Dalton spun, tube at the ready, but even before his avatar completed the turn, the RVer had shown him what was happening. A group of the blue silhouette targets had dropped their covering and were now red.

That lasted for less than a second as all six Special Forces men fired into the new targets.

Dalton paused. There were no more targets. The other members of his fireteam "jumped" to his position. Then Anderson's team was there. He could see Raisor's avatar floating to the north, watching, and he knew where the surprises had come from.

"Let's go home," Dalton ordered.

On the hillside, the two officers lowered their binoculars after watching the ten men's arms shift into wings before they simply blinked out of existence.

"That couldn't have been real," one of the men whispered.

"Those targets are all destroyed," the other noted. "That's real."

The first officer headed for the door of the bunker. "We weren't supposed to be here. As far as I'm concerned, we didn't see anything. We didn't hear anything. We don't know anything."

"We wasted them!" Egan, the intelligence sergeant, was ecstatic as he toweled off the embryonic fluid.

Dalton didn't say anything, letting the adrenaline flow run its course. The trial run had gone far better than he'd expected. He'd had to reevaluate his outlook on the upcoming mission and accept that Raisor was mostly right–they would have a tremendous advantage and they were the best force for this mission. Not only were they a potent fighting force once they arrived on target, but the ability to infiltrate and exfiltrate a foreign country through the virtual field was unparalleled in its possibilities. Dalton saw Raisor and Hammond by the master control console watching.

"You see how I hit that tank and the fireball went right through the armor!" Barnes was using his hands like a fighter pilot to show what had happened. "Then I 'jumped' about twenty meters to the left and hit the tank again. Unbelievable."

"Just remember nobody was shooting back at you," Dalton noted.

That brought a moment of silence.

"What exactly happens if we do get shot?" Trilly wanted to know.

"You slip back into the virtual world," Dr. Hammond said, "and allow Sybyl to reconstitute you."

"Far out!" Monroe yelled, raising his hand for a high five from Egan.

"You go on the real thing in six hours," Raisor said. "I suggest you get some rest."

As the team filed out, Dalton cornered Lieutenant Jackson. "What do you think?" he asked her.

"I think it was too easy," Jackson said.

Dalton nodded. "Two things worry me. First, we still don't really know what happens when the avatar gets shot or blown up or run over, or any of the other things that can happen to it."

"And the second?" Jackson asked.

"Murphy's law," Dalton said succinctly. "Whatever can screw up will. I'm concerned about the Russian psychic capability. What if they *are* on top of this?" He could see the look in Jackson's eyes and knew she was thinking the same thing. "What if this demon, this Chyort, shows up? Or if what happened to the first team happens to us?

"We don't know much about what we're doing," Dalton continued. "We really don't know diddly about the Russian capability. What about this Dr. Vasilev? You said he worked in Moscow. Do you think you can find him?"

Jackson looked tired, black lines under her eyes, but she nodded. "I can give it a shot. He's published in some journals that give some bio information. I can go to the Institute in Moscow and try to find him from there."

"I'd really appreciate it," Dalton said. "I know you need to rest, but—"

Jackson held up her hand. "No problem. I'll go back in."

Dalton ran a hand through his goo-filled hair. "I'll go with you."

Feteror sensed a presence down the computer path he was on. A shadow where there shouldn't be one. He paused, uncertain for the first time in a very long time.

The shadow moved.

Feteror raced down a side path, his essence flowing through the circuitry, and he popped out behind the shadow. He froze, seeing his grandfather looking about in amazement at the hardware inside of the computer.

"Opa!" Feteror exclaimed.

The old man turned, a bright smile above his bushy gray beard. "Arkady!"

Feteror edged forward, uncertain. "How can you be here?"

Opa shrugged. "That is what I wanted to ask you. And where is here?" His frail arms waved about.

Feteror stepped forward. "But you aren't real."

Opa reached out and grabbed Feteror's virtual arm. "Does that feel real?"

"But–" Feteror shook his head. "How can this be?"

"How can you be?" Opa said. "I don't know. I was asleep. And now I'm awake."

"But I didn't summon you," Feteror said.

"Summon me? Summon me?" Opa glared at his grandson.

"What happened to wake you?" Feteror asked.

The old man frowned. "Someone tried breaking in." He looked about, confusion crossing his face once more. "But I was home. In the cottage. Someone was at the window. I woke and yelled. They ran. But this isn't the cottage."

Feteror nodded. Rurik's prying had woken the old man. But what he didn't understand–and knew the figure in front of him wouldn't know either–was how his grandfather's image had come "alive" and escaped its memory cell. This was something new and unprecedented.

Feteror checked the time. He knew that General Rurik would exhaust all the normal channels to try to find his wife and children. When they failed–and they would, given Oma's and his own thoroughness–he would reluctantly turn to Feteror. He estimated he had a little while before the call came.

"Where is the cottage?" Opa asked.

Feteror reached out and took his grandfather by the arm. "I will take you home, Opa."

Chapter Seventeen

Dalton's lungs filled with liquid. His body spasmed, tired muscles fighting the foreign substance, then giving way.

The process went faster and shortly Dalton was back on the virtual plane. Jackson's falcon avatar swooped past, over his left shoulder, startling him.

"Ready to go?" Jackson asked.

"Where's the first point?" Dalton asked.

An image from Sybyl appeared in his mind as Hammond spoke. *"You'll be taking the polar route to Russia. Your first jump point will be in central Canada right above this lake."*

Dalton's arms flowed into wings and he took flight, catching up to the falcon.

"First jump," Jackson said.

"First jump," Dalton acknowledged.

He concentrated on the lake point in Canada. Everything went blank; he felt disoriented and then he was there, about five hundred meters above the water.

He looked around. Jackson was close by. Dalton felt awkward and huge next to her small, graceful form.

"Second point," Jackson projected.

It took them four points to get to Moscow. Dalton had no idea if that many were necessary—if they could have gotten there with one jump. He also had no idea how much time passed. Between some of the points the transition was not instantaneous. He felt as if he had flown a distance between some of them in the gray fog of the virtual plane.

He was grateful for Jackson's presence, as he wasn't sure he could have made it this far this quickly without her keeping him oriented.

"The Russian Physiological Psychology Institute is that building." Jackson nosed down toward a large, square building, built of dark stone. Dalton followed. He paused as Jackson's avatar blipped into the roof and disappeared, then he did the same. He was in an office. There were three men in uniform inside the room. Dalton staggered backward before he realized that he was still in the virtual plane and the men couldn't see him.

"This is Dr. Vasilev's office." Jackson paused. *"I don't know who they are. They have GRU tabs on their shoulder boards."*

"Seems like they're looking for something," Dalton noted.

That was an understatement, as the large desk was turned on its side, spilling papers. Two men dropped to their knees, searching both the papers and the underside of the desk. The third, obviously an officer of higher rank, watched the other two.

One of the men on his knees said something to the senior officer in Russian. The officer replied.

"Vasilev is missing," Jackson told Dalton. *"They're trying to find out what happened to him."*

"You understand Russian?" Dalton asked.

There was an amused tone to Jackson's projection. *"Yes. And so do you."*

Dalton didn't have a chance to pursue that as the senior officer pulled a cellular phone out of a deep pocket of his greatcoat. He punched in and began talking. Dalton watched with interest as Jackson dissolved her falcon shape and became a small glowing sphere on the virtual plane. She floated over to the officer, enveloping the cell phone and the hand holding it.

The officer completed the call. Jackson came back to

Dalton's position, re-forming to her avatar on the virtual plane. *"Let's go,"* she said.

"Where?" Dalton asked.

"He just called his higher headquarters to say their search has turned up nothing and they have no idea where Vasilev is. We're going to that headquarters to see what else they know."

"How do you know where that headquarters is?" Dalton asked.

"I went into the cell phone's memory. The address was listed there inside of the encryption lock. It's a trick I've learned while doing this," Jackson said. *"Here's the site."*

Dalton received the image.

"The phone he called is inside this room," Jackson told him. *"It's not far away. Let's go."*

He flashed out of the room behind Jackson.

When he came to a halt, he was in a conference room, hovering directly above a large wood table. Startled, he pushed himself over to a corner of the room, joining Jackson.

"They can't see you," Jackson reminded him, the edge of laughter in her tone.

"I'm glad you're having fun," Dalton said.

A GRU officer was at a lectern, speaking quickly in Russian.

"Can you understand him?" Dalton asked.

"Yes," Jackson said. *"As I told you earlier, you can too, if you ask Sybyl to do the translation for you. It's practically instantaneous."*

"Another thing no one's told me about," Dalton said.

"It's hard to get you up to speed on everything in a couple of days," Jackson noted. *"I've been remote viewing for six years and there's still so much I don't know about it. So many capabilities I haven't even thought of, never mind tested."*

"Sybyl?" Dalton prompted.

The voice of the Russian faded for a brief moment, then

Dalton could hear him in English, through the medium of Sybyl. It was disorienting—as pretty much everything else that had happened so far had been—to watch the man's lips move, but hear words that didn't exactly correlate with the movements.

"We must assume there is a connection between the attack on October Revolution Island and Dr. Vasilev's disappearance," the officer said. "The phased-displacement generator is missing. Without Vasilev's expertise, the weapon would be practically useless. With his expertise—" The officer paused, the words sinking in.

"What is a phased-displacement generator?" Dalton asked Jackson.

"A hypothetical weapon," Jackson responded. *"A mechanical device that integrates a space inside of it into the virtual plane, and then is capable with psychic help of sending a mass through the v-plane to any location on the planet. There were intelligence reports years ago that the Soviets were trying to develop such a weapon."*

"Doesn't sound very hypothetical to these guys," Dalton noted.

"The generator is no good without nuclear warheads," one of the officers at the table noted.

"Not necessarily," the officer at the lectern said. "The phased-displacement generator projects mass. The possibilities for its use are limitless. Whoever has it can project a biological agent directly into the aqueduct for a major city and cause an epidemic. They can project a conventional explosive to exactly the right location to cause a tremendous disaster. Say a pound of C-4 into the American space shuttle's fuel tank when it launches?"

"If this weapon is so damn effective, why was it left lying in that godforsaken place?"

Dalton focused on the man who had said that. His uniform was different—camouflaged fatigues, a blue beret tucked in his belt. His face was hard, the eyes cold: a killer. Dalton recognized the insignia of the Spetsnatz on the beret.

"Colonel Mishenka," the man at the end of the table with the four stars of an Army general on his collar acknowledged the Spetsnatz officer. "The weapon was abandoned because it malfunctioned, killing everyone involved in the project."

Mishenka fingered a folder. "This Vasilev wasn't killed, General Bolodenka."

"*Almost* everyone," Bolodenka clarified. "Vasilev barely escaped. The information he gave us indicated that the risks involved in a weapon such as the phased-displacement generator would not be worth taking." The general indicated for the briefer to continue.

"The generator requires computers in order to operate. Another key to the phased-displacement generator is that it will require a tremendous amount of energy. This will limit where whoever has it can set up. They would have to tap directly into a major power line, and the draw would clearly show up. I've already alerted those who would be affected to keep an eye out."

"That's if they stay inside our borders," General Bolodenka noted.

"The Mafia is most powerful inside our borders, so I will assume that is where they will operate," Mishenka noted. "How do you know this thing—this generator—works?"

General Bolodenka swiveled in his heavy leather chair. "Because in its last field testing, the phased-displacement generator destroyed an American nuclear submarine in 1963 just before it malfunctioned, killing all those who were running the test and also destroying what I understand were some critical biological components."

"Critical biological components?" Mishenka repeated.

"The generator required the mind power of psychically attuned individuals to operate," the briefer said.

"Then that's another parameter that whoever has it will need for it to operate, correct?" Mishenka asked.

"Correct."

"Perhaps, then," Mishenka mused, "the good doctor is involved with this. Wouldn't he have access to such people at his Institute?"

"We're checking into that," General Bolodenka said.

"You said that this generator required computers," Mishenka said.

"That is correct."

"And the computers need a special program?" Mishenka prompted.

The briefer glanced at the general, who nodded for him to speak.

"A CD-ROM with the programming for the phased-displacement generator was stolen from GRU records last week."

Mishenka shook his head in disgust at the information. "I was informed of that attack, but I was not told what was taken. I cannot operate efficiently if I am kept in the dark." He leaned forward. "The attack was most brutal. From what I understand, one of your GRU agents was ripped in half. How could this happen?"

"We don't know," the briefer said.

"How could the Mafia have found out about this weapon? About the CD-ROM?" Mishenka asked.

"We don't know that also."

"There has to be a leak inside your organization," Mishenka said.

Any comment on that was forestalled when the door opened and an enlisted man walked in, handing the briefer a piece of paper.

The briefer quickly scanned the message and said,

"We've just received word that General Rurik's wife and children have been kidnapped. They were picked up by a squad of Omon, but the bodies of those men were found in a warehouse in the river district. There are no further clues." The briefer glanced up. "The injuries to the bodies are similar to those we found at the site in Kiev."

"Who's General Rurik?" Colonel Mishenka asked. "And what does he have to do with this generator?"

"Rurik is the head of SD8," General Bolodenka said. "That is the department that was in charge of the generator."

" 'Was'?" Mishenka asked. "What does SD8 do now?"

"It runs the successor to the phased-displacement generator program," Bolodenka said.

"Which is?" Mishenka pressed.

"That, Colonel"—General Bolodenka's voice had turned chilly—"is none of your concern."

"I disagree, General," Mishenka said. "I do not think this kidnapping can be a coincidence. All of this information is most definitely connected. Anything you withhold from me will hinder any action I take."

"Let us deal with one problem at a time," Bolodenka said.

"What do you want me here for, then?" Mishenka asked.

"When we find the generator, your men will go in and secure it," Bolodenka said. "You will also neutralize all those involved with extreme vigor."

"Just say 'kill,' " Mishenka said. "It does not bother me to deal in the truth."

"Kill, then," Bolodenka said.

"And how do you propose to find the generator?" Mishenka asked.

"That is not your concern." Bolodenka smiled, revealing expensive capped teeth. "But rest assured we will."

"I need to know what is going on," Mishenka said. "Or I will not accept this assignment."

Bolodenka stood. "Alert your men, Colonel Mishenka. Be ready to move at a moment's notice." The general walked toward the door and paused. "Contact my scientific adviser. He will update you on SD8's current status." Bolodenka went out of the room, the others following.

Mishenka pulled a cell phone out of his breast pocket.

"Can you get that phone's number?" Dalton asked Jackson.

"Yes."

"Do it," Dalton ordered.

She coalesced into the glowing ball and slid over Mishenka's hand. In a moment she was back at Dalton's side.

"Let's go," Jackson said.

Dalton followed her out of the room, into the feature-less virtual plane. They paused as they both considered what they had learned.

"You really believe the Russians destroyed one of our subs in 1963 with this thing?" Dalton asked.

"It's long been an unsubstantiated rumor that the Thresher, *an attack submarine, was destroyed by some sort of psychic force,"* Jackson said.

Dalton was concerned with something else. *"Do you think this Chyort is the successor to the generator?"*

"Yes," Jackson said.

"So the Chyort is an avatar, just like us?"

"Like us," Jackson acknowledged, *"but more powerful. They've done something different than Psychic Warrior."*

"What the hell is going on?" Dalton wondered. *"This doesn't make much sense. If all this is true, and you met the Chyort in the railyard, then the GRU should know that the Mafia plans to take down the nuke train. But those guys in there acted like they didn't have a clue."*

"Maybe the information is compartmentalized?" Jackson suggested.

"That was the head of the GRU in there. If he doesn't know, who does? Hell, Chyort, whoever the hell he is, should be stopping all this."

"Let's get home," Jackson said. *"I'm tired and this doesn't change anything. In fact, it makes it all the more critical that we stop the nuke hijacking, now that we know that the Mafia will have a means of projecting those warheads anywhere on the globe."*

"One billion dollars. U.S. currency, of course." Oma lit a foul-smelling Russian cigarette and watched the two men across the expanse of her desk. There was no external response on their part to her quoted price or the odor she blew across the desk.

"I will be most reasonable about payment," Oma said. "One hundred million due in the next twenty-four hours to insure targeting. The balance to be paid on completion of the task."

"For *one* nuclear bomb?" the head of the delegation asked.

"For one nuclear bomb placed anywhere you want it on the face of the planet and detonated there, Mr. Abd al-Bari," Oma clarified. "You want the bomb inside of Israel's secret nuclear weapon storage facility in the Negev Desert? I will put it there and detonate it." Oma's steel teeth shone as she smiled. "The world will think it an accident. The Israelis will have to go public and admit what they have so fervently denied for so long. Their nuclear arsenal will be destroyed. The military forces based nearby will also be destroyed. A rather spectacular coup, and there is no way they can trace it to you."

"No one can get inside Negev," the younger of the two men protested, before he was shushed by Abd al-Bari.

"I can put the weapon anywhere you want and detonate it," Oma repeated. "That is why the price is set as it is."

"Still rather high for one weapon," Abd al-Bari said.

"How much do you spend on your military each year?"
Oma didn't wait for an answer. "Buy a few less fighter jets
and you won't even tweak your budget."

"The money is not the critical factor," Abd al-Bari said.
"I want to know how you can do this."

"That is not part of the deal," Oma said.

Abd al-Bari laughed. "Then there is no deal." He stood.
"I have listened to many fools make many outrageous
promises over the years. I do not need to waste any more
time."

Oma spread her hands out on her desktop. "You fail to
understand the true nature of what we are discussing. I am
trying to be courteous. To give you something for your
money."

"I do not need to listen to your blustering." Abd al-Bari
turned for the door.

"I understand you enjoy gambling," Oma said.

Abd al-Bari paused.

"According to my sources, you play the cards," Oma
continued. "That means you understand the difference between a bluff and someone holding a strong hand."

"I am very good at everything I do," al-Bari said.

"If you have the imagination, I would suggest you turn
this all around and picture my deal for one billion dollars
per bomb as a winning hand." Oma smiled once more. "I
do not wish to offend you, but please, understand that I can
put those nuclear bombs anywhere, including the center of
your largest oil field. There are some who would pay the
money I am asking for that to happen. Of course, I have not
contacted them yet. If I am bluffing, then no harm done if
you walk out that door. But if I truly hold the cards I am
telling you I hold—"

Abd al-Bari's skin flushed a shade darker. "Do not threaten me."

"I am trying to be reasonable," Oma said. "I would like to continue to be reasonable. But I thought it best that all the possibilities be put on the table, so to speak, so that we have complete understanding."

Abd al-Bari said, "And if you fail? If you do not do what you say you can after I have paid you the money you ask for down payment?"

Oma spread her hands wide, taking in her office and the building. "Then you know where to find me and you can play *your* winning hand. I understand you have those in your organization who are most willing to die for your cause. I have no doubt that if you wanted me dead, one of those people would find a way to accomplish that."

"I have to confer with others," Abd al-Bari said.

"Please do." Oma's voice chilled the room. "But I need an answer in twenty-four hours."

Chapter Eighteen

A dreary rain was falling, turning the ground around the railhead into mud. Colonel Verochka, head of nuclear security for the GRU, watched from the interior of the BMD armored vehicle through a bullet-proof portal on the side. Led by two T-72 tanks, four BMDs rolled through the mud, their treads giving firm traction. The armored personnel carriers were followed by two more T-72s. Overhead, above the sound of the rain falling on the metal and the roars of the armored vehicles, Verochka could hear the sound of helicopter blades. She knew that four MI-28 Havoc gunships, the most advanced helicopter in the Russian inventory, were flying cover.

The four BMDs slid next to a heavily armored railcar hooked to two oil-burning engines. As dozens of infantrymen, weapons at the ready, spread out around the train, the back doors on the lead BMD swung open. Two men carried a plastic container out, up a concrete ramp and in through the heavy metal doors on the side of the car. Four more bombs were off-loaded, then the next BMD moved up and the process was repeated.

Colonel Verochka waited until all twenty warheads were loaded and the train was secured. Then she ordered the driver of the BMD to head to the nearby airfield. She sat down in one of the web chairs along the inner wall of the APC. Between her knees a metal briefcase was secured.

A steel chain ran from the case to a titanium cuff around her left wrist.

Overhead, two of the Havocs flew cover as they approached the airfield.

"Goddamn those Russian sons of bitches!" Raisor exclaimed. "We thought they might have had something to do with the *Thresher* going down!"

"We?" Dalton was bone-tired, and there was less than four hours before they had to go. But Raisor had demanded a complete report on what they had discovered on their reconnaissance mission. "You weren't even born when the *Thresher* sunk."

"The CIA suspected Soviet involvement in the sinking at the time," Raisor said.

"That really doesn't matter right now," Dalton said. "The important thing is we now know there's more to this theft of nuclear weapons than it appeared. If these Mafia people have the phased-displacement generator, and they have Vasilev, and the programming code, and they can get the bombs, we've got a big problem on our hands."

"They still need remote viewers to aim the weapon," Jackson noted.

"If they're gathering all the other pieces," Dalton said, "I'm sure they have a handle on that too."

Raisor checked the digital clock overhanging the room. "We don't have much time."

"If you can get an idea where Vasilev is or what happened to this generator," Dalton said to Raisor, "it would help."

"Just concern yourself with your mission," Raisor said.

"I'm trying to do that," Dalton said, "but nobody seems to have a clue what is really happening."

"We know the warheads are going to get stolen in four hours," Raisor said. "That's all we need to know."

"Dr. Hammond," Dalton said, giving up on the CIA man.

Hammond had a cup of coffee in her hand. "Yes?"

Dalton noted that the hand holding the cup was shaking very slightly. "What if you wanted to destroy an avatar? How would you do it?"

"On the virtual plane or in the real?" Hammond asked.

"Either one."

Hammond took a deep drink from her mug, then put it down. "I've thought about it and I've had Sybyl put some time into it. But I really can't tell you. The key thing to remember is that the avatar is a projection. Even when it coalesces into the real world and transfers power into matter, it is still a projection. So what you want to know is sort of like asking how one would destroy an image on screen in a movie."

"Where am *I* then, when I'm on the other side?" Dalton asked.

Hammond looked at him quizzically for a few seconds, then realized what he meant. "We have to assume that despite traveling on the virtual plane, the essence of who you are remains with the body."

"I don't buy that," Dalton said. "When I've been out there, I've been out there."

"You're asking where the mind exists," Hammond said, "and that's something that's more philosophical than–"

Dalton cut her off. "I'm asking where the soul exists," he said, slamming his fist into his own chest. Then he pointed at his head. "This only takes you so far, then something else takes over. I want to know if we're putting that something else out there."

"I don't know," Hammond said. "I don't think so, but . . ."

"What do we do if we come up against an enemy avatar during our mission."

"What enemy avatar?" Raisor asked. He gave a hard look to Jackson. "Has she been filling your head about her devil?"

"It's a possibility," Dalton said. "General Bolodenka said that SD8, which deals with the same thing you at Bright Gate deal with, has come up with a new-generation weapon, something beyond the phased-displacement generator. I think they may have developed a similar ability to Psychic Warrior, and I think we need to be as prepared as we can be for the possibility we might run into something."

"I don't know what to tell you," Hammond said. "We really have no experience in this area."

A thought occurred to Dalton. "What if something happens to Sybyl while we're out in the virtual plane?"

"We have a backup computer that we can put on-line," Hammond said.

"And while you're waiting to go on-line, what happens to us?" Dalton demanded.

"The switchover is automatic."

"But if there is a time gap?"

Hammond put her hands in the air, more from frustration than anything else. "I don't know."

"Why are you so worried?" Raisor asked.

"Because we think this Russian avatar, Chyort, knows about the nuke takedown. And we might trip over each other trying to stop it."

"If your goals are the same, then there shouldn't be a problem," Raisor said.

"But if they aren't?" Dalton didn't wait for an answer. "Remember, this Chyort probably works for the agency that killed every man on board the *Thresher*. Even if our goals are the same, we're still on opposite sides, as you pointed out to me when you justified not giving the Russians your intelligence about the takedown."

"Why not focus on your mission, Sergeant Major?" Raisor suggested.

"What about the first Psychic Warrior team?" Dalton asked. "Are they dead?"

Silence filled the room. Finally Raisor stood up. "Come with me, Sergeant Major. I want to show you something."

"Agent Raisor–" Hammond began, but the look he gave her froze the next words in her mouth.

Dalton followed as Raisor headed to the side of the control room, to a door that Dalton had never seen opened yet. Raisor punched in a code on the small pad next to it and the metal slid to the side.

"Come on," Raisor said, waving Dalton in.

The door slid shut behind them. The room was almost a duplicate of the control room, full of ten tubes. And inside nine of them were bodies, floating in the green fluid. Six men, three women.

"That's the first Psychic Warrior team," Raisor said. "*My* team."

"Are they alive?" Dalton could see small placards on the front of each tube listing the name of the occupant.

"The bodies are," Raisor said. "The minds, or soul, or whatever you want to call the essence of a person, that we don't know about. Hammond thinks they're dead. The government thinks they're dead. We were supposed to pull the plug on the bodies a week and a half ago."

"What happened to them?"

"We were betrayed," Raisor said. "I've seen your classified file, Dalton. You fought in Vietnam, were captured and held prisoner. You know about being betrayed, don't you? About being given a mission and then having the plug pulled? Well, that's what happened here, literally. They were on a mission and my superior had Sybyl shut down while they were still out. I was in DC, playing politics with the Select Committee on Intelligence, trying to keep our funding flowing. And I came back to this."

"Why?"

"That's a complicated story which you don't have the clearance for," Raisor said.

Dalton had seen it before—personnel abandoned because some bureaucrat or politician thousands of miles away and safe behind their desk made a decision. In Vietnam they'd sent teams of indigenous infiltrators into the north, and when Nixon had halted the bombing campaign, all air traffic over the north was grounded, including the resupply and exfiltration flight for those men. They all died. And life in Washington went on. The Marines in Beirut who'd been placed in an untenable position with unclear guidance. And thus they died. Delta Force in Mogadishu. The SEALs in Panama.

Dalton stopped in front of one of the tubes. A dark-haired woman floated inside, fluid slowly flowing through the tubes. The name on the placard was Kathryn Raisor. Dalton turned toward the CIA man. "Is this your wife?"

"My sister." Raisor held up his left hand. "This is her ring from the Air Force Academy. She went from the Air Force to the NSA. We were both pegged for this program because we maxed out the psych tests when they were screening for personnel for this program. We were good psychic ability candidates. It must be genetic, don't you think? Hammond and the other brains think so." Raisor was standing next to his sister's tube, looking up at her, his voice low, as if he were in a trance. "Oh yes, that's what they think."

"Hammond did this?" Dalton demanded.

Raisor shook his head. "Her predecessor." The cold smile crept around his lips. "He is no longer with us."

"Who ordered it?"

"That's my concern," Raisor said.

"It's mine too," Dalton said. "It will be my team in the tubes next. I want to know if the son of a bitch who did this to your team can do this to mine."

"The source of that decision is not wired into the chain of command for this mission," Raisor said.

"So this is why we were brought in?"

"Replaceable parts in the big machine," Raisor said. He looked at his watch. "I suggest you get some rest. We go over very shortly."

As Dalton walked out of the room, the last thing he saw was Raisor silhouetted against the glow from his sister's tube.

"Who is that?" Opa asked.

The sound of General Rurik's summons echoed across the glade, into the woods and the fields beyond.

Feteror was seated with his back to one of the trees. He reluctantly stood. "I have to go on a mission," he said.

Opa reached out a wrinkled hand and placed it on Feteror's shoulder. "I enjoyed talking with you."

Feteror nodded, not sure what to say.

"Will you be back?"

Feteror paused. "I do not know." He looked at the glade and the area surrounding them. He could hear birds chirping in the trees, the sound of the water rushing by. He could even smell the odor of manure coming from the nearby fields. It felt more real than anything he'd experienced in almost a decade and a half, but he knew it wasn't.

"I have to go."

"Arkady–" Opa paused.

"Yes?"

"There are good things in the world." Opa spread his hands, taking in the glade. "This is a good place."

"This is not real," Feteror said. He paused, almost adding that the old man he was talking to was not real either.

"Are you here?" Opa asked.

"What do you mean?"

"If you are here, then this is real," Opa said. "You don't believe me. You don't believe that I am here, either, do you?"

Feteror felt the tug of the plan he had worked so hard to put into effect pulling at him.

"Hatred is not the way," Opa said. "I fought for years and I know that."

"Do you know what they did to me?" Feteror didn't wait for an answer. "They cut away my body and kept me in darkness. They took away everything!"

Opa shook his head sadly, his thick gray beard brushing against his aged chest. "They took much, but not everything, Arkady. Some things *you've* given away and you can get them back." He reached up with his hand and placed it on Feteror's chest. "You're missing something there. You can get it back."

Feteror shrugged the hand off. "I will make them pay."

Feteror dissolved from Opa's view.

The old man stood alone in the glade. He looked up into the blue sky, a tear slowly making its way down his leathery cheek.

Feteror accessed his outside links, forcing himself to block out the image of his grandfather, and focusing on what was to come.

"Yes?" He could see General Rurik standing at the master console. He was pleased the see the wild look in the other man's eyes. He had hoped the pig cared for his family.

"I have a mission of the highest priority for you," Rurik said.

Feteror waited.

"There are two tasks." Rurik paused, collecting himself, then continued. "The steel cylinder you saw being taken from October Revolution Island—you must find it." He paused, not speaking.

"And the second task?" Feteror pressed.

Rurik's hands came down on the edge of the table in front of him, the whites of the knuckles clear to Feteror's cameras. "My wife and children have been abducted. I want you to find them."

"Which of the two tasks has the higher priority?" Feteror asked.

The look in the general's eyes told Feteror the answer to that, even as the old man lied. "I want you to accomplish both."

"You must give me the power and time to accomplish both, then," Feteror said.

His electronic eyes could see the anger on Rurik's face. "You will have all the power we can send you."

"I will do as you order."

"Do not cross me," General Rurik said. "I will reward you if you get my family back."

What could you possibly offer me? Feteror choked the words back. He focused on the pain he could see on the general's face, relishing the sight.

"I'm loading all the data we have on both the phased-displacement generator and my family's abduction," Rurik said.

"Let me get started."

The window to the outside world cycled open. Feteror felt a wave of power, more than he'd ever experienced before, shoot through him. He leapt for the window and was out.

Barsk looked out the window as the cargo plane banked. The ground below was snow-covered in places and looked rather bleak. He could see the large dam and the hydroelectric plant behind it in the gorge where a plume of water cascaded down from the overflow spillway.

To the east, high above the power plant, a landing strip had been laid down years ago, but it looked desolate and empty, with a group of hangars lining the runway. Three sets of power line towers ran by the edge of the airfield after climbing out of the gorge.

Vasilev had spent the entire flight rocking back and forth in his seat, his eyes unfocused. Barsk had serious doubts about whether the man was going to be of any use once they landed.

Barsk turned his attention back into the plane as they descended. "There's one thing I don't understand."

Vasilev, despite being dressed now in a one-piece black jumpsuit borrowed from the mercenaries and despite having been given a good meal on the flight, still looked rough. Barsk slapped him on the shoulder. "Hey!"

Vasilev slowly rubbed a hand along the gray stubble of his beard. "What?"

"This Chyort—the demon that is helping my grandmother. Why is he doing it?"

Vasilev gave a laugh that bothered Barsk. "He is trying to get back at those that use him."

"To what end?"

Vasilev stared down the length of the plane along the gleaming steel tube that filled it. "So we will all go to hell."

"One hundred million dollars."

Oma steepled her fingers and peered over the top of her reading glasses at the young man sitting across from her who had just spoken. He wore a tailored three-piece suit and his Russian was flawless, without an accent. He was of the new breed of international broker, representing the interests of the United Nations, using economic leverage and payoffs instead of force.

The young man smiled, revealing very white and straight teeth. "Half now, half upon delivery of the warheads."

"I do not have any warheads," Oma said.

"Not yet. But I believe you plan to come into ownership of some shortly. I thought coming here before you finalized some other deal to, shall we say, dispose of them, would be best for all involved in case you are successful in your endeavors."

"Your NATO already has thousands of nuclear weapons among the various members," Oma noted.

"And we prefer not to have to use them," the young man said. He leaned forward, his false friendliness gone. "Listen. I know who you are. I know what you do. I know you've been putting feelers out for buyers of nuclear weapons. That tells me you either have them or are planning to get them shortly. I've also heard that you are promising delivery of those weapons anywhere in the world along with detonation. You must be a fool to think you can get away with that. We have dealt with people like you before. We will never let you get a warhead out of the borders of Russia. And we will squash you like an irritating bug."

"Then why are you offering me money instead of squashing me?" Oma asked.

"We are trying to be civilized."

"If you are so smart and informed," Oma continued, "you would know that one hundred million dollars is one tenth of the price I am asking."

"You have to be alive to be able to enjoy your money. I'm offering you life and one hundred million. That's better than lining your coffin with a billion dollars."

"I could have you killed for five dollars on the streets," Oma said. "That would leave me with a considerable profit margin."

"I am only a representative," he answered. "Killing me will not make your problem go away."

"Actually," Oma said, "I believe you are the one with the problem. You came to me."

The man said nothing, simply staring across the desk at her.

Oma waved her hand, signaling the meeting was over. "I will consider your offer."

The young man stood. "Do more than consider." He flicked a card onto the desk. It was blank except for a cell phone number.

Leksi was standing behind the two pilot seats in the MI-8 Hip, watching through the windshield as two of the Hind gunships swept over the field a half a kilometer ahead of them.

When both gunships turned and commenced to circle, Leksi ordered the pilot of the helicopter to land there. They swept in to a landing in the tall weeds. Leksi could see two fuel trucks in the treeline, exactly as Oma had told him there would be. The FARP, forward arming and refueling point, had cost them over five hundred thousand American dollars to have ready, but it was worth it. All the choppers would be topped off and fully armed, prepared for the upcoming action.

As the blades of the MI-8 began slowing, Leksi exited the chopper and walked to the side of the clearing. The other MI-8 came in for a landing, followed by the Hind gunships. As the sound of the rotors and engines began winding down, Leksi stretched his back.

He looked to the west where a range of high hills loomed. On the other side of those hills was a river. And along the thin level space between water and mountains ran a rail line.

Leksi shivered, not from the damp chill in the air, but

from excitement, almost a sexual feeling. His right hand slid down to the butt of the nine-millimeter pistol strapped to his thigh and the fingers flexed around it, feeling the cold plastic and metal. He looked at the watch strapped to his left wrist.

Two hours.

Chapter Nineteen

Colonel Verochka walked quickly from the back ramp of the BMD to the left side door of the MI-14 transport helicopter. As soon as she was inside, the door was swung shut by the loadmaster.

She checked her watch. It was time. She gave a thumbs-up signal to the loadmaster, who relayed the order through his headset to the cockpit, and the helicopter took off.

Other than the loadmaster, who sat down across from her, she had the spacious interior of the cargo bay to herself. She set the metal case down between her feet, making sure that the chain wasn't tangled. She twisted in the seat and looked out one of the small glass portals as they gained altitude. She saw one Havoc gunship about fifty meters away, and she knew the second was on the other side. She also knew that four Mig-24 jet fighters were taking off at this moment and would provide overhead cover.

She leaned back in her seat and relaxed for the first time since she'd signed for the metal case.

The lights were off, leaving only the dim reflection from the half-open door to illuminate the room. Dalton was sitting on his bunk, back against the cold wall, listening to the nervous rustlings in the room. Some of the men were asleep from sheer exhaustion, but he knew most were awake, unable to sleep. No one had taken Hammond's sleeping drug, not wanting to have anything in their system that could interfere with their ability to operate. There was slightly under ten minutes before they had to go to the experimental chamber and prepare to launch.

Dalton turned his head as someone slipped in the door. He recognized the slender figure of Lieutenant Jackson. She wove her way through the bunks until she arrived at his location. Dalton slid over, giving her room to sit at the foot of the bed.

"You okay?" he asked in a low voice.

"No."

Dalton smiled in the dark. "Me neither."

Jackson's head came up. "But you've been in combat. Don't you get used to it?"

"You never get used to it," Dalton said. "Plus, this is different than anything else I've ever done. One time I sat down and figured it out. I've fought on every continent except Australia and Antarctica. I guess I should be grateful there's no native population in Antarctica and we haven't gone to war with the Aussies, or I'd be seven for seven. Vietnam. El Salvador. Lebanon. Somalia. Panama. Antiterrorist work in Berlin. Other places. Other times. Each one a little different, each one pretty much the same.

"I've jumped in, walked in, been flown in, swum in, ridden in—you name it—I've gone into combat every way I thought was possible. And now here's a new way."

"I've never fired a shot in anger," Jackson said.

Dalton chuckled. "Hell, neither have I. I've fired a heck of a lot in fear, though." He stretched his legs out. "It feels strange to be this close to infiltration—I guess we can call it infiltration—and not be doing something. Usually we would be cleaning our weapons, loading magazines, sharpening knives, memorizing call signs and frequencies and doing radio checks. But we're just sitting here waiting."

Dalton knew some of the men were listening in. He also knew there wasn't much he could say to make them feel better. In his experience, he never knew how someone was going to react in combat until they were there. Training helped, but no training could prepare someone for the ultimate test. He'd seen men he'd thought he could count on flake out and others he hadn't thought much of do the most incredible feats of arms.

His watch began beeping. Dalton stood. "Rise and shine. Another great day in airborne country."

The members of the team got out of their bunks.

"Let's do it." Dalton headed for the door.

Feteror looked down on the rail line. The armored train was twenty minutes from the border checkpoint between Kazakhstan and Russia. He noted the Havoc helicopters flying cover, and on the train the number of guards and their weapons.

Then he swept north searching, doing quick jumps through the virtual plane, peeking into the real. After six tries, he spotted the MI-14 helicopter with its fighter and gunship escort, heading northwest, toward Russia. The aerial convoy would cross the border in six minutes, but he knew its destination and it had another hour and twelve minutes of flight time. More than enough, Feteror knew.

He jumped, through the virtual plane, and poked into the real above the FARP. He could see the men preparing their weapons, the helicopters warmed up. Leksi was yelling orders, getting everyone moving.

Feteror settled down on a mountain peak, between the FARP and the rail line. He slowly materialized into the real world, keeping his form colorless so he couldn't be spotted. He felt the spatter of the light rain on his wings.

Like a huge vulture perched on the rocky crag, he waited.

Oma turned the card the NATO representative had given her over and over in her liver-spotted hands.

The phone rang and she put the card down and picked the receiver up.

"Yes?"

"We accept."

She recognized Abd al-Bari's accent.

"In fact," the voice continued, "we would like delivery of four packages."

Oma closed her eyes. She had dealt with large sums of money, but the thought of four billion dollars staggered even her.

"The money?" she asked.

"The first payment has been transferred to the account you indicated. As we discussed, the balance will be paid upon our satisfaction that you have completed your terms of the agreement."

With her free hand, Oma began typing into her computer, accessing her Swiss account. She knew al-Bari was not lying, but she had to see the numbers for herself.

"Where do you want the packages delivered?" she asked as her fingers worked.

"That data is being transmitted via encrypted fax as we speak."

Oma looked up as the bulky secure fax machine she had appropriated from the defunct KGB buzzed, then hummed, spilling out a piece of paper.

"We will be waiting," al-Bari said, then the phone went dead.

Oma looked at her computer screen. Four hundred million dollars was credited to her account. She slowly walked across the room to the fax and picked up the paper.

You will destroy the following targets:

1. Washington, D.C., the Capitol Building zero point
2. Inside the Israeli Negev Desert nuclear weapon
    storage facility
3. The Pentagon
4. New York City, the United Nations zero point

Oma's hand shook as she read the list and realized the
implications of the targets and the order of destruction. One
word sprang to mind as she carried the paper back to her
desk: *jihad*. Abd al-Bari's people were preparing for the
Holy War they had always dreamed of, crippling the abili-
ties of the Americans and Israelis to fight against the storm
of fanaticism they hoped would arise.

She placed the target list on the desktop next to the
card. She looked once more at the computer screen and the
flashing dollar figure there.

She opened a drawer and pulled out a cellular phone.
She punched in memory one. It was answered on the second ring.

"Yes?"

"Barsk, are you ready?"

"We have off-loaded the weapon and Vasilev is setting it
up, hooking it into the computers you had waiting here. I
have men working now on splicing into the power lines."

"Good. Wait until you hear from me again." Oma cut
the connection and put the phone on the desk in between
the card and the target list. Then she leaned back in her seat
and closed her eyes.

General Rurik paced back and forth, bathed in the glow of
the flashing red light that indicated that Feteror was out.

"Anything further on what our friend has been up to?"
he asked the senior technician.

The man looked up from his computer screen with a troubled visage. "It is most strange, sir."

Rurik halted in his pacing. "What is?"

"Feteror is gone, but I'm picking up indications that he isn't gone."

"How can that be?"

The man shook his head. "I am not certain. There is a presence inside of Zivon that I cannot pin down."

"Well, pin it down," Rurik snapped.

Dalton felt the embryonic solution slide up his legs as he was lowered into the isolation tank. He knew the other members of his team were being lowered at the same time into their own tanks, but he could see nothing with the TACPAD helmet securely fastened on his head. He gave a thumbs-up as the solution came up over his waist, then chest.

"All right." Dr. Hammond's voice echoed in his ears. "All systems are green on all tanks. We are ready to proceed."

Raisor's voice replaced hers. "We have final approval from the National Command Authority. Psychic Warrior is a go for its first operational mission."

Dalton felt the first tinglings of the TACPAD being activated.

From his rocky aerie Feteror watched Leksi move his forces out. Then he leapt into the air, sliding into virtual space, and jumped.

He came out where he thought the air convoy with the PAL codes should be. He twisted in the air, searching, and spotted it moving at 140 knots to the northwest. He focused on the MI-14 in the center. He knew that to act too early would be to alert the troops guarding the train, so he flew alongside.

Chapter Twenty

Fifth time wasn't much better. Dalton's lungs tried to expel the liquid coming in, but lost the battle. His mind was focused on other matters though, noting the pain and nausea with almost a detached feeling.

"Give me the latest satellite downlink," he asked Hammond, through Sybyl.

"This is live feed from a KH-14 over the target," Hammond told him as a picture formed in Dalton's mind. He saw a bridge over a river. A train on the western side, approaching. There was only one very long car with two engines pulling. He could also spot two gunships flying cover.

"Expand," Dalton ordered.

Hammond had Sybyl relay the request to the NSA computer, which forwarded it to the spy satellite.

As Dalton waited he ran down the checklist for complete interface with Sybyl. A new picture was forwarded. The river crossing was a small spot in the lower left corner. Dalton traced the rail line as it moved into Russian territory along the east side of the river. He knew the resolution wasn't good enough to be able to spot the planned ambush, but that wasn't what he was looking for.

"The immediate rally point–the IRP–will be here." Dalton picked a hill on the west–Kazakhstan–side of the river. He searched further. *"The emergency rally point–the ERP–will be over this mountain."* He designated the spot he wanted. *"Use the ERP if you become separated or things go to shit. If it's*

really bad, come all the way back here to Bright Gate. Is that clear?"

He received an affirmative from the other members of the team and Raisor.

"All right," Dalton said. *"RVers, head for the first jump point."*

Leksi leaned down and placed his head alongside the rail. He could feel the slightest of vibrations. He stood, gesturing for his demolition men to work more quickly.

This section of track curved left, following the river. The demo men were placing two sets of charges on the rail. A pressure trigger was wired to the first set of charges. When fired, the explosives would take out a forty-foot section of track.

Leksi had carefully chosen this site. He knew that blowing a straight section of track would be fruitless—he had seen a train cross over sixty feet of blown track and pick up the track on the other side. But with the curve gone, the engine would smash into the mountainside on the east side.

He looked up the steep slope. His missile teams were settling in, throwing small camouflage nets over their positions. The FM radio hooked to his combat vest was crackling with noise.

"This is Tiger Flight. In position. Over."

Leksi spoke, the voice-activated boom mike in front of his lips transmitting. "Hold until I call you in. Over."

"Roger. Over."

Leksi took one last look around, then sprinted for cover. He paused just before sliding off the embankment and looked up. He scanned the skies, but there was nothing he could see. Still, as he got behind the concealment of a large boulder, his eyes went once more to the sky, then to the rail.

"We've spotted the ambush site," Jackson reported through Sybyl. *"The train is only about two minutes from passing through the kill zone."*

"Roger. We're coming," Dalton relayed back to her. *"Jump point one. Let's go!"*

Dalton concentrated on the first point that had been relayed back by the RVers.

He was there. He paused only long enough to make sure the other members of the team came in. Then he was on to the second jump point.

Leksi pulled a set of night vision goggles out of his buttpack. The mercenary next to him stared at him in confusion. Leksi ignored him. He had learned early to trust his instincts.

He slipped the goggles over his head and, making sure they were turned to the lowest possible setting so they wouldn't overload in the daylight, he switched them on. He scanned the sky. Nothing. Then he turned the switch to infrared.

Leksi paused in his scanning. There was something up there, a disturbance as if something was passing through the air, but he couldn't see anything solid. Leksi frowned. He pulled the night vision goggles off and pulled his binoculars up and looked in the same direction. Nothing. He put the goggles back on and the sky was clear.

A tap on his arm brought his attention back to earth. He could hear the train now. The lead engine was in sight, a half mile away. Leksi reluctantly took the goggles off, the mystery of the disturbance having to be put off for the time being.

Dalton was the first one into the immediate rally point. He materialized, feeling the rocky ground under his feet. Other forms appeared all around.

"The train is about to enter the kill zone," Jackson reported. Along with the message came the view she had. Dalton could see the train. And the ambushers.

He looked about the IRP. Everyone accounted for. Except Raisor.

"Anyone seen what happened to our CIA friend?"

The responses were all negative. There was no time to wait or to devise an elaborate plan.

"Captain Anderson. You hit the side of the hill and work your way down. My team, we'll go right on top of the train. Clear?"

"Clear!"

The train hit the trigger. The explosion was relatively small, just enough to cut the track in both spots. The lead engine raced off the embankment and slammed into the rocky mountainside two hundred meters from Leksi's position with an impact he could feel through the rubber soles of his boots.

The second engine buckled on top of the first, gushing steam forth.

The lone cargo car smashed into the back of the second engine, bounced off, broke its coupling, then rolled three times before coming to a halt, between the engines and Leksi.

Leksi jumped to his feet, waving with his free arm for his men to follow.

Overhead, the lead Havoc came racing in for a gun run. Two SAM-7 missiles flashed out of the hidden positions on the mountainside, and the gunship became a fireball.

The second one had been about a quarter mile behind the first, and the pilot desperately tried to pull out of his run.

Two more missiles fired. They closed the distance and hit the remaining Havoc.

Leksi put his AK-74 to his shoulder and fired a burst, killing a dazed soldier climbing out of the armored cargo car.

Feteror was still in the virtual plane. It was interesting keeping himself fixed in the center of the cargo bay of the MI-14 as it flew. He was watching the female colonel who had the case attached to her wrist. The army had changed much since his time. To trust such an important thing to a woman!

It was time.

He entered the real plane.

Colonel Verochka looked up, sensing the change in the inside of the cabin, the hair on the back of her neck rippling as if she had been touched by an electric shock.

Feteror materialized, letting color flow into the form of his avatar.

Verochka pressed back against the hard seat back in disbelief. The loadmaster ran for the cockpit, screaming into his microphone, but Feteror reached out and grabbed him around the throat with one massive hand. Feteror squeezed with that hand while he slammed the other into the man's chest and through. The man screeched. Blood exploded out the back, splattering Colonel Verochka. The loadmaster's head popped off with a horrible ripping and snapping sound.

Feteror threw the body to the floor and turned to the woman. Her right hand was scrabbling at her side, trying to draw the pistol strapped there, but her wide eyes were focused on him.

Feteror slashed out with his right hand, forefinger extended, a six-inch razor-sharp claw at the end. It sliced through Verochka's wrist, cleanly severing her gun hand.

The door to the pilot's compartment opened. The co-pilot stuck his head in, saw the demon and the carnage, and the door immediately slammed shut, the lock clicking.

Feteror drew back, pulling his wings up high, his most frightening pose. Thus he was caught off-guard when Ver-ochka darted forward, blood still spurting from the stump of her right wrist. She ducked under his left wing. Feteror whirled.

Verochka had her left hand, briefcase tucked under the arm, on the lever that opened the side door. Feteror paused, confused.

Verochka opened the door, the wind ripping it away. She dove out with the briefcase.

Feteror roared and dematerialized. He re-formed, streaking down, following Verochka's body. He was impressed, not only with the decisiveness of her actions, but the way she kept a tight body form on the way down, her arms tight at her side, head down. It was all so clear to Feteror; he could even see the thin trail of blood spurting out of her wrist into the air behind her.

He spread his arms, unfurled his wings, and scooped her out of her fall.

Feteror came to a hover, leaning his demon face into the colonel's. "Very brave," he hissed.

He felt her slam the briefcase against his back as she struggled. Her face was pale, from fear and loss of blood.

The first thing Dalton saw was green tracers ripping by just inches to his left. Hammond's assurance notwithstanding, he rolled right, and fired at the source of the tracers. His first fireball hit the man in the chest, blowing a hole straight through.

He continued firing, seeing in his mind the other members of the team materializing.

"Shit!" a voice yelled. *"Something's wrong!"*

Dalton knew immediately that it was Trilly, both from the voice and the tactical update that Sybyl was constantly playing in the background of his mind.

"I'm losing form," Trilly said, the surprise evident in his voice.

"Get out of here," Dalton ordered.

"Going to ERP," Trilly confirmed.

Dalton continued to fire at the attacking mercenaries.

"Hammond, what's going on?" Dalton demanded.

"We're having trouble keeping track of everyone. There's a divergence. Someone's split off."

Goddamn Raisor, Dalton thought. *"You keep power to my team, do you understand?"*

"Yes."

An explosion flashed on the hillside as Captain Anderson's team took out one of the SAM sites.

Feteror stiffened. He turned his head from the frightened face of Colonel Verochka. Something was wrong.

"It was nice to meet you," he hissed to her. He let go of her body, snapping his claws shut on her left arm, severing it–and the attached metal briefcase–from her body.

He listened to her scream, both from the fall and the loss of her arm, her body tumbling to the ground far below.

Still hovering, Feteror ripped the case open, the metal parting easily. He dropped the empty case as he held the single piece of paper inside between two claws. He scanned the PAL codes listed, matching them to the warhead serial numbers, putting the information into his database.

Then he dematerialized and jumped.

Raisor floated above the limousine as it cruised down Constitution Avenue going from the Capitol toward the White House. He wanted to wait, until the limo was directly across from the White House, on the south side of the Ellipse, before striking.

It was difficult, though, to hold back. To keep at bay the anger, the passion of revenge he had nurtured ever since finding out what had happened to his team, to his sister.

It had taken this, an international crisis, for him to be able to go back on the virtual plane with the power to use the weapons they'd developed for the psychic warriors. Now he was bringing those weapons home to the woman who had so casually tossed away the first team of psychic warriors.

It was night in Washington and Raisor began to allow his avatar to form in the real plane, directly over the closed sunroof of the limousine.

Leksi pressed his back against the railbed. Another fireball flashed by overhead, catching one of his men in the head, blowing it open like an overripe melon.

He looked up the slope. More of these monsters were coming down the hillside. All of his missile teams were dead.

"Tiger Flight!" he yelled into the mike to be heard above the sounds of firing and screaming.

"Tiger Flight. Over."

"Get in here for support now!" he screamed.

"Roger."

Dalton carefully stood. The surviving attackers were scattering, some hiding, others running.

"Captain Anderson," Dalton projected. *"I want you to secure—"*

Dalton halted in mid-sentence as a scream seared through his brain like a red-hot spike. He staggered, losing all sense of his surroundings.

On the hillside, Feteror had come into the real plane directly behind one of the attacking avatars. He had a very good idea who they were, and he didn't hesitate. With all the power of SD8-FFEU being directed through him, he grabbed the form and crushed it in his claws.

The energy/matter of the avatar in his hands vanished in a flash of light.

At Bright Gate, Dr. Hammond stared at her control panel in dismay.

"What's happening?" Dalton demanded, his voice echoing out of the speakers.

Hammond typed furiously on her keyboard.

"What is going on?" Dalton repeated.

"Sybyl's overloading. Something's affected two of the avatars. I'm trying to pull them back, but Sybyl can't do that and keep everyone else going at the same time. Also the power split, going to two different locations—we've never done that before and Sybyl is having trouble maintaining all your forms." Hammond ran a hand across her forehead. *"It's all happening too fast."*

Dalton became aware of his surroundings. He staggered back, feeling a pounding in his head. A line of green tracers burned through the air, right by him. He sank to his knees.

"Get out of there!" Jackson's voice echoed through his brain.

Dalton snapped out of existence at that place, into the virtual plane. He could hear more screams in his head. He checked tactical but there was nothing coming from Sybyl.

"What the hell is going on?" he projected toward Jackson.

"Chyort!" was the quavering answer. *"Choppers–gunships inbound from the east!"* she added.

Dalton came back into the real plane fifty meters from where he had been and behind the man who had shot at him. Dalton fired, the fireball blasting through the man.

"We're interdicting the choppers!" Jackson informed him.

Dalton looked up. He could see the two eagles and Jackson's falcon head east.

Looking down, he saw two of his teammates backing up, firing their energy tubes. Dalton followed their aim and saw what had scared Jackson.

Feteror felt the energy bolts hit him. He wanted to laugh, to shriek his glee. The energy poured into him, strengthening him beyond anything he had ever experienced, beyond anything SD8-FFEU had ever given him.

He dove forward, arms outstretched, into one of the American avatars. The white head was sliced off, the round shape bouncing onto the ground, then slowly shrinking and disappearing as it lost its energy shape.

He struck out at another and it staggered and collapsed to the ground under the blow.

"Status!" Dalton screamed. *"Hammond, I need status!"*

"I'm hurt!" the avatar at Chyort's feet called out—Barnes; Dalton recognized the yell.

"Go to the ERP!" Dalton ordered.

He shot a fireball at the demon as it bent over Barnes's form. The ball hit Chyort directly in the back. The surface there briefly glowed, then faded.

Two blazing red eyes turned to look directly at Dalton. Barnes's form disappeared as he jumped. At that moment Captain Anderson's avatar came winging down from above and smashed into Chyort's back. The two forms tumbled together.

Another scream resounded in Dalton's head. He knew now that each scream meant one of his people was dead.

Or their avatar was. He didn't and couldn't take his thoughts further than that right now.

"We took out the gunships," Jackson informed him. *"But both of my partners got shot up. Williams and Auer are gone!"*

"Get out of here, Jackson. To the ERP!" Dalton ordered. *"Everyone, to the ERP!"*

Dalton turned back toward the smashed cargo car. He could see mercenaries climbing over it, placing charges on the steel doors. Dalton fired, cutting down the demolition men.

Another scream. Dalton looked over his shoulder. The Chyort had Captain Anderson's avatar over his head, ripped it into two pieces at the waist. Chyort threw one piece in each direction, the parts fading as they tumbled to the ground.

The Chyort leapt into the air, spreading its leathery wings, and headed straight for Dalton.

Dalton jumped into virtual space. The Chyort was there also, still coming. Dalton jumped fifty meters left. It gained him a half second as Chyort pivoted on its wings.

Dalton jumped to the ERP, hoping he would lose Chyort in the process.

Raisor was completely in the real world, a ghostly white form above the limousine. Another quarter mile and they would be there.

Leksi yelled orders to his surviving and shocked men. The demon flashed out of sight, which made his job a little easier. He directed men to finish placing the charges. Using the radio, he ordered forward the lift helicopters and also learned of the destruction of his gunships.

There was a quick snap of plastique firing. Leksi

climbed up on the cargo car. Scattered on the down side of the car lay twenty plastic cases.

"Get them out!"

Dalton knelt next to Barnes. Trilly was standing to the side, nothing apparently wrong with him.

"I can't move, Sergeant Major," Barnes whispered. *"I jumped here, but I can't do anything more."*

"I'll get you back," Dalton promised. *"Hammond! Where the hell are you?"*

Lieutenant Jackson was circling overhead, keeping an eye out, flashing in and out of reality as she checked both the real and virtual plane.

There was no one else. Five gone. Half the team was wiped out. Dalton thought of Lang Vei, the tanks rolling through the wire, then banished that nightmare from his mind.

"Jackson," he said, reaching up with his mind.

"Yes?"

"Can I take Barnes back somehow?"

"I don't know."

"Give me a suggestion," Dalton said. *"You're the expert."*

"Try to meld into his psyche. Attach him to you emotionally. That might allow you to take him into the virtual plane and back."

Dalton reached down, cradling Barnes's avatar in his arms. He was concerned to see the form fade from view slightly before coming back.

"I'm going," Trilly said.

"No, you're not," Dalton said. *"You're a soldier, and a sergeant. You stay here with us and we all leave together."*

Dalton didn't have time to worry about Trilly, or the energy to stop him from running. A voice echoed inside his head.

"This is Hammond. I can't keep Sybyl on track for both locations."

"Where is Raisor?"

"I don't know."

Dalton thought she was lying, but this wasn't the time for it. *"Cut his power and concentrate on my team. Get us out of here. Then you can bring him back on line."*

"But–"

"Do it!" Dalton turned his attention to the form in his arms. *"You're coming back with me,"* Dalton said. *"You're coming back with me, Barnes. You understand?"*

Barnes's avatar weakly nodded.

"But if I–" Hammond's voice wavered.

"Do it!" Dalton screamed with the power he had. *"We're dying here. Most of my team is already dead."*

"All right," Hammond said. *"I'm focusing power on your team."*

The Ellipse, the lights of the White House just beyond, appeared to the right. Raisor landed on the roof of the limo with a solid thump that could be heard inside. He knew bodyguards would be reacting, but it was too late. His right arm switched from wing to six-foot-long blade. He poised it above the roof, directly above where he knew his target was sitting. He relished the feeling, the anticipation of payback, and then began to thrust the arm down, when his form vanished and he was in darkness.

He screamed, his anger and frustration echoing into the virtual plane.

Dalton focused as he had in the hospital room with Marie. A myriad of emotions raced through him like a fast-moving stream of quickly varying temperatures.

"Dalton!" Jackson screamed.

Dalton looked up as Chyort materialized in front of him. Dalton stared into the dark red eyes.

"Who are you?" Dalton demanded.

The demon took a step forward and Dalton felt the earth shake beneath him. He turned, putting himself between the demon and the body in his arms.

Dalton closed his eyes and focused only on Barnes. Dalton felt pain slice into his back. He focused on the isolation tanks in Bright Gate as he took a glance over his shoulder. A form came leaping between him and Chyort. Trilly!

Dalton jumped, Barnes with him.

Chapter Twenty-one

Feteror hesitated. He looked down at his right hand. The claws had torn into the American's back, going in over six inches, yet the man had ignored the pain and jumped. The other American who had jumped between them had died with one slice, the head neatly separated.

Feteror knew he could follow the Americans into their hole in the Rocky Mountains. He felt he now had the power to break through their psychic fence. Like a wolf among the sheep, he could rip them to shreds.

He turned and looked back toward the east, where the battle had occurred. With regret, Feteror jumped back.

He came into reality on top of the wreckage of the cargo car, scaring the wits out of the men pulling the bombs out.

Leksi yelled, telling the men to keep working, to ignore the demon. Then the naval commando climbed up to face Feteror.

"You were late," Leksi said. "Who were the others? The ones who fight like you?"

"Americans." Feteror liked the way his demon voice sounded, like boulders rubbing together, underlaid with the treble of the screams of the damned. "And I was not late. This was your job, not mine."

"And I will finish it if you would stop frightening my men."

Feteror snapped into the virtual plane.

Barsk kept a safe distance from the men reeling the thick black cables.

"Are you ready yet?" he demanded of the scientist.

Vasilev sighed and looked up from the computer terminal he'd been working at for the past hour. "This program was written for top-of-the-line computers in 1963. Computers have come a long way since then. This was upgraded several years ago but it is still out of date. I am trying to integrate the old software with the new hardware, but it is difficult."

"I don't want to hear excuses," Barsk said.

"I'm not giving you excuses," Vasilev replied. "I am telling you what is happening." He ran a trembling hand through his gray hair. "I can assure you I want this to work more than you do. It will put an end to the nightmare my life has been."

"Then get it working," Barsk snapped. "I'm beginning to—" He halted as he felt a wash of cold through his stomach. He turned.

The Chyort coalesced into being inside the hangar.

"Are you ready yet?" the demon hissed.

"We still have to hook up the power cables," Barsk said.

A long claw pointed toward Vasilev. "Is the program for the phased-displacement generator ready?"

Vasilev shrugged. "I am working on it."

Chyort blinked out of existence and then reappeared, looming over the old man. "You're working on it?"

"I am doing my best." Vasilev took an involuntary step backward, bumping into the computer console. "It has been many years and—" He paused as a claw touched his neck, pressing against the pulse that beat on one side.

"There are things worse than death." Chyort's words swept over the scientist. "You know that, don't you?"

Vasilev nodded.

"I know you don't fear death," Chyort continued. "But what I will do to you if you fail me will be worse than anything you can imagine. I will—" The demon paused, the head turned.

Then the creature was gone.

Dalton swam in the pain, his entire body awash in it. He tried to push his mind through the overwhelming tide of agony. He remembered the bayonet; he focused on it, the feeling of ice sliding into his back. Then the butt stroke from the NVA soldier holding the AK-47.

Awakening in the prison. Weak from loss of blood. Reaching, feeling blood still soaking through the dirty rag tied over the wound. Pressing his back against the concrete wall, stopping the bleeding. Holding the position, even when the guards came in and kicked, he pushed against the wall, knowing if he didn't, he would bleed out.

"Sergeant Major?"

No, Dalton thought. I'm just a Spec/4. Junior team member.

"Sergeant Major?"

Dalton tried to open his eyes but there was only darkness. And the pain.

"Sergeant Major! This is Dr. Hammond."

Hammond? Why was it so dark? Even in the cell there had always been a little light seeping in from the corridor.

A white dot appeared, so tiny and so far away.

"Focus on the dot."

Dalton tried to scream, but instead he gagged. Something was in his throat, blocking.

"We're bringing you out, but you have to be aware." The voice was insistent.

Dalton wished the woman would just shut up. He slid

down the concrete wall and rolled onto the floor into the fetal position. He was so tired and it hurt so badly.

A new voice ripped into his skull, louder than the other one.

"Damn it, Sergeant Major! This is Lieutenant Jackson. I'm ordering you to get back here. Don't you give up!"

Dalton shivered, feeling cold seep into his body, strangely lessening the pain. He saw Marie, the same as when he had first met her, the skin on her face smooth, flawless. She was beckoning to him to go in a different direction. Dalton pushed himself to his hands and knees. He began crawling toward Marie.

"Come back, Sergeant Major Dalton."

Dalton felt the opposing tugs, Marie and the warmth and comfort of just going to her, and Lieutenant Jackson's voice grating on his mind, his conscience, his sense of duty. He looked toward Marie and he knew she knew. She smiled sadly and faded from view, mouthing something that he couldn't make out.

Dalton stared in her direction until there was nothing there. The other voice kept nagging at him. Then he remembered.

The team was gone. Massacred. He couldn't do it again. He couldn't fight again. The last time, he had left Marie alone for five years. He couldn't do that to her again.

He let go of his grip, sliding toward where Marie had been.

He saw her once more.

"Why did you summon me?" After the glorious feeling of power during the battle with the Americans, being contained inside Zivon was unbearable to Feteror.

"Because the situation has changed," General Rurik said. "Twenty nuclear warheads have been stolen."

"You have already tasked me to accomplish two missions. Yet you bring me back here to inform me of this?"

"Did you find the phased-displacement generator?" General Rurik demanded.

"No."

Rurik stepped closer to the speaker. "Did you find my family?"

"I have a lead that I was tracking down when you called me back."

"Give me the lead," Rurik ordered.

"I am forwarding the information through Zivon," Feteror said. "But it would be best if you allowed me to continue on the mission."

"I do not trust you," Rurik said. "You are up to something. You will wait while I verify what you have learned."

Feteror remained silent, itching to get away. He forwarded information through the electronic channels of Zivon. He watched as General Rurik took it off the computer screen and then grabbed a phone, calling Moscow, shutting down the psychic wall for a moment.

A spear of pain slammed into Dalton's chest. It felt like his lungs were getting ripped out through his throat.

"Goddamn it, Sergeant Major, you've got to hold on."

The words were coming from outside, from a great distance, but the fact that they were external was so novel to Dalton, he marveled at it for a few moments. So much had been inside his head for so long now.

Another voice—it was Hammond's, a part of his mind recognized—spoke: "He's in arrest. Stand clear."

Dalton screamed as a jolt of electricity through the microprobe lanced his chest. The pain was bad, but the real hurt was seeing Marie fade again with each pulse of his heart in response to the electric shock.

"No!" Dalton yelled, the word garbled by embryonic

fluid sputtering out of his mouth. He rolled to his side vomiting, knocking away Hammond, who was getting ready to shock him again.

"He's got a pulse," Hammond announced.

Dalton pushed away Jackson's hand as she tried to hold his head.

"Leave me alone," he whispered. He turned to his other side, his back to those in the room, and kept his eyes closed. He searched for another glimpse of Marie, but there was nothing.

Leksi swung his arm around his head and pointed up. The pilot responded by increasing throttle and pitch on the blades. Laden with ten of the nuclear bombs, the first Hip rose into the air.

Leksi ran to the second and jumped on board. It followed the first.

Leksi flipped open his cellular phone and punched in memory one.

Chapter Twenty-two

"Sergeant Barnes made it back, thanks to you," Jackson said.

Dalton's hands were cradled around a steaming mug of coffee. He had ladled in several heaping teaspoons of sugar. He took a sip, relishing the burning feeling on his tongue. He was seated at the table in the small conference room off the experimental chamber. He couldn't bear being in there, looking at the bodies of the rest of his team floating inside their isolation tanks. Jackson was seated next to him. Hammond was on the other side of the table.

"Where is he?" Dalton asked.

"In the dispensary. He's sleeping, but the doctor gives him a clean bill of health."

"One out of nine. And the rest of the team?" Dalton asked.

Jackson shook her head, not able to answer him.

"Their bodies are still viable in their isolation tanks," Dr. Hammond said.

"Like the first team?" Dalton said.

"Yes," Hammond said.

Dalton rubbed his forehead. "So they're probably dead, as far as they're concerned, right?"

"We don't know that for certain," Jackson said.

"And Raisor?" Dalton knew he had to ask.

"We don't know," Hammond said. "His body is also in stasis. I restored his power, but there's been no contact. I think we might have lost the connection when I diverted all power to your team."

"Where did he go?" Dalton demanded.

"We don't know," Hammond said, "but we have a larger problem on our hands. I just got a call from Washington. Your mission failed. The nuclear warheads have been stolen. Combining that with the information you brought back about the phased-displacement generator, we have the biggest danger this country has faced since the Cuban Missile Crisis. The National Security Council is very concerned. They are considering their options."

Dalton looked up at the doctor, recognizing the panic in the clipped sentences. "Very concerned? Is that what you call it? They should be crapping in their pants. Options? What options? What are they going to do?"

Dalton took a deep drink of coffee, feeling the burning liquid hit his bruised throat. He relished the pain because it sharpened his mind, brought it out of the fog of near death and despair. The issue of Raisor's disappearance bothered him, but it was a msytery that wasn't a priority right now.

"For starters, they can now work with the Russians, given that the warheads have been stolen," Hammond said.

"That's like reuniting the Three Stooges," Dalton said. "The Russians had to have known about–" He paused, realization hitting him like a punch in the gut.

"What is it?" Lieutenant Jackson asked.

"Something's not right about all this," Dalton said.

"What do you mean?" Jackson asked.

"This Russian avatar, Chyort, it's not right." Dalton's mind was racing as he considered all he had experienced. "Chyort attacked us, not the mercenaries taking down the train."

"Maybe he thought you were the greater threat?" Dr. Hammond suggested.

Dalton shook his head. "No." He turned to Jackson.

"Chyort was in the railmaster's shack the same time you were, right?"

Jackson nodded.

"So he knew about the change in the timing of shipment. Yet the Russian guards weren't ready. They ran right into the ambush. And Chyort attacked us, not the ambushers.

"He's with them. I don't know why, and I don't know how, given that this Chyort is supposed to be part of the GRU, but he *is* with the Mafia, helping them. And we aren't going to recover those bombs or stop the phased-displacement generator from being used, until we stop Chyort."

Dalton turned to Dr. Hammond. "If you had to destroy your own project—stop Psychic Warrior—and you couldn't defeat it on the psychic plane, how would you do it?"

Hammond spread her hands, taking in the complex. "To make sure I succeeded, I'd take out Bright Gate."

"Which leaves you with the opposite situation from what we have right now," Dalton said. "What happens to me if I'm on the virtual plane and my body here is destroyed? Or Sybyl is taken off-line?"

"I don't know for sure what happens to your psyche if your body is killed, although I assume it would also be killed," Hammond said. "But if Sybyl is taken off-line, then you will lose all the power and support you get from the computer. Your psyche might still be floating around out there, but it won't be able to do much."

Dalton nodded. "All right, then. That's what we'll do."

Oma put the phone down. They had the bombs. They had the phased-displacement generator. But it had almost been a disaster. She thought about Leksi's account of the strange beings that had attacked him—Americans, working in the same manner as Chyort. Yes, Chyort had won, but . . .

Oma knew the playing field had changed, she just wasn't sure yet what the changes meant.

She looked at the computer screen on which she had left the information from her Swiss bank account. Four hundred million dollars. With 360 billion pending.

Her gaze shifted to the desktop, on which two things sat: the target list and the card from the NATO representative.

The phone rang. She grabbed it. "Speak."

"We have dropped the child off as instructed," the voice on the other end informed her.

"Very good." Oma held the receiver in her hand as the other end went dead. Another piece in the puzzle that she didn't quite understand. She'd assumed that Chyort had had her kidnap General Rurik's wife and children for revenge. But if so, why had he told her to free one of the children in a place where the GRU would find him quickly?

She pushed down on the receiver button and got a dial tone. She punched in the number off the card. It was answered on the first ring.

"Yes?"

"Do you give this number to everyone or do you know who I am?" Oma asked.

"I know who you are," the NATO representative replied. "Are you calling to chat about the weather or do you accept my offer?"

"You know about the warheads?"

"You have many people's attention now," the man acknowledged. "You might not enjoy the heat of the spotlight that is now shining in your direction. In fact, I'm not sure I can keep my offer on the table much longer."

"I have four hundred million in an account already," Oma said. "An advance against four billion. Do you understand my situation?"

There was a brief silence before the man spoke again.

"We can match the four hundred now that you have the bombs. But we also want the name of the original bidder and all other information you can give us."

"I cannot do–" Oma began.

"I would think that would be in your best interest," the NATO representative interrupted. "Even if you give back the advance, they–whoever they are–will not be happy about your reneging on a deal. Give us the name and perhaps we can clip their wings so they don't come after you."

Oma knew that NATO was willing to pay ransom to get the bombs rather than launch a military mission that could easily be as costly in financial terms and more importantly costly in the arena of NATO blood spilled and public image. It was overall cheaper, more direct, and more in line with the realities of the world to pay. It was the way the real world worked.

"Deposit the money and we can discuss this," Oma said. "Right now, this is only talk."

"You are playing a very dangerous game and the clock is ticking. This deal requires all the bombs to be turned over. Every single one. I will have the money in your account inside of the hour. Then we will talk again. It will be the last time we talk, one way or the other."

"You should learn to relax. To enjoy life."

Feteror stopped his "pacing" and looked at his grandfather's image in amazement. They were in the clearing near the stream. Feteror was beginning to worry that something had gone wrong. That Rurik would not let him out again. That Oma had the bombs now and had betrayed him.

"This is *not* life," Feteror said.

Opa raised his bushy gray eyebrows. "What is it then?"

"This"–Feteror waved his hands around the glade–"is all an illusion. It isn't real. We are inside a computer."

"A computer? What is that?"

"*You* aren't even real." Feteror had no patience for this. He needed to get out, or all that he had worked for would go to naught. He knew he could not trust Oma to keep her end of the bargain without looking over her shoulder. She needed him to operate the phased-displacement generator, but he knew that she might make a deal that didn't require the generator now that she had the bombs. Of course, he reassured himself, she didn't have the PAL codes.

Opa didn't look angry, merely puzzled. "How can I not be real?" He stretched his arms. "I feel real."

Feteror stopped and walked over to his grandfather, who was seated on the tree stump where he had always sat. Feteror thumped his chest. "I am not real either. None of this is. I am a monster. I'm supposed to be dead. You are dead. And I am going to join you soon—and bring those who did this to me on the journey. They will pay for what they inflicted on me. For betraying a loyal soldier.

"Like you said, Opa, the generals don't care about the common man. They use us like a sponge until we are soiled and dirty and can work no longer, then they throw us away. They have betrayed the entire country. I gave everything, *everything*, for Mother Russia, and she kicked me in the face. You gave everything. Millions gave everything. And now criminals and bootlickers run the country. I am going to end that and make them all pay."

Opa looked at him. "How can you do that if we are not real? Is this a dream? I do not understand."

Feteror shook his head, knowing there was no way he could explain this to his grandfather. "Trust me, Opa. I will do all that I say."

Opa frowned. "But why? I fought in the Great Patriotic War. I came home to you and my daughter, your mother. I raised you. I did not seek vengeance. What was done in the war was done for necessity. I still had my life to live."

"I *don't* have mine!" Feteror exploded.

Opa waved his hands around the glade. "But you have this!"

"It isn't real!" Feteror screamed.

Opa reached out and touched Feteror's arm. "There is good in everyone, grandson. You must–" Opa began, but he was interrupted by the bright flash of General Rurik's summons.

Despite his anxiety to get going, Feteror paused. He put a hand on his grandfather's shoulder. "Opa, I have to go now. We will not meet like this again."

Opa smiled, revealing his yellowed and stained teeth. "I do not understand what this place is or why I am here. I don't understand why you feel you must do what you feel you must, but you are my grandson, so I will be with you in spirit. Good luck, Arkady. Godspeed."

Feteror nodded, then flashed through the circuits to access his line to General Rurik. As he did so, his grandfather's last words echoed in his mind. God? There was no God as far as Feteror was concerned. No God would allow what had been done to him to happen.

He spoke into his circuits. "Yes, General?"

"We found my youngest son, exactly where you said he would be."

Feteror waited.

"Find my wife and other son," Rurik ordered.

"I will."

The door opened and Feteror was free. As he raced out the window into the virtual plane, he realized that if all went well, this would be the last time.

"We can't beat Chyort in the virtual plane." Dalton's voice was firm.

"That makes Psychic Warrior worthless." Hammond was shaking her head. "The whole purpose of this program was–"

Dalton slapped his hand in the tabletop. "Look in the chambers. My people and yours are just empty shells, and the essence of those people is dead!"

Dalton watched the doctor with no sympathy. Her little world, her pet project, had fallen apart and failed. A black mark on her efficiency report. Dalton was more concerned with the bodies in the tanks and the twenty nuclear weapons heading toward the phased-displacement generator. And Chyort.

"As I said, I've already been in contact with the National Security Council," Hammond said. "They're using a satellite to search for the phased-displacement generator and to track down the nukes. They are also opening contact with the Russian government to offer support."

"It won't be that easy," Dalton said. "Things are as screwed up on their end as they are on ours. The clock is ticking and by the time the official world reacts, it will be too late."

"They'll contact us as soon as they discover anything," Hammond said.

Dalton stood. "Find where Raisor went. And where he is now." He walked out without another word. He went to the dispensary and looked in on Barnes. The sergeant was sleeping, his body wrapped in blankets.

Dalton looked down at the younger man. He reached up and unpinned his own sergeant major's insignia from his collar and put it on the small stand to the left of the bed. Then Dalton pulled his wedding band off his ring finger. He looked at the inscription on the inside for several seconds, then placed it next to the rank.

Dalton left the dispensary and went to the main chamber and up to the closest isolation tank. Captain Anderson's body floated listlessly inside. The breathing fluid was moving slowly through the clear tubes, and the monitor said that the machine was keeping his heart going. But staring at the body inside the tube, the head covered with the TACPAD, Dalton felt little hope. Even if their psyches were recoverable, he knew that Chyort still waited on the virtual plane, ready to stop him from succeeding in any attempt to recover them.

Dalton stood for a long time, staring and thinking.

"I have a question." The voice startled Dalton out of his morbid reverie.

Lieutenant Jackson had come up behind him unheard and unnoticed. She looked past him at Captain Anderson's body.

"What's your question?" Dalton asked.

"The story you told me—about the pilot who was brought in wounded while you were a POW and how you stayed up with him all night?"

"Yes?"

"What happened to him?"

Dalton sighed. "He died within a month. He just gave up."

"But *you* didn't, right?"

"No, I didn't."

"Don't give up now, Sergeant Major. We need you."

Feteror popped into the GRU main conference room and maintained a silent presence for ten minutes. More than enough time to know that the Americans were now putting their cards on the table and talking to his government through the GRU, preparing a conventional response to the bombs' being stolen.

Feteror had not expected such a quick reaction, but he also had not expected the assault at the ambush site by the Bright Gate personnel. He saw the Spetsnatz colonel sitting quietly at the conference table, listening to the various reports coming in.

Feteror came closer to the man. He knew him. Years

ago, in Afghanistan. Then it had been Captain Mishenka, a ruthless and efficient leader of an elite hunter killer team. A fool to still be sitting here serving a new government when the old one had betrayed his fight in Afghanistan.

Despite Mishenka's presence, Feteror's own government acting alone did not worry him. By the time they discovered where the phased-displacement generator was, it would be too late. And the only way they would find the stolen nuclear weapons was when they exploded at their targets.

But the Americans—that was another story. They had capabilities that could pose a threat either acting on their own or helping the GRU. Feteror slid along the virtual plane, out of the room.

Inside the conference room, Colonel Mishenka shivered, looking up at the ceiling. He'd felt a cold draft down to the very marrow of his bones for just a second. His eyes narrowed, the deep lines etched at the sides indicating the years he had spent fighting in the brutal elements.

The chill was gone. He returned his focus to the briefer at the front of the room.

In orbit, 285 statute miles above the surface of the earth, thrusters on *Warfighter 1* fired, maneuvering the 850-pound satellite toward the target grid area. On board, doors slid open, revealing the hyperspectral imaging equipment bay. It was the most advanced spy satellite in the American inventory, launched just the previous year and capable of all-weather, all-condition viewing across a large number of frequency bands at extremely high resolution. Some of its imagers could even "see" through ceilings into bunkers and hangars by using certain bandlengths.

Just as important as the imaging equipment was the on-board computer that could be programmed to look over wide swaths of terrain for a specific image. The RHC3000, a 32-bit, 2-gigabyte, high-density mass-memory command and data handler, was currently being updated with information sent by the Russians regarding the makeup of the phased-displacement generator and with the exact composition of the twenty missing warheads.

It would be in position in six minutes to begin searching outward from the site of the ambush into central Russia.

Feteror had never gone this high–there had never been a need to and it had never occurred to him to try. As he passed out of the atmosphere, he wondered if he could travel far in space, or if his virtual link to Zivon and SD8-FFEU had a limit.

It was dark here in this netherworld, not the grayish white of the virtual plane closer to the planet. More a dim area, desolate, empty even of the whispering of the souls of those close to the surface. Feteror found it quite soothing.

He reached out through the virtual plane with his senses. He picked up the approach of *Warfighter 1* as it closed on the ambush site. He closed on the satellite. It was a spectacular piece of machinery. He noted the imagers pointing earthward out of the bay, the small maneuvering thrusters firing slight puffs, orienting the vehicle.

Feteror slid his being into the satellite. He became part of it, using its imagers as his own senses. He looked down at the earth, able to see the curving horizon of the planet in all directions. It was so spectacular that he almost forgot his task, but not quite.

He processed a picture through the main camera. Then he accessed the thruster control program.

"Sergeant Major."

Dalton heard the resignation in Hammond's voice before he turned and saw the defeat etched across her face.

"Yes?"

Hammond wordlessly held up a glossy piece of paper.

Dalton took it, Lieutenant Jackson looking over his shoulder. The demon's face was etched against a black background, as horrible as Dalton remembered it.

"Chyort," Dalton said, handing the imagery back. Jackson was nodding, also recognizing their foe from the ambush.

Hammond spoke in a monotone. "He took out the satellite the NSA was sending over to find the generator and the nukes."

"Took out," Dalton repeated. "How did he do that?"

"They don't know, but they have no communication with it and the tracking station can't even pick it up in orbit. It's gone. The Russians"—Hammond's voice betrayed her admiration in the face of the disaster—"they must have done something completely different than us to come up with this thing, this Chyort."

Dalton considered the photo. "He wanted us to know he did it. There's no other reason for him to allow his image to be processed."

"Any more information on who or what Chyort is?" Lieutenant Jackson asked.

"I'm working on getting that information, but my best guess is that he's the end result of their version of the Psychic Warrior program."

Jackson gave a derisive laugh. "They've got something going that we don't have a clue about. It's far beyond what we're doing here."

Dalton shook his head. "We don't have time for this." He pointed at the imagery. "Allowing himself to be photographed like that means he's confident that he can accomplish what he wants to and he's not worried about us stopping him." He turned to Hammond, who was still staring at the picture. "I want communication with the National Security Council."

Hammond nodded. "We have a direct link in the control room."

"How can we stop them?" Jackson asked while they walked to the control room.

"I'm an old soldier," Dalton said, "so I say we do it the old-fashioned way. With some new-fashioned help."

Chapter Twenty-three

Feteror's roar vibrated the metal in the hangar. "How can you not be ready! You have the program!"

Vasilev watched the demon pace about. "I have done my best. I am trying to update the language of the program to work on these new computers, but I am not a computer expert."

A claw flashed out, stopping just short of Vasilev's neck. The old man didn't even flinch.

"I thought the program had already been updated when it was switched to the CD-ROM."

"Somewhat, yes," Vasilev agreed. "But that was three years ago and already computers have advanced beyond that."

"How long will it take?"

"Anywhere from a couple of hours to a couple of days."

"We do not have a couple of days."

"Whether you have the time or not makes no difference in how long updating the programming will take," Vasilev said. "There is also the additional problem of, once the base programming is running, having it synched with a psychic projection. We need a way to target the warhead once it is on the virtual plane." He spread his hands. "I don't see that part of the system here."

"*I'm* that part of the system," Feteror said. "You get it working. I'll take care of the rest."

"I will try."

Feteror shook his wings, sending a breeze through the hangar. "Try is not good enough. The problem is the computer? I will take care of it."

He slid out of the real plane and flowed into the computer Vasilev had been working at. He raced along the electronic pathways. There was much he understood here from his time inside Zivon.

He came to the place where Vasilev had been working. To his virtual eyes, there was a logjam of data, the pieces not fitting, turned the wrong way.

He worked like a madman, twisting the data to fit, putting the pieces in place. He cleared up what he could see, then reversed his path out of the computer, re-forming into the real world in front of the old man.

"Get back to work," Feteror snarled. "It should take you less time now."

Feteror's head twisted on his gnarled shoulders as the sound of inbound helicopters made its way through the metal siding of the hangar. Feteror flashed outside and watched as Leksi's two helicopters landed and the bombs were off-loaded.

All was in place, but they could not act until the advanced computer could process the old program. Feteror would have found it humorous except for the stakes involved.

"Is everyone clear on what they have to do?" Sergeant Major Dalton was dressed in the camouflage fatigues he had worn to Bright Gate. He was striding down the corridor that led to the hangar. Lieutenant Jackson and Dr. Hammond were having to run to keep up with him.

"Clear," Jackson said.

Hammond reluctantly nodded.

Dalton glanced at Jackson. "You remember what you have to do, right?"

She nodded.

"And?" Dalton prompted.

"We don't do anything until you clear the way," Jackson said.

"Roger that." Dalton continued walking. "But the minute I take care of Chyort, you have to move quickly." He glanced at Hammond. "Is everything set to get this started?"

"They're still trying to get through to the Russians."

"What about my ride?"

"It will meet you at DIA." Hammond looked troubled. "This is going to cause a hell of a stink."

"The stink has already started," Dalton said. "Let's hope we can keep it at that level. One of those nukes goes off somewhere and everything you're worrying about right now will be insignificant. Any idea where Raisor went?"

"I've had Sybyl scan but no sign."

A technician came running down the hallway. She held a small metal case in her hand. "Here's the SATCOM link you asked for."

Dalton took it. He walked through the door into the hangar. The blades were already turning on the Blackhawk, and the side door was open.

"Good luck!" Jackson said.

"Don't go over until it's clear," Dalton warned her one last time.

"I won't."

Dalton climbed on board the chopper. As he slid the door shut, the platform began sliding out of the side of the mountain. The last thing he saw as they lifted off was Lieutenant Jackson watching him fly away.

———

Oma stared at her computer screen. Two deposits of four hundred million were sitting side by side in their separate accounts. Her husband had always told her to have her options open, to never play her hand until the last minute.

She leaned back in her chair and looked at the clock. There was still time to play this just right.

Chapter Twenty-four

Sergeant Major Dalton woke as the Blackhawk settled down onto the grass next to the concrete runway at Denver International Airport. Several phone calls from the National Security Council had shut down one of the runways twenty minutes ago. Police cars, lights flashing, were parked near the end of the runway.

"Your ride is about two minutes out," the pilot informed Dalton through the headset.

Dalton opened the side door and stepped off the chopper, carrying the com link. He could see the white-capped peaks of the Rocky Mountains to the west. The airport itself was surrounded by miles of open rolling plain. The white peaks of the uniquely designed terminal were about two miles away, but Dalton had no intention of going there.

He scanned the sky and was rewarded when he spotted a small dot rapidly approaching from over the mountains. It closed swiftly, the shape not that of a normal plane, but more a solid V-form without wings.

As it got closer and slowed on its approach, Dalton could make out details. It was over 250 feet long and a hundred feet from tip to tip at the widest part. The best Dalton could describe the aircraft was that it was shaped like a stretched-out B-2 bomber.

Nose up, it came down toward the far end of the runway from Dalton. He knew that many in the terminal and waiting planes were getting the first public glimpse of one of the most classified projects in the Black Budget, but apparently the decision makers on the National Security Council felt that was a small price to pay for the mission he had to accomplish. Besides, a toy manufacturer had already designed and was selling a model that looked very similar to what was landing; they even had the name right: the SR-75 Penetrator, developed under the project code name Aurora.

The wheels touched down and the plane decelerated. Dalton could see smoke coming from the tires as they tried to halt the forward momentum. He knew about the plane from classified briefings he had attended while assigned to a top secret antiterrorist task force. At its home base at Groom Lake in Nevada, near Nellis Air Force Base and the infamous Area 51, the plane used a runway–the longest runway in the world–over seven miles long to take off and land. It was straining to stop even on DIA's longest main runway.

But the pilots accomplished the task, slowing to a roll about five hundred yards from Dalton's location, then bringing the plane toward him. The skin of the craft was a dull black, the small windows in the front hard to spot. The design lines were smooth and sleek.

The plane halted and a hatch opened in the belly between the two large sets of landing gear. Dalton started forward as a ladder extended down. He grabbed the bottom rung and climbed on board.

The man who greeted him was wearing a high-pressure suit, the mask on his helmet swung open. "I'm Major Orrick, recon officer. I don't know who the hell you are, but you sure got some pull to get us out in public like this."

Dalton shook the man's hand, introducing himself. They were standing in a small space, another ladder leading out of it. Orrick pulled the bottom ladder in and sealed the hatch. He pointed up. "Follow me."

Dalton climbed behind him into a room crowded with

electrical gear and computer screens. There was barely
room for both of them to fit.

"This is my area," Orrick said. He handed Dalton a
pressure suit and helmet. "One size fits all when the size is
extra large." He jerked a thumb toward a four-foot-high
opening in the front of the compartment. "Cockpit is that
way. Better get that on and get up there. The pilot would
really like to know what he's doing and where we're going."

The entire plane was vibrating from the engines. Dalton
could feel the small movements indicating it was taxiing. He
quickly stepped into the pressure suit and pulled it up. He
crouched down and made his way down the tight corridor.
There were dim red lamps lighting it and the glow of daylight about twenty-five feet ahead. He poked his head out
the corridor.

The pilot and copilot were strapped tightly into their
form-fitting crash seats, half reclining back, the seats canted
up so they could see out the four small windows. The rest
of the front was taken up with instrumentation.

The man in the right seat turned his head slightly, seeing movement out of the corner of his eye.

"You Dalton?"

"Yes."

"I'm Colonel Searl. World War III starting or something?"

"It could," Dalton said.

Both men twisted in their seats to get a better look.
"What the hell does that mean?" Searl said.

The SR-75 was pointing down the main runway, holding. "Maybe we ought to get airborne, then I'll fill you in."

"Where are we going?" Colonel Searl asked.

"That's something else I've got to find out once we get
airborne. All I can tell you right now is, we're heading for
someplace in Russia." He held up the case holding the

SATCOM. "I need to hook into your commo system to find out exactly where we're going."

Searl returned his attention to the front. "You better get back there and settled in. We'll be airborne in less than a minute. We'll head for the polar route; it's the quickest way to Russia, but you need to give us a more specific location pretty quick because Russia is a damn big country."

Dalton returned down the corridor to the recon officer's space. Orrick had folded down a small seat, and he helped Dalton settle onto it, buckling him into it just as the plane began moving.

Colonel Searl rolled up the throttle on the plane's conventional turbojet engine, and the large plane began accelerating down the runway. It took the plane over two and a half miles, just about to the end of the runway, before the delta wings produced enough lift for the wheels to separate from the ground.

With the turbojet engine at max thrust, the pilot continued to gain altitude and speed. Dalton was slammed back into the seat, the straps holding him cutting into his suit. He could feel the strong vibration of the engines.

"We're passing through Mach 2 now," Orrick informed Dalton. "We're already over the Colorado-Wyoming border."

It had been less than five minutes since takeoff. Dalton opened up the SATCOM and tossed one end of the cable to Orrick.

"We're going high," Orrick continued as he plugged in the cable. He looked down at his console. "We're passing through fifty thousand feet. When we get close to sixty thousand, the pilots switch over to the PDWE. Pulsed-detonation-wave engine," he clarified. "It's pretty simple—we've got a bunch of high-strength compression chambers in the back. We pump a special mixture into them, they explode in sequence, forming a high-pressure pulse, and they are guided into a combustion chamber which channels it out the rear."

Dalton checked the small board on the SATCOM. It was functioning and he had a link back to Bright Gate. "How fast can you go?" he asked. That was something that had been left out of the briefing he had been given on the plane, the aircraft's top speed simply listed as being something over Mach 5.

"Mach 7," Orrick said proudly. "Over five thousand miles an hour."

Dalton hoped that would be fast enough. He put the small headset on. "Dr. Hammond?"

"Here."

"Do you have the link into the Russian secure military network?"

"Yes. The GRU just authorized it."

"Lieutenant Jackson there?"

"Right here."

"You got a cell phone number when we went to Moscow. For a Colonel Mishenka."

"I have it," Jackson said.

"Can you punch it up?"

"Wait," she said.

There was a hiss of static, then Dalton heard a buzz. A voice answered in Russian.

"Do you speak English?" Dalton asked.

"Who is this?"

"Is this Colonel Mishenka?"

"You called me. You know who I am," Mishenka said. "I want to know who you are. This is a classified Spetsnatz line."

"My name is Sergeant Major Dalton, U.S. Army Special Forces."

There was just the sound of the static for a few seconds.

"Very interesting," Mishenka said. "People here are talking to the Americans. Most worried. Quite a bit of excitement. To what do I owe the honor of your call, Sergeant Major?"

"I believe we have a common problem," Dalton said.

"We do?"

"Twenty nuclear warheads," Dalton said succinctly. He saw Orrick's head snap up across the small compartment.

"I'm not—" Mishenka began, but Dalton cut him off.

"I don't have time to argue or play games. I am heading toward Russia right now."

"We do not need your help," Mishenka said. "The situation is under control."

"No, it isn't. I also know about the phased-displacement generator. You don't have a handle on either the bombs or the generator, do you?"

Dalton felt the plane seem to stutter, then he was slammed back in his seat once more.

"P-D-W-E," Orrick mouthed the letters to Dalton with a thumbs-up.

Dalton nodded.

"Sergeant Major, you are speaking about things which—"

"Don't lie to me or waste my time," Dalton snapped. "This is *our* problem. And it's worse than you know."

"The official word here is that we do not need your help," Colonel Mishenka said. "This is an internal problem that will be dealt with using our own resources."

"The phased-displacement generator makes it our problem," Dalton said. "And if you are counting on SD8's secret weapon to find the bombs or the generator, you are very badly mistaken."

The tone of Mishenka's voice changed. "Why?"

"Because someone in SD8 is helping the Mafia."

"How do you know all this?"

"Because I was there when the bombs got stolen," Dalton said. "My team was wiped out and I barely escaped."

"How could you have been there? How do you know all this? We are getting very confused reports from those who have gone to the train site."

"Listen closely," Dalton said. He quickly told Mishenka about the Bright Gate program, witnessing the briefing inside KGB headquarters, and the battle at the train ambush. He ended with his belief that Chyort was a creation of SD8 and was helping the Mafia.

"Chyort," Mishenka repeated the name. "I have heard of this creature. I thought it only a rumor, a myth."

"Chyort is real," Dalton said. "And you know what it is. I heard General Bolodenka authorize you to be briefed on Department Eight's current operation. It has to be Chyort. And if it is on the other side, any action you take will be thwarted by it. Chyort just took out our *Warfighter I* satellite that was trying to track down the generator and the bombs."

"How could this creature do that?"

"I don't exactly know, but you should be getting a fax into the GRU war room any second now. It shows Chyort just before he destroyed *Warfighter*. He wanted us to know it was him."

"Wait a second."

Dalton impatiently listened to the hiss.

"Your fax arrived a few seconds ago. What is this thing?" Mishenka asked. "I have never seen anything like it."

"A monster your people created and now it's turned against you."

"What is your plan?" Mishenka asked.

"Do you have communications with SD8?"

"I'm not sure."

"We have to take out SD8; it is from that base that

Chyort is able to work. We have to destroy its ability to project onto the virtual plane."

"How do you propose to do that?"

"We must attack it at the source. Do you know where that is?"

"Yes."

"Send me the coordinates. I'll head straight there. Then call whoever you have there and get them to stop this thing."

"I'm having the coordinates of the base sent to you. I will be heading that way myself shortly. I will try to make contact with Department Eight."

The screen flashed with numbers. "Major Orrick!" Dalton called out.

"Yes."

"Here's our target area." Dalton read off the numbers.

"I have partial system running," Vasilev said.

"What does that mean?" Feteror growled.

"We can try a test run," Vasilev said.

The phased-displacement generator gleamed inside of the hangar, reflecting the glow of the lights set up around it. Leksi had put all the helicopters under cover of the other old hangars. He'd deployed his men in an efficient perimeter, antiair and antitank missiles ringing the airfield. Feteror knew without the help of the Americans, the GRU would never find them in time.

He was also aware, though, that once he started drawing power from the lines, someone at the closest monitoring plant would notice. He was tired of having to worry about all these potential problems. He had spent years considering all the possibilities, and his plan would take care of that problem.

For a moment, he considered running the test against SD8. That would bring it to a conclusion. But his anger forestalled that. There were many who must pay first. He had been trained always to stick with the plan, and he would do so here.

"Load the generator," Feteror ordered.

"We must wait until we hear from Oma," Barsk protested.

"We must test the generator," Feteror said. He smiled, noting that Leksi was moving behind the boy, weapon at the ready. As if that could achieve anything.

"I need to call Oma before you do anything," Barsk said.

"Oma and I are partners." Feteror resisted the urge to just take the man-child's head off. He needed these people for a while longer. Instead, he pointed a long claw at the generator. "Do not worry. I plan to run the test in a manner designed to gain us some time. Your Oma would approve."

"I must call Oma." Barsk was sounding like an irritating tape, playing over and over.

"Call her then!" Feteror snapped. "In the meanwhile, load the first warhead in the generator. We do not have forever. If I know her well, and I believe I do, your Oma will want to know it works before committing to a course of action."

Leksi looked to Barsk, who reluctantly nodded. Leksi snapped orders and his men uncrated one warhead.

"What do I have to do, old man?" Feteror leaned close to Vasilev.

"The computer will integrate the physical material inside the generator into the virtual plane. Your job will be to target it. The computer will then fire it across the folded space and into the real. The bomb will be on a timer which I will activate prior to its leaving the generator."

"That will not be a problem," Feteror said.

"Where will you be sending the warhead?" Barsk asked.

"Do not concern yourself," Feteror said.

He noted that Barsk had his cell phone out. Feteror

slipped into the virtual plane for a moment and reached out to the phone.

Colonel Mishenka climbed on board the helicopter waiting on the roof of GRU headquarters, his mind racing with what he had just learned. In the distance he could see the few skyscrapers that dotted the Moscow skyline. The fools below him were still scrambling, searching desperately for the bombs and the phased-displacement generator. They couldn't accept that someone in SD8 was involved.

They had tried to call General Rurik, the commander, but the base was shut down to all outside communications and had missed its last contact. That in itself had Mishenka convinced that what the American Green Beret had told him was true—someone in Department Eight had gone over to the other side. And Mishenka had a very a good idea who that person was—he had been truly startled and shocked to learn the identity of the man behind Chyort: Major Arkady Feteror.

Mishenka remembered Feteror from Afghanistan. A brilliant and ruthless warrior. A man who took only the hardest missions. But Feteror was supposed to have died. Mishenka remembered hearing that they had found the major's body in a village, torn to pieces. What had these GRU people done to him?

There wasn't the slightest doubt in Mishenka's mind that Feteror was behind all this trouble, the last report on General Rurik's son being found notwithstanding. Feteror would use a boy like a pawn with not the slightest twinge of conscience. The Feteror that Mishenka remembered would gut a child as easily as another man would give a piece of candy. A most formidable foe.

The helicopter shuddered and headed toward the air-field where a jet was waiting. Mishenka hoped only one thing—that this American Special Forces man who was coming was up to facing down Feteror or the psychic cyborg—the term the briefer had used—that Feteror had been made into—and had a plan to stop this madness.

"We're two hours out from the grid you gave us," Major Orrick said. He pointed on a chart. "It's here."

Dalton nodded. He spoke into the boom mike. "Jackson?"

"Yes?"

"Any change?"

"Nothing has occurred."

"Raisor?"

"Nothing there either."

"Notify me if anything happens."

"I will." There was a pause. "I'm sorry."

Dalton leaned back in the seat, closing his eyes in weariness. "What for this time?"

"For the men of your team."

"Let's just do this right."

"I've been looking over the information Sybyl gathered from the battle. I think we've learned some things about this Chyort."

Dalton opened his eyes. "Like what?"

Hammond's voice came over the radio. "The Russian projection—the Chyort avatar—is different from what we are doing here."

"No shit," Dalton said. "How?"

"The interface is purer than what Sybyl can accomplish through Psychic Warrior. Our TACPAD is efficient, but ultimately there is a degradation in power and focus. Sybyl doesn't read that degradation in Chyort. The interface of human and machine seems to be almost perfect."

"How do you think they are able to do that?"

"I asked Sybyl that," Hammond said. "The computer thinks they have created a cyborg."

"Come again?"

"Chyort appears to be the result of a human brain being directly wired into a computer full-time."

"Can that be done?" Dalton asked.

"We could do it here"–Hammond almost sounded jealous–"except that the process would not be reversible and that would cross an ethical line we aren't even allowed to contemplate."

It all clicked for Dalton then, what Chyort was doing and why. "They've created their own Frankenstein and it's turned on them."

"Warhead loaded and armed," Leksi said.

"Setting?" Feteror asked.

"Two kiloton as directed. Ten-second delay from phase displacement."

Enough to cause absolute devastation in an area about three kilometers wide and collateral damage for five times that distance. More importantly, the EMP–electromagnetic pulse–emitted by the explosion would fry every electric device within fifty kilometers.

Feteror turned, claws grating on the concrete floor. "The program?"

Vasilev's face looked even more haggard in the dim glow of the computer screen. "In phase. Ready to phase bomb into virtual."

"Power," Feteror ordered.

One of Leksi's men threw a switch. The entire hangar hummed as the power lines going into the phased-displacement generator fed it the energy it needed.

Barsk edged closer to Vasilev. "You are sure this will work?" He had given up trying to dial out to reach Oma. The phone wasn't working.

"I am sure of nothing except that I will die shortly," Vasilev said, "and this will all finally be over."

Feteror was preoccupied. "A speedy and painless death is what you are working for."

Vasilev shook his head. "No. That is not why I am doing this. I am working for atonement. To pay for what I have done. To pay for trying to play God."

Feteror focused his red eyes on the gleaming metal tube. The warhead rested in the top chamber. There was no vent here. If the warhead failed to project and detonated–well, there would not be much left for the authorities to find.

Feteror lifted a large, scaly arm. He began to slide over the line into the virtual plane. He stretched his self out, toward the generator. He could sense the bomb inside, flickering on the edge of the virtual plane also. He dropped his arm and snapped entirely into the virtual plane at the same moment as Vasilev hit the final control to send the bomb over.

The bomb was there, totally in the virtual plane. He could see the red digital clock counting down on the control face of the timer Leksi's armament man had attached. Ten seconds.

Vasilev knew where he wanted the bomb to go, and he had planned the path many times. There were two jumps. He focused on the bomb and the first jump point. The bomb disappeared. The timer was frozen in the virtual plane and Feteror knew it would only start once he deposited it on target and it passed through to the real.

Feteror raced northwest, following the bomb's path. He jumped, saw the bomb, projected the second and final jump point, and the bomb was gone.

Feteror jumped again. He was exactly where he wanted to be. The bomb appeared right in front of him in the virtual plane. He reached out and wrapped his claws around it. He moved in three smaller jumps to the exact position, high over a tall roof with the X of a helipad directly below.

The target. The bomb slid through the wall between the virtual and real. The timer clicked to nine.

Feteror jumped twenty kilometers away to the south. He slid into the real plane, hovering in the air a thousand feet above the ground, and looked back in the direction he had come from.

A tremendous flash lit up the early morning sky.

Feteror knew that in that second, GRU headquarters was nothing but a smoking hole in the earth: ground zero.

Colonel Mishenka was only twelve kilometers from the epicenter; the helicopter he was on was in final approach to land at the military airfield. He heard the startled yells of the pilots and caught the flash as it washed over the helicopter.

The fireball and shock wave were next, rolling out from ground zero. The pilots were shouting, stunned by the sudden loss of all electrical equipment on board the aircraft, flying by the seats of their pants, bringing the chopper down as quickly as they dared, seeing the wave of fire that was coming toward them.

Mishenka watched the approaching wave dispassionately through the Plexiglas window on the side of the cargo bay. It would either dissipate or kill them.

The chopper slammed into the edge of the runway, the shocks on the wheels absorbing only part of the impact. Mishenka was thrown against his seatbelt, which he rapidly unbuckled. He threw open the side door and stepped outside, facing directly into the wave.

But he already knew it was losing power. He'd seen films of nuclear blasts before, and this one wasn't big. Somewhere under five kilotons, his mind calculated. By the time the wave hit him, it was like a strong, warm wind.

Mishenka also knew with that wind was a very unhealthy dosage of strontium 90, cesium 137, iodine 131, and carbon 14, the makeup of a nuclear weapon's fallout having been drummed into him during the many training sessions he had gone through. He also knew that the pills in his antiradiation kit were placebos, designed to allow the soldier to keep fighting until he became incapacitated.

He looked at the runway. A Mig-1.42, the cutting edge of Russian aerospace technology, was waiting as he had ordered. It was shaped like a dart, with two large engines, each below a tall vertical tail. He could see the cockpit was open and the pilot was yelling at a ground crew man. Colonel Mishenka walked across the concrete runway to the plane.

The pilot looked down. "We cannot fly! No circuits. No radio. Nothing."

"Do the engines work?" Mishenka asked.

The pilot stared at him. "Yes, but–"

"If the engines work, you can fly, correct?"

"But I will have no instrumentation, Colonel!"

"Your compass works, correct?"

"My ball compass, yes, but my navigational computer is completely fried."

Mishenka held up his briefcase. "I have a map. We can fly low and navigate by watching the ground beneath us. I also have a shielded satellite phone in here, so we will have communications."

The pilot shook his head. "Flying low. It will be very dangerous, Colonel. Perhaps we should wait until–" He stopped as Mishenka laughed. "What is it?"

"Dangerous?" Mishenka spread his arms wide. "Did you see that nuclear explosion?"

"Yes."

"Don't you understand?" Mishenka didn't wait for an answer. "We are all dead if we stay here. It will just take a day or two. So I would much rather die flying into a mountain than wasting away." He pointed at the small packet on the man's right shoulder. "Have you taken your pill?"

The pilot was still struggling to understand the impact of what he had just been told. He could only shake his head.

"Take your pill," Mishenka said. "You'll feel better and you'll be all right as long as we get out of here in time."

The pilot ripped open the packet and pulled out the pill, gulping it down without the benefit of water. He grabbed the inset ladder and flipped it down. "Let's be on our way."

Chapter Twenty-five

Dalton received word of the nuclear explosion outside of Moscow as the SR-75 crossed the north pole. He leaned back, uncomfortable in the hard jump seat, and closed his eyes. Lieutenant Jackson was tapped into the secure intelligence network, and the extent of the devastation was still being assessed, but there was no doubt thousands were dead.

"Jackson?"

"Yes?"

"Where is GRU headquarters in relation to the blast site?"

"Seismic readers have fixed the epicenter," Jackson said. "GRU headquarters would roughly be right where they have triangulated the center of the blast."

"Try to get in contact with Colonel Mishenka."

"I have been trying to. There is no answer."

Dalton ran a hand across his forehead. "Great."

Oma listened to the sirens racing to the southwest. The mushroom cloud had loomed high in the sky for minutes after the explosion, then slowly dissipated. She had stared out her armored windows at it, before finally picking up the phone. She tried Barsk's cell phone but she got no reply. She called on the secure fax line, overriding the fax signal when it came on, until someone on the other end picked it up. She told the man to get her grandson.

"Barsk!" she yelled when he finally answered.

"Yes, Oma? I have been trying to get a hold of you, but my phone has not been working. I think—"

Oma cut him off. "What the hell have you done?"

"What are you talking about?"

"A nuclear weapon just exploded outside Moscow!"

There was no immediate answer.

"Did you use the generator? Did you fire a nuclear weapon?"

"It was Chyort, Oma. He said he had to take care of something. Test the weapon."

"You let him activate the generator?"

"Let him! How would I stop him?"

Oma realized the futility of the conversation. "Put Leksi on."

There was a short pause, then a gruff "Yes?"

"Do you have control of the situation?"

"No. Barsk is letting this monster run crazy."

Oma rubbed her forehead. "All right. Listen to me. I am sending you a target list by the secure fax. I want you to make sure Vasilev targets all the sites listed in order. Is that clear?"

"Clear."

"Put Barsk back on."

"Yes?" Her grandson's voice was petulant. Oma was tempted to simply hang up, but she knew she could not do that.

"Barsk, listen very carefully. I am sending a target list to Leksi. He will insure that it is carried out. I want you to leave there. Get as far away as possible as quickly as you can and meet me at my lake house."

"But, Oma!" Barsk protested. "This is my responsibility here. I am in charge. If you do not trust me to accomplish this, then what—"

"Shut up!" Oma yelled into the phone, silencing her grandson. "Do what I say or I wipe my hands of you."

"Yes, Oma."

She turned the phone off. Then she went to her desk and picked up the list Abd al-Bari had sent her. She went back to the fax and punched in the number for the fax in the hangar. When the tone screeched, she fed the target list in.

She watched as it disappeared into the machine, then reappeared in the feed tray. She took it back to her desk and sat down. She fed the list into the shredder.

Then she picked up the phone and punched in the number for the NATO representative.

Colonel Mishenka finally got the satellite radio working ten minutes after they were airborne. It took him another five minutes to punch through the jumbled calls of the Russian military reacting in shock to the nuclear detonation. The fact that since the breakup of the Soviet Union and the attempted coup against the President, the GRU had increased its stranglehold on the control of intelligence and the communications capability of the entire military, meant that destruction of GRU headquarters virtually decapitated the Russian military's ability to act.

Listening to the confused chatter, Mishenka was aware that there were many officers who were convinced the nuclear attack had been a surgical strike by the Americans—a prelude to an all-out attack. Missile forces were going on alert and the strategic bomber forces were opening their hangars and unlocking the vaults on nuclear weapons that had been mothballed years ago.

The old ways died hard, and the only ones—other than the President's office—who had known about SD8, Chyort, and the American cooperation in tracking down the twenty nuclear weapons, were all glowing ash in the Moscow countryside.

Mishenka punched in the number he had been given by the American. It was answered immediately.

"Dalton here."

"This is Colonel Mishenka."

"I was afraid you'd been caught in the explosion," Dalton said.

"The stakes have been raised," Mishenka said. "Not only has GRU headquarters been taken out, but SD8 is totally isolated now."

"Our enemy is very smart," Dalton said.

"I know who it is—or who it was—and he is indeed very smart. And ruthless."

"Taking out a couple of square miles of Moscow goes beyond ruthless."

"Let us hope that is the limit this goes to."

"What do you mean?" Dalton asked.

Mishenka quickly filled him in on the reaction of the Russian military.

"Goddamn," was Dalton's summation.

"We have to secure the nuclear weapons and this phased-displacement generator," Mishenka said. "Who knows where the next target will be."

"As I told you," Dalton said, "we have to destroy Chyort in order to be able to find and then get to the generator and bombs."

"What is your plan?"

"Are your men moving?"

"I have a company of Spetsnatz at the closest airfield to SD8. My time to that location is twenty-five minutes."

"I'm forty-five minutes out," Dalton said.

"I'll alert them that you're coming," Mishenka said. "And once we are there?"

"We go in and take the station out."

"Hell of a plan," Mishenka said. "I have the defense setup for the station and it will not be that easy."

"I didn't say it was going to be easy," Dalton said. "I said we were going to do it."

Mishenka smiled inside his oxygen mask. "Very good. I will see you shortly."

"As you now know, what I told you was true," Oma said.

"I grant that you have proved you have the nuclear warheads," Abd al-Bari said matter-of-factly, "but you have not proved your capability to put them anywhere. You could have driven that one in a truck to Moscow."

"I just want to insure that you will pay the balance," Oma said. "I am putting everything on the line."

"You do what we agreed, the balance will be there," Abd al-Bari said.

"Good." Oma put the phone down. She stood and looked about her office. She knew it was the last time she would be here. There was nothing in it she wanted. She had prepared long for this moment. She went to the door and walked out without a backward glance.

"Where is Barsk?" Feteror hissed at Leksi.

The navy commando shrugged. He could care less where the boy was.

"Let me see that," Feteror demanded.

Leksi stared at the demon for a few seconds before holding the fax out.

Feteror leaned over, blood-red eyes close to the writing. He laughed as he saw the targets, the sound causing those in the hangar to wince. "Beautiful! The beginning of the end for everyone."

He pointed a claw at the generator. "Load another warhead. We have some other business to take care of before we proceed with your master's list."

Chapter Twenty-six

Lieutenant Jackson and Dr. Hammond were alone in the control chamber–other than the bodies in the isolation tubes. Hammond was having Sybyl run through various projections about a possible connection to the lost psyches–if they still existed on the virtual plane. So far they had come up with nothing. She was also continuing the search for Raisor.

Jackson was monitoring communications between Sybyl and Sergeant Major Dalton while keeping an eye on the small television set to the side of the master control panel. CNN was broadcasting the first reports of the nuclear explosion outside of Moscow. Confusion seemed to be the common denominator in all the reports, with the source of the bomb being the most speculated-upon aspect.

"That's strange," Dr. Hammond suddenly said.

"What is?" Jackson asked.

"I'm picking up something through Sybyl. Something on the virtual–" She paused, staring at her readouts.

A loud screech ripped through the room, echoing off the walls, the sound piling on top of itself. Red warning lights flashed, pulsing, adding to the confusion. Jackson looked up in shock as in the center of the room, above the isolation tanks, a small black sphere appeared, the surface pulsating, glistening, straining to expand.

Hammond's panicked voice punched through the noise.

"The psychic wall has been breached. I'm reverting all power to interior containment."

"Oh my God!" Jackson whispered as she checked the infrared scanner. It showed a nuclear bomb hanging in the center of the room in the virtual plane. She looked up. A square inch of the top tip of the bomb appeared in the real plane. Then another inch.

Chapter Twenty-seven

"Sybyl's holding it, but I don't know how long she can keep it contained." Lieutenant Jackson's voice was on the edge of hysteria, but her training and discipline were holding. Dalton had heard radio calls like this before—from an A-Camp being overrun in Vietnam; from the trapped Delta Force soldiers in Mogadishu; from pilots shot down in the Gulf War calling for rescue as Iraqis closed in.

"But Sybyl *is* holding, right?"

"If she wasn't, we wouldn't be talking. The bomb must be on some sort of timer that is on hold until it clears into real space."

"Can you clear out of there?" Dalton asked.

Jackson gave a wild laugh. "To go out we'd have to shut down the psychic wall. If Sybyl turns off the wall, we'd be destroyed instantly. We're caught between two walls. The bomb is inside the outer wall, but Sybyl used the backup containment program to stop it before it came into the real plane inside. The psychic wall and the containment program work off the same system. Turn one off, you turn the other off."

Dalton looked at Major Orrick. *"How long?"* he mouthed.

Orrick flicked his ten fingers at Dalton. Ten minutes.

"How long can the wall hold?" Dalton asked.

"Dr. Hammond is putting every bit of power she can into the computer. But we have no idea. Every time Sybyl ups the containment, it seems like the other side ups too. Jesus, Sergeant Major, the damn nuke is just hanging there above our heads, slowly coming into reality. It's about a fifth in now. It comes all the way in, we're done for. I don't want to put any extra pressure on you or anything, Sergeant Major, but could you *hurry the hell up!*"

Feteror had put the bomb into Bright Gate without much trouble. The outer virtual wall had been relatively easy to pierce. But that damn computer had reacted with startling speed. The bomb had been caught in a virtual containment field.

He'd left the bomb there, operating off the program from the phased-displacement generator. It was going into the real world, much slower than Feteror would have liked, but it would get there eventually.

"Two minutes out," Colonel Searl announced over the intercom. "Slowing to recon speed."

"Extending surveillance pod," Major Orrick said. He looked up at Dalton. "We have to slow down or else we'd rip the surveillance pod right off. We're down to about two thousand miles an hour right now." He leaned forward and placed his eyes into a set of eyepieces that had cycled up from the console. "We'll get a good shot across the spectrum. Someone's farting down there, we'll pick it up."

Dalton waited. He looked down, noted that his left foot was tapping impatiently against the wall of the recon room and forced it to stop.

"Missile launch." Orrick mentioned it as if he were saying the sun had come up in the morning.

"We're tracking red," Colonel Searl acknowledged.

Orrick hit a button. "Pod in. Clear to boogie." He smiled at Dalton as they were both slammed back in the seat. "We're faster than any missile made."

"Tracking green," Searl announced. "We're all clear. Entering approach to destination airfield." He laughed. "Damn Russkies are gonna be surprised to see this baby land."

Dalton clicked on the SATCOM link. "Jackson?"

There was no reply.

"Jackson, I don't want to take anything from what you're doing, but if you can answer me, let me know."

"I can talk," Jackson said.

"How's the wall holding?" Dalton asked.

"It's a losing battle. The bomb is sliding from virtual to real at the rate of three percent per minute. At this rate, it will completely be in the real plane in twenty-two more minutes."

Chapter Twenty-eight

"Sergeant Major." Colonel Mishenka snapped a salute, which Dalton automatically returned.

"Colonel Mishenka."

Mishenka unrolled a blueprint and put it on the hood of the four-by-four he'd driven out to the SR-75's taxi point. "This is Special Department Number Eight's Far-Field Experimental Unit." His finger touched several points. "Surface-to-air missiles that fire automatically if the airspace is encroached upon."

"We already had one of those fired at us as we came in." Dalton put the imagery the SR-75 had taken next to the blueprint. He checked his watch: twenty minutes.

Mishenka looked over the photos, then back at his blueprint. "Automatic guns cover the entire perimeter using heat sensors. Anything registering over a certain size is fired on. I understand many a deer has lost its life there. The perimeter is also mined; the mines are pressure activated. The only map of the minefield is kept in the facility, so we are going to have to breach it.

"Everything is controlled by the master computer inside SD8. And General Rurik, even if we could get through to him, can't turn it off as long as Feteror–Chyort–is out of his cage."

"So we have to get in."

Mishenka pointed across the runway. Two heavy cargo planes waited. They were surrounded by a large number of men in camouflage fatigues preparing weapons and gear. "The Twenty-third Spetsnatz company is ready. We're only a couple of minutes from SD8 by air." He waved and several officers came over and gathered around the hood. Dalton noted in them the same hard, competent look he had seen in Special Operations soldiers the world over.

"How do we get in?" Dalton asked.

Mishenka frowned. "There is a bigger problem than the automatic defenses."

"What is that?" Every nerve of Dalton's body was screaming for them to load the planes and get going, but he knew a couple of minutes spent planning was more important than rushing in with guns blazing.

"Just before I left Moscow, I was fully briefed on SD8's base. Two things struck me—one good, one not so good. The not so good thing is that there is a wall—a psychic wall—completely surrounding the facility. I saw a videotape of a prisoner who was forced to walk into the wall." Mishenka tapped a finger against his skull. "His brain was destroyed."

Dalton nodded. "Bright Gate, where I came from, has a similar wall around it."

"Do you know of a way to get through it?"

"I will check with my base once we're airborne. What was the good thing?"

"General Rurik did not trust Feteror. Because of that, the general wears a wristband that monitors his own heartbeat. If his heartbeat ceases for ten seconds, the wristband shuts down the central computer, Zivon, which shuts down Feteror, trapping him inside the cyborg machine that keeps him alive."

"So we get to General Rurik—" Dalton began.

"And stop his heartbeat—which means kill him—we stop Feteror," Mishenka finished.

Lieutenant Jackson remained in the chamber where the bomb hung over the isolation tanks. It had materialized over 40 percent. As she watched, another small piece flickered into reality.

"Dr. Hammond?" Dalton's voice cut through the air.

"Yes?" Hammond answered.

"How do I get through a psychic wall?"

Hammond gave a bitter laugh. "You don't. Not if you want to keep your brain from becoming mush."

"I've got to get through the wall here or we can't stop this thing."

Jackson watched the bomb produce another square, but listened as Hammond thought out loud to Dalton. "The wall is an electromagnetic projection on the psychic plane. Think of it as a field of deadly electricity. You touch it, you're zapped."

Jackson could hear the sound of turboprop engines in the background coming from Dalton's end.

"How do I get through it, Doctor?" Dalton's voice was insistent. "Wear rubber-soled shoes? Wrap tinfoil around my head? Think! There's got to be a way."

"There's so much we don't know!" Hammond protested. "We aren't even really sure if our wall works or not!"

"Well, the Russian one does, that's for damn sure," Dalton said.

"Jesus Christ!" Jackson exploded, pushing Hammond aside and typing into the keyboard. The answer was back in a second.

"Sybyl says there aren't any options," Jackson relayed.

"Not good enough," Dalton's voice echoed out of the speaker. "There's got to be a way."

"Here." Hammond regained the keyboard and typed. She stared at the results. "I've had Sybyl run a multitude of possibilities and probabilities. Your best chance of success is that you might be able to short it out for a very brief period of time."

"How do I do that?" Dalton asked.

Hammond closed her eyes and thought for a few seconds. "You would have to put a conductor in the field. It would draw power for an instant before the field snapped back to normal operating parameters. For the short period while the field focused on that conductor, most likely less than a second, you might be able to get through close by."

"What would be a conductor?"

"There is only one conductor that works for a psychic field," Hammond said. "The human brain."

Oma's cell phone rang for the third time in five minutes. Reluctantly she opened it.

"Yes?"

"I said every warhead had to be accounted for," the NATO representative hissed at her.

"Every warhead is accounted for," Oma said. "You know for certain where one is—or was—and I can tell you where the other nineteen are."

"Don't be a fool. Detonating one doesn't count."

"It took out GRU headquarters, you should be grateful."

"Grateful? Grateful? Every country that has nuclear weapons is in DEFCON Four alert status. There's a lot of itchy fingers out there and you've put them over the button."

"Do you want the location of the rest of the warheads or not?" Oma pressed. "The one that just went off proves we have the warheads and we have the means and the will to use them."

"Give me the location."

"If I give it to you, you must promise that you will not pursue me."

The man laughed. "Fine. We won't. But I'm sure your countrymen will be after you until the day you die."

"Perhaps," Oma said. "Here are the coordinates of the remaining weapons and the phased-displacement generator."

"What will happen to the bomb here if Sergeant Major Dalton does succeed?" Jackson asked Hammond.

"I do not know," Hammond answered.

"Best guess," Jackson pressed.

"It will explode right where it is, some of it into the real plane at approximately the percentage it is in your world when it detonates."

Jackson looked at the half of a bomb that hung in the air. "So we're dead no matter who wins."

There was no reply from Hammond, nor had she expected one.

Jackson nodded to herself. "All right then. There's only one thing to do." She tapped Dr. Hammond on the shoulder. "Get my isolation tank ready. I'm going over."

"What are you going to do?" Hammond asked.

Jackson pointed at the bomb. "The only thing I can do. Defuse that thing."

Colonel Mishenka leaned close to Dalton in order to be able to hear inside the noisy cargo bay of the AN-24 transport. Dalton relayed Hammond's course of action.

"Short-circuit the field with a brain?" Mishenka asked.

Dalton nodded.

Mishenka laughed. "That is great. Simply great. You Americans have such a great sense of humor."

"It's not–" Dalton began, but he paused as Mishenka put a hand on his arm.

"I know it is not a joke, but it is the Russian way to laugh when things are the worst. It is how we have survived much misery. Besides, before we worry about the psychic wall, first we have to get to it. We will deal with the psychic wall if we live long enough to get there."

"What is your plan?" Dalton shouted. The Spetsnatz men were rigging parachutes on each other as the plane banked.

Mishenka pointed at the map. "We will parachute in the only place we can—here in this open field. Then work our way up the hill and then in. Not much of a plan, but it is the best I can do with such little notice."

He stood and grabbed a parachute off the web cargo seat and held it out to Dalton. The sergeant major took it and slipped it over his shoulders. There were AK-74 folding-stock automatic weapons, and Mishenka indicated for him to take one, along with ammunition, grenades, a demolitions pack, and other weaponry.

Dalton checked his watch. Sixteen minutes.

Chapter Twenty-nine

Feteror formed himself in the real plane inside the hangar. He looked about. Leksi and his men waited by the generator with eighteen plastic cases holding nuclear weapons lined up. Vasilev was at the computer console. Barsk was gone.

That last fact started to truly register on Feteror. Why would Oma's grandson have left? He knew the answer as soon as he considered it: She was double-crossing him. He laughed, the sound startling everyone in the hangar. She was double-crossing everyone.

But it did not matter. His revenge had begun. He only needed to complete it.

He was adapting, changing. The link back to Zivon was as strong as ever, and the computer was helping deal with this unusual situation with regard to the phased-displacement generator and the bombs. What else could he accomplish? Feteror wondered. Might he be able to actually direct more bombs while the one still was out there, not detonated? He saw no reason why not.

"Load the generator," Feteror ordered.

The back ramp of the Antonov AN-24 was down, the wind swirling in the back, adding to the roar of the engines.

"One minute!" Colonel Mishenka yelled to Dalton and the Spetsnatz men lined up behind him. The Colonel knelt down, grabbing the hydraulic arm that lowered the ramp on his side.

Dalton went to the other side and assumed a similar position. He looked forward, blinking in the 130-knot wind that blew in his face.

The peak that held SD8 base was directly ahead. As he watched, there was a flash and a line of smoke streaked up into the sky.

"Missile launch!" one of the crewmen yelled. The man was seated on the center edge of the back ramp, a monkey harness around his body hooked to a floor bolt keeping him attached to the plane. He pointed a flare gun out the back and fired in the direction of the oncoming missile.

He continued firing as quickly as he could reload. It wasn't high-tech, but it worked. At least for the first two missiles launched at the lead plane as the infrared seekers in their nose went after the hot flares.

"Stand by!" Mishenka yelled.

Dalton stood and shuffled closer to the edge of the platform.

"Go!" Mishenka stepped off on his side, Dalton on his.

Dalton tucked into a tight body position as his static line was pulled out. The chute snapped open. Dalton looked up, checking to make sure his canopy had deployed properly, and he saw a SAM-8 explode in the right engine of the second AN-24 cargo plane as the first jumpers exited.

The cargo plane's right wing sheered off and the plane canted over. Dalton watched as desperate parachutists tried scrambling out of the open rear. A couple made it before the plane impacted with the ground, producing a large fireball.

Dalton turned his attention to his situation, forcing his feet and knees together, bending his knees slightly—as he'd been taught almost thirty years ago at Fort Benning by screaming Blackhats—and he prepared for his own impact with the ground.

His feet hit; he rolled and came to his feet. The wind was taking his chute upslope, so he cut lose the shoulder connects. The chute, minus his weight, took off. Forty meters away a machine gun chattered, stitching holes in the nylon.

There was a terrible scream. Dalton looked up. One of the last men out of his plane had hit the top of the psychic wall. He was still descending, but the man had both hands wrapped around his head. Even at this distance, Dalton could the blood gushing out of the man's ears, nose, and mouth.

The scream ended just as the man hit the ground like a sack of potatoes. An automatic machine gun fired twenty rounds into the corpse. The man lay there, his parachute anchored by his body and flapping in the breeze.

Dalton watched as two Spetsnatz commandos slapped down a tripod, slid a tube onto the top, loaded a missile, and fired, all in less than ten seconds. The missile streaked right into the source of the firing that had shot up Dalton's parachute. The small mound hiding the machine gun exploded.

Colonel Mishenka was yelling orders, but the men were well trained and needed little direction. Other Russian soldiers were opening their bundles, pulling equipment out.

Three men ran forward to the minefield warning signs and opened up a large satchel. They pointed a thick plastic tube upslope. There was a flash, then a thick line flew out of the end of the tube, soaring high through the air until it landed, a hundred meters away. One of the men pulled a fuse ignitor on the close end of the line, then all three dove for cover.

The cord of explosive detonated, blowing a five-foot-wide path through the minefield. The three men dashed into the path, made it ten meters, then were cut down by another automatic machine gun.

A rocket destroyed that bunker.

And the bloody process continued as Colonel Mishenka's Spetsnatz worked their way up the hill, closer and closer to the shimmering psychic wall.

Dalton ran forward and threw a grenade at a bunker housing a machine gun that had just killed a soldier. He knelt and checked his watch. Nine minutes.

Zivon alerted Feteror to the attack, even as the computer battled the attackers with the automatic defense system. Leksi's men were loading the third warhead into the generator.

"How soon will you be ready?" Feteror demanded of Vasilev.

The professor looked up at the demon. "You still have the second bomb in stasis in the virtual field. That's affecting the computer. Slowing it down."

Feteror frowned, dark ridges coming together on his demon face. "Can you fire the next one?"

Vasilev didn't look up from his keyboard. "I am trying to get the program to accept the new mission."

"How long?" Feteror demanded.

Vasilev ignored him. Feteror stepped forward.

The professor looked up. "We can fire the third now."

Jackson felt the liquid pouring into her lungs, but her focus was elsewhere. She had Sybyl access everything in the database on Russian nuclear weapons. She contacted Hammond through the computer.

"Anything from Sergeant Major Dalton?"

"He is on the ground. They are assaulting SD8's base, Chyort's home."

"Any other nuclear explosions?"

"Not yet."

"How long can you keep the bomb from coming through completely?"

"I estimate 8.4 minutes."

"Come on, Dr. Hammond!" Jackson yelled. *"Get me over there!"*

Dalton fired on full automatic, right into the open end of a machine-gun bunker, his bullets smashing into the weapon. He rolled twice to his right, pausing at the edge of the path blasted by the line charge.

He was less than twenty feet from the psychic wall. He could not only see it shimmering now, but he could feel something. A thrumming on the edge of his consciousness. A feeling that made him want to turn and get away as fast as possible.

He looked over his shoulder. Over three quarters of the Spetsnatz were dead, but the survivors were still moving forward, wiping out the last of the automatic weapons.

Colonel Mishenka ran forward and threw himself into the dirt next to Dalton. He peered ahead at the wall, then glanced at Dalton.

A Spetsnatz soldier ran past them.

Mishenka yelled for him to stop, but too late as the man hit the psychic wall. His body spasmed, arms flying back. They could hear his spine snapping in a row of sharp cracks.

The man tumbled to the ground, his head canted at an unnatural angle, blood flowing from every visible orifice.

General Rurik pounded his fist in frustration against the console. "What is going on?"

"I cannot access the surface," the technician said.

Rurik looked up at the red flashing light. He had missed the last contact with Moscow because Feteror was still out.

He had violated procedure for the first time in his career. He had no clue what was going on. But they knew something was happening above them. The dull sound of explosions echoed through the stone walls.

Someone was attacking them. But who?

There was only one answer—it had to be Feteror and help he had recruited. No one else would dare go up against the psychic wall. No one else could be this far into Russia and assaulting this most secret of bases.

"Captain," Rurik said, turning to the chief of security. "Have your men ready to stop an assault."

"But, sir—" The man hesitated, then continued. "They cannot get in."

"Oh, they will get in. Feteror is helping them! Now move!"

"The generator is in phase," Vasilev announced. "The program is working slowly, but it is working."

"Fire this one," Feteror ordered, "and load the next one."

Leksi stepped forward. "You are doing as Oma ordered now!"

Feteror looked at the huge naval commando. He smiled, revealing his rows of sharp teeth. Without a word he sliced forward with his right claw.

Leksi surprised him with his speed. The commando rolled forward, pulling up his submachine gun as he did.

Feteror jumped through the virtual plane to right behind Leksi, even as the man pulled the trigger. Feteror swung down with both hands. Leksi again surprised him by bringing back the submachine gun and blocking the right claw, but the left ripped into Leksi's back.

Feteror relished the familiar sound of tearing flesh. He lifted Leksi as the commando tried to bend the gun back, to fire at his attacker. Feteror solved that problem by slicing off Leksi's right arm.

He tossed the dying commando against the wall and stood over him. "I *will* destroy Oma's targets but I do not need you to tell me to do it."

"The bomb is in phase," Vasilev reported.

Feteror turned to the cowering mercenaries. "Load the next bomb as soon as the generator is clear."

He jumped into the virtual plane and connected with the bomb. He directed it west toward America.

"Time for your plan to get through the wall, if you have one," Dalton said.

Mishenka spit and rubbed a hand covered in blood across his face. "I have one. You need a short?" He tapped the side of his head. "I've got one right here."

Dalton wasn't sure he had heard right.

Mishenka stood and walked toward the shimmer that indicated the boundary of the psychic wall. "I suggest you stay close to me," he called over his shoulder.

"I can't let you do that," Dalton said.

Mishenka was standing right in front of the wall. Dalton came up next to him. He could feel the pain now, the fear, pulsing through his brain.

Mishenka laughed. He ripped open a packet on his combat vest and pulled out a small red pill. He held it up to Dalton. "My antiradiation pill. Perhaps it works, eh?"

Dalton knew the Russians issued the red pill as a placebo and that anyone with the slightest common sense knew that.

Mishenka tossed it away. "I am a dead man anyway. Let my death be worth something." He looked at Dalton. "Are you ready?"

Dalton met the other man's eyes. "I'm ready."

Mishenka pulled his belt off and handed one end to Dalton. "I go, you follow."

Dalton found he could not speak, so he simply nodded.

"Now!" Mishenka yelled.

He stepped forward into the wall, pulling on the belt. Dalton was pulled through behind him.

The Russian jerked straight up, his mouth open, a cry issuing forth that chilled Dalton's heart.

Dalton hit the wall. He staggered, feeling a spike of pain rip into the base of his skull. His skin crackled, felt as if it were on fire. He kept moving his legs, going forward. He fell onto the ground, the pain receding.

Dalton rolled and looked back. There was a glow around Mishenka's head. The Russian was looking straight at him. The mouth twisted from the open scream into a fleeting semblance of a smile, then a river of blood spilled over the lips and Mishenka fell to the ground dead.

Dalton looked down at his hand. He was still holding the belt. The other end was in the Russian's dead hand. Dalton let go of the belt and stood. He headed toward the base.

Feteror's head snapped to the left. He was halfway toward Washington, but something halted him at the jump point.

He opened to the flow of data from Zivon. Someone was through the psychic wall!

Feteror jumped for home, the bomb going with him.

Chapter Thirty

Lieutenant Jackson floated next to the bomb. It was the inverse of what she had witnessed from the floor of the experimental chamber. Here, on the virtual plane, a small square disappeared every few seconds. There was less than a third of the bomb remaining in the virtual plane.

"Dr. Hammond?"

"Yes?"

"I need the specifications for this type of nuclear weapon."

"I have specs for our version of it."

"Stay with me."

"I will."

Jackson let go of her avatar and became pure psyche. She flowed into the bomb.

Dalton threw the backpack Mishenka had given him to the ground in front of the large steel door that blocked his way into the underground complex. He pulled out the long black tube. He worked fast, his watch telling him that less than four minutes were left.

He peeled the tape off the end of the tube and pressed it against the center of the left steel door. He swung down the two thin metal legs to the ground, centering the tube horizontally against the door. He pulled the firing tab, ran twenty feet away, and dove for cover behind a berm.

The tube fired, the shaped charge producing intense

heat that burned a three-foot-diameter hole through the door in an instant.

Dalton ran forward. He slammed against the door, next to the hole, the edges still simmering. He pulled a flash-bang grenade off his vest and threw it in. Counted to three. The grenade went off. Dalton dove through the hole, rolling forward onto the concrete floor inside, coming up to his knees with his AK-74 at the ready.

He fired at the two stunned guards, knocking them backwards. Then he was on his feet, running along the corridor that sloped downward.

Feteror came into being above SD8-FFEU. He could see the bodies littering the ground below. He recognized the uniforms of the dead. Spetsnatz. It had come full circle.

He clearly saw the psychic wall. There was only one way he could get in, through the window allowed him. And once he was inside he would be trapped inside Zivon.

He roared, a demonic dragon circling on leathery wings, his lair below being invaded. Impotent to stop—Feteror paused. He had the bomb. It had to end now.

Mishenka had told Dalton that the guard force inside SD8's base was minimal—they counted on the automatic defenses and the psychic wall.

So far Dalton had encountered six guards. He edged between two large stacks of supplies. The door from the supply room to the brain center lay ahead. He paused and looked at his watch. Less than two minutes.

Throwing caution to the wind, Dalton sprinted forward and was slammed back as a bullet ripped through his left shoulder.

Jackson was in the center of a jumble of wires in the core of the bomb. She had gone into machinery and computers before, but only for data, for information. Never to do anything real to the machine. She didn't even know if she *could* do anything.

"*How much time?*" she asked Hammond.

"*A minute and twenty seconds.*"

"*What do I do?*"

There was a short pause. "*According to Sybyl, you must stop the detonator. The conventional explosion that initiates the nuclear reaction.*"

"*Where is it?*"

Hammond had Sybyl project the vision to Jackson.

Feteror took the bomb with him through the window into the underground complex.

Inside the hangar, the next bomb was loaded inside the generator.

Vasilev looked around. Some of the men were tending to Leksi, leaning the dying man against the wall. Chyort was nowhere to be seen, nor did Vasilev sense his presence.

"Fire the next target!" Leksi spit the words out along with a dribble of blood down his chin. "Damn you, do as you're told."

Vasilev smiled. He knew without Feteror, the bomb would not go anywhere. "Yes, sir."

He hit a button on the console. "Atonement," he whispered.

The hangar disappeared in an instant, destroying the immediate area and the approaching Russian forces that had been alerted by NATO intelligence using the information Oma had called in for her four hundred million.

Dalton looked at his watch. Under a minute. He could hear the man who had shot him moving on the other side of the pallet.

Dalton stood, blood streaming from his shoulder. He yelled in Vietnamese at the top of his lungs and came around the pallet firing. The man was still turning toward him when Dalton's first bullets hit, splattering him against the wall.

The bolt slammed home. Dalton tossed the gun aside and ran into the corridor, pulling a pistol out of its holster. He kicked open the door at the end and staggered into the brain center.

A Russian general holding a pistol in his hand stood in front of Dalton, soldiers flanking him, their weapons also at the ready.

Feteror looked down from his virtual perch. He saw the American Green Beret and General Rurik pointing their guns at each other. He knew the bomb he had would explode in ten seconds after he released it into the real world. There was nothing they could do to stop it.

"Why?"

Feteror spun about, startled. Opa was shaking his head. "Why must you destroy?" Opa said. The old man's right arm stretched out toward Feteror, who jumped back, startled. But the arm went right past him, into the virtual window.

Feteror turned to follow it. The arm kept growing until it reached the half-materialized bomb. It flowed into the bomb. The red digital readout blacked out.

"What have you done!" Feteror screamed.

"Do not move!" General Rurik ordered Dalton. The two guards flanked the general, their weapons pointed at Dalton.

The sergeant major could feel the flow of blood down his side from his wound. His head pounded from the after-effects of the psychic wall. He could see that the barrel of the pistol he was holding was shaking. He knew there was no way he could get all three before they gunned him down.

"Jimmy," a woman's voice whispered in his ear. *"You know what you have to do."*

Dalton let go of the gun.

Feteror saw the American drop the gun.

"What have you done?" he demanded of Opa. "They have won!"

"No," Opa said. "I do not think so."

"Who are you?" General Rurik demanded.

Dalton focused on the Russian general, pushing away all distractions. He used the power of over fifteen hundred days and nights of captivity, the skills he had learned during six months of Trojan Warrior and the past two days at Bright Gate, what Sybyl had shown him of the virtual world and the line between it and the real. He put the white dot right between the Russian's eyes and then he probed with his mind.

Rurik grabbed his temples, a surprised look on his face. He staggered, tried to say something, then went down to his knees. He wavered there for a couple of seconds, still trying to mouth words that wouldn't come through the pain in his head. Then he keeled over and smashed into the hard floor, face first.

Feteror saw General Rurik hit the floor, the body slack. He'd seen the psychic force go from the head of the American into the general's—a golden burst of light on the virtual plane. The light on the general's wristband changed to red.

"We'll be trapped in here forever!" Feteror grabbed Opa by the shoulders and shook him.

Opa shook his head, the gray beard wagging back and forth. "It is best."

Feteror screamed into nothingness as his power drained from him, leaving him floating in inky darkness.

The nuclear warhead hanging over the center of Bright Gate snapped completely into reality.

"Oh God!" Hammond yelled as it dropped to the floor of the control room with a thud. It lay there.

"Bring me back," Lieutenant Jackson's voice echoed out of the speakers.

Epilogue

"Are they alive?" Barnes asked.

"Their bodies are," Jackson answered. "Their psyches—their selves . . ." Her voice trailed off.

Sergeant Barnes was in a wheelchair next to her, looking at the tubes holding the rest of the second Psychic Warrior team. "You don't think we're going to find them, do you?"

Jackson shrugged. "I don't know. We're getting different readings off of Raisor. Sybyl doesn't know what to make of it. We think he's definitely out there somewhere, but we haven't been able to make contact."

Barnes had a gold ring that he was rubbing between two fingers. "What do you—" He paused as the door to the outside corridor swung open.

Sergeant Major Dalton slowly walked in, his arm in a sling, his face drawn and tight from exhaustion. He'd returned to Denver via Aurora as soon as the surviving Spetsnatz had secured the SD8 base. Then he'd been flown to Bright Gate by a Blackhawk.

"Sergeant Major!" Barnes and Jackson said it at the same time.

"You have something of mine." He held out a hand.

Barnes passed him the wedding band and the sergeant major's insignia.

Dalton sat down in a chair with a wince. "The Russians are shutting down SD8," he informed the others. He felt the metal ring in his palm, fingers of the other hand running over the worn metal.

"Chyort?" Jackson said the word in a low voice.

Dalton shook his head. "His physical remains–the brain–is isolated. The Russians are saying they'll make sure he never gets out." Dalton held up the ring and looked at the inscription on the inside. *Love Always, Marie.*

"I have to go to Fort Carson for a funeral." Dalton slowly stood. He headed for the door, then paused and turned. "Are you going to be all right?"

Jackson forced a smile. "I'm fine."

Dalton nodded. "Hold the fort. I'll be back as soon as I can. We're not done here yet."

Robert Doherty is a pen name for a best-selling writer of suspense novels. He is the author of *The Rock; Area 51; Area 51: The Reply; Area 51: The Mission;* and *Area 51: The Sphinx.* Doherty is a West Point graduate, a former Infantry officer and a Special Forces A-Team commander. He currently lives in Boulder, Colorado.

For more information you can visit his Web site at www.nettrends.com/mayer.